THE TOMB OF DRAGONS

Also by Katherine Addison

The Goblin Emperor
The Witness for the Dead
The Grief of Stones
The Angel of the Crows

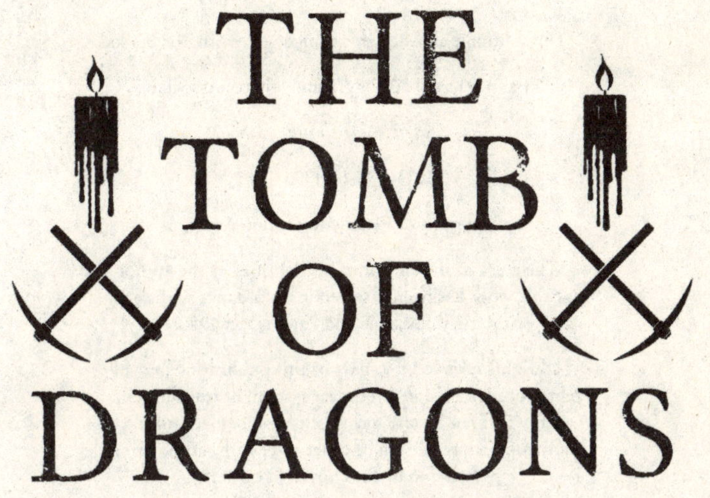

THE TOMB OF DRAGONS

KATHERINE ADDISON

SOLARIS

Published 2025 by Solaris
an imprint of Rebellion Publishing Ltd,
Riverside House, Osney Mead,
Oxford, OX2 0ES, UK

This edition published by arrangement with Tor Books

First published 2025 by Tom Doherty Associates

www.solarisbooks.com

ISBN: 978-1-83786-439-3

10 9 8 7 6 5 4 3 2 1

A CIP catalogue record for this book is available from the British Library.

Designed & typeset by Rebellion Publishing Ltd

Printed in Denmark

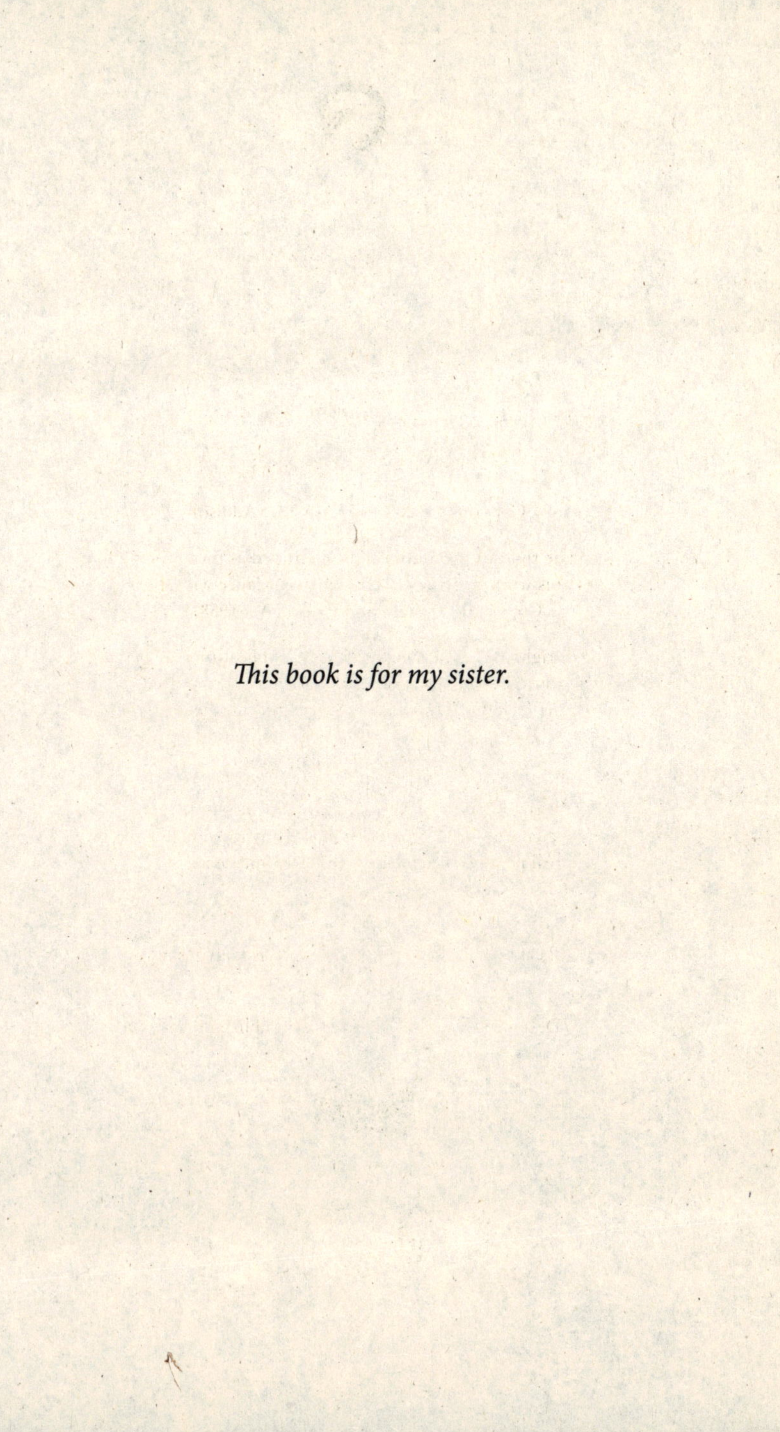

This book is for my sister.

"WHY DO YOU feed the cats, othala?"

The question came from the landing above me; I stepped back onto the stairs to get a better look. The asker was a child, a part-goblin girl almost old enough to start pinning up her hair, with skin that was not quite black and eyes of a vivid grass green. There was nothing accusatory or contemptuous in her voice, just curiosity.

"I like cats," I said.

"My mother says you must have an eitheiavan."

"It is true that all cats are prelates of Noranamaro, and she is a goddess whose favor is shown in strokes of luck and success against long odds. But really, I just like cats."

She considered that for a moment, her green eyes solemn. Then she said, "My father says that cats are pests and you are wasting good sardines."

"They are my sardines to waste," I said mildly, since the child was not to blame for her father's opinions. "But if cats are pests, what are the mice and rats they catch?"

"Oh," she said. Another moment's consideration and she said, "My name is Thenavo Shelenin."

"I am Thara Celehar, a Witness for the Dead."

"We read about you in the newspapers. My mother says you are a good man."

"I follow my calling," I said, even though I wasn't sure I had one anymore.

"Is it true you're taking a sabbatical?" She took care with the pronunciation of the unfamiliar word.

"Of a sort," I said cautiously. "The Archprelate of Cetho has another task for me. But Othalo Tomasaran will be Amalo's Witness for the Dead while I am busy."

"What will you do?"

"I don't know. I'm still waiting for the Archprelate's instructions to arrive."

"I hate waiting," she said sympathetically.

"Yes," I said, although I was careful not to say it with the weight of sleeplessness and bad dreams it actually carried. "But his letter will arrive soon, and in the meantime I feed the cats." I guessed suddenly why she had spoken to me in the first place. "Would you like to come help?"

Her face lit with an amazing smile, and she said, "Oh yes, please, I would like that very much." She came scrambling down the stairs and said, "Do you think they will come while I am here?"

"I think if you stay back, you will not bother them, although the shyest of the queens may flee from you all the same."

"Have you named them?"

"No," I said. "Names have too much power, and I do not pretend that they are *my* cats. Only my friends." Which was not something I had meant to say and certainly not to a child.

But she only nodded and said, "Where do you keep the sardines?"

I WOKE IN the middle of the night and did not know where I was.

I lay still, staring into the darkness, and sorted through the possibilities. It was not my bed in the dormitory at Tavolaree. It was not my bed in the terrible apartment I had shared with three other prelates in Lohaiso. It was not Aveio—please let it not be Aveio—and it was not the closet-sized room my cousin Csoru had grudgingly given me out of her household in the Untheileneise Court. It was a rented room in Amalo, and after a moment's fierce thought, I was able to remember *which* rented room in Amalo and orient myself. There the outer door, there the table, there the cold-water sink, there the closet I had turned into a michenmeire with an old dressing table, a threadbare black coat, and the coil of Evru's hair—the only thing I had of him and the only precious thing I owned. I knew this room. I rolled over and, for a wonder, fell easily back to sleep—

—Only to be woken, sometime before dawn, by a harsh pounding that reverberated through the room. I grabbed my dressing gown from the back of the chair, scrambling it on over my nightshirt, and answered the door.

There were two members of the Vigilant Brotherhood standing outside my door, one elven and one goblin. The goblin was carrying an owl-light. They both looked grim and tired.

"Can . . . can I help you?" I said. I could hear my neighbors' doors being pounded on up and down the hall.

"I'm sorry," the elven man said, clearly by rote, "but we need to search this room. Prince's orders."

"Search?" I said. "For what?"

"Dach'osmer Coralis Clunethar," said the goblin.

I yielded the doorway and did not tell them I did not know who they were talking about. They seemed unlikely to explain, and all too likely to think I was joking.

They were, at least, efficient. The goblin raised the owl-light to illuminate the room; the elven man checked under the bed and in the closet and behind the door, those being the only places in the room a person could conceivably be hiding. I stood and watched, since I could do nothing else.

"Nothing," said the searcher. They nodded to each other and left the room without taking any further notice of me. I heard their boots clomping up the stairs to the next floor, where they would doubtless do the same thing all over again.

I shut the door and sat down blankly on the bed. I had not lived in Amalo long, but predawn searches seemed out of the ordinary.

And who in the world was Coralis Clunethar?

I HAD ALREADY been pledged to eat breakfast with my friend Anora Chanavar, which spared me the bother of going to find him. Everyone I passed on the streets looked tired and nervous, as if they, too, had been woken by banging on their doors in the middle of the night. In the Chrysanthemum, the elven server who greeted me and led me to Anora's usual table looked as if she'd been crying.

I had purchased the newspapers—the *Arbiter,* the *Standard,* captain, a tall, scar-faced part-goblin man with a soldier's topknot, gave me a polite nod as I went past. I nodded back, thinking that unless they actually established a choke point (which would almost certainly cause a riot among the people it made late for work), it was ridiculous to imagine that posting guards here would accomplish anything—except to ensure that a great many people saw that the Principate Guard were out in force. And maybe that would help, even if I couldn't see exactly how. It was, mercifully, not my problem.

The thought that recurred to me through the day was the pale orange fire of the captain's eyes.

THE NEXT MORNING, I had almost reached the great marble archway when there was a commotion ahead of me: a heavy thump, a sudden swirl in the crowd. Someone screamed.

There were innocent interpretations, but years of service in the prelacy of Ulis had ground certain assumptions into my reflexes. I pushed forward, ducking under the elbow of someone trying to back away, and, yes, I was right. The noise had been a massive goblin man hitting the floor.

"A prelate!" someone said, and a little space cleared for me to reach him.

I knelt beside him and hesitated. He was lying on his front, and I was not quite sure of my ability to roll him over on the first try. The last thing anybody wanted was for this to become the spectacle of me wrestling with the body of a man easily more than twice my size.

"What do you need?"

I looked up into the pale orange eyes of the Principate Guard captain. At closer range, he looked to be in his early forties, with the crow's feet of a man who spent a great deal of time squinting against sunlight. The white scar across his white face looked like the reminder of an ugly wound. "Captain Hanu Olgarezh," he said. His accent was Ezheise, rather than Amaleise, which I put aside to find interesting later.

"Thara Celehar, prelate of Ulis," I said, "and I could use a little help."

"Of course," he said at once, even as his eyebrows went up at the harsh sound of my voice, and together we rolled the goblin man over.

He was already dead. At a guess, he had been dead before he reached the floor. I said the prayer of compassion for the dead. It hurt not to be able to do anything else.

The captain said, "What can we do?"

"Move him out of the way," I said, "and send someone to the Sanctuary to get them to come pick him up. He'll have to go in the morgue and we hope somebody misses him enough to come identify him. Unless someone here knows him?" I looked up at the faces surrounding us, white and black and every shade of gray.

"He got on at Creivorn'ostro, every day," someone volunteered.

"Do you know his name?" the captain asked.

"No," the part-goblin woman said sadly. "We just nodded to each other. So I guess that's not much help."

"It doesn't narrow things down very much, no," the captain said, but I noticed that he said it ruefully, joining her in regret, rather than being harsh. He straightened up and raised his voice in a sudden shout: "C'mere, boys!"

Four elven guardsmen pushed politely through the knot of people, and the captain said, "Put the body in the watchstation and then, Cazenar, you run down to the Sanctuary and let them know."

"Yes, Captain," they said, and he surprised me by turning to offer me a hand up. His hand was harsh with sword calluses and very strong. I didn't need the help, but I appreciated it.

"Thank you, othala," the captain said.

"I follow my calling."

He smiled, lopsidedly because of the scar, and said, "That doesn't mean you shouldn't be thanked."

THE ARCHPRELATE'S LETTER arrived by courier from the Untheileneise Court the next day, a crisp, cold, late-fall morning. The courier, a young goblin man with blazing orange eyes, found me in the Prince Zhaicava Building, in the Witness for the Dead's office that had been mine and now belonged to Velhiro Tomasaran. Tomasaran, who had learned that she was a Witness for the Dead when she touched her husband's corpse, was a tall, sleekly elegant elven woman, my own age or a little older. She had come to Amalo in pursuit of her calling and had been determinedly learning everything I could teach her.

I was not surprised at the courier's arrival, for all the empire's couriers shared information with each other, and the prince's couriers here in Amalo would have been able to tell him exactly where I was.

He delivered the letter with a courteous bow and was gone again, leaving Tomasaran and me staring at the letter—which was written on good rag paper and sealed with gold wax—as if it was something poisonous.

The Archprelate had promised me a task in Amalo, and I had no reason to doubt him, but three nights of patchy sleep had left me with an overabundance of time to imagine terrible possibilities.

After a few moments, Tomasaran said, "Are you going to open it?"

She knew the answer—we both knew the answer: I had to

open it because the Archprelate was my superior and I owed him obedience and also because the Amal'othala was not going to pay me at the start of the new month—having lost the necessary ability, I could no longer be Amalo's Witness *vel ama* for the Dead. If the Amal'othala could have taken money back from me without looking inexcusably petty and avaricious, he would have.

I opened the letter.

> *To Thara Celehar, prelate of Ulis, greetings.*
> *It has been brought repeatedly to our attention that the municipal cemetery Ulnemenee is being very poorly administered and has been for a number of years. Both the Amal'othala and the Ulisothala assure us that the problem does not lie with the beneficed prelate, but they profess themselves unable to ascertain where the problem does lie. Therefore, we find it necessary to appoint you as a special investigator for the Archprelacy to determine what the problem is and to implement a solution.*

I stopped reading to shut my eyes for a moment. Ulnemenee was the municipal cemetery of the Veren'malo, and while its current beneficed prelate, Ulsedra Shalicar, was an inoffensive, nervous man, the previous prelate, Anlevis Drinimar, had been, by all accounts, a nightmare, quarreling with the other prelates, quarreling with the Ulisothala, quarreling with the Master of the Catacombs, and entirely untouchable because he was the brother of one of Prince Orchena's—and later Prince Orchenis's—most trusted councilors.

"Celehar?" said Tomasaran. "Are you all right?"

"Yes, I'm fine," I said. "I just . . ." I read the rest of the letter more quickly—noting with relief that the Amalomeire was being ordered to pay me again—and handed it to

Tomasaran, since there was nothing in it unsuitable for her to see.

She read it, frowning, and said, "Ulnemenee? Isn't that . . ."

"The municipal cemetery of the Veren'malo, yes," I said. Tomasaran was learning the city's cemeteries, but she was finding it a slow task.

"That's Othala Shalicar."

"Yes."

"That's . . . awkward?"

"Yes." Shalicar had been the prelate of Ulnemenee for nearly five years and done nothing. "Although the Archprelate is correct that something needs to be done. And the problem predates Othala Shalicar, if what Anora has told me is accurate. He's just failed to solve it."

"The Amal'othala isn't going to like this."

"Nor is Vernezar. But they already dislike me, so it isn't as if this will change anything."

"But it is not comfortable."

"That isn't really much of a change, either. I have found that being a Witness for the Dead is usually uncomfortable one way or another."

"That explains a great deal about you," said Tomasaran.

"What do you mean?"

"You never expect to be comfortable, so you don't complain when you aren't."

"Is that a criticism?"

"No, not at all. But I worry that it means you will be taken advantage of."

"By whom?"

"The Amal'othala, for one. Amalo is a wealthy prelacy. He could pay you better."

"You've been talking to Anora," I said. "I recognize this line of thought."

"And?"

I shrugged uncomfortably. "My stipend is sufficient."

"And that's why you're wearing a coat of office with visible mends?"

"It's still respectable," I said and heard the defensive note in my own voice.

"Barely," said Tomasaran. "Considering that you defeated a revethavar, I think the least the Amal'othala could do is buy you a new coat."

"I hope you don't intend to say that to him." Tomasaran's inevitable audience with the Amal'othala was scheduled for that afternoon.

"I'm not brave enough," she said with a shrug of her own. "I never made any of the impassioned speeches to my husband that I imagined, either."

THIS WOULD HAVE been a notable day without the letter from the Archprelate, for it was the execution of Osmin Esmeän Tativin for the murder of the Marquise Ulzhavel. Tomasaran came with me without my having to ask. The plaza before the Ulistheileian was packed with people, even more (I thought) than had been present for the execution of Broset Sheveldar. It was rare to have a woman executed—women either murdered less often than men, or were less frequently caught. Or both.

Tomasaran paid a half-zashan for a confession pamphlet, complete with a woodcut of the execution on the title page. "It will not say anything unexpected," I told her.

"How can it, being printed before her death?"

"Just so long as you know what you're buying."

"Oh, yes," she said. "I'm just curious about—"

She broke off at the sound of a shriek from within the Ulistheileian, and then another, and when the doors swung wide, it wasn't two Brothers escorting a condemned person, it was six Brothers trying to contain a frenzy. I barely recognized Osmin Tativin in the haggard, raggedly crop-headed woman screaming like an animal and struggling at every step against the men who held her.

Everyone in the plaza fell silent, shocked at Esmeän Tativin's complete abrogation of every shred of formality, decorum, or dignity.

It was pure misfortune that she caught sight of me, but she did, and she howled like the werewolves in a wonder-tale: "Thara Celehar! I curse thee, Thara Celehar! May thy days be restless and thy nights be sleepless! May thy calling fail thee! May thou murder thy love! May—" One of the Brothers gagged her with a handkerchief, and before she could get it out of her mouth, they had brought her to the dais, and she forgot about me entirely in her desperate, clawing attempts to avoid the reveth-atha waiting for her. The Brothers flung her down, one of them grabbing her ragged hair to hold her head while the executioner dropped the stock into place. She was still screaming, muffled behind the gag, when the reveth-atha dropped.

Mercifully, no one in the crowd had identified me as the person at whom she was shouting, and as the plaza slowly warmed back to life, Tomasaran and I were able to make our way unregarded back to the tram stop.

We returned to the Veren'malo and had ordered lunch at my usual zhoän before Tomasaran said, "You're awfully calm for someone who's been cursed."

"She had none of the training she would have needed to make a curse that would actually work," I said.

"There's *training*?"

"Of course," I said. "Every prelate has to be taught the curses of their god. Ulis has only death curses, and we only learn them when we're old enough to understand why we must never use them."

"But surely the curse of a condemned woman has some power, even if it's . . . purely an amateur effort."

I shrugged. "Maybe so. Maybe not. It doesn't matter. Everything she cursed me with has already happened."

Tomasaran stared at me, and I realized what I had said.

"The insomnia I knew about," she said. "And your calling. But *murder*?"

"Not a literal murder," I said. "But my lover committed murder, and I was the Witness for the victim."

"What? Celehar—"

The server came with our food, chicken tobasthas with yogurt-garlic sauce, and when she left, Tomasaran said, "But how terrible. I am surprised you are still a Witness, having had that happen to you."

"I tried not being a Witness," I said. "I thought I had no choice. But being a Witness is better by far than not being a Witness. It gives me . . ." "Purpose" sounded embarrassingly pompous, even just in my head. "Something to do."

"You follow your calling," Tomasaran said thoughtfully.

We ate in silence for some time before she said, "Do you think the Archprelate's task will be enough?"

I knew what she meant, although I wished she had not asked the question.

"It will have to be," I said. "At least I have no fears that it will not keep me busy."

I WALKED TO Ulnemenee through the narrow streets of the Veren'malo. This was the original site of the city of Amalo (as opposed to various other gatherings of people who had lived along the Zhomaikora and the shores of Lake Zheimela), so it had been built on—an endless cycle of building and demolishing and building again—for more than two thousand years. Nothing of the original city remained except the walls.

Ulnemenee was walled like a copy in miniature of the Veren'malo itself and was beautifully maintained, even if essentially nonfunctional.

A junior prelate emerged from an arched doorway and started briskly across the tiled floor of the atrium, only to come to a dead halt when he saw me.

"Othala? Can we help you?" He sounded flustered, and I wondered if I had startled him that badly or if he had a reason to be alarmed by a visiting prelate.

I said, "We must speak to Othala Shalicar. Is he here?"

The junior prelate hesitated.

I said, "If he is not here, we will wait for him. The matter is an important one."

He tried to hide his wince and said, "We will go fetch Othala Shalicar immediately."

"Thank you," I said.

He exited the atrium through the door by which he had entered. I waited, but I did not have to wait very long before I heard a thin, peevish voice saying, "Well, he'd better be quick about it, whatever it is," and Othala Shalicar came in.

He was taller than I was, an elven man of about medium height, with near-sighted green eyes and a receding chin. His hair was thick and glossy and almost certainly a wig. He, too, stopped when he saw me. He tilted his head to look at me through his pince-nez, his ears flattening, and said, "Othala Celehar," without any enthusiasm.

"Othala Shalicar," I said. "We have been ordered by the Archprelate to investigate matters at Ulnemenee."

"Investigate?" he said weakly. "We don't understand."

He understood well enough. Every prelate in Amalo knew about the problems at Ulnemenee; it was not as if they could be a surprise to the beneficed prelate. I said nothing, and his ears flattened further. "What do you want, othala?"

"To understand why the deceased of Ulnemenee do not progress."

"Because there is no room for them," said Othala Shalicar.

"The Archprelate desires that this problem be resolved."

"*How?* We cannot dig more catacombs with our bare hands!"

That was true enough. But no other ulimeire in the city had outpaced the construction of catacombs; moreover, Ulnemenee had stopped being able to take new corpses fifty years ago.

I said, "Clearly, we must talk to someone in the Catacombists' Guild."

"Oh, you can't!"

"We . . . *can't*?"

"Dach'othala Vernezar was very explicit when we were granted this benefice that any discussion with the Catacombists' Guild had to go through him. We were *not* to make inquiries on our own."

"And you haven't?"

"We are obedient to our Ulisothala."

"*Has* there been any discussion between Vernezar and the catacombists?"

"Not to our knowledge."

"Then we suppose we must begin by talking to Dach'othala Vernezar."

"Yes," said Shalicar unhappily. "We suppose you must."

THE ULISTHEILEIAN OF Amalo was a new building, barely two hundred years old, the previous one having been destroyed in a fire. It wrapped around three sides of the plaza, tall and gray and forbidding—which was certainly a reasonable choice for Ulistheileneise architecture, although it made me think more fondly of Lohaiso, where the Ulistheileian was long and low and the warm colors of terra-cotta and brick.

The novices on duty at the front door looked pinch-faced and cold, and I was not surprised that their first response was to tell me I could not possibly see Dach'othala Vernezar today. I reminded myself that patience was one of the virtues all prelates were supposed to teach by example and explained about the Archprelate's letter.

It was wrong to be amused by the horror on their faces. One fled into the depths of the building to find Vernezar; the other stayed grimly on duty, although the set of his ears said he wanted to be anywhere in the world but here.

The younger novice returned and said, panting only slightly, "Dach'othala Vernezar will see you, othala. Do you know the way?"

"We do," I said. I had been in Vernezar's office before.

The halls of the Ulistheileian were full of busy prelates; I blended in well enough and got to Vernezar's office without anyone asking me what I thought I was doing. Vernezar's secretary—the most harried-looking of any of the secretaries I had met in Amalo, including the Amalomeire's legion of canons—nodded at me resentfully and said, "You're to go in."

I nodded back and went.

As befitted the Ulisothala of Amalo, the office was large, graciously appointed in the tall, grim style of two hundred years ago, and boasting an excellent view of the reveth-atha in the center of the plaza. I wondered if Vernezar watched executions or if he drew the heavy plum-colored drapes and got on with his work.

Aiva Vernezar, a tall and skinny elven man with a long nose and close-set eyes, had been Ulisothala for twenty years (which, Anora frequently said, was nineteen years too long). He was standing behind his desk, and he watched me approach with an expression somewhere between irritation and dread. "What is this about a letter from the Archprelate?"

I explained, once more, that the Archprelate desired the ulimeire of Ulnemenee to become functional again. Before Vernezar could say what was perfectly visible on his face, I extracted the letter from my inside waistcoat pocket and gave it to him. He read it carefully, scowling, and I saw his fingers tighten as if he wanted to rip it in half. But he was no Tivaris Urnashar to defy the Archprelate, and in any event, Ulnemenee was hardly the sort of thing one defied the Archprelate over. He gave the letter back to me, and I put it carefully away again.

"We suppose we cannot stop you from talking to the catacombists," Vernezar said, "but we doubt you will find them helpful."

They cannot be less helpful than you, I thought but did not say.

We exchanged minimal bows.

There were many entrances to the catacombs beneath Amalo, some public, some private. The official entrance was in the Veren'malo, actually built into the city wall as if it were a gate—but instead of the other side of the wall, what one discovered was a great descending staircase, wide enough for ten abreast.

I had never been here before, but I knew that the main office of the catacombists was on the first level down; aside from the darkness and the looming rock walls, it looked very like the office of the Cartographers' Guild in the Prince Zhaicava Building, though much larger, with maps everywhere and busy clerks, most of them female and split relatively evenly between elves and goblins.

The nearest clerk, a very young goblin woman, looked up and said, "Can I help . . ."—she faltered for a moment when she realized she was talking to an Ulineise prelate, then rallied—"you, othala?"

All of the other clerks turned to stare. I said, "I need to speak to someone about the revethmerai of Ulnemenee."

"Just a moment," she said, getting up. She wove through the desks to a door at the back of the room. I stood and tried to pretend I didn't know that half the clerks were still staring at me. It wasn't very long before she came back, accompanied by a young elven man wearing his Catacombists' Guild pin very prominently.

"This is Sol Terenar," the clerk said.

Sol Terenar and I bowed to each other, and I said, "We are Thara Celehar, a prelate of Ulis. We have come about the revethmerai of Ulnemenee."

"What about them?" said Sol Terenar.

"Why aren't there any?"

He looked offended. "We have received no request for revethmerai from Ulnemenee."

"Then how do we make a request?"

"We are sorry, othala, but you cannot do that." He clearly wasn't sorry. I recognized this smugness as pleasure in being unhelpful. The Ulistheileian was full of it.

"Why not?"

"Only the prelate of the ulimeire can request revethmerai."

"Then how do we do *that*? Do we have to drag him here? Can he write a letter?"

"Um." He looked suddenly much less sure of himself. "We are not quite sure. Ulnemenee's case is peculiar."

"How so?"

"We . . . we cannot tell you that."

"Why not?"

"It's Guild business." The smugness returned.

"If it relates to the problem of Ulnemenee's revethmerai, it is *our* business. We have a letter from the Archprelate of Cetho requesting us to solve the problem." I showed him the letter, although I didn't think he saw anything but the seal.

"Oh dear," he said. "We're afraid we cannot help you."

"Then who can?"

The question seemed to stymie him. Finally he said, "Let us ask Sol Uprashar."

He hurried off between the desks. I carefully refolded the Archprelate's letter and put it back in my inside waistcoat pocket (with my pen, my notebook, the pilgrimage token from a pilgrimage I had never been on, a tile from the Hill of Werewolves, and two white stones from the corn maze of Orshan), which was the safest place I had to keep it.

More than a quarter of an hour later, Sol Terenar returned, followed closely by a part-goblin man probably twice his age. They both looked disappointed that I was still there.

"This is Sol Uprashar," said Sol Terenar.

Sol Uprashar and I exchanged bows, and he said, "We understand that you are interested in Ulnemenee, but it's not clear to us why you're here."

I explained myself again.

Uprashar's eyebrows went up. "But why hasn't Othala Shalicar come himself?"

I hesitated over telling them about Vernezar's obstructionism and decided not to. Instead, I explained about the letter from the Archprelate, getting it out again to show him the seal.

He was stubbornly unimpressed. "That doesn't give you any special authority here. Only the beneficed prelate can request revethmerai."

"How does he do that?" I asked again. "Must it be in person or will a letter suffice?"

Sol Uprashar seemed as thrown by that question as Sol Terenar had been. He stammered a little, then said, "We must consult Dachensol Idrinezh. Pardon us." He and Sol Terenar hurried away.

Again, it was a long time before Sol Terenar, alone, came

back. "Dachensol Idrinezh says that the procedure is quite clear. Either the beneficed prelate must come himself or his representative must bring a properly witnessed statement of need."

"All right," I said. "Thank you."

He looked surprised, but answered my bow.

I RETURNED TO Ulnemenee and again sent the junior prelate after Shalicar, whose ears were set sullenly when he came into the atrium.

I picked up our conversation where it had left off. "Either you must come yourself or you must make a witnessed statement."

Shalicar said, "We can't *go* there!"

"Why in the world not?"

He lowered his voice to a whisper and abrogated formality: "Vernezar would kill me."

Fortunately, I didn't have to insist. "Then you must make a witnessed statement."

"A witnessed statement of *what*?"

"Of Ulnemenee's need for revethmerai."

"Can you not come back tomorrow?" Shalicar said, almost plaintively.

"The problem will not have changed," I said.

"No, but we . . . we need time to think."

"About what?"

He was reddening but said, "About framing a statement of need to the Catacombists' Guild."

That was almost certainly not what he needed time to think about, but calling Othala Shalicar a liar seemed like the worst of my possible choices. I said, "Very well. We will come back tomorrow. If you could have the statement of need ready, that would be of great help."

"Of course," Shalicar said. "Tomorrow."

I wanted to leave almost as much as he wanted to be rid of me. I said, "Yes." We bowed to each other and I, gladly, left.

I WENT TO the Vermilion Opera, where they were rehearsing *The Dream of the Empress Corivero.* My friend Iäna Pel-Thenhior, the director of the Opera, was part goblin and wore his hair in long beaded Barizheise braids; that, along with his bright brocade coats and golden eyes, made him difficult to miss and difficult to forget. He saw me as soon as I entered the auditorium and called from the stage, "Did it come?"

Naturally, everyone turned to look at me, and my face heated. But Iäna had been deeply interested in the question of what the Archprelate wanted me to do, and staunchly encouraging about the possibilities. He was already striding up the aisle, telling his singers to take a rest, and he swept me easily back out of the auditorium and up the stairs to the privacy of a box on the third floor.

"Unless thou wantst all the singers of the Opera to be privy to thy business," he said as he sat down in the other chair.

"No," I said. "Thou'rt quite right."

"But it *did* come?"

"Yes," I said and told him about the Archprelate's letter and Ulnemenee and Vernezar and the Catacombists' Guild.

"Many people seem to be trying to put thee off," Iäna observed.

"Yes, but I don't think there's anything sinister in it. At least not yet. But what of thee? How fares the Opera?"

"No," said Iäna.

"No?"

"We aren't changing the subject just yet. What in the world happened to thy coat?"

"My coat?"

"I'd noticed thou hadst not been wearing it, and now I understand why. I can see the mends in the dark. What *happened*?"

I explained that after it was damaged in the tomb of the revethavar, I had asked my laundress to mend it. She had returned it the previous evening. "She did not do a bad job."

"Thou needst more exacting standards," said Iäna. "And honestly thou shouldst have given it to me."

"To thee? Thou art no tailor."

"No, but I have an entire department of them. Thou shouldst take it to them now and let them fix it."

"It's not that bad."

"But it could be so much *better.* No, I know thou wilt not unless I drag thee, and I don't have time to drag thee down there right now. But the instant I *do* have time, I promise thee, we are getting that coat fixed. But now, to answer your question, the premiere of *The Dream of the Empress Corivero* is in two days. Nanavo is panicking—the last time we did *Corivero,* she was still the junior principal, so she watched Aiatho sing it, but it is very different, as she quite rightly says, to be singing the role oneself."

"Is it so difficult?"

"*Difficult,* no. But it means being on stage for three of three acts, and there's not a great deal to hide behind. And the famous arias are like honey traps for sopranos—easy to get in, but another matter entirely to get out." He must have sensed my puzzlement, for he elaborated, "There will be, in the audience, children who have never seen *Corivero* before, but they will be the only ones. And everyone will be comparing her to Mindaran and Sheplezhen and all the other famous Amaleise sopranos who've taken a whack at it. And of course Sorbescin at the Amal'opera. They did it last year."

"I begin to understand."

"Nanavo is thinking too much. She's nearing the end of her career as a principal, and it's making her more and more twitchy."

"What happens to opera singers when they can't sing principal roles any longer?"

"We take them down to the basement and bash their heads in with a carpenter's maul," Iäna said, so matter-of-factly that it was a moment before I caught on.

"You do not," I said, and his laughter pealed out, probably loud enough to be heard on the stage three stories below us.

"Some singers go back into the chorus or take character roles. We have an endless need for old women to be soothsayers and loyal servants and witches and so on."

"What about those who leave the Opera?"

"They vanish. Thoramis can barely keep up with the singers *in* the company. I can't ask him to try to keep track of everyone who leaves. I wish we could give them pensions, but Parzhadel would never agree to it, and even if he *did* agree, I fear we would bankrupt the Opera in very short order." He sighed. "It's a terrible way to earn your living, really, but none of them would trade for anything anyone could offer."

"And thee?"

"Oh, I'll go on composing until the prelates come for me, and they'll probably have to pry the pen out of my dead fingers. What of thee?"

"What dost thou mean?"

"What wilt thou do, if thou art no longer a Witness for the Dead, which is thy calling?"

"I have my task from the Archprelate."

"And after that?"

"I have no idea. Unless the Archprelate has another task. I hope he would not ask me to return to court, but he might."

"Mightst thou find another calling?"

"I would be undeservedly lucky if I did. Many people don't even find *one.* And I have never felt about anything . . ." I stopped, for I lacked words to continue.

"Thara," Iäna said. "I would find thee a calling if I could."

"I know. But it's not something anyone can do *for* me."

"No, I suppose it isn't."

On stage someone called, their voice pitched to carry to the ceiling, "Iäna! Are you coming back or not?"

Iäna muttered something in Barizhin, then leaned over the box railing and yelled, "*In a minute!*" To me, he added, "I would not leave thee on such a note, but this scene does need work, and it's unfair to the singers to keep them waiting any longer. Wouldst meet me for dinner at the Torivontaram?"

On the brink of a reflexive refusal, I hesitated. I had no business to conduct this evening, no one whom I had promised to meet. There was no reason I couldn't have dinner with Iäna. "Yes," I said. "I'd like that."

"Is six o'clock too early?"

"Not at all," I said. "I will meet thee there."

BUT AT SIX o'clock, when I arrived at the Torivontaram, there was no sign of Iäna. "I am meeting Mer Pel-Thenhior," I said to the young goblin woman who showed me to a table along the wall with the mural of trees.

"Of course," she said, and her smile was reassuring.

I ordered a four-cup pot of isevren and settled in to wait with no idea of how long I might be waiting.

But when the tea came, Merrem Pel-Thenhior, Iäna's mother, came with it. She was short for a goblin woman; unlike her son, she preferred severely practical colors and wore her hair pulled back in a single braided bun. Iäna had inherited his golden eyes from her. She said, "Iäna will be here in a very few minutes. His zhornuzai needed his help." She used the plural of "zhornu," but nothing to indicate whether these were literal cousins or merely close confederates, as in the Curneisei usage.

I said, "Have you many zhornuzai in Amalo?"

She gave me an odd look and said, "Amalo is a good city for the Barizheisei," which did not answer my question.

Iäna came in before I had decided whether or not to try again.

"Thara, a thousand apologies," he said as he crossed the room to our table. "Hello, Mother." There was a warning in the way he said it, but Merrem Pel-Thenhior just raised her eyebrows, unimpressed. "I was dealing with a very irritating problem."

"I told Othala Celehar that you were helping your zhornuzai," Merrem Pel-Thenhior said pointedly.

"So I was," said Iäna. "That doesn't mean it wasn't profoundly annoying. *And* made me late." He took the chair opposite mine, draping his overcoat over the empty chair. "But no matter. I see you have answered the tea question."

"I hope isevren is all right," I said.

"It's a better decision than orchor," Iäna said. "Mother? Was there something you needed?"

"Not at all," said Merrem Pel-Thenhior. "Shall I tell you our menu for today?"

"No need," said Iäna. "I recognize the smell of sonvolot, and I think we can assume the rest."

It was true; the rich smell of potato soup filled the Torivontaram.

"Very good," said Merrem Pel-Thenhior and added something in Barizhin that I did not catch, but that made Iäna's ears twitch.

"Yes, Mother," he said, his tone long-suffering.

She laughed and went back to the kitchen.

"She seems to think I'm a bully," Iäna said, "for she says I'm not to bully thee."

"I hope thou wouldst not," I said.

"Certainly not," Iäna said. "And in any event, I am *not* a bully, though I admit many people have told me I am overwhelming. Sometimes, they mean it as a compliment."

"Sometimes," I said.

He smiled and said, "But in any event, tell me about Ulnemenee."

"Hast never been there?"

"The Veren'malo is not my parish, and I understand that those who *are* its parishioners don't go there either."

"Since they have been unable to hold funerals there for fifty years, I am not surprised."

"Why has no one complained?"

"I'm sure someone has," I said. "The trouble is, who is there to do the complaining? Ulnemenee is a poor ulimeire in a poor district, and it is an unfortunate truth in Amalo that money is what gets one heard. Money and family, as always in the empire."

"So the complaints have been ignored."

"Most probably. It's taken fifty years for the ripples to spread far enough that the Archprelate has noticed it."

One of the servers came up with two bowls of sonvolot and a round loaf of bread already split and the white cheese beside it thinly sliced.

I poured more tea for us both, and we talked while we ate.

I said, "It is a disgraceful situation, and it says nothing flattering about the Amal'othala that he's let it continue."

"I notice that thou dost not mention Dach'othala Vernezar."

"There are so many other reasons to consider Vernezar a poor Ulisothala, it hardly seems worth it."

"Why has he not been replaced? Either of them?"

"Family," I said. "They both have connections that make them almost invulnerable. I know that the Archprelate wants to change things, but he has few allies and cannot proceed as ruthlessly as one might like."

Iäna was frowning. "*Thou* hast connections. Why hast thou not used them?"

"I was disowned," I said, as neutrally as I could.

"*Disowned?* Why?"

It was a good question, and it was only fair that he should know.

"In my last benefice," I said, "I was having an affair with a married man who murdered his wife." "Having an affair" was a tawdry and inadequate way to describe my relationship with Evru, but I did not know a better. I looked carefully at my teacup to keep from having to look at Iäna.

"What happened?"

"The body was found, I witnessed for the corpse, and on my testimony my lover was executed," I said, trying to place each word carefully and not rush. Having to repeat myself would be as bad or worse than having to say it in the first place. But I kept my gaze on my teacup, not Iäna's face.

"Thara," Iäna said. He put his hand over mine, which startled me into looking at him. "That is a terrible thing, and I am sorry it happened to thee."

"Thou art kind," I said and blinked against the sudden stinging in my eyes.

"And of course thou art still grieving," Iäna said, like a man solving a ring-and-nail puzzle.

"It was . . ." I tried to reckon back and found that I simply could not, that between Evru's execution and the summons from the emperor to witness for his father and brothers, there was a black jagged crevasse that could have been a month or could have been a year.

"Thou needst not," Iäna said.

We were silent over our food for several minutes, before Iäna said, "I have been forgetting to ask. Was that woman who dragged thee into the revethavar's tomb . . . Osmin Temin. There, I knew I'd think of her name. Was she successfully buried?"

"Yes," I said, "along with the twenty-two other bodies from the tomb."

"Nothing interesting happened?"

"Her family stayed away exactly as they had said they would. They truly want nothing to do with her."

"I wonder what she did."

"Something horrible, no doubt," I said.

Iäna's eyebrows went up.

"She was a dreadful person," I said. "I know of nothing good that can be said about her."

"I'm certainly not arguing," Iäna said, although he looked a little worried. "But it does lead me to ask about thee and thy situation."

"My situation is unchanged," I said, "and I think is unlikely *to* change."

"Thou'rt a pessimist."

"So Tomasaran tells me. But I cannot help the truth being the truth, and the truth is that if Othalo Rasaltezhen cannot help me, there is in all likelihood nothing to be done."

"Here I am plaguing thee again," Iäna said. "I merely wish for a better outcome."

"So do I," I said with considerable feeling. "For after this task for the Archprelate is complete, I . . . I have no idea."

"The Archprelate may have more ideas," Iäna said.

"I cannot hang on the Archprelate's sleeve for the rest of my life," I said.

"Is that what thou'rt doing? This is no mere makework that he has asked of thee in the matter of Ulnemenee."

"No, but it is my profound hope that Ulnemenee is unique."

Iäna laughed. "Somehow I feel sure that the Archprelate has a list of Ulnemenees and has merely been waiting for the person he could entrust them to."

"What a horrid thought," I said. "Let us talk of other things." Which was something Iäna was both happy and well equipped to do.

As we were putting our overcoats on to leave, Iäna said, "You must come to the Opera tomorrow night. It's the premiere of *Corivero*."

"Of course," I said. "Is the company ready?"

"Never ask a director that," Iäna said, smiling a little ruefully. "But I think they'll do."

I SLEPT UNUSUALLY well that night, with no dreams that I could remember on waking. I dressed and meditated on my fear of the revethavar who had destroyed my ability to hear the dead. Then I went to the Red Dog's Dream for oslov and orchor, then up the Zulnicho line to the Amal'theileian, a nod to the orange-eyed Captain Olgarezh, the Prince Zhaicava Building, and the office that was no longer mine.

I had promised Tomasaran that I would not desert her, and I knew *she* still thought of the office as mine, even though she was the Witness for the Dead and I, after the revethavar, was not. Things could have been painfully awkward between us, but Tomasaran staunchly pretended nothing had changed, and I was too much of a coward to argue.

We had been afflicted by a run of days without petitioners, our only visitors being the newspapermen, Goronezh, Thurizar, and Vicenalar, hungry for a story and guessing that there was one here to be had. I lied to them, almost reflexively at first, to keep them away from the wound I did not want to discuss, and then—the trouble with lying—I was committed to the story and had no choice but to keep telling it. It had settled into the lie that Tomasaran was "minding the shop"—as Thurizar insisted on phrasing it—while I did something unspecified for the Archprelate. No mention was made of the revethavar, and although I was never quite forced to the lie direct—that of course I was still a Witness *vel ama* for the Dead and why would anyone think otherwise?—I came at times awfully close. Goronezh in particular was extremely difficult to shake off, but Tomasaran backed me loyally, and the newspapermen came away with nothing. I had read the stories in the *Arbiter,* the *Standard,* and the *Herald* about the tomb beneath the Hill of Werewolves and been pleased to be almost unmentioned, Osmer Ormevar, like water behind a dam, expanding to fill all the empty spaces.

I beat Tomasaran to the office and thus waited for several minutes in the hallway, glad that I had been assigned an office in one of the back corners of the building, where there was almost no traffic. Tomasaran arrived, as immaculate as ever, and unlocked the door, but we had barely sat down before a petitioner arrived.

It was a simple matter of a man's last wishes; Tomasaran went and was back within an hour. "Nothing interesting," she said.

"What about your audience with the Amal'othala?"

"That, on the contrary, was almost *too* interesting. He does not like me."

"He doesn't like anyone except the canons who pander to him. What did he say?"

"He went through all the irregularities in my situation, with extensive discussions of what I should have done instead. And then at the end, and he said it as if he found it physically painful, he confirmed that the Amalomeire will pay me to act as the city's Witness for the Dead."

"That's splendid news!"

"And he gave me a chit to take to the Ulistheileian to get a prelate's coat." She sounded dubious.

"Also splendid news."

"I thought you had to buy them?"

"If you have a coat like yours, a canon's coat in good repair, and a chit from the Amalomeire, you can trade. After that you have to buy them, either from the Ulistheileian or a secondhand store, depending on the wealth of your benefice."

"Oh," she said, ears flat and disheartened. "Does the Amalomeire do nothing free?"

"You would have to ask Anora. But in my experience, no."

"How," a pause while she searched for a word, "parsimonious."

"Amalo is a wealthy prelacy and intends to stay that way."

"But all priests swear vows of poverty!"

"And individually that remains true," I said and sighed. "But there's nothing in that to keep the Amalomeire from amassing wealth."

"Shouldn't there be?"

"That's a reformer's question. So the answer is probably yes, but it would take consensus among the great prelates to implement, and that has not happened for at least a thousand years."

"So, never?"

"Probably not? Certainly not today."

"Meaning I should go get a new coat."

"Yes, and I should get to Ulnemenee."

It was cold and clear; I walked very briskly from the Prince Zhaicava Building to Ulnemenee where, as I had expected, they were not expecting me. The junior prelate—a different one, this time, a young elven woman—went running to fetch Othala Shalicar, who came out looking flustered, both junior prelates behind him.

"The statement of need?" I said.

"Oh!" said Shalicar, as if surprised. "Yes, just a moment." He beckoned to his junior prelates, and they disappeared together through a different door.

I waited, for long enough that it was evident Shalicar was writing the statement of need at that moment. I wondered if he had seriously believed I would not come back.

Shalicar returned, junior prelates still in tow, and handed me a folded and sealed paper. "We hope that this will be sufficient."

"We hope so," I said, tucking the document into my inner coat pocket. Shalicar and I bowed to each other, and I departed.

Ulnemenee was surrounded by what had once been the dwellings of the great noble families of Thu-Athamar; in some streets in the Veren'malo, their palaces had been converted into luxurious apartments, "town residences" for those same noble families, all of whom now had their principal estates well out of the city. In other streets, which once had been the gardens of the nobility, the land had been built on, becoming row houses and secondhand clothes dealers and pawn shops. The noble families were not Ulnemenee's parishioners and had not been for five hundred years; they had private cemeteries or exclusive cooperatives. The people Shalicar was failing to serve were the workers—the servers and maids and gardeners, the page boys and tram conductors—who kept the Amal'theileian functioning as a seat of government. Vernezar did not consider it necessary to listen to such people, and apparently his predecessor had felt the same way. The complaint had probably never formally made its way to the Amalomeire; working people could not afford the investment of time required simply to *get* to the Amalomeire, never mind finding someone there to listen to them. They found other ulimeirei instead.

It made me pointlessly angry—pointless because Vernezar was hardly going to listen to me, either. But the Archprelate was giving me a chance to set things right, to get the great wheels of devotion turning again.

I descended into the catacombs, and the same young goblin woman said, "Can I help you, othala?" in a tone that said she knew she couldn't.

"I believe I need to speak to Dachensol Idrinezh," I said.

"Oh, you can't!" she said, and then, her ears flat with embarrassment, amended it: "That is, Dachensol Idrinezh is very busy."

"I thought he might be," I said, pretending I hadn't heard her gaffe, and stepped up a level of formality. "How about the Master of the Catacombs? Might we speak to him?"

The young goblin woman looked helplessly at one of the older clerks, a stern-faced elven woman in black bombazine and pearls: a widow, one of those who took pride in not remarrying. She gave me a long, cool, considering look and said, "We will go see. Could we have your name, othala?"

"Thara Celehar," I said and bit off the words that wanted to follow.

"Just a moment."

I stayed where I was. The other clerks slowly got back to work, the young goblin woman slowest of all, as if she feared I might attack.

It was longer than "a moment" but probably not more than ten minutes before the elven woman returned and said, "The Master of the Catacombs will see you. Please follow us."

I followed her back between the desks and then down a long, narrow passage that twisted along what had to be an original fault in the rock and then through a cavernous workroom full of catacombists, all of whom seemed to be arguing with each other. Several of them turned to stare as we passed. Then there was an even narrower set of stairs going up, and we climbed high enough that I realized we must have come back up inside the wall. At the top of the stairs there was a door, on which my guide knocked.

From the other side, a voice roared, "Come in!"

She opened the door and stepped inside to let me pass. "Good luck," she said, so softly that I almost didn't hear her, and started back the way we'd come, leaving me staring at the Master of the Catacombs.

He was full goblin, black-skinned and red-orange-eyed and so massive that I was surprised he could squeeze himself small enough to reach this room. His clothes were drab and practical denim, and he wore his hair in a single bun at the back of his head, unadorned. The studs in his ears were diamonds—I was quite sure they were not glass—and they caught the light sharply as he moved. "We are Dachensol Harumenad, and you are the Witness for the Dead, although we forget your name." He had a strong Barizheise accent.

He was lying—he had to have recognized my name in order to know that I was a Witness for the Dead—probably as a ploy to emphasize his status relative to mine. Or just to see what I would do.

Was I a Witness for the Dead? Not for these purposes. I said, "Our name is Thara Celehar. We are here simply as a prelate of Ulis."

He raised his eyebrows. "And what brings you here, O simple prelate of Ulis?"

"We have come about Ulnemenee."

He nodded. "You have the statement of need?"

"We do. And we thought that rather than being handed from Sol Terenar to Sol Uprashar to Dachensol Idrinezh, only to be told there was something wrong with it, we would speak to you."

"We cannot fault your reasoning. Might we see the statement of need?"

I gave it to him. He broke the seal and skimmed it quickly. "Yes, this is perfectly in order. How *did* you get it past Dach'othala Vernezar?"

"We were appointed to this task by the Archprelate. Dach'othala Vernezar has no say in the matter."

"Well, thank all the gods for that," said Dachensol Harumenad. "We will write orders for Ulnemenee's dead to be received, and you will have Othala Shalicar—or his juniors, yes?—bring the dead to the Violet Street entrance to the catacombs. And the thing will be solved."

"We hope so," I said.

I WALKED BRISKLY back to Ulnemenee, where I found Shalicar watching one of his junior prelates cleanse the courtyard.

I explained my success.

"That's splendid," Shalicar said unenthusiastically.

I said, "Is there a problem?"

Shalicar hesitated for so long that I thought he wasn't going to say anything. The junior prelate whispered, "You should tell him."

I waited, and Shalicar said abruptly, "Come with us."

He led me into the ulimeire, along a narrow hallway, and dragged open a heavy, carved door. "This," he said.

The room was clearly someone's study—or, more accurately, had clearly *been* someone's study, before the stacks and piles and mounds of paper had made it impossible for any work to be done.

I looked at Shalicar.

"It was like this when we arrived," he said. "And we . . . we just don't . . ." He abrogated formality in a rush: "I don't even know where to begin."

"The registers are in there somewhere," the junior prelate said.

"And the map of the cemetery and the timetables of reveth'osrel and all the apparatus of maintaining a ulimeire. I can't find any of it, and I'm afraid that looking is going to bring the whole mass down on my head."

"A sensible concern," I said. "I think you can't start by looking for anything."

"What do you mean?"

"I think you have to start by picking up the piece of paper on top of the nearest stack and finding out what it is. And then deciding what to do with it, whether to burn it or to keep it. And then you move on to the next piece of paper."

"Celehar, that's going to take months!"

"Yes. Did you have something better to do?"

"And it won't *help*."

"What do you mean?"

He looked at me for a long moment, face and ears unreadable, then said, "Come with me."

I followed him deeper into Ulnemenee, the junior prelate trailing us both with a worried look on her face. Down a short hall, and then through another heavy carved door. Shalicar paused to light a candle and led me down a staircase, narrow, twisting, and steep. At the bottom, which came just as I was wondering if this was another entrance to the catacombs, Shalicar flung open the first door we came to and said, "There, you see? Impossible!"

The storeroom was full of the linen bags prelates used to house defleshed bones. Judging by the contours, all the bags contained skeletons.

"And it's not just the one room," Shalicar said, almost triumphantly. "We can never hope to catch up."

"Did you also discover this situation when you assumed the benefice?"

"Yes. I think Othala Drinimar must have started putting bones down here when he first quarreled with the Master of the Catacombs and then just . . . never stopped until he ran out of room."

"How long was he prelate of Ulnemenee?"

"More than fifty years," Shalicar said.

"And his relationship to Dach'osmer Drinimar protected him from investigation, never mind remediation."

"Yes," Shalicar said.

"And you have been protected by Dach'othala Vernezar's unwillingness to admit the problem exists."

Shalicar's ears flinched, but he said, "Yes. I am glad you are here, Celehar, don't mistake me. But I just don't know how much good you're going to be able to do."

"Well," I said. "We'll have to find out."

I WAS GRATEFUL to leave Ulnemenee, even knowing I would have to come back next afternoon. I took the tram to the Ulvanensee stop and went to talk to Anora.

He was watching one of his juniors conduct a funeral. I stood beside him and watched without comment until the funeral was complete and the mourners had left. Then I said, "I need to talk to thee."

"Of course," said Anora. "What about?"

"Ulnemenee."

"Ulnemenee? What has thou been doing to come across Ulnemenee?"

"It is the task the Archprelate has assigned me," I said. "To solve the problem of Ulnemenee."

"Gracious," said Anora. "And thou hast accepted the charge?"

"I can't say no to the Archprelate!"

"Thou canst if he sets thee an impossible task."

"It isn't *impossible,*" I said, but honesty forced me to add, "At least, I don't think so."

"Come," Anora said. "Let us sit in my office where we can be out of the wind, for it seems to me this conversation may take a while."

I was glad to follow him into the comparative warmth of the main building. We sat across from each other at his massive desk, and Anora said, "All right. Tell me the tale from the beginning."

I obliged to the best of my ability. Anora listened closely, without speaking. When I was done, he said, "Art thou sure the Archprelate has not set thee an impossible task? How dost thou plan to proceed?"

"That's why I wanted to talk to thee," I said, "for I have no idea."

That made him laugh, though ruefully. He said, "I don't know what help I can give thee. I have never encountered a situation like this." He considered a moment. "Thou canst not hope to count all those bones."

"Not without the registers," I said.

"Dost think the registers will even be correct?"

"I don't know. I hope Drinimar was not so lost to all sense of duty as to let them lapse."

"Or throw them out."

"Anora!" I said, deeply shocked.

"It's a possibility, when someone has let things get as bad as they are in Ulnemenee, that he *was* lost to all sense of duty. In which case, who knows what he might have done?"

"I'm going to proceed on the assumption that the registers are in Ulnemenee somewhere," I said. "Until I am forced to believe otherwise. At least Drinimar or his junior prelates or *someone* thought to label the bags. Otherwise there would be nothing for it but to petition the Archprelate for a revethilagrat held for these hundreds of people."

"Are you sure a revethilagrat is not the correct answer regardless?"

"It is my last resort," I said. "But I must at least *try* to sort things out."

"Thy notion of duty is uncomfortably broad, Thara. I do not think the Archprelate meant that thou shouldst throw thyself at an unscalable wall."

"If it proves to be unscalable, I will stop throwing myself at it."

"I will hold thee to that promise," said Anora.

THAT NIGHT I fed the gas meter with five-zashan pieces and read one of my brick-like Barizheise novels until nearly dawn. When I did fall asleep, I slept only a couple of hours, and then was awake again, but at least by then it was morning enough to go to the Red Dog's Dream for oslov and bitter black tea.

Up the Zulnicho line, past my flame-eyed captain (*Don't be silly, Celehar, he does not belong to thee*), I arrived later than usual at the Prince Zhaicava Building, which I did not expect to be problematic, although perhaps I should have known better. I heard the raised voices from the end of the hall and walked rather faster than was decorous to the office door, where an elven man in his forties was standing and loudly insisting that Tomasaran had to help him. He broke off when he realized I was there and said, "At last! Are *you* the Witness for the Dead?"

I looked at Tomasaran, whose ears were flat. She said, using the plural "we," "I have explained to Mer Bolorezh that we cannot help him, but he does not believe me."

"I assure you," I said, "if Othalo Tomasaran cannot help you, then neither can I."

"But you *are* the Witness for the Dead, the one the newspapers talk about."

"Yes," I said reluctantly, "that is I, but Othalo Tomasaran

"No, but the longer you put off starting, the longer it will be." I picked up the next item on the stack. "This is water-damaged and illegible. Othalo Ostilin, would you be so kind as to burn it?"

She gave me a shy smile and followed Hadrinar.

"Obviously," I said, "we can't do this one piece of paper per trip, but the principle is clear enough."

"Celehar . . ."

"I will do it all myself if I have to. But it will certainly go quicker if you help."

Shalicar's ears were flat. "Is this not dishonoring the dead?"

The question was completely unexpected. "What?"

"Going through Othala Drinimar's papers like this. It doesn't seem respectful."

"Shalicar," I said, "there's respecting the dead and then there's chaining the living to the past."

"Is that not the very definition of a Ulineise prelate? A person chained to the past?"

"Does it seem that way to you?"

"How can it *not*?"

We stared at each other in silence for several moments.

Shalicar burst out: "You're a Witness for the Dead! Is not your entire calling a chain binding you to the dead? Do you not feel dead yourself?"

I said, "If you feel that way, why did you become a Ulineise prelate?"

"What choice did I have?" And when I said nothing, he continued, "My mother died at my birth, and I am my father's fifth son. One I might have escaped, but not both. I was destined for the prelacy from the moment I was born."

"You feel no calling?" I said hesitantly.

"Calling!" Shalicar snorted. "'Delusion' is a better word."

I had known, of course, that there were prelates who felt

no calling—it could hardly be otherwise—but I had never met anyone who openly admitted it. "Is that how you ended up at Ulnemenee?"

"Was it a convenient place to put me, do you mean? Yes. Yes, it was. And Dach'othala Vernezar knows I will do what he wants, because Ulnemenee is better than being assigned solitary devotion, which Dach'othala Vernezar could do."

"And what Dach'othala Vernezar wants is for Ulnemenee to stay nonfunctional?"

"Dach'othala Vernezar wants Ulnemenee to be untroublesome. Which, given that it is perfectly stagnant, it is."

"But any effort to improve things is going to make it troublesome again," I said, understanding. "Well, Vernezar knows it's my fault, not yours."

Hadrinar and Ostilin returned, each carrying an empty flour sack.

"What an excellent idea," I said. "Shalicar, this is going to happen whether you help or not. But if you aren't going to help, you would probably be more comfortable somewhere else."

He sighed and said, "No, Ulnemenee is my ulimeire. I will help."

"Thank you," I said and picked up the next piece of paper.

When I emerged from Ulnemenee, I was startled by how late it had gotten. I was lucky enough to find a tobastha cart still doing business and dined on chicken tobastha, eaten while walking to the Opera. My luck held, and I did not drip anything on my clothes.

The front office staff behind the ticket windows waved to me, and I waved back. I made my way around to Iäna's box to see what was happening on stage.

It was all stagehands this evening, doing last-minute checks of the complicated scenery for *The Dream of the Empress Corivero,* which was a sort of series of nested boxes that opened one at a time, drawing the audience farther and farther into the garden. Anyone who was asked would have heard at least one story of a production of *Corivero* going wrong, and I could understand the stagehands' obsessive care.

I watched them peacefully for some time, until the box's second door opened and Iäna came through from backstage. "Oh good, thou'rt here," he said and dropped into the other chair. "I will be wretched company, but I am glad thou cam'st."

"I am looking forward to it," I said.

"It will be either magnificent or disastrous," Iäna said and got out his notebook.

The Dream of the Empress Corivero was a beautiful opera, sometimes whimsical, as with the children's chorus singing tree frogs, sometimes full of grandeur, as with the great procession at the end, always exquisite. The appeal of the opera was the richness of its score and, frequently, in the opulence of its staging. In the first act, Corivero talks to the flowers—the Chorus of Roses, the Lily, the Ordenna, the Aivalo, the Lilac—then, accompanied by the Chorus of Rooks singing the last song of twilight, the Lily takes Corivero through to the bower of the Queen of the Night Garden. I knew the Queen was Min Lochareth, the senior principal alto, but I would never have recognized her beneath the Queen's maquillage and elaborate wig. The Queen presents for Corivero the Masque of the Garden, in which the Ordenna and the Lilac are joined by the Mailin and the Elesth to perform some stunning four-part harmony and Corivero sings her delight. I remembered what Iäna had said about Corivero's arias—easy to start, difficult to end—and glanced sideways at him, but could read nothing from his face.

In the third act, accompanied by the Chorus of Tree Frogs, the Queen of the Night Garden brings Corivero down to the River, where she listens to the River's handmaidens singing, and then talks to the River and to the Great Willow until the Queen reappears, this time escorting the Light of Day, and with a cavalcade of flowers behind them. When they have crossed the stage and the lights rise, Corivero is back in her bedroom.

I listened with great pleasure to the tripartite River's aria, the two tenors and the baritone blending their voices to create the effect of running water. The bass playing the Willow Tree was too young for the part, but that was not his fault, and he was doing an admirable job. And the set and costumes were magnificent, the River wearing silk in shimmering layers of blue and turquoise and teal and the Willow splendid in brown velvet with green embroidery. Corivero's elaborate white dress—supposedly her nightgown, but I thought even empresses probably didn't wear quite that much lace to bed—stood out beautifully among the deep greens of the garden set, the masses and masses of silk flowers. And at the end, as the Light of Day and her lantern left the stage, the entire set simply lifted away, leaving Corivero standing alone. And as she turned, her skirts flaring wildly around her, the original set—the Empress's bedroom—moved out from the wings to enclose her.

The applause was tumultuous and I was glad to join in, glad that it had not been the disaster Iäna had half predicted. After the curtain calls, for which a beaming Iäna joined his singers, I hesitated, unsure whether I should wait for Iäna or simply go home. The backstage door swung open and Iäna leaned in. "Wait. I have not forgotten the matter of thy coat."

"But it—"

"*Wait,*" he said urgently and the door closed again.

I waited. It was not very long before Iäna reappeared and said, "Sorry about that. Wilt thou come with me to Wardrobe?"

"It's not necessary," I said.

"A plague upon 'necessary,'" said Iäna. "It will please me and all of thy other friends, and I think thou canst not be entirely happy that thy coat of office looks like a secondhander."

He saw he had caught me and said, "Ha! Come, Thara. It will not take long."

I followed him through the labyrinth of the Opera's backstage, down a narrow staircase so steeply pitched it was nearly a ladder, and along a hallway I was sure I'd never seen before, to come out in front of the doors painted WARDROBE. One leaf was propped open with a chair, and in the chair was sitting Ulsheän Adalharad, the part-goblin mistress of the Vermilion Opera's Wardrobe, who was sewing bright silk flowers onto the skirts of a severe black dress.

"Hello, Ulsheän," Iäna said. "Did Deniän rip her dress?"

"Hello, Iäna," Merrem Adalharad said, anchoring her needle to look up at him. "No, this is the understudy's dress. I'm only just now getting around to finishing it, which tells you what kind of a week it's been down here. And my girls are all out helping the singers. What can I do for you?"

"My friend," said Iäna, waving a hand at me, "has a coat."

She looked at me. "Good evening, Othala Celehar."

"Good evening, Merrem Adalharad," I said. I had encountered her only once before, in the search for Arveneän Shelsin's killer, but she had been cooperative and had told me a good deal about how the backstage of the Opera, which was in truth most of it, functioned.

I saw that her attention had been caught by my coat and said, "It was badly damaged a couple of weeks ago, but I do not think my laundress has done a bad job of the mending."

"In justice to your laundress," said Merrem Adalharad, "no, she didn't do a bad job. But I have girls who can give you better than 'not bad.' Let me see that coat."

I took it off and handed it to her across the spread of the understudy's dress. She promptly turned it inside out and inspected it, grumbling under her breath. I tried not to feel awkward about being in my shirtsleeves.

Finally, Merrem Adalharad said, "Othala, it would be much easier to make you a new coat."

"I cannot let you do that," I said, "for I cannot possibly afford it. For that matter, I cannot afford—"

"Stop," said Iäna. "I think it is not unfair to say that the Opera owes you a debt for uncovering the murderer of Min Shelsin."

"I follow my calling," I said. "There is no debt." Besides, although I did not say it, he and I both knew that I had also been the cause of Tura Olora committing suicide.

"Will you trade?" said Merrem Adalharad.

"Trade?"

"I'm sure we've got a prelate's coat back here that will fit you."

"I can't wear a *costume* as my coat of office."

"No, no, it's perfectly genuine," said Iäna. "We get all kinds of things from secondhand stores."

"But it's not . . ."

"Is the coat sacred?" Iäna said.

"Not as such, no. But I am expected to treat it with the dignity befitting my office."

"There's nothing undignified about it," said Iäna. "It's

a Ulineise prelate's coat of office, the same as if you had bought it from the secondhand store yourself. And don't pretend you wouldn't have, either."

"I don't want a new coat," I said.

"Don't be a bully, Iäna," said Merrem Adalharad.

"Sorry," Iäna said. "I get overenthusiastic."

"We could still do a better job with the mending," said Merrem Adalharad, using the plural "we," "but we would have to lend you a coat, for it can't be done tonight."

"I thank you," I said, "but I think I would rather just keep my coat as it is."

She handed me the coat and said, as I shrugged back into it, "If you change your mind, othala, you are welcome to come back."

"Thank you," I said. "I do appreciate the offer."

"It wasn't a bad idea," Iäna said.

"No, but I would rather not," I said, and he nodded acquiescence. Merrem Adalharad freed her needle and returned, with neat, quick stitches, to securing a purple silk flower to the dress. "Good night, Merrem Adalharad."

"Good night, othala," she said.

"I confess I have no idea how to get out from here," I said to Iäna.

He laughed. "It is a little like the giants' castle in the wonder-tale. This way."

It was not the way we had come. I followed him.

I FELL EXHAUSTED into bed that night and slept like a lead weight until dawn, when I crawled reluctantly out of bed, meditated barrenly on my fear of the revethavar, and went to the municipal baths, where the hot water did its work. I felt, if not precisely refreshed, at least less fatigued, and I used the full-length mirror in the changing room to pin my hair back into a neat braid. I looked at my coat in the mirror and decided that I had been an idiot not to accept Iäna's offer.

But, really, the coat would do. I walked to the Red Dog's Dream for breakfast, then caught the tram up to the Amal'ostro, nodded to Captain Olgarezh as I passed, and walked to Tomasaran's office in the Prince Zhaicava Building. Soon, I would have to stop doing this and let her do the work on her own.

Tomasaran was already there. "Good morning, Celehar."

"Good morning," I said, sitting down.

We heard someone running down the hall and were both staring at the doorway when a panting part-goblin boy appeared and said, "Please, you must come."

"Come where?" said Tomasaran.

"The Vermilion Opera."

"The *Opera*?" I said. "What has happened?"

"Please," the boy said again. "Ortanis has found a dead man in one of the boxes."

Tomasaran and I exchanged a horrified look, and Tomasaran said, using the plural, "We will come."

"Does Mer Pel-Thenhior know?" I said.

"Zhana was sent to find him," the boy said. "Mer Kalmened was already in his office."

"Do you know who the dead man is?" I said.

"No," the boy said. "Just that he is dead."

That being the only real criterion we had, Tomasaran and I followed the boy out of the Prince Zhaicava Building, north and east around the Amal'theileian to the Plaza of the Armistice, and then up one block on Indigo Street to the Vermilion Opera, where there was a clump of extremely distressed people standing in the lobby. I recognized Mer Kalmened, the administrator of the Opera, and one of the others was clearly the man who'd found the body, given his agitation.

"Othala Celehar!" said Mer Kalmened, part goblin and very tall. We had spoken to each other only once before, when I was questioning everyone about the death of Arveneän Shelsin, and I had thought then that he did not think very much of Witnesses for the Dead. "Thank goodness you've come."

I said, "This is Othalo Tomasaran, who will be fulfilling my duties while I am traveling." I had settled on that, finally, as the simplest way to explain Tomasaran without having to explain myself. And if it was a lie, it didn't matter, because I wasn't a Witness. "Othalo Tomasaran, this is Mer Kalmened, who runs all the parts of the Vermilion Opera that Mer Pel-Thenhior does not."

"Othalo," said Mer Kalmened, and they exchanged bows. "Will you come with me?"

"Of course," said Tomasaran, and the two of us followed Mer Kalmened into the auditorium foyer and up the stairs to the first row of boxes. He turned right and stopped at the first door we came to, which had the Parzhadeise crest of a wolf and three stars on it. I had a sudden horrible certainty of who the dead man was.

"It's Mer Dravenezh," said Mer Kalmened as he unlocked the door.

Tomasaran glanced at me, her eyebrows raised. I said, "Mer Dravenezh is the secretary of the Marquess Parzhadel. He attends the Opera faithfully."

"Yes," said Mer Kalmened. "He attended the premiere of *The Dream of the Empress Corivero* last night and . . . well, someone is supposed to check all the boxes before we lock the doors, and didn't." He held the door open so we could enter the box.

The inside was as lavish as the gilded outside. Mer Dravenezh was slumped over in one of the elegant chairs, a knife hilt protruding from his back.

"He would've been dead before he realized what was happening," I said. "This person either knew what they were doing or got very lucky."

"Should I?" said Tomasaran.

"Yes," I said. "You never know what you may find."

She murmured the prayer of compassion for the dead and stepped forward to touch the dead man gently on the shoulder. I had never realized, when I was the one speaking to the spirits, how awkward the silence was. I folded my hands and contemplated the view from the Marquess Parzhadel's box.

At the moment, it was an excellent view of the curtain, which was painted with an elaborate pattern that made it look like wrought iron. The auditorium lights were at half, presumably so that the maintenance crew could see what they were doing. The rows of seats in the pit seemed endless.

Tomasaran stepped back. "You were correct," she said. "He was watching the opera and didn't even have time to feel pain. He certainly didn't know there was anyone else in the box with him."

"Yes," I said. "There was no disturbance last night. Whoever did this chose their moment very carefully."

"Oh dear," said Mer Kalmened. "I admit I was hoping for a quick answer."

"I'm sorry," said Tomasaran.

"You can't find answers that aren't there," I said.

"I did not mean to imply blame," said Mer Kalmened. "Just that . . ."

"Yes," I said. "It would have been better to have no mystery."

"Othala Celehar," said Tomasaran. "May I speak to you for a moment privately?"

"I need to go back to the office in any event," said Mer Kalmened. "Can you find your way out?"

"Yes," I said. "Thank you."

He hurried away, and I said to Tomasaran, "What is it?"

"When Mer Dravenezh died," she said carefully, "he was thinking about his lover."

"And?"

"His lover was Tura Olora."

I almost did her the discourtesy of asking if she was sure, and I knew my ears betrayed my shock.

"I cannot be mistaken," she said. "But I remember your telling me that Tura Olora was the man who killed Arveneän Shelsin."

"To protect his lover, yes."

"Do you think that is why he was killed? Not that he was Mer Olora's lover, but the reason that Mer Olora thought he needed protection . . . I'm not explaining myself well."

"No, I understand you," I said. I looked back at the corpse. "And it certainly looks as though Mer Dravenezh needed protecting."

The clatter of someone coming very quickly up the staircase proved to be Iäna.

"This is dreadful," he said. "Who in the world would want to murder poor Mer Dravenezh?"

Tomasaran hesitated.

I said, "Mer Pel-Thenhior knows that Tura Olora died to protect his lover."

"Why are we talking about Tura?" said Iäna.

"Tura Olora was Mer Dravenezh's lover," said Tomasaran.

Iäna was as taken aback as I had been. "Tura? And Mer Dravenezh? I didn't even know they *knew* each other. But why should that make anyone want to murder Mer Dravenezh, especially when Tura has already killed himself?"

"I think that depends on what was in the letter," I said.

"The letter?" said Tomasaran.

"The letter that Arveneän Shelsin stole and Tura Olora killed both her and himself to keep secret."

"Ah," said Iäna. "You think there was something more than just the secret of the love affair between Ema Dravenezh and Tura."

"Mer Dravenezh's murder certainly suggests so," I said. "*He* can't have been killed to keep the fact of the relationship secret, for I cannot see that he had any reason to disclose it, nor that he could harm anyone but himself in so doing. But it seems highly unlikely that the two deaths—three, counting Min Shelsin—are unrelated."

"I see your point," Iäna said. His ears dipped; he said, "What must we do? There's never been a dead body *in* the Opera before. When Tura killed himself, the Brotherhood was already there and didn't need any help from us."

"I think we are still waiting for a messenger to return from the Marquess Parzhadel," I said. "He will know if Mer Dravenezh had family in Amalo—he may wish to see to the burial himself. If not—"

"No, he almost certainly will," Iäna said.

"It would be one fewer problem," I admitted. "Because otherwise the body ought to be taken to the municipal ulimeire and that . . . won't work in this case. He'll probably end up at Ulvanensee as Mer Olora did."

"Are you witnessing for him?" Iäna asked, looking from me to Tomasaran.

I was on the verge of replying when I thought better of it. I certainly *could* continue to direct the business of the office, but that was not necessarily in anyone's best interest, including mine.

Tomasaran gave me a stricken look and said, "I don't know. Mer Kalmened merely asked if we could find out who did it."

"From the fact that you're still standing here, I gather that you couldn't," Iäna said.

"No, Mer Dravenezh didn't even know there was someone in the box with him. But that's not witnessing *for* him, is it?"

"No," I said. "To witness for him, you first have to be petitioned, and no one has petitioned you yet."

"It is very confusing," Tomasaran said.

"It becomes easier with practice," I said.

"True of so many things," Iäna said, "including, I suppose, the company of dead bodies. Must you stay here, or can we go somewhere more comfortable?"

"You needn't stay," I said.

"It is very likely that the marquess's envoy will have a message for me," Iäna said. "It only makes sense to wait for him somewhere that I know he'll have to go. I am quite certain that the marquess will petition you on Mer Dravenezh's behalf."

"I have to stay with the body, don't I?" Tomasaran said.

"It depends on who you ask," I said. "Some funerary rites practiced in this city demand that the body be watched from death until burial, and then the vigil dinner after. Others don't. Ploraneise rites—and he's most *likely* Ploraneise—are content with stipulating that the body must be brought to the ulimeire as promptly as possible. Which in this case means not until we know which ulimeire to bring him to."

"And thus not until the messenger arrives from the marquess," said Iäna.

"Correct," I said.

"And until then, you don't know," said Iäna. "He might *not* be Ploraneise."

"It would be better if I stayed with the body," Tomasaran said, not asking this time. "But you need not."

"Come down to the lobby," Iäna said. "That's the way the messenger will have to come in any event."

I looked at Tomasaran. She said wryly, "It's not the body that bothers me."

"All right," I said and went with Iäna back down the stairs to the foyer.

"Let's stop here," Iäna said. "Unless thou want'st to talk to the front office staff."

"No," I said. "I have no need to talk to any of them. Tomasaran may."

"Thara," he said. "Do not torment thyself."

"It's just the custom of thought," I said. "I keep tripping over things that aren't my duty any longer. But I'm not tormenting myself. I don't *mind* it. I just keep having to remember it again."

Iäna did not look as if he entirely believed me, but he said, "I'm trying to think if there are other people Mer Dravenezh might have known. But he kept very much to himself. Never had a guest in the Parzhadel box, never tried to insinuate himself backstage—although now I suppose *that* makes sense—never caused any kind of fuss. It's frankly shocking that he should have had this much effect on someone."

"To drive them to murder?"

"Yes. At least, I assume that the person who did it felt strongly about it."

"They were certainly firm of purpose," I said. "They killed him with one blow."

"How ghastly," said Iäna. He looked at me curiously. "Do you become inured to the details with practice?"

"I suppose so. I've been preparing bodies for burial since I was thirteen."

"Death holds no mystery for you."

"Only the mystery of who did it."

THE MESSENGER TO the Marquess Parzhadel made good time, but it was still nearly noon before he returned, sweating and exhausted, with the marquess's message.

"As I thought," said Iäna, skimming the contents. "He wants the body brought to the estate so they can bury it in the Parzhadeise graveyard."

"That's an honor for a secretary," I said.

Iäna made a face. "He's also the bastard child of Parzhadel's mother's brother."

"Cousins," I said.

"Yes. *And* he served Parzhadel faithfully and well. I don't know if they liked each other, but Mer Dravenezh was fiercely loyal."

"Yes," I said, thinking of the one time I had spoken to him.

"So now we just have to arrange transportation. The Parzhadada do not happen to have a hearse."

"Thou'lt be able to rent one," I said.

"And a coachman, I hope. Unless one of the company has a skill they haven't told me about."

"I can drive it," I said. "That was one of my duties in Lohaiso."

"Wouldst thou?" said Iäna.

"Of course," I said. "I will go obtain the hire of a hearse if thou wilt find someone—or probably two—to carry Mer Dravenezh down to the lobby."

"Yes," said Iäna. "I'll have to find Grolana. He owes me a favor."

"I'll just tell Othalo Tomasaran the plan," I said and went back up the stairs to the Parzhadel box, where Tomasaran was sitting in the second chair, contemplating the corpse.

"You don't literally have to keep your eyes on it all the time," I said.

"No, I know. I was just thinking about how horribly easy this murder was. He wouldn't have gotten any blood on him, and he didn't have to worry about what to do with the knife."

"And he could just return to his box and no one would be the wiser," I said.

"You think he has a box?"

"Or he rented one for the night. He'd run the risk of encountering a page boy if he had a seat in the pit. A box would make everything much easier."

"And maybe he does have a box," said Tomasaran. "Rich people can be murderers, too."

"Yes, they can," I said. "But I came up to tell you the messenger has come back from the Marquess Parzhadel, and we need to take the body out to the estate."

"We?" she said.

"You can go alone if you like," I said, surprised. "And if you can drive a team."

"That's not what I meant. Are you saying I have to go?"

"You're the Witness for the Dead," I said patiently. "The marquess may very well want to petition you on behalf of Mer Dravenezh. Certainly he will want to talk to you."

"I can't solve a murder!"

"You've watched me do it."

"But—"

"I will not desert you," I said.

"Can't you just . . ."

"Do it myself?"

"Well, yes," she said, almost defiantly.

"I'm not the Witness for the Dead."

"You're splitting hairs."

"No. It is important. You are the only person in Amalo who can be a Witness *vel ama* for Mer Dravenezh."

"But I learned nothing from his corpse!"

"Not entirely true," I said.

"Celehar—"

Iäna said from the door of the box, "Is this a bad time?"

Tomasaran and I both startled.

"Sorry," said Iäna, "but I found Grolana, and we're ready when you are." One of the stagehands, a goblin with a goblin's hulking shoulders, was standing behind him.

"Very good," I said. "Tomasaran and I can argue all the way out to Gulanee, but I'd better go get the hearse."

THE NEAREST LIVERY stable, which I found with directions from Mer Kalmened, had one hearse and a team of dark bay horses, who were close enough to black to suit. I was unlikely to find better, so I paid the deposit, wincing at the cost even though it was the Opera's money, not mine, and waited while the ostlers harnessed the horses.

I swung up on the box and took the reins and whip. The horses proved mercifully placid beasts, and pedestrians and traffic gave way for us. When I pulled up outside the Vermilion Opera, Iäna was watching for me. "The props and sets crew built him a coffin while we were waiting for the messenger," he said. "So it's more a prop than a real coffin—I wouldn't want to try to take it up or down stairs, for instance—but it's better than nothing."

"Yes, it is," I said. And they brought him out very solemnly, Iäna and a handful of stagehands whose names I did not know, all goblins and part-goblins. Tomasaran came out behind them and climbed up beside me on the box, while the men lifted the coffin into the hearse.

"*Are* we going to argue all the way there?" she said.

"Not by choice," I said.

"No, you're right," she said. "I must speak to the marquess. Although I can still hope he will want a judicial Witness instead of me."

"We're set," said Iäna. "We've latched the door and everything."

"Thank you," I said, and we started for the Marquess Parzhadel's estate.

ON THE WAY out, I told Tomasaran about Tura Olora.

She already knew part of it, that he had murdered Arveneän Shelsin and then committed suicide, but she had not known what he had said about keeping his lover safe.

"He was right," she said. "Clearly, Mer Dravenezh *was* in danger."

"Yes. But from whom? Who would care enough about an affair between an opera singer and a marquess's secretary to do murder?"

"A jilted lover," Tomasaran suggested.

"Yes, but Mer Olora's suicide couldn't have protected Mer Dravenezh from that. There was some secret he was trying to keep *beyond* the fact that they were lovers."

"Perhaps they were Curneisei."

It was a good idea—after three Curneisei were found to have assassinated the Emperor Varenechibel IV and his heirs (all save Edrehasivar VII), anyone subscribing to that philosophy would have good reason to keep it secret—but, "No, Tura Olora was not Curneisei. The opposite, if anything. His complaints about 'riffraff' in the Opera were heartfelt."

"Did Mer Olora have any family? Someone who might be angry at Mer Dravenezh because of their affair?"

"He had no one who cared enough to come to his funeral," I said, "so I don't think so."

"How sad," said Tomasaran. "At least Mer Dravenezh has someone who cares that he is dead."

"No one wants to be seen mourning for a suicide," I said.

"As if it were contagious," she said, and made a warding gesture just to be sure that it was not.

THE GATE IN the wall was open when we reached Gulanee, the Parzhadeise estate. The gatekeeper came out and asked, "Are you the Witness for the Dead?"

Tomasaran said, "Yes," without my having to prompt her.

"The marquess wishes to speak to you right away." He looked uncertainly at me, and Tomasaran said quickly, "Othala Celehar is our colleague. He comes with us."

"All right, othalo," said the gatekeeper. He held the horses while Tomasaran and I got down, and by then a groom had appeared to climb up and take the reins.

We were led up to the house by an elven page boy. It was a massive building stuccoed a soft gold color; inside, the walls were a chaos of paintings hung so close together they almost overlapped, and the floor was an intricate parquet, rather like a quilt pattern but done in pale woods. The page boy led us swiftly down a long, well-lit hall to an open door, where he said loudly, "The Witness for the Dead," and gestured us inside. Tomasaran gave me an apprehensive look, then straightened her shoulders and went in. I followed.

The first thing one noticed about the bedroom of the Marquess Parzhadel was the bed, a great hulking four-poster made of purple-black renazbeth wood. The bed was hung with silks in light colors, and the counterpane was pale green embroidered with a garden of elaborate flowers.

The second thing one noticed was the marquess, who sat back against the headboard, propped and protected by an infinity of pillows. Even by elven standards he was very pale, and his cheekbones stood out harshly in his thin face. But his gray eyes were bright and his hair, dressed in braids and buns and hanging loose over his shoulders, was clearly *not* a wig. He was much younger than I had expected, only a few years older than the emperor.

The first thing he said, frowning, was, "But why are there two of you?" His voice was as light as his eyes—and as sharp.

Tomasaran, to her credit, said promptly, "Othala Celehar is teaching us how to be a Witness for the Dead."

"We did not know Witnesses for the Dead had an apprenticing system."

"Ordinarily we don't," I said, "but Othalo Tomasaran has come late to her calling."

"Ah," said the marquess. "We understand, then, that one of you is the Witness for our cousin."

"Not formally," I said, "although Othalo Tomasaran has witnessed to his death."

"What must we do to make your witnessing formal?" the marquess said patiently.

"Oh!" said Tomasaran. "You must petition us."

"Thank you," said the marquess. "Then we petition you to witness for our murdered cousin, Ema Dravenezh." His voice did not waver, but it was obviously an effort.

"It is a rightful petition," said Tomasaran, "and we are honored to accept it." I had to admire her acting ability; she neither sounded nor looked nervous.

"Very good," said the marquess. "Now, what can we do to help you in your witnessing?"

Tomasaran shot me a pleading glance.

I said, "Is there anyone you can think of who would have wanted to harm him?"

"No," said the marquess. "No one. He was a very quiet person."

"Anyone who might wish to harm *you* by killing him?"

He made a warding gesture. "What a terrible thought." He considered it carefully, though, before saying, "We have . . . perhaps 'antagonists' is the best word. But no one who would murder an innocent man merely to wound us."

"Do you know of anyone else we could talk to? Someone who might have seen a different part of him?"

"Well, yes, of course," said the marquess. "You should talk to his sister."

"His sister?" said Tomasaran.

"His mother and our uncle were long-term lovers, and they had two children: Ema and Orazheän. Ema was fostered with us so that he might find a place in our household. Orazheän was apprenticed to the Procurers' Guild. She's a brothel manager in Paravi. The brothel is called the Verashme Circle, but that is all we know about it."

"That is very helpful," I said.

"Is it?" said the marquess. "It seems like pitifully little to go on. Paravi is not a small district."

"The postal service will know how to find it," I said.

"Ah," said the marquess. "We would not have thought of that."

"We must find her anyway," I said. "To notify her of the death."

"Yes, we suppose you must." The marquess looked both very young and very weary. "Any help you need, please come to us. We desire more than anything—well, more than anything other than to have Ema back—we desire more than anything to have this murderer caught."

"No matter who it is?" I said.

"Yes," said the marquess. "No matter who it is."

We returned the hearse to the livery stable, and there was time to go to the postal service's main office and get the location of the post office of the Verashme Circle. Tomasaran did the talking.

"You'll have to go out there tomorrow afternoon," I told her as we came down the stairs of the Prince Thuvenis Building.

"Me?" she said. "What about you?"

"Back to Ulnemenee," I said. "I can play truant for one afternoon, but not more than that."

"Celehar, I've never notified anyone of a death before."

"Sadly," I said, "it isn't hard. Make sure she's sitting down. Don't draw it out. 'We regret to tell you that your brother, Ema Dravenezh, has been murdered.' She will have questions, which can lead naturally to you asking questions of her. You want to get as much as you can from her the first time. If you have to go back, she's unlikely to be welcoming."

"Experience?"

"Experience. Most people will want a murderer caught, but they won't want to be involved in any way with the process. With good reason. It is an ugly business."

"You say that of your calling?"

"Absolutely," I said, surprised. "Murder is ugly. Uncovering the truth of a murder is therefore also ugly. And so often the answer is not what people want it to be."

"You think the marquess didn't mean what he said?"

"He meant it," I said. "But he may not be aware of what it means."

In the morning, Tomasaran and I arrived at her office at the same time. (The captain was busy when I passed him, and I was unreasonably disappointed.) She had stopped on her way in to collect the post. "There's a letter for you. From the Sanctuary."

No need to ask how she knew when the letter was sealed with the Sanctuary's sigil.

"It's probably from Dach'othala Ulzhavar," I said as I opened it and was immediately proven wrong. It was from Othalo Rasaltezhen and said, *My friend Doret Athmaza and I have thought of something. If you can come to my workroom today or tomorrow, I think perhaps we can help.*

Tomasaran insisted I go to the Sanctuary at once, as if there were some danger of Othalo Rasaltezhen forgetting her idea. I took the tram down to the Sanctuary, where I found young, part-goblin Othalo Rasaltezhen in her workroom, along with an elven man in a blue maza's robe.

"Othala Celehar!" she said, smiling. "This is Doret Athmaza, who often collaborates with me. We think we may have found a way to repair the damage done you by the revethavar."

"That is good to hear," I said cautiously. Doret Athmaza and I bowed to each other; he was more what I had thought Othalo Rasaltezhen would be before I met her: elven and middle-aged. "I admit I was not expecting anything."

"And we may be wrong," said Othalo Rasaltezhen. "This is all hypothesis and speculation."

"But worth a try," said Doret Athmaza. "Even if it does not work, we will have gained much valuable information for the next try."

The way he spoke of a next try was both discouraging and heartening.

"What do you need me to do?" I asked.

"Come sit over here again," said Othalo Rasaltezhen, "and then I am afraid that most of what you have to do is be patient."

I sat in the chair she indicated. She sat in the other chair and Doret Athmaza stood behind her.

"Meet my gaze," said Othalo Rasaltezhen. I did and was aware immediately of her looking through my eyes into my mind. It was no less unpleasant than it had been the first time.

Othalo Rasaltezhen and Doret Athmaza began a low-voiced, elliptical conversation of which I could make no sense, but I could tell, after about five minutes, when they both started getting cautiously excited. I felt nothing, which was far preferable to the agony of the revethavar's attack, but before long, Othalo Rasaltezhen said, "It is working. The damage is repairable—although, like anything mended, it will not be the same as it was."

"I would not expect it to be," I said. To distract myself from the naked feeling of Othalo Rasaltezhen and Doret Athmaza knowing where I was hurt, I said, "Can you tell me anything of what you are doing?"

"Only in metaphors," said Othalo Rasaltezhen, "and those probably not very accurate. But I could say there is a wall in your mind, like the wall of a house, that the revethavar has torn down. We are going through the rubble and putting the wall back together."

"It sounds rather tedious."

"Not at all!" said Othalo Rasaltezhen. "The revethavar did not actually *destroy* anything, in the sense that there don't seem to be any pieces missing. Which is good."

"Yes," I said.

"Maybe a document is a better comparison. The revethavar tore it to pieces and scattered it around the room, so to speak. We are putting the pieces back together as we find them, and I do think that this would have happened eventually on its own, although I have no idea of how long it might have taken. The pieces adhere to each other as we put them together."

"So it isn't . . ."

"Isn't what?" said Othalo Rasaltezhen, when it became clear that I was not going to finish the sentence without prompting.

"Isn't unnatural, I was going to say, but that's a foolish question."

"The revethavar was unnatural," said Doret Athmaza.

"Yes, I take your point," I said.

"Healing is the most natural thing imaginable," said Othalo Rasaltezhen. "And I follow my calling just as you do, Othala Celehar."

"Yes," I said. "I apologize, I don't know why I said that."

"It's understandable to be concerned," said Othalo

Rasaltezhen. "We're trying something none of us has done before, and there are always those who will say that anything new is against nature."

"My teacher was one such," I said. I did not remember Othala Pelovar with any fondness.

"Then there you are," said Othalo Rasaltezhen. "But it is not unnatural."

"Thank you," I said, and in truth I was relieved that she said it so readily. I had been accused often enough of being unnatural for being marnis, a man who desired other men. I did not need another reason.

The document-mending was a slow process. Othalo Rasaltezhen's penetrating gaze did not become more comfortable, but I became more accustomed to it. It was still unnerving that I could not feel what she and Doret Athmaza were doing, but I reminded myself that I was lucky—it could have been as painful as the revethavar's attack, in which case I would not have been able to bear it and I did not try to pretend otherwise.

When at last Othalo Rasaltezhen sat back, releasing me from her gaze, I felt no different. "Is it done?" I asked.

"We have repaired everything we can see to repair," said Othalo Rasaltezhen. "Which does not exactly answer your question, but it is the best I can do."

"The only way to tell will be to try," said Doret Athmaza.

"I suppose there are enough bodies in the mortuary that Dach'othala Ulzhavar will not begrudge an experiment," I said.

"We will come with you," said Othalo Rasaltezhen, and she and Doret Athmaza accompanied me around the spiral hallway and down the stairs to the mortuary, where Ulzhavar, the Master of the Mortuary, middle-aged, elven, and as usual wearing workman's boots beneath his cleric's robes, said, "Yes, absolutely," before Othalo Rasaltezhen had finished explaining. He took us to the newest body he had, an old woman who had died that morning of a charcorsa.

I said the prayer of compassion for the dead without letting myself rush through it like a novice, and touched her forehead.

Nothing.

I waited, although it had never been anything but instantaneous, but there was nothing. I might just as well have been trying to talk to the table.

Othalo Rasaltezhen said, "We will have to try again, but not, I think, today. I am exhausted, I am sure Doret Athmaza is exhausted, and forgive my saying so, Othala Celehar, but you look like you have a headache."

She was correct, now that I let myself think about it.

"You all need food," Ulzhavar said firmly. "Come to lunch with me at the Glass Phoenix."

I hesitated, and he said, "They're not nearly as expensive as they sound. Come, Celehar, you have to eat *somewhere*."

"Yes, all right," I said.

The Glass Phoenix was a converted row house, narrow but tall. We found a circular booth on the second floor, padded, backed by the walls, and curtained for privacy. Ulzhavar and I sat on one side, and Othalo Rasaltezhen and Doret Athmaza on the other, and Ulzhavar tied the curtain back so that the servers would know we were there. Ulzhavar recommended the house specialty, which was Cairado-style albarat. "The owners are from Cairado," he said, "so it really is 'Cairado-style.'"

Ulzhavar did most of the talking, and it was mostly about Coralis Clunethar. The newspapers were full of him—he'd been spotted in Amalo; he'd been spotted in Ezho; he'd been spotted on the South Road. He was going to raise his banner; he was going to seek asylum in the Untheileneise Court; he was going to renounce his claim to the principate. "No one knows anything," said Ulzhavar, "which means that the newspapers can say whatever they like. You may be sure that whatever he *is* doing, he won't tell the newspapers about it. He is both too canny for that and not canny enough."

"What do you mean?" said Doret Athmaza.

"Well, it's obvious why you wouldn't share your plans to overthrow your cousin's government with the newspapers, but a *truly* canny man—and I am grateful Coralis Clunethar is not one—would be wooing the newspapers to get them on his side. Because Prince Orchenis certainly isn't going to. And the more popular you are with the newspapers, and with the newspaper readers, the harder it is, for example, for your cousin to become fed up with your antics and have you executed. But Coralis is like his father, who never forgave Prince Orchena for building the Amal'ostro and never saw the point of it. He took after *their* father, who felt that it was the sacred right of the Clunethada to rule Thu-Athamar, and everyone else was just here to be ruled. Prince Orchena had many flaws, but he did at least understand that ruling the principate was an obligation, not merely a source of money and power, and thankfully Prince Orchenis has in that way followed his father's lead."

"It would be to everyone's benefit for Prince Orchenis to have a son," said Doret Athmaza.

"And soon," agreed Ulzhavar. "The more there is standing between Coralis and the principate throne, the better."

"Do you think it could be true that he's heading for the Untheileneise Court?" said Othalo Rasaltezhen.

"Possible but unlikely," said Ulzhavar. "He will not find a sympathetic listener in Edrehasivar." He glanced at me.

"I am no expert on the emperor," I said. I had hoped to be left out of the conversation entirely, left to lick my wounds in peace.

"Yes, but you've *met* him," said Ulzhavar, "which is more than anyone else in this establishment can say. And the newspapers say that you have his favor."

"I wish they would not," I said. "But, no, I do not think the emperor would give Coralis Clunethar any support. Prince Orchenis has been unwaveringly loyal, and anyone whose reign begins with two coup attempts is going to appreciate that."

"Rather," said Ulzhavar.

"That is some comfort," said Othalo Rasaltezhen. "Without the chance of the emperor's support, there is much less damage Coralis can do."

"Except assassination," said Doret Athmaza, and we all made warding gestures.

"No need to knock down my house of cards," Othalo Rasaltezhen said, although she did not sound resentful. "But, yes, you're right. If you have people to help you—as Coralis does—assassination requires nothing but idiocy."

"But *who* is helping him?" said Doret Athmaza. "That's the question the newspapers are afraid to answer."

"He is, of course," said Ulzhavar, "popular with those who dislike Prince Orchenis's policies, such as the Cambeshada, who follow like sheep where Dach'osmer Nedeva Cambeshar leads."

I shivered, remembering the interview with Dach'osmer Cambeshar in which I had all but accused him of Arveneän Shelsin's murder, remembering how cold his eyes were.

"And I don't know," Ulzhavar said. "Some people fall for Coralis's particular kind of romantic reactionary nonsense. He claims to be following the ideals of Prince Azorna, who ruled the principate two hundred years ago and was much beloved. Some people who don't like the way things are now want to go forward, even though we don't know exactly what 'forward' is going to look like, but some people want to go backward to where they think they know *exactly* what it will look like, even though they're wrong."

"Some people will do anything to stop change," said Doret Athmaza. "And yet change always happens anyway."

At Ulnemenee, I found to my surprised pleasure that Shalicar and his junior prelates were at work in Othala Drinimar's study, Shalicar passing judgment on each piece of paper and handing it to either Hadrinar or Ostilin, who would put it in one of the flour sacks. When a flour sack was full, it was carried off to the refectory fireplace and emptied into the flames. Progress was slow—every so often, Shalicar said, he would find a piece of paper that was relevant to the running of Ulnemenee, and that made him reluctant to hurry—but it was progress.

"Can I help?" I said.

"I don't think there's room," Shalicar said. "There's barely room for *me,* and Hadrinar and Ostilin have to have a clear path to the door."

Clearly, he did not want help, and I found the change in attitude so marvelous that I did not want to do anything that might change it back. I decided to go home early and sweep my room.

I took the Zulnicho line south (a different captain on duty) and walked from the ostro to my tenement building, hurrying because it was cold and the wind made the tips of my ears sting.

I was almost there when a man came barreling out of an alley and nearly knocked me flat. He was elven, about my age, and wild-eyed with desperation. "Oh, othala, come quickly!" he said, clutching at my sleeve.

"What's wrong?" I said, trying to disentangle myself from his grip. But he got an arm around my shoulders and shoved me into the alley. "What is it?"

"My brother," he said, crowding me further into the alley. "Oh, do please hurry!"

In the narrow alley, I couldn't get around him back to the street, and he kept pushing me forward.

"Wait," I said, trying to plant my feet. "Just a minute!"

"Sorry, othala," said a new voice. "No time to lose." And someone dropped a bag over my head.

I tried to fight them, but when I raised my hands to get the bag off my head, someone looped a rope around my wrists, and when it pulled tight, all I could do was kick. I landed one solid blow on someone's shin and was rewarded with a yelp, but there were more of them, too many hands, and I was half carried sideways and then terrifyingly down a flight of narrow, uneven stairs that seemed to go on forever. At the bottom, it was only a hard hand on my arm that kept me from falling.

"This way, othala," someone said, and I was dragged off to my left, away from the stairs. After that, I lost all hope of keeping myself oriented; I did well to keep myself on my feet as I was dragged relentlessly along. I was carried down at least two more staircases. "Lost" would have been a kind word for my state when I was finally yanked to a halt.

Someone pulled the bag off my head, and I was dazzled for a moment by lantern light. As my eyes adjusted, I saw that we were somewhere in the catacombs—self-evident by the plaqued revethmerai surrounding us—and that I was outnumbered five to one.

One of them said, "Are you all right, Othala Celehar?" He was part goblin, middle-aged, and there was nothing about his face I would have looked at twice if I'd passed him in the street.

For a moment, I could not answer him in my horror that they knew my name. They had targeted me deliberately, and I had no idea of who they were. Then I said, "Yes. I am all right. But I don't understand. Who are you? What is it you want?"

"My name is Delthonar. And we have a job for you."

"A petition?" I said, if possible more bewildered than before. "Why did you not come to the office?"

"You'd never agree to it," said Delthonar.

"But then . . ."

"You have a choice," Delthonar said, and his smile was not a pleasant one. "We have a tisane of tulavero root. You can either drink it, or we can beat you senseless and pour it down your throat. Or we can leave you here in the catacombs to die. You decide."

"But what do you *want*?" I said desperately.

Delthonar shook his head. "Not until we're there. Will you drink the tulavero?"

"But if you have a petition—"

"No," he said. "Will you drink the tulavero or not?"

They were all bigger than I was, and I was no great fighter to begin with. It wasn't actually a choice except insofar as I could choose to be beaten senseless. Or not.

Or left in the catacombs to die.

"I will drink the tisane," I said.

Delthonar produced a canteen with a red-and-black warning sigil painted on it. "Drink the whole thing," he said, "and we shouldn't have to dose you again." He gave me the canteen.

I took a mouthful of tepid, strongly anise-flavored tisane. For a moment I didn't think I was going to be able to swallow it, but the look in Delthonar's eyes convinced me he was sincere in his threat.

I drank the whole canteen, although it nearly choked me. The tulavero worked quickly; I began to feel as if I were floating. The men began a conversation in Barizhin. It was hard to piece together any sense through the tulavero and my incomplete grasp of the language, but I recognized the word for a mine and the word for a priest and the word for death ("reveth," the same as in Ethuverazhin). Those were bad auspices, as was their violent method of getting my attention.

Then the words went from incomprehensible to mere noise and I was ensnared in dreams. I knew I was dreaming, but I could not escape them. The tulavero was not strong enough to make me sleep, but it was too strong to let me wake.

I dreamed of my novitiate, which had taken place in an ancient castle in Thu-Tetar: Tavolaree. I dreamed of the courtyard where we were allowed to congregate in good weather. It was the final year of my novitiate, because I was standing with Zhemena and Milharis and Dava, and it was both the courtyard of Tavolaree and the director's box at the Vermilion Opera. The auditorium was full, every seat taken up with a neat pile of bones, skull resting on top with its empty eye sockets pointed toward the stage, the bones of Ulnemenee. I knew that we were all waiting for the curtain to rise on a production of *The Grief of Stones,* which was an opera not about a lighthouse, but about Evru. And me. I kept looking for Iäna, to try to persuade him to perform something else, but he was nowhere to be seen. Zhemena said, "Thou wilt not find him. He's on the other side of the curtain."

I understood that he meant that Iäna was among the living actors, not the dead audience, and protested, "Thou art not dead."

"Am I not?" said Zhemena. "Really, Thara, how wouldst thou know? We haven't seen each other for more than a decade. I might be dead and long buried for all the knowledge thou hast."

"I would have heard," I said, but it was a feeble counter and only made him laugh.

but Delthonar was remorseless until finally he judged I had drunk enough of it and let me go. The man holding me up let go, too, and I flopped back down like a rag doll. And dreamed.

For a long time, I dreamed that I was trying to escape from the revethavar through the corn maze at the Sanctuary of Orshan, the whole time knowing how futile it was; all the revethavar had to do was wait by the entrance, which was also the exit, and it would catch me without the least exertion. But I kept going, fear and tulavero making it impossible for me to heed my own knowledge, and the corn maze changed character around me, getting darker and darker, until finally I realized it wasn't a corn maze at all, but the funerary complex beneath the Hill of Werewolves. Even as I recognized this, I came to the two snarling wolves that guarded the entrance to the crypt. They rolled their eyes at me but did not move.

I froze, afraid both of stepping between them and of what might be waiting for me in the crypt, and we all stood there unmoving until a voice called from within the crypt, "Thou mightst as well come in."

"But the wolves," I said.

"Will not harm thee. Ata! Eira!"

The wolves whined and grumbled, but they lay down, resting massive heads on stony paws, and I nerved myself to walk between them and enter the Crypt of the Praeceptors of the Wolves of Anmura.

The crypt was empty except for a tall elven man standing in the middle of the room. He wore armor that I recognized, both from the ghosts on the Hill of Werewolves and from the tailor's dummy in Osmer Ormevar's workroom. He wore his hair in a thick braid down his back, and his face was at once ascetic and cruel. I knew who he was.

"Hasthemis Brulnemar," I said.

"I was," he agreed, "and thou art Thara Celehar, a Witness for the Dead."

"I was," I said. "I don't know what I am now. A prelate of Ulis, maybe."

He looked me up and down, a cursory summing up that made my face burn, and said, "Ulis has not released his hold on thee, if that is what thou fearest."

His phrasing left it up to me whether I feared Ulis *had* let me go or whether I feared he *hadn't*. "Thou'rt a dream anyway," I said. "Hasthemis Brulnemar is long dead, and the revethavar is destroyed."

"Then why dost thou dream of me?" said Brulnemar, not at all discomfited by being told he was dead.

I had no answer, and he continued, "Thy spirit clings to my memory, for I came nearer than any ghoul to destroying thee." The thought clearly pleased him.

"Thou didst not succeed," I said.

His eyebrows went up. "No? Wert thou not destroyed, when thou foundst thyself deaf to the speech of the dead? Art thou not in truth destroyed still?"

"I am not destroyed," I said, although I wondered if it was a lie.

Brulnemar looked amused. "Bravely spoken. And thou dost continue to move and speak, but tell me truly, Thara Celehar, dost think thyself anything more than a puppet whose master has not yet cut the strings?"

"If Ulis still has need of me, I will be a puppet," I said. "Thou canst not destroy that."

"Thy master uses thee cruelly," Brulnemar said, eyes bright and very watchful. "For is not a revethavar a creature of Ulis's making?"

"No," I said. "A revethavar is made by mortals who think to cheat death. Was it a good bargain?"

That stung him on the raw. "Watch thy tongue," he

snarled, and I was sure he was going to hit me, but he did not move from his place in the center of the crypt. *Could* not move.

"Thou canst not hurt me," I said, and then realized the truth of what I had said. I said it again, "Hasthemis Brulnemar, thou canst not hurt me," and woke.

WHEN I WOKE clear-headed, I was again by a fire, this one in a three-legged brazier burning coal. I was curled on a kind of pallet, not padded enough to disguise the fact that I was lying on stone. The light of the brazier was negligible, but there was a big lantern hanging from a thick wooden beam nearby, and it cast enough light to show me the ceiling was stone as well, stone that had never been touched by tools. I was underground.

I lay for some time trying to make sense of this information, but there seemed to be none to be had. I had been kidnapped from the city and brought to a cave—but why? And by whom?

I had found no answers by the time a voice said, "Oh good, you're awake," and a big goblin man with eyes of a clear amber yellow crouched down beside me.

"Where am I?" I said, my voice a hollowed-out whisper.

"Right to the point," he said. "There are several answers, but the first one is a warning. You're the better part of a mile from the world. If you try to escape, we won't save you—not because we won't look, but because we won't be able to find you. *No one* knows the full extent of these tunnels. You don't have a rabbit's chance of finding the way out, and even if you did, you're still more than a day's travel from the nearest town. Do you understand me?"

"Yes," I said and swallowed painfully.

"Water," he said. "Just a moment." He got up and stepped

around me. I wanted to sit up—or, at least, roll over to be able to watch him—but my body seemed as heavy and inert as lead.

It was only a few moments before he returned and offered me a canteen. I eyed it suspiciously. "You are wise to be cautious," he said, "but it's just water. Here. Watch." He unscrewed the cap and took a mouthful. I watched him swallow.

This time when he offered the canteen, I forced one heavy hand to reach out and take it. He helped me sit up, and I gratefully drank from the canteen. Just water, flavored by nothing but darkness.

"Thank you," I said, "but *where am I*?"

"Ah," he said. "You are under the mountain Revethora Vezvaishoroi."

"The Tomb of Dragons."

"Yes."

"Why?"

"Ah," he said again, this time uneasily. "That's harder to explain."

"You've gone to a great deal of trouble to get me here. There must be a reason."

"In point of fact, I didn't know Delthonar was going to do this insane thing until it was too late to stop him."

"It's not insane, Halhathvered," said another goblin. "We need the thing quieted."

"Thing?" I said.

"We don't know what it is," said Halhathvered, "because no one's ever gotten a good look at it and survived to tell anyone else. But we know it's big, it tears its victims to pieces, and it spends much of its time in a part of the mine where we can't go, because the air is bad."

"And you've brought me here because . . . ?"

"Isn't it obvious?" said Delthonar from behind me. "We

want you to quiet it like you did in Tanvero."

"In Tanvero?" I said, and my body was tightening in dread before my mind understood what they were talking about. "You mean you think there's a ghoul in the mine."

"A dragon ghoul," said Halhathvered.

I startled all of us by laughing.

"It's not a laughing matter," said Delthonar. "Men are dying."

"Oh, but it is," I said, "and if you'd just *asked* me, back in Amalo, I could have told you. I can't help you."

"What do you mean, can't?" said Delthonar.

"I mean I can't do it. I've lost the ability."

"That's ridiculous," said Delthonar. "If you could do it in Tanvero, you can do it here. Or were the newspapers lying?"

"No, for once the newspapers told the exact truth. But I can't do it any longer."

"Just like that?" Halhathvered said.

"Essentially," I said. "I encountered a revethavar."

"You did what?" said Delthonar with an incredulous laugh. "We're a little old for wonder-tales, othala."

"I wish it *were* a wonder-tale," I said. "But it is not."

"Then why wasn't *that* in the newspapers?" Delthonar said triumphantly, as if he'd caught me in a lie—which of course he had.

"Because I lied to the newspapermen," I said.

For some reason, that reached them. "You lied?" said Halhathvered. "I thought Witnesses *vel ama* were forbidden to lie."

"They are," I said. "But I am no longer a Witness *vel ama*. I'm just an unbeneficed prelate, and no one cares if I tell lies or not."

"Then you're no use to us," said Delthonar.

"Delthonar," said Halhathvered in a warning tone.

"No use at all," I agreed and could no longer contain

the sick, hysterical laughter that had collected behind my breastbone. I rolled away from them, curling up like a hedgehog, and laughed until I couldn't tell whether I was laughing or sobbing. And they at least believed me enough that they left me alone.

THE MINERS OF Revethora Vezvaishoroi were an independent consortium; they did not work for any of the big mining companies. Mostly this was to their advantage: everyone was a shareholder, so that any ore found benefitted them all. But it also meant that when something went wrong, there was no one they could ask for help—or even advice—and thus they ended up doing stupid things like kidnapping a (former) Witness for the Dead.

I learned the story in bits and pieces, mostly by listening to their conversations as they tried to figure out what to do.

They had not dug most of the tunnels under Revethora Vezvaishoroi themselves, but had taken them over from earlier miners who had in turn taken them over from the dragons for whom the mountain was named. The dragons had all been killed 120 years ago by the Clenverada Mining Company, which then decided, when the best vein of gold played out, that the mountain was not rich enough to suit them and sold it at auction. Rumors were already circulating that the mountain was haunted, and the story was that the Clenverada didn't make back the amount they'd paid to ensure that the principate government looked the other way. There had been treaties made between the principate government and the dragons, though those turned out not to be worth the paper they were written on.

The stories about Revethora Vezvaishoroi being haunted continued to circulate and the mountain changed hands several times before Halhathvered and Delthonar formed their consortium and began mining and exploring in the unshakable belief that there were unimaginable riches *somewhere* in the mountain waiting to be found.

They had had some success in following ore veins earlier miners had dismissed as played out or not worth the bother of excavating—enough that they continued their operations, always pressing deeper and deeper into the tunnels. Earlier this year, they had found a vein of silver that had promise of fulfilling their dreams of wealth and began mining it wholeheartedly. It led them into a part of the tunnels deep beneath the surface of the world, and while most of the miners were working that vein, a few had started exploring to see where the vein was going to lead them and just how far they might be able to follow it.

And then one of them didn't come back. The others searched and found him, dead and torn to pieces, at the head of an unexplored tunnel that, following the vein of silver, led sharply back and down from the main tunnel. It was clearly not an accidental death, and as they could see the track of blood leading back down into the dark, it was not difficult, even without a Witness for the Dead, to figure out what had happened.

They agreed not to explore that particular tunnel. The vein of ore had other branches. They carried the remains up to the surface to bury them by their watchtower, and that was that.

But then it happened again. Another miner didn't come back and was found, torn to pieces, in the mouth of another tunnel leading further down. The problem was clear, and I thought—as Halhathvered was explaining to me why I had ended up under the mountain with them—that the solution was clear as well. "Why did you not just avoid all tunnels going further down?"

All the nearby miners scowled at me, and Delthonar said,

"It is not that simple."

"What makes it complicated?"

"This vein of silver is the richest vein we have seen in five years," said Halhathvered, as if that explained everything.

"Ah, so the actual problem is greed," I said.

"You have no right to judge us," said Delthonar.

"You had no right to kidnap me," I said.

"We had to do *something*," said Delthonar.

"But what makes you so sure it's a ghoul?" I said. "There might be other creatures down here that would defend their territory. In fact, it can't be a ghoul."

"Why not?" Halhathvered said, almost indignantly.

"Because you're all still alive," I said. "A ghoul—and how there could even *be* a ghoul down here also makes no sense. There are no cemeteries."

"It's a dragon ghoul," said one of the other miners.

"How in the world do you know that? Has anyone *seen* it?"

"It has to be," said someone else. "This mountain is the tomb of dragons."

"Surely that's mere poetry," I said.

"No," said Halhathvered, "it's quite true. As the dragons were dying, they all came here."

"How did the Clenverada Mining Company kill them?"

"With eisonsar."

"Eisonsar?"

"Aside from being lighter than air, eisonsar is poisonous to dragons," said Delthonar. "So they flooded the mines with it, one at a time."

"They flooded the mines with eisonsar," I said.

"Yes."

"Does that not mean that all of the mines are filled with explosive gas?"

"The eisonsar dissipates upward everywhere it can," said

Halhathvered. "You just have to watch out for the pockets where it has no egress."

"They could also call this mountain Revethora Ethuverai," said an elderly elven miner. "There was an explosion that killed a dozen miners, only a week or two after they started mining here. It's that that made the Clenverada give up on this mine more than anything else."

"Showing good common sense," I said and got an array of scowls.

"In any event," said Halhathvered, "we know that there are dead dragons in the tunnels below us, and one of them has clearly turned ghoul."

"Then why are you all still alive?"

"Its movements must be restricted in some way," said Delthonar.

"I've never heard of a ghoul that did not wander as freely as it liked," I said, but even as I said it, I remembered the revethavar, who had indeed been restricted to his tomb. But that was nonsense. There couldn't be such a thing as a revethvezvaishor'avar.

Could there?

"You know a lot for someone who says he can't help us," said Delthonar.

"I *have* quieted ghouls," I said. "I just can't do so any longer."

"That's awfully convenient for you," said Delthonar, "seeing as how it means you don't have to help us. And we have only your word for it that you can't."

"It's not something I can prove," I said. "You can't prove a negative."

"I know one way you could," Delthonar said darkly. "And it would leave us no worse off than we are now."

"You're talking about murder," I said.

"Not if you can quiet ghouls," said Delthonar.

"But I *can't*."

They had surrounded me as we argued, and Delthonar said, "Let's throw him down the drop! Let him make his way back if he can!"

"Now wait a minute!" said Halhathvered.

"But I'm telling you—" I started, and then they grabbed me.

There were too many of them to fight, although I tried, and I could hear Halhathvered yelling at them to stop. They dragged me down a tunnel that ended after a short distance in a steep drop-off, and without any further discussion, they pushed me over the edge.

I stumbled over something at the lip of the drop-off and ended up rolling wildly, unable to stop or slow down or control my fall, until I came up hard against the ground again at the bottom of the drop.

Something rolled down the drop-off and mercifully came to a stop mere inches from me. One of the thick miner's candles, nearly too thick to be held comfortably. I did not have my coat of office, for I had been using it as a pillow, but a quick search of my waistcoat and trouser pockets showed that I still had my lighter. It would have helped to have a candlestick, but I was able to light the candle and see at least a couple of feet around me. I did not thank them.

There was no possibility of climbing the slope I'd just fallen down, and in any event that would just land me back in the miners' camp where I had no desire to go. I turned right and found myself very shortly faced with a dead end. The path to the left was the only feasible option—which meant that the dragon or the ghoul or *whatever* it was, was also somewhere to the left.

Without any weapon except a candle and without the ability to find its name, I had no hope of defeating a ghoul. My death seemed assured.

I extinguished the candle and stood in the utter darkness beneath Revethora Vezvaishoroi. I began the prayer of acceptance of death; it was a short prayer, designed for repetition, and as I repeated it, I felt myself moving into a deep meditative state such as I had been unable to reach since my encounter with the revethavar.

As if the thought had summoned it, the memory of the revethavar surged up, pain and chaos and fear. I said, "Hasthemis Brulnemar, thou canst not hurt me," as I had said in my dream, and I felt something shift in my head, like a key turning in a rusted lock. I felt very strongly the presence of Ulis, as I had felt him in the dream that had first brought me to Amalo; I said again, "Hasthemis Brulnemar, thou canst not hurt me," and the memory of the revethavar crumbled away to nothing. Ulis's strength was greater than mine could possibly be. I switched to a prayer of gratitude. If nothing else, the burden of fear had been lifted from my shoulders, which might prove to be nothing but irony, but I was grateful all the same—and it might be that Ulis had chosen to restore the ability that most clearly marked me as his.

The only way to find out was to try. I finished the prayer of gratitude and came carefully out of my meditation. Opening my eyes made no difference in this absolute darkness, and I made haste to light the candle again. It couldn't do much, but I was glad to have a tiny bubble of light against the great, cold darkness of the mountain.

I proceeded down the left-hand path with considerable caution, and I had not gone far before I encountered the first ghost, an elven man who came screaming toward me and vanished almost as soon as I had realized he was there. I jerked back a pace, but there was nothing there, nothing but my own jangled nerves to suggest anything had been there at all.

But as I stood there, another screaming elven ghost emerged from the darkness and disappeared with nothing to show why he was screaming or what had happened to him. I knew the ultimate answer to that—there was a reason he was a ghost—but what had killed him remained a mystery. This deep in a mine, there were all sorts of potential accidents, and then there was whatever had happened—not accidental—to Delthonar's fellows.

I did not so much nerve myself to continue as realize that there was no point in standing still. I kept close to the wall, though, in the hopes that it would prevent the ghosts from running straight through me. And indeed the next ghost, this one goblin, did not run straight at me, but ran a chord on the circle of my candlelight and was gone.

I proceeded slowly—I was at least as wary of another drop-off as I was of the ghosts—and I lost all sense of time or direction. I did notice after a while that the wall I was following had great scorch marks on it, as if there had been a fire.

Or, I supposed, an eisonsar explosion.

There was a rush of screaming, staggering ghosts, at least one of whom was actually on fire, and then there was a gust of wind and my candle went out.

I froze. There hadn't been enough air movement before to make the candle do more than flicker, and thus there was nowhere that gust of wind could have come from.

Nowhere except a being like the revethavar, who could shape the air in whatever way it chose.

I said wildly, "Are you there, dragon?"

And the darkness blinked great moonlight-colored eyes and said, *We are here. What are you that seek to speak with us rather than destroy us?*

"We are Thara Celehar, a Witness for the Dead." I had to blink hard against tears, for I had thought I would never be able to say that truthfully again.

You cannot find restitution for us. The people who murdered us and all our kin are long dead.

"The Clenverada are still wealthy on the profits of their company. We think they are not blameless."

You can do nothing about them.

"No, but we can speak to the Prince of Thu-Athamar."

His ancestors were paid handsome bribes not to interfere.

I felt like a mouse being toyed with by a cat. I said, "We can speak to the emperor."

And she paused.

Can you? she said after a long silence. *Truly? The Clenverada revered their emperor. He could have made them stop if he had known.*

Depending on the emperor, he, too, might have been easy to bribe, but I was not about to say that. And in any event, Edrehasivar VII was well known to be incorruptible.

He can make the miners stop.

"Yes," I said.

He can order the mines sealed, so no one can start mining again clandestinely. The Tomb of Dragons—for we know your people call it that—can truly be a tomb.

"Yes," I said again.

All the mines, she said. *All the dragonholds.*

I wondered if anyone knew any longer which mines were dragonholds and which were not, but I wasn't going to say that either. "It is within his power," I said.

And you will speak to him? You swear it?

"Yes. We will witness for you."

Her eyes drew back a little. *Then we will let you live, although we did not intend to.*

There seemed to be nothing to say to that, and after a moment she said, *The question then is how to get you out from beneath Revethora Vezvaishoroi alive.*

"That is a good question," I said.

Back along the Main Trunk won't do. That will just bring you to the people who threw you down here.

"Who will almost certainly murder us," I said, for really, what else could they do?

Our strength does not reach that far, or we would kill them for you.

That also seemed unanswerable.

Most of the other exits we know are blocked—they blocked them to keep the eisonsar in, you understand—and the remainder are too far up the mountain. You would never make it back down. . . . But you might be able to use Jormentauren's Door. It too is beyond our strength, though not beyond our sight.

"How far does your sight reach?"

Throughout the mountain. We know everyone who comes here.

That revelation was unsettling, that she had seen me being lugged into the mine like a parcel. I said, "Where is Jormentauren's Door? Since we have neither food nor water nor horse, we had best move quickly."

Though we can do nothing about either food or horse, we can take you to water, said the dragon. *It is not significantly out of our way.*

"Then that would be an excellent first stop." My mouth had gone dry with fear some time ago.

Very well, said the dragon, and her eyes disappeared. Instead there was a ball of light about the size of my clenched fist. *You will want your candle. We can make this luminescence, but we cannot illuminate.*

I lit the candle, marveling a little at how steady my hands were, and set out, following Ithalpherix's ball of light.

Although nothing but the light was visible, I had a very strong sense of a giant creature in the tunnel with me. I almost heard her scales rubbing against the opposite wall. I almost felt the furnace heat of her body.

We proceeded for a long time in silence. I noticed the floor of the tunnel was gradually sloping down and wondered about the route we were taking, but I did not dare ask. She could still change her mind and decide to tear me to pieces, and I had no sense of how close she was to that tipping point.

Endless, silent darkness . . .

And then I fell over the first bone. I landed hard on one shoulder because I was desperately trying to save the candle. It went out, but I did not drop it, and then the darkness was absolute except for the ball of light, which, as Ithalpherix had said, cast no illumination.

I felt her watching me, but she said nothing.

It took me a moment to collect my thoughts, another moment to find my lighter and light the candle again. When I did, I looked at the bone. It looked like a vertebra, but much too large for elf or goblin. I guessed it at a foot tall and roughly the same in width and depth. It was black and reflected the light, as if dragon bones—for it could be nothing else—were made out of obsidian.

I stood up carefully. Nothing seemed to be broken. I said, "Is this, then, the tomb of dragons?"

Yes, said Ithalpherix. *It is as far beneath the surface as any of us had tunneled. We thought we would be safe here, but it was already too late. You are standing amidst the bones of Aglathenning now.*

I raised the candle a little. More black shining bones surrounded me. I saw that I had actually been walking parallel to the tail for some time before it crossed the tunnel and blocked my path.

We are coming to the vault, said Ithalpherix, and her light went bobbing ahead, so that I had to find a path through the dragon's bones to follow it. *It was a natural cavern which we made wider, so that we could meet comfortably without having to expose ourselves to our enemies on the surface.*

"How many dragons . . ."

Does it hold? Or how many dragons could *it hold? There are seventy in the vault now, each of them curled as tightly as possible. It held fifty comfortably.*

I tried to imagine a space large enough to hold fifty dragons and failed utterly. "What about the other one hundred twenty-two? For you said, did you not, that one hundred ninety-two dragons were killed by the Clenverada?"

Yes. Most of them never made it this far. The others, like Aglathenning, crept off in various directions to die alone.

We had reached the skull, which was much longer than I was tall. It was comparatively narrow for its length, and the teeth I could see were intimidating, even though their owner had been dead for more than a century.

Come, said Ithalpherix. *We still have far to go.*

I felt the gaze of Aglathenning's empty eye sockets for a long time.

We came to a crossroads, and although I wondered what lay to right and left, I again did not ask. Ithalpherix led me down an even steeper tunnel into the dragons' vault. My candle showed me nothing, except the glints of dragon bones, but I could feel that I was in a great open space, and I had to shield the candle against drafts.

We are skirting the vault, said Ithalpherix. *It will take longer, but dragon bones are not safe to wander among.*

"Haunted?" I said.

Yes, and sharp in unexpected places. You are familiar with hauntings?

"Elven cemeteries are often haunted, too. Little more than

disturbed earth and the occasional thrown rock usually, although sometimes there are other signs."

The bones will move slightly or there will be a fall of pebbles. We have hoped many times that it was a sign that there was somehow another like us, even though we knew it could not be. The Rite of Living Death was only performed once. We do not think anyone but Hascepolor knew it.

"You are lonely," I said.

We are. It is ironic. We are surrounded by our kin and yet have no one to talk to.

"We can . . . we have forced dissolution on a revethavar. We think we could help you end your existence. If that was what you wanted."

There was a tick of silence, in which I knew I had said the wrong thing, and her ball of light disappeared.

Are you telling us you can end us?

"Only if it was what you wanted! That was not a threat!"

There was a much longer silence, in which I felt her presence even more strongly, as if she were coiling around me where I stood. *Presumably,* she said at last, *if you intended to do this, you would have done it already.*

"Yes," I said, trying not to sound as desperate as I felt. "We would have done it at once. Certainly, we aren't going to do it *here*."

No, she said thoughtfully. *For you would condemn yourself to death as well.*

"Yes," I said, now trying not to sound relieved.

Very well, she said, and the ball of light returned. I followed it doggedly, even though I was shaking enough to make the candlelight waver and jump. Either Ithalpherix did not recognize this as fear or she did not choose to comment on it. I walked in silence for a long time as we skirted the edge of the vault. Once I had to venture out away from the wall to walk around a pile of dragon bones, and that was perhaps the worst yet, walking among piles of bones taller than I was and feeling the hauntedness of them. I heard bones shifting twice, and as I approached the wall of the vault again, I was pushed violently to the side—so violently that I fell against the massive vertebrae of the next dragon—and a bone I could not identify, but that was easily twice the size of my head, crashed against the floor where I had been, hard enough that it bounced a little.

We apologize, said Ithalpherix. *There was no time to warn you.*

"No," I said, "we understand. Thank you very much."

You cannot witness for us if your skull is crushed, she said matter-of-factly, and her ball of light bobbed, beckoning me onward again.

I lost my sense of time, so I could not tell how long it took, nor did I have any sense of how much of the circumference of the vault I walked, but eventually, the ball of light led me to turn right and start up another tunnel. After a minute, I could hear water.

We called the river Psalythenor, which means "clear flowing," said Ithalpherix. *Fortunately, it flows deep beneath the mountain and never rises before it meets the greater river, Phanasabren. The miners have never found it.*

The tunnel veered gently left and then widened a little to become the bank of a river. My candlelight was not strong enough to reach the opposite bank, but I could see that the river's name was well-earned, for the pebbles on the bottom were as clearly visible as if the water had not been there.

We regret, said Ithalpherix, *that we cannot give you a vessel in which to carry water with you.*

"It cannot be helped," I said. I knelt carefully and dipped my free hand in the water. It was fast-flowing and bitingly cold. Even more carefully, I set the candle down beside me; then I cupped my hands and drank from the Psalythenor. I could feel the coldness of the water down my throat and into my stomach, and I welcomed it.

I drank as much as I could, for who knew when I might get another chance? Then I picked the candle up again, noting with dismay how little of it was left, and stood.

Ithalpherix said, *We also regret that the way to Jormentauren's Door is across the river.*

"Of course," I said, for I had ceased to be surprised at the misfortunes which befell me beneath Revethora Vezvaishoroi. "How deep is it?"

It will come up to your knees perhaps, she said; I set down the candle again and took off my shoes and stockings and rolled up the legs of my trousers as far as I could. I tucked my stockings into the toes of my shoes, then got a good grip on my shoes with one hand and picked up the candle with the other, and, bracing myself for the cold, I stepped into the Psalythenor.

Even though I had tried to be ready, I yelped at the touch of the water on my feet, but I did not drop the candle or my shoes. The current pushed against me, and I made sure my position was stable before I took another step. The water deepened, but Ithalpherix was correct that it never came above my knees. I kept looking ahead for the opposite bank, but the Psalythenor made up for its shallowness here by being extremely broad. My feet were numb almost immediately, and the numbness had crept up to my shins before I was finally able to set foot on the bank. I gasped with relief and took only two clumsy steps before I sat down, setting my shoes and stockings down and clutching my left foot with my free hand, then my right.

I thought that I had never fully understood the expression "bone cold" before.

It was several minutes before I was able to pull myself together and put my shoes and stockings on again.

Ithalpherix, who had waited in silence, said, *Are you ready, then?*

"Yes," I said. "Pray continue."

The tunnel now began to slope sharply upward, and it was in the middle of a series of hairpin turns that the candle burned my fingers and I dropped it. It went out, and although I immediately bent and tried to pick it up, it was nothing more than a hot blob of wax. And although I *could* get out my lighter, its reservoir had not been full to begin with. It would last . . . maybe a minute? Maybe less?

I said none of the things I wanted to say.

Ithalpherix said, *We can still lead you, if you can still follow.*

"Our only other option is a slow death from starvation," I said. "Or, we suppose, we could grope our way back to the river, throw ourself in, and drown. No, we will follow."

You have promised to help us, she said. *We will not lead you wrongly.*

It was a relief that she said it. "Thank you," I said.

The ball of light came closer. It illuminated nothing, but at least it was something to look at instead of the darkness pressing against my skin. I found the wall of the tunnel with one hand and, lacking other options, followed the ball of light.

Ithalpherix went much more slowly and did not complain at the hesitancy of my steps. I wondered how the dragons had illuminated these tunnels, and finally, to distract myself from the utter blackness surrounding me, I asked her.

We could breathe fire with every breath. And the darkness held no fear for us, for each dragon knew their own hold perfectly, and we all knew this hold, which we did not *know as the Tomb of Dragons. It was . . . "sacred" is not the right word. "Held in common" is closer, for in general dragons do not share.*

That was part of the little I knew about dragons, that they were solitary and defended their holds against all comers, even their own kind. "We think we understand," I said.

I had heard stories of miners who had gotten lost and gone mad for lack of light; I had been skeptical, but I was coming to believe the stories were true, for the darkness was complete and heavy, and I could feel it pressing against my eyes even as I looked resolutely at Ithalpherix's ball of light.

I did manage, after a time, to stride out more confidently, for the tunnel was smooth-floored and its slope was constant, and as she had promised, Ithalpherix led me carefully, warning me of each turn and keeping her ball of light as close as she could. And after a length of time I had no way of measuring, she said, *Go carefully, for we are coming up on Jormentauren herself.*

"Is that why you call it Jormentauren's Door?"

Yes. Once we get past her, we will be nearly at the surface.

"Does she lie next to the wall?"

"No, but you will have to step over her forelimb, and her bones will not welcome you."

I stopped and got my lighter out, but after so long in the dark, the light merely dazzled my eyes, and I put it away again. I proceeded slowly and felt forward with each foot before I took a step. It was well that I did, for even with that caution, I stubbed my toes painfully on what Ithalpherix told me were Jormentauren's wrist bones, and I had to feel my way over them. One bone shifted as I touched it and sliced a line of pain across my palm. For a hallucinatory moment, I thought I saw the pain shining bright, and then it was gone, and I could only feel the wetness of blood.

Did she wound you? said Ithalpherix.

"We did not expect to get out of here unmarked," I said and finished my careful traverse of Jormentauren's wrist. The rest of the way past the skeleton was clear except for a moment when I had to squeeze between her eye socket and the wall. I could feel the edge of the bone raking across my back, and for the length of one indrawn breath, I thought I was stuck, but I managed to force my way clear. I staggered several steps and fell, though I succeeded in staying close enough against the wall that I did not land on Jormentauren's snout.

I picked myself up again and lurched several steps further.

Ithalpherix said, *That is the last of her skeleton,* and I felt as if I could breathe again.

I was tiring but was reluctant to say anything, irrationally afraid that Ithalpherix would leave me stranded in the dark. I kept climbing and climbing, and then in front of me I thought I saw a pinprick of light that was not Ithalpherix's doing. That brought me fresh energy, especially since the pinprick grew as I climbed, becoming larger and larger and at last resolving into the mouth of a tunnel.

"Is that the way?" I asked Ithalpherix.

Yes, but it will not be easy.

I climbed up the last bit of the slope to the tunnel mouth and saw immediately what she meant. Sunlight poured down from a hole in the ceiling of the tunnel and illuminated very clearly the jumbled mass of boulders between me and the even brighter pinprick, barely visible, of what had to be Jormentauren's Door.

"Is this not impassable?" I said.

That is what the miners think, said Ithalpherix, *and because it is higher up the mountain than is convenient, and because they have other entrances, they have never bothered to do more than look in. But if you are determined, there is room for you to climb through the boulders.*

Determination I had, for I still refused to let Delthonar and his men be my death. "All right," I said and began the work of getting to Jormentauren's Door.

I WAS BRUISED and scraped and squashed and pinched by the time I extricated myself from the boulders, but Jormentauren's Door was only fifty feet away. Ithalpherix had stayed with me the entire time, often able to tell me whether my next move had to be over or under or around. Now, she said, *Our sight does not extend to the surface of the mountain. We cannot help you further.*

"You have already saved our life," I said. "We thank you."

We remember that there is a stream due south from Jormentauren's Door. Turn right as you come to the surface and go as straight as you can.

"Thank you again," I said, for the water of Psalythenor had been a long time ago.

We cannot bind you to keep your promise, she said, almost angrily. *Were we still living, we could bind you to return to us, but that would require that we be able to look into your eyes and you into ours.*

"We will return," I said. "When they come to seal the entrances to Revethora Vezvaishoroi, we will come with them. We swear it by the moon, the mirror, and the maze." The slice across the palm I had received from Jormentauren's bones, which had been painful and hindering throughout my progress through the boulders, was easy to make bleed again. I picked a spot on the tunnel wall and smeared blood in a rough rendition of a circle, which could mean moon, mirror, maze, or, as in this binding vow, all three. "We swear it."

There was a long silence before she said, *We believe you. You need only come beneath the surface of the mountain, and we will find you.*

"Very well," I said and I walked out from beneath Revethora Vezvaishoroi into the lengthening purple shadows of dusk.

My first problem was water. Ithalpherix said there was a stream to the south, and south was, in any event, the direction I wanted to go. I turned right and began walking south down the mountain. There was something that might be a trail, and I decided to follow that for as long as I could.

My second problem was hunger, but there was nothing I could do about that.

My third problem was the cold, for which I was not dressed. I could walk briskly for as long as there was light, but when full dark came, I needed at least to be out of the wind.

I almost turned back to find Jormentauren's Door again, but I needed water. I was actually still debating the point when the ground sloped down abruptly and I found myself on a road—not a paved road, of course, but a track that had been worn from a path to a trail to a clear road. It had to be the way the miners came and went from Revethora Vezvaishoroi, which meant that if I followed it one way, it would take me to the mountain, and if I followed it the other way, it would take me, eventually, to Tanvero.

Tanvero was for tomorrow. I kept going south and was shortly rewarded for perseverance by the sound of running water. I followed the sound to the stream and there lay on my stomach and drank the clear, cold water, as dark in the dusk as drinking shadows.

I found my way back to the road and turned northwest around the mountain rather than southeast away from it, walking as quickly as I could, for daylight was ebbing with every moment, and came before very long to the watchtower that the miners kept out of fear that one day the Clenverada would return and demand their mountain back. What they intended to do in that contingency, I had no idea, and suspected they did not, either, but it meant that there was a tower on the outcropping somewhere above my head and here, directly by the path, a structure that one might call either a shanty or a cabin, depending on how generous one was feeling. Next to it was a long stable for the miners' mules.

I was not feeling generous, but the lantern light shining through the one window was warming, poetically if not literally. The watchman would know who I was, so I could not knock on the door and beg shelter, but it could not be far to the mountain, and I had learned from the miners that if one went far enough into the mine, the temperature would even out at a bearable level. Even pleasant, if one was used to it. It was certainly the best I could hope for tonight.

I kept walking, even more briskly now, and it was not far before the road turned and came to what was clearly the Clenverada's main entrance to the mine, for the stone had been worked into an arch and there were great wrought-iron letters spelling out **R E V E T H O R A V E Z V A I S H O R O I.** I shivered as I passed under the arch, and not from cold.

I wanted to go no farther than I had to, and I wanted if possible not to be on the Main Trunk, where I ran double the risk of being found. Both these wishes were granted by a side spur, only wide enough for one person, that snaked back into the mountain, twisting without branching, and I was soon in pitch blackness again.

But the temperature had risen enough that I felt warm by comparison, and I was glad to stop and sit down, even to lie down, staring up into the blackness. I wished for my coat of office, not for any reason of propriety but so that I might have folded it up beneath my head as a pillow again. As it was, I oriented myself carefully so that my feet were pointing back toward the Main Trunk, and then lay still and wondered how I would know when morning came.

I MUST HAVE fallen asleep, although I did not expect to,

because I was woken by a great noise of rattling and banging coming from the direction of the Main Trunk. I crept cautiously back down the spur, and stopped in blank surprise when I found that the Main Trunk was as lit up as any street in Amalo. I dropped to my stomach to crawl to the last bend in the spur, figuring that I was filthy enough not to be easily distinguishable from the rock, and discovered that the banging and rattling were ore carts, and the men with them were Halhathvered and three others, one elven man and two part goblin, whose names I did not know.

This was a piece of good fortune, for Halhathvered, of all of them, was the one who might regret my presumed death.

I waited until Halhathvered came close to the spur and said as quietly and distinctly as I could, "Halhathvered, I must speak with you."

His entire body jerked with the shock, and then he was on his knees beside me, practically lying flat himself. His face was haggard, almost more gray than black, and he did not look as if he had had any better sleep than I. "Othala Celehar! But how . . . ?"

"It is a very long story," I said, "and I am not sure I care to tell it to you. But I think you owe me some help."

He winced, but said readily, "Yes, anything I can do."

"But first, what are you doing?"

"Leaving."

"Leaving?"

"I'm a greedy man," he said, "but I am not a murderer, and I'll not partner with murderers. Morgorad and Chelinvar and Nolharad and I are leaving Revethora Vezvaishoroi."

"But no one else minds."

"They are all Delthonar's creatures," Halhathvered said. "But no matter. How can I help you?"

"If you are leaving, my problems become much simpler. May I come with you?"

"Of course! We will have to smuggle you past Orplenar in the tower, but that's easily enough done. Come." He stood up and offered me his hand. After a moment of consideration, I accepted his help.

Morgorad and Chelinvar and Nolharad were equally as shocked as Halhathvered, but seemed sincerely delighted to see that I was alive. Halhathvered said, "I am sorry I cannot return your coat of office to you. Delthonar burned it."

"*Burned* it?"

"He wanted nothing that might show you had been there," said Nolharad.

"Delthonar seems to have thought of everything," I said dryly.

Halhathvered said, "Yes, and it worries me that he may have done murder before. As I said, I want no part of any enterprise with him. We are taking our share of the mined ore and our share of the mules and leaving."

"You must be going to Tanvero first," I said.

"There's nowhere else we *can* go," said Halhathvered. "Yes, Tanvero first, and then I suppose we look to see who's hiring. But let us get out of here safely before we worry about that."

Between the five of us, we came up with a plan—a simple plan, but it did not take anything fancy. I would make my own way past the watchtower and wait for them at the first bend in the road beyond.

"This time of day, Orplenar's feeding mules," Halhathvered said, and I set out at once, with Chelinvar's borrowed coat flapping around me. I crossed to the side of the road opposite the watchtower; daylight was beginning to spread on this side of the mountain and I could see that the watchtower was empty.

I went swiftly and at the bend, I retreated behind the first line of trees, just in case, and observed to myself that even if everything went wrong, I now had a coat. And in the pocket of the coat was one of the miners' biscuits—Chelinvar's breakfast, which he had also sacrificed to me without complaint. I gnawed the biscuit until there were only crumbs left, and then I licked the crumbs off my palms. And I waited.

I waited and waited, and just when I was beginning to think something really *had* gone wrong, I heard the sound of mules approaching. I did not come out though, until the mule train (if you could call six mules a train) stopped and Halhathvered called, "Othala Celehar?"

Then I came out. Halhathvered was walking in the lead, with one mule saddled for riding, with Nolharad and Morgorad walking behind. Chelinvar was riding the second mule and leading the last four, which were laden with bags of ore.

"Thank goodness," said Halhathvered. "Come, you shall ride Orchid."

"Orchid?" I said. The mule regarded me with one sad brown eye.

"Halhathvered named them all after flowers," Morgorad said, coming forward to hold Orchid's head.

"Orchid, Ordenna, Clematis, Bargarasta, Hyacinth, and Rose," said Halhathvered. "Orchid and Clematis are the only two that are broke to saddle, and Clematis likes Chelinvar and no one else in the world. Here." He made a stirrup of his hands and boosted me easily into the saddle. "Are you a rider, othala, or would you prefer me to lead? Orchid is good-natured and willing."

"I can ride," I said, and Morgorad gave me the reins.

Orchid was indeed good-natured and seemed happy to follow wherever Halhathvered led, sure-footedly keeping us out of the worst of the ruts. The most serious problem I faced was not falling asleep.

may be beneath Revethora Vezvaishoroi, but the limits of her strength are much narrower, which is why any of us is alive at all, and it is *possible* that Delthonar and the others will continue to survive—I should have warned them."

"They tried to kill you."

"And you didn't stop them."

"Ten to four," said Halhathvered. "And I didn't truly believe Delthonar would do it until it was too late."

He walked in silence for a long time, then said abruptly, "You've no reason to forgive me, but I am sorry. I should have insisted we take you back to Tanvero at once. And I'm sorry I didn't stop Delthonar. I seem to have made a lot of mistakes this past week."

"At least you were smart enough to get out." I sighed. "I do not know if I can forgive you, but I do not blame you for being desperate. It was an ugly situation to be trapped in, even if it was your own greed that kept you there."

Halhathvered's ears twitched, but he did not argue.

"The dragon said that greed drives our peoples insane," I said, "and I think she is correct."

"I can offer no evidence to the contrary. Certainly I think Delthonar is a madman." A thought struck him. "And you *cannot* warn them, for they will believe that your survival brands you a liar. They will not credit this talk of a vision."

"Do you think me a liar?"

"No. But Delthonar would tell you I am a fool."

As Halhathvered had predicted, we reached Tanvero just before it got too dark to see the road. As we started into town, I looked for faces or buildings I recognized. I found nothing—which was in all honesty not surprising, as I had spent very little time in Tanvero in daylight—and I was beginning to wonder if Halhathvered and I would ever be able to escape from one another when I glanced down a side street and saw a door with a green lantern over it. "There!" I said. It was either Coralezh or the other Tanvereise cleric, and at that moment I did not care which.

"Othala?" said Halhathvered.

"I have need of the services of a cleric," I said, "and from there I can make my own way. I have friends in Tanvero."

"You are sure?" said Halhathvered, although he was already halting. Orchid halted with him and all the train halted.

"Yes," I said, "I am quite sure." Halhathvered caught Orchid's reins and I dismounted, which was painful and almost embarrassing, when my knees threatened to give way. But I clung to the saddle for a moment and became steadier.

I gave Chelinvar his coat back.

Halhathvered and I looked at each other. "Safe travels, othala," he managed at last.

"And to you," I said, since that much at least I could say sincerely. I turned down the side street. Halhathvered said, "Come on, mule," to Orchid, and the train started into motion again.

I found with great relief that I did recognize the side street, and I opened Coralezh's door with something resembling confidence.

There was one person waiting in the front room, a young elven woman with her hair in braids wound round her head, who glanced at me, looked away, and then looked back in disbelief. *"Celehar?"*

"Chonhadrin?" I said, nearly as shocked. Although I knew my friend Chonhadrin had been planning to visit her grandfather, Osmer Thilmerezh, in Tanvero, I had not imagined she would still be here. Not with her job at the Amal-Athamareise Airship Company waiting for her.

"Merciful goddesses," she said, "what has happened to you? You look like you've fallen down a mine shaft."

"That's because I have." I sat down beside her. "But what are you doing here?"

Chonhadrin shrugged a little. "Merrem Olharad does not approve of me, but she admits that I am useful to run errands when Grandfather is poorly."

"Merrem Olharad?"

"Grandfather's housekeeper."

"And Osmer Thilmerezh is not well?"

"He says his arthritis says the first of the big fall storms is coming."

Coralezh emerged from the back room carrying a small wooden box. His eyebrows went up when he saw me, and he said, "You *do* look like you've fallen down a mine shaft."

"It is an accurate description of what happened," I said.

"Is anything broken?"

"No."

"Are you bleeding to death?"

"No."

"Then wait five minutes while I give Min Chonhadrin the instructions for brewing this tea."

"Of course," I said.

Coralezh wrote the instructions on a piece of foolscap, his handwriting precise and legible. "Osmer Thilmerezh and Merrem Olharad should know this, but I find that it never hurts to repeat instructions one more time."

"Thank you," said Chonhadrin, accepting the paper and the box. "Celehar, shall I wait for you? Or do you have . . . ?"

"At the moment I have nothing except the clothes I'm wearing," I said ruefully. "If you think Osmer Thilmerezh might have—"

"Absolutely," said Chonhadrin. "His house is ridiculously large for one man, and I know he will be happy to see you."

"Then, please, wait."

"Come," said Coralezh, "and let's see what's what."

He had me take off my ruined trousers, shirt, and waistcoat, and made disapproving noises over my bruises and scrapes. He cleaned the cuts across my shins and the long slice across my palm. "If I'd seen this sooner," he said, "I might have stitched it. As it is, you are going to have quite the scar. You're lucky it didn't go deep enough to cut a tendon."

"Yes," I said, thinking of Jormentauren's bones. "Quite lucky."

"As for clothes," he said, "I seem to be making a habit of outfitting you. Let us see what I can provide."

He kept the clothes that came variously into his possession in two large trunks against the wall. He came up quickly with a shirt, stockings, and, surprisingly, a waistcoat, but had to dig several layers deep to find a pair of trousers that would fit me. Of coats, he had none that did not envelop me like a blanket.

"Can't be helped," I said and put on the smallest one, which was a subdued plum embroidered in brown and gray. It fit well enough across the shoulders, although the cuffs hid my hands almost to my fingertips. It was still better than roaming Tanvero in my shirtsleeves. I made sure to transfer all my belongings from one set of pockets to the other.

"I regret that I have no overcoats," he said. "They do not come into my possession as often, and I gave the last one I had away last week."

"Can't be helped," I said again. "Thank you. This time I truly have no means of payment."

"I would not accept it if you did," said Coralezh. "Tanvero is still in your debt, for who can say how many the ghoul might have killed without you?"

In the front room, Chonhadrin tactfully said nothing about the coat; she with her box and paper, and I with the clothes I stood in, bid Coralezh good evening and set out into what was now night.

Tanvero did not have streetlights, so our way was lit by the moon, the stars, and the puddles of light from occupied rooms in the buildings we passed. Chonhadrin walked confidently; I said, "Have you done this often?"

"Not *often,*" said Chonhadrin, "but Merrem Olharad has sent me to Coralezh before."

"How long have you been here? I would have thought you'd be back in Amalo by now."

"Oh, me, too," said Chonhadrin. "I meant to stay only a week, but Grandfather asked me to stay longer and hasn't yet gotten around to asking me to leave, and it's not as if A3 Co. is going anywhere. They'll be there when I do get back, and Grandfather is very lonely."

"You must have taken to each other."

"Yes," she said, "and I find that I enjoy cemetery maintenance, which is about all there is to do for fun in Tanvero. Weeding is very meditative."

"I know many prelates who would like to hire you," I said.

She laughed. "I'll get bored with it soon enough—or the snow will come and there will be no weeding to do."

"Is the snow expected soon?" I said, a little anxiously, for snow would make the trip from Tanvero to Amalo twice as long and mean there were only half as many caravans making it. And the cold was biting through my plum-colored coat in a way that suggested fall was nearly over.

"Soon," said Chonhadrin. "*How* soon depends on who you ask."

We came to a tall clapboard-sided building; even in the dark I could see its irregular shape against the stars. Chonhadrin went up the stairs and in the door, and I followed her. "Grandfather!" she called. "I met someone in Coralezh's!"

"Met someone?" said Osmer Thilmerezh from the front room. "What in the world art thou talking about, Amiru?" He came to the door and saw me. "Great goddesses! Othala Celehar, what are you doing here again so soon?"

"It is a very long story," I said.

"You must be hungry," Chonhadrin said, not asking. "I will see what Merrem Olharad has to feed you with, and then you can tell us both the whole thing."

"Food sounds like a very good idea," I said.

Chonhadrin said, "It won't take long," and disappeared into the back of the house.

"Come," said Osmer Thilmerezh. "Be welcome in our house. We have a good fire going. It's getting quite cold at night."

"Yes," I said and followed him into a room that seemed to be half parlor and half study, with chairs grouped around a fireplace and a desk in the corner, clearly built to fit in exactly that space.

"It made no sense to keep heating the study, with a good fireplace in here," said Osmer Thilmerezh. "Sit down, Celehar, you look like you're going to fall over."

Which was untactful, but I could feel the truth of it. I sat down in the chair that did not have an abandoned newspaper on its seat. Osmer Thilmerezh folded the newspaper tidily and took the other chair. "All the caravan masters bring us newspapers now," he said. "We suppose if one has been asking for forty years, word does spread."

"Yes," I said, although I was almost too preoccupied with the warmth of the fire to follow his words.

"There's been quite a lot about you in them," he said.

"Much of it is nonsense," I said.

"That's true of any newspaper."

Chonhadrin came in and said, "The soup from dinner will be ready soon. It wasn't all the way cooled. And I—we told

"We have no one else to tell."

"Surely you plan to see Vera and Valta while you are in Tanvero," he said in surprise.

"Yes," I said, "but if they ask us, we must tell them the truth."

"What?" said Osmer Thilmerezh and *"Why?"* said Chonhadrin over each other.

"We cannot lie in the service of our calling," I said.

"But this isn't about your calling," said Chonhadrin. "This is about you getting kidnapped by a bunch of—"

"Amiru," said Osmer Thilmerezh.

"We are witnessing for Ithalpherix," I said.

"Oh," said Chonhadrin. "And you can't separate the two? No, no, you're right, I see where that doesn't work."

"No, it does not," I said.

"Is it a lie if you wear a coat other than the one Coralezh gave you?"

"No, but we have no such coat."

"You are not so different from Grandfather in size. Grandfather, do you not have an old coat you could lend Celehar?"

"We suppose," said Osmer Thilmerezh, "but how do you think it will make a difference? Anyone meeting Othala Celehar—except Coralezh, who is so lacking in curiosity that we sometimes wonder if he has a pulse—is going to want to know why he's in Tanvero, and if he will not lie to them, it does not matter what coat he's wearing. On the other hand, we can certainly provide you a better-fitting coat, othala."

"We would greatly appreciate it," I said.

"In the morning, though," said Osmer Thilmerezh. "It would be cruel to keep you from sleep any longer. And we must recommend that you not leave the house. We will arrange with Baltivar to take you and . . ." He gave me a long, thoughtful look. "Are you opposed to other people lying on your behalf?"

"It is not a situation we have encountered before," I said. "But we have no control over what you choose to do."

"Then we will tell him you have come to Tanvero to escort our granddaughter back to Amalo."

"Grandfather!" Chonhadrin said in great indignation. "We do not need an escort!"

"Maybe not," said Osmer Thilmerezh, "but Othala Celehar needs a plausible story. And you should most certainly return to Amalo before you get snowed in here."

She eyed him with suspicion. "Were you *waiting* for some way to give me an escort home?"

"Of course not," Osmer Thilmerezh said blandly.

I yawned involuntarily.

"We can argue about it once poor Celehar is in bed," said Chonhadrin. "Let me show you where your room is, Celehar."

"Yes, please," I said, for I felt very ragged and as if I might start dropping parts of myself soon.

Chonhadrin picked up a candlestick and lit the candle, then led me back into the hall and up the stairs, which twisted sharply twice and then produced a wide landing. Chonhadrin opened the middle of the three doors and led me down a short hallway.

"My room's at the end," she said, "and you're in here."

The room was small and dark, but the bed was the only thing I really noticed.

"Thank you, Chonhadrin," I said. "Good night."

"Good night," she said and, having lit the candle in the wall sconce, she closed the door.

I took off my shoes and the plum-colored coat, but otherwise slept in my clothes—and used the coat as an extra bedcovering.

I did not remember my dreams.

In the morning, I put the plum-colored coat back on. Downstairs, I found Chonhadrin and Osmer Thilmerezh once again in the front room, drinking tea and arguing amiably about something in a Barizheise novel. Chonhadrin bounced to her feet when she saw me and led me back, this time past the staircase, to the kitchen, where Merrem Olharad had made a pot of oatmeal with dried currants and honey. I sat at the kitchen table, and she ladled me out a bowl.

"Come back up front and find us when you're ready," said Chonhadrin and exited.

Merrem Olharad made a noise between a laugh and a snort and said, "She's good for him, though. She can talk almost as much as he can."

"Have you worked for Osmer Thilmerezh long?" I said, since that seemed safer than commenting on Chonhadrin.

"I was ten when he came to Tanvero," she said, "and my mother was his housekeeper until she got too old for the stairs. So when Olharad died, it just seemed natural to come work for Osmer Thilmerezh."

Years of experience as a prelate of Ulis had taught me not to ask her if she liked him. She would not feel comfortable being truthful with me, or—even worse—she would, and I would learn more about Osmer Thilmerezh than *I* was comfortable with. Instead, I asked a leading question about her family, and ate my breakfast to the easy accompaniment of Merrem Olharad's sisters and children and grandchildren.

When I came back into the front room, Osmer Thilmerezh had, in addition to an overcoat that was starting to go threadbare at the elbows, two coats that he suggested I try. One was a deep blue embroidered in gray with silver buttons; the other was a burgundy embroidered in shades of red and violet with buttons covered in gold cloth. The coats were quite a bit fancier than I was used to—even my silk coat of office had not had silver buttons—and I gave Osmer Thilmerezh a doubtful look.

"They're the darkest coats we have," he said. He was wearing green embroidered lavishly with flowers so I supposed that was probably true. The burgundy was quite eye-catching, but at least neither of them was the mustard-yellow coat Coralezh had given me the last time I was in Tanvero. I shrugged out of the plum-colored coat and tried the dark blue.

"That's an improvement," said Chonhadrin, and I could not deny that she was correct. The blue coat came quite a bit closer to fitting me properly than the plum-colored one did, and I no longer had a nagging feeling that I looked like a child playing dress-up with his father's coat.

"This plum-colored coat is really quite handsome," said Osmer Thilmerezh. "We imagine Merrem Cencharan could take it in for us, and Min Elovanin the embroiderist could make it brighter."

"Easily," I said.

He shrugged one shoulder and said, "We decided when we'd been here ten years that we were going to stop pretending we didn't like bright colors. It was hopelessly unfashionable at the time, but our case was hopeless anyway, and we try to provide work to as many Tanvereisei as we can."

We prefer not to be noticeable, I did not say.

"Well, very good," said Osmer Thilmerezh. "We will go talk to Mer Baltivar."

He left, and Chonhadrin said, "Are you all right?"

"Much better after an uninterrupted night's sleep in an actual bed."

"Which is good," she said, "but not quite what I meant. Are *you* all right?"

"Yes," I said. "A little daunted at what witnessing for Ithalpherix seems likely to entail, but I am well." I could acknowledge to myself that the return of my ability to speak to the dead was buoying me up despite the terrible story of the dragons and the miners. I would burn out—it was truthfully only a matter of time—but it hadn't come *yet*.

She said, "I'm afraid you *will* be stuck with my company on the way back to Amalo. Grandfather's right that it's a good lie."

"I don't mind your company," I said, and her ears lifted with her smile.

We rode from Tanvero to Amalo with a late caravan that was hurrying to beat the snow. Baltivar the caravan master, a burly part-goblin with honey-colored eyes, raised his eyebrows a little bit when I said I was a Witness for the Dead, but he did not ask me why I was wearing a blue coat with silver buttons. Chonhadrin and I picked a wagon, made ourselves comfortable on the cargo—which, judging by the softness of the bales, was furs—and spent the first day of the trip back to Amalo talking lazily about my work and about hers. We'd been talking about her work on airship crews, where one of her jobs was often to search the rigging and armature for stowaways before the airship took off. "People freeze to death," she said. "If you ever want to stow away on an airship, come to me first." And she laughed. "No, the real horror of a job is cleaning the pipes that run hot air from the engines under the cabin. Because you have to crawl *under* the airship, the pipes are always filthy, and they may not have cooled off very much when your crew chief sends you to clean them. Most ashenoi have burns like this." She unbuttoned her cuff and pushed her sleeve back to show an oblong patch of scar tissue running down her forearm.

"Sometimes you can't avoid brushing against the pipes, no matter how hard you try. I *will* say that you try a lot harder after the first time you burn yourself."

"It must have been very painful," I said.

"Oh, it was," said Chonhadrin. "I was lucky in that we were working on the first airship in the line, and it was only a quick dash to the workroom of the Csaiveise, who slathered it with aloe and told me to be more careful."

"I don't suppose working for the Amal-Athamareise Airship Company encourages tact or sympathy in its Csaiveisei," I said.

"Not at all." And she went on to tell me other stories about that particular Csaiveise, who was a tremendous healer in the hands, as the Csaiveisei put it, but as brusque and indifferent in manner as a person could possibly be.

The second day started off much the same way, but it was just after midmorning when the wagon abruptly stopped. Someone was shouting, but I couldn't make out any words. Then our wagon driver scrambled back off the seat into the cargo and hissed at us, "Bandits!"

Chonhadrin and I stared at each other.

"What should we do?" she said.

"Hide. Unless you have a weapon and know how to use it?"

"No. But shouldn't we, I don't know, get away from the wagon train?"

"We're more likely to draw attention if we do. Better to stay put."

"Makes sense," she said and we crawled further into the wagon, where we found an awkwardly shaped space among the bales and barrels in which to wedge ourselves.

After some miserable time of listening to shouts and the clash of metal and the thwap of arrows, we heard Baltivar shout, "Those of them that can still go are gone!"

I stood up and made my way back to the end of the wagon. "Where are you going?" Chonhadrin said.

"I have a duty with the dead," I said, shrugging out of my overcoat.

"They're bandits."

I took off the blue coat and folded it carefully.

"Ulis doesn't care," I said and leapt down.

There were two dead bandits; I judged one by his clothing to be their leader, which perhaps explained why the others had been so ready to flee. I said the prayer of compassion for the dead for each of them, and was standing up again when Baltivar came running from the back of the caravan.

"Othala Celehar?"

"Yes?"

"Will you hurry? Othira isn't dead yet."

"Show me," I said and followed him at a run back down the wagon train to the very rear, where a goblin man was lying in the road with an arrow sticking straight up from his chest. The men surrounding him made way for me, and I knelt beside him, saying one of the prayers of hope for the dying. The arrow was through his lung, and it wasn't likely to be much longer before he drowned in his own blood.

Like the dragons.

I took his hands, getting blood on my shirt cuffs, which was unfortunate but couldn't be helped. He met my eyes, and his mouth opened, clearly with the intent to say something, but instead he coughed, a gout of blood, and his eyes rolled back in his head. I thought that was it, but somehow he collected himself again, his eyes meeting mine and his hands clutching desperately, painfully, at my hands, and he tried to speak. This time I felt the heat of blood spraying across my face; I blinked involuntarily, and when I opened my eyes again, he was dead. His hands fell away from mine.

I said the prayer of compassion for the dead and stood up.

"What did he say?" Baltivar asked me.

"Nothing."

"But it looked like . . ."

"He tried, but he couldn't."

Baltivar looked at me speculatively. "You said you are a Witness for the Dead."

"I am."

"Can you Witness for Othira? I hate to think of him being buried with some business unfinished."

"Of course," I said. "I can't do it right away—the death is too fresh and I wouldn't be able to find anything else—but I could do it this evening."

"That would be very helpful, othala, thank you."

"Do you know if he was Ploraneise?"

"Oh," said Baltivar. "Oh dear. Brasa!"

A big part-goblin with jade-green eyes stepped forward from the clump of guards and drivers. He looked as if he might have been weeping, although he was calm enough when he said, "Yes, Baltivar?"

"Was Othira Ploraneise?"

"He was Tahareise. I thought you knew that."

"He was very quiet about it," Baltivar said.

"It is not a popular sect," said Brasa with dry understatement. The Tahareisei, whose sect originated in eastern Barizhan, believed that all gods were equal. They believed the priests of their kelkinorai, their congregations, were direct conduits for the speech of the gods. They were almost considered heretics in Amalo.

"It means we do not need to keep vigil," I said.

Baltivar and Brasa looked at each other. "Should we maybe keep vigil anyway?" said Baltivar.

"Certainly, if it will make you more comfortable," I said. "I don't know of any sect that *forbids* keeping vigil."

"We'll take shifts," said Brasa. "Just in case."

Chonhadrin came around the side of the wagon, holding a canteen, and said, "Celehar, you're going to want to wash your face."

"Yes," I said. "Thank you." I took the canteen, soaked my handkerchief, and wiped the blood off my face and hands as best I could. Without a laundress immediately to hand, there was nothing to be done about the stains on my shirt and waistcoat, but those at least would be covered by my coat—which reminded me that I was wandering around in my shirtsleeves.

Chonhadrin and I went back to the wagon we had been riding in, and I put my coat and overcoat on. "Give me that handkerchief," Chonhadrin said. "You missed a spot."

I gave her the handkerchief and held still. I'd apparently missed several spots; lacking a mirror, I was glad to have a friend willing to clean blood off my face.

Once the three bodies had been wrapped in spare tarpaulins and stowed atop the barrels in the second-to-last wagon, we were able to get moving again. Chonhadrin and I sat in silence for several miles before she said, "Do you ever wish you didn't have to follow your calling?"

I hesitated over my answer. "Following my calling is sometimes unpleasant, but I much prefer it to having no calling at all."

"How so?"

"I thought for several months that I had lost my calling, and it was . . . if I say I didn't know what to do with myself, it sounds trivial, but it isn't. I don't have words for how hopeless it was. If I follow my calling, I know that my actions have purpose."

"Do you think someone can have purpose *without* a calling?"

"I suppose I believe that 'purpose' and 'calling' are the same thing. A calling doesn't have to be religious."

"So anything you're passionate about, you could describe as a calling?"

"It depends on the passion," I said. "There's a difference between being passionate and being . . . well, 'driven' I suppose is the right word."

"You feel driven?"

"Oh yes. I follow my calling because I must."

She hesitated.

"Ask," I said.

"What will you do when you can't follow your calling any longer? You told me Witnesses for the Dead burn out."

"We do," I said. "I suppose I pray for Ulis to find me another purpose."

"Could you just go out and find one yourself? Like . . . oh, like teaching foundling children to read."

"I could do that, and I believe it needs doing. But it would not be a calling. You don't choose your calling. You only choose to follow it."

"Oh," she said. "Perhaps I understand."

"It does not go into words well."

"Do you . . . are you *happy*?"

"What does happiness have to do with any of it?" I said, startled.

"I SUPPOSE THAT answers my question," said Chonhadrin.

That evening, I returned to Othira's body; Baltivar and Brasa both came with me, although Baltivar told the rest of the guards and drivers to leave me alone.

I scrambled up into the wagon where the bodies were resting. The guard keeping vigil was part goblin; I didn't know his name.

It was easy to tell Othira's goblin bulk from the other two, and I observed that whoever had wrapped the bodies knew how to wrap a shroud, suggesting previous employment as a sexton. I folded the tarpaulin back from Othira's face, said the prayer of compassion for the dead, and touched his forehead. I did not allow myself to hesitate, although the thought had occurred to me that perhaps I was wrong. Perhaps it was not that my ability to hear the dead had been restored, but rather that the dragon, being a revethvezvaishor'avar, could speak to anyone, if she chose to do so rather than rending them limb from limb.

But as soon as I touched him, I knew.

The death was still vividly present, the suffocating pain, but it was possible to push it aside and look for the thing he had wanted so desperately to say.

After a moment, I stepped back.

"Well?" said Baltivar.

"'Give Brasa my pay,'" I said.

"What?" said Baltivar.

"That's what he was trying to say before he died. 'Give Brasa my pay.'"

Baltivar looked affronted. "What? He didn't trust me to give the money to his widow?"

"He was very worried about his wife," I said.

"Who is my *sister*," Brasa said pointedly. "Giving it to me makes sense."

Baltivar grumbled, but I thought with this many witnesses, Othira's final wish would be honored.

CHONHADRIN AND I parted ways at the Glassmarket ostro. She was headed south, to the Taravar stop and her apartment, while I knew, much as I dreaded it, that I had to see Iäna first thing. I could not pretend that I did not know he (and Anora and Tomasaran, but I could only deal with one at a time) would have been desperately worried about me, especially since I had lost count under Revethora Vezvaishoroi and had no clear idea of how many days I had been gone.

There was no one at all in the lobby; when I pushed through into the auditorium, I found Iäna and the children's chorus practicing the Chorus of Tree Frogs from *The Dream of the Empress Corivero*.

Iäna turned when he heard the auditorium door swing shut. I came down the aisle and watched his face go from puzzled to shocked as he identified me: he had thought I was dead.

"Thara!" He jumped down and came to meet me, catching me in a bear hug that nearly lifted me off my feet. "Where hast thou been?"

"It is a very long story," I said. "But I am sorry to have worried thee. I did not leave by choice."

He released me, frowning. "If thou didst not leave by choice, that implies that thou didst leave by force."

"Correct," I said.

He stared at me for a moment, then turned and yelled, "*Thoramis!*"

"I don't want to take thee from thy work," I protested.

"Thara, please don't be ridiculous," said Iäna. "We will go up to the third-floor boxes, and if they need me, they can yell. But they won't. Thoramis knows how to do my job at least as well as I do."

He said this last loud enough for his assistant Thoramis to hear as he came out of the wings. Thoramis grinned and said, "That might be true. Go on. We'll be fine."

We did not speak on the way up the stairs; it wasn't until we were seated in the darkness of a third-floor box that Iäna said, "Now. Tell me what happened."

I told the story for a second time. When I described the vision in which I regained my ability to hear the dead, Iäna found my hand and held it for the rest of the story. When I was done, he said, "And thou art well?"

"My calling has *not* been taken from me. Yes, I am well."

"Not, for example, worried about the Clenverada?"

"Not yet."

He snorted with laughter. "Wilt thou be?"

"Oh probably," I said. "I need a favor."

"Name it."

"My coat of office was destroyed beneath Revethora Vezvaishoroi—"

"And thou need'st a replacement. Of course! Let us go talk to Ulsheän."

MERREM ADALHARAD WAS surrounded by a swarm of seamstresses. One of them saw me and gasped, "Othala Celehar!" It was Balaro, one of the girls from the foundling school.

All of them turned, green eyes and red eyes and orange eyes and blue eyes. And Merrem Adalharad's eyes, which were a vivid pumpkin color.

"Othala Celehar!" she said. "Oh, thank goodness!"

I glanced at Iäna, who said, "We asked everyone we could think of to look for you."

"We?" I said, for he had distinctly used the plural.

"Othala Chanavar and Othalo Tomasaran and I. They came to me when your friend at the Chapterhouse said it wasn't within his remit to search for a missing person."

"But what can I do for you?" said Merrem Adalharad. "I observe that that very handsome blue coat is not a prelate's coat of office."

"No," I said. "It is not. I was hoping that I could trade for one that is."

"You don't have to trade," Iäna said.

"I would rather," I said. "And I will never wear this coat anyway. It's much too gaudy for me."

"Oh those gaudy silver buttons," Iäna murmured, mocking but not unkindly.

"Exactly," I said. "So I wish to trade."

"Certainly," said Merrem Adalharad. "We have several coats of office, as it happens. All from secondhand stores, so you need not worry that they are not the real thing. One of them I think will fit you quite well. And if it does not, we can always alter it." As she spoke, she walked down the long aisle between the racks of clothing. She turned into a side aisle and then reappeared with a coat of office.

I saw as she came closer that it was indeed a real one, made of silk and a much deeper black than my old coat of office had been by the end. The black-on-black embroidery was minimalist and severe and the black silk buttons were each embroidered with a circle symbolizing the moon. Merrem Adalharad gave it to me and said, "If you would prefer, we have a room with a mirror just down there." She pointed.

I said, "Yes, thank you." I gave my overcoat to Iäna to hold. The room was very small, but it had a door that latched and one wall was a mirror. I took off the blue coat without regret and shrugged into the coat of office. It was a surprisingly better fit than I had expected: the shoulders were wide enough and the sleeves were not enough too long to matter. And I looked like myself in the mirror, which was a tremendous relief.

I came out, and Merrem Adalharad and two of her seamstresses were immediately on me, like wolves with tape measures.

"It's fine," I protested.

Merrem Adalharad said, "By which you mean, *it'll do*. But we can provide you a better coat than that, Othala Celehar."

Unless I fled, pursued by wolves, I did not seem to have a choice. I let them measure, went back into the little room and changed back into the blue coat, came out and let Merrem Adalharad politely snatch the coat of office from my hands.

"How long?" asked Iäna.

Merrem Adalharad thought for a moment. "The day after tomorrow, probably in the afternoon. I promise it will be worth the waiting, othala."

"Merrem Adalharad," said Balaro.

"Yes?" Merrem Adalharad said.

"We have another coat that should fit Othala Celehar. It's not a coat of office, but it's not . . ."

"Gaudy," Iäna said.

"And maybe Othala Celehar could borrow it?" finished Balaro.

"Well, run and get it," said Merrem Adalharad, and the goblin girl standing next to Balaro, whom I belatedly recognized as one of the other girls from the foundling school, ran down the main aisle and disappeared among the racks. I even came up with her name, although it took me a moment. Her name was Kelmaru.

She returned almost as quickly as she had gone, with a plain dark blue coat. It had even less embroidery than the coat of office, and its buttons were made of black-lacquered brass. The brass was starting to show through on several.

"Is that more to your taste, othala?" said Merrem Adalharad.

"Yes, thank you," I said and smiled at Balaro, who smiled back.

Back to the little room with the mirror, where I changed quickly from the blue coat with silver buttons to the blue coat with black buttons, transferring the contents of my pockets as I did so. As Balaro had said, it fit me—not perfectly, but as well as any secondhand coat was likely to. I came out again and gave the blue coat with silver buttons to Merrem Adalharad.

"Thank you, Merrem Adalharad," I said, and Iäna said, smiling, "We'll be back."

I HAD KEPT Iäna from his opera long enough, and I had other people I had to see. He said, "I would come with thee if my afternoon was not a solid block of rehearsals and we did not perform tonight."

"And I thank thee for the thought," I said. "But it is not necessary."

"And thou wouldst rather only one person made a fuss over thee at a time," said Iäna.

He had caught me fairly, and I felt my face heat. "I would rather no one made a fuss at all, but I cannot have that."

"No," Iäna said. "Thou canst not."

MOST OF A frustrating hour in the Office of the Treasury of the Amalomeire (which once had been the chambers of the Princess of Thu-Athamar), and I had my stipend again, though only because one of the canons on duty happened to recognize me. It was by then too late to find Tomasaran in the Witness for the Dead's office, so I took the tram to Cemchelarna and Merrem Nadaran's boardinghouse, where a skinny teenage goblin girl let me in, and I found Tomasaran in the parlor with ancient Min Nadin, the one deep in the newspapers, the other sewing blue squares to gray squares to green squares with an unrelentingly perfect, tiny stitch.

Tomasaran looked up at my knock on the door. For a moment, she didn't seem to recognize me, and then she started up out of her chair, newsprint pages sliding in all directions, shouting, "Blessed goddesses, where have you *been*?"

"I was—"

"We searched Amalo from top to bottom for you! I thought you were surely dead!" She'd shoved her way free of the hindering paper and now flung her arms around me.

I was not certain how to react. "I am not dead," I offered. "I was kidnapped."

"Kidnapped?" And then she realized what she'd done and hurriedly let me go. We were both blushing.

"By miners," I said. "They'd run afoul of what turned out to be a revethvezvaishor'avar."

"A what?" said Tomasaran.

"A what?" said Min Nadin, who was not pretending not to be able to hear us.

"A revethvezvaishor'avar," I said again. "Like the revethavar under the Hill of Werewolves, only a dragon."

"How can there even *be* such a thing?" said Tomasaran. We both sat down.

"They had a Rite of Living Death and were desperate enough to use it."

She stared at me. "How in the world do you know *that*?"

"She . . . ah, the dragon told me."

"The *dragon* told you? Oh, Celehar, please begin the story from the beginning and tell it properly."

"I will try," I said.

Min Nadin said, "It is a wrench, but I feel that this is not my story to hear. I will go into the kitchen and tell Vinsu you are back."

Tomasaran and I both watched her leave, frail but unconquered by her great age.

"Now," said Tomasaran.

I told the story again.

Tomasaran could not keep from exclaiming at several points, most notably at the reinstatement of my ability to hear the dead, and we lost the thread entirely for some time at Nesairis Clenverar's murder of nearly two hundred dragons.

I was surprised at her outrage. I had expected a woman from a small northern town in Thu-Athamar to consider dragons to be dangerous beasts, the villains of wondertales, not creatures who could be wronged by a clever man's scheming.

I said something of the sort, and Tomasaran said, "A hundred years ago, women were considered beasts with no legal rights. It is still"—her mouth twisted—"the father's right to dispose of his children as he sees fit, whether sending them to apprentice or making advantageous marriages, or simply the question of by whom they will be raised." She paused a moment, clearly wrestling with bitter memories, then said, "My husband was considered a clever man."

We were both silent for a long time; to simply continue my story seemed unfeeling, but to offer sympathy seemed presumptuous. Finally, she said, "But I have shunted our conversation onto a side track. Pray continue."

Her next outburst was when I admitted I had agreed to witness for the dragons. "Are you insane?" she said in horror. "The Clenverada will chew you to pulp and spit you out."

"I did not know you knew the Clenverada," I said.

"Everyone knows *of* the Clenverada," said Tomasaran. "They don't have the power in Amalo that the Amal-Athamareise Airship Company has, but their power stretches up into the mountains to the north and to the refineries to the south. And all the people in between who work for them in one capacity or another."

"I am going to seek an audience with Prince Orchenis," I said.

She shook her head. "He will not help you. He relies too much on the Clenverada's support."

"No, I know," I said. "But it is the first step I must take regardless, before I seek an audience with the emperor."

"Is that your plan?" she said. I was not sure whether she was horrified or admiring; probably, she was not sure, either.

"Insofar as one can call it a plan, yes."

"All right," she said, although the look she gave me said she thought I was insane. "Then go on. Once you agreed to witness for one hundred ninety-two dead dragons, what happened?"

I told her about the long underground journey, about the great tomb of dragons, about the Psalythenor, about Jormentauren's Door, about meeting up with Halhathvered again and the deal we had struck.

She said, "How could you bring yourself to have anything to do with him?"

"A lack of choices," I said dryly.

"Well, yes, but even so!"

"I do not . . ." I trailed off, trying to figure out a way to explain my feelings. "I do not forgive him, but I also don't resent him. I believe that he was doing the best he thought he could in a bad situation. I do *not* believe that of Delthonar."

"Then you think Halhathvered would have stopped them from throwing you to the dragon if he could?"

"Yes. Certainly if he had wanted to murder me, he had every opportunity to do so."

"That is not comforting, Celehar."

"Perhaps not, but it meant that I got to Tanvero alive, and there I unexpectedly met a friend, who traveled with me back to Amalo."

"A friend?" Tomasaran said, as if doubting that I had such things.

"A friend," I said. "Her grandfather had been worried about her traveling from Tanvero to Amalo on her own, so we were mutually convenient for each other. And then I told the story to Mer Pel-Thenhior and now to you, and I still have to tell it to Othala Chanavar."

"And you would very much like to be done telling it," she said.

"I would," I agreed. "But I am not."

I HAD TEA at the boardinghouse—Tomasaran and Min Nadin and Merrem Nadaran all insisted, and I was grateful. Then back to the tram, back to the Dachenostro, down the Zulnicho line and so to Ulvanensee.

As I came into Ulvanensee, the three junior prelates were conducting a cleansing, as they had to do periodically to keep the haunting activity down. Vidrezhen saw me, lost her place in the ritual, and yelled, *"Anora!"*

I stopped where I was.

Anora came running, surely thinking that his junior prelates had encountered a revethavar. He skidded to a stop when he saw me and said, "Great blessed goddesses, Thara, where hast thou *been*?"

I said, and heard the uselessness of it, "It is a very long story."

"Then I pray thee," said Anora, who looked as if he didn't know whether he wanted to hug me or to throttle me, "that thou wilt begin to tell it. Come into my study, for thou lookst as if thou hast need of a chair."

"Yes," I said, for I was still very tired from meeting the dragon under the mountain.

I followed Anora into his study, gratefully sat down, and once again told my tale. Anora listened like a prelate, deeply and without interrupting, and when I was done, he said, "Thou hast picked up a new burden. I only hope it may not be more weight than thou canst carry."

"I hope that, too," I said.

"We will go to the Chrysanthemum," said Anora, "and celebrate thy safe return. For that thou *hast* returned safely is—after the story thou hast told—truly a surprise."

"Yes," I said. "It is more than I expected, to be perfectly honest."

"All the more reason to celebrate," said Anora. "May the juniors come with us, or wouldst thou prefer not?"

"They are welcome," I said. Their presence would prevent Anora asking any of the searching questions I knew he would think of.

"I will yell at them to hurry with their cleansing, then," said Anora and left the study. I put my face in my hands for a moment, trying to find some reserve of strength I hadn't tapped yet, then pushed up out of the chair and followed him.

ANORA'S JUNIOR PRELATES also wanted to hear the story of where I had been, and they had many questions about dragons which I, having been brought up in the flatlands of the south, where there were no dragons, could not answer. Anora knew the answers—or at least knew what the wonder-tales said. He knew that dragons were solitary, that they dug great tunnels beneath the mountains of Osreian's Spine, following the veins of ore: gold, silver, copper. "They were supposed to be very wise," he said, "if you could keep one from eating you long enough to ask it a question."

"Did they *really* eat people?" said Daibrohar.

"That is what the stories say," said Anora. "I have no idea if it's true or not."

"Ithalpherix did not *speak* of eating elves or goblins," I said, "although that does not mean she didn't."

Vidrezhen said, "It makes a convenient excuse for killing them."

"Yes," I said, "and they were clearly very much in the way."

"It speaks of a shameful degree of greed," said Erlenar.

"What is a gold rush about, if not greed?" said Anora, and to that none of us had an answer.

"But what are you going to do?" said Vidrezhen. "How do you witness for one hundred ninety-two dead dragons?"

"I must try to speak to the emperor."

"You can't imagine he's going to make judgment in favor of dead dragons, no matter how many of them there are," Erlenar protested.

"I learned very early in his reign not to try to predict what Edrehasivar will do," I said. "All I can do is ask."

BEFORE HE LET me leave that night, Anora made me promise that I would visit Subpraeceptor Azhanharad as soon as I could.

"Well, of course I will," I said, puzzled, "but why should the subpraeceptor—"

"He's been watching the Mich'maika for a week," said Anora, "expecting thy mangled corpse to be pulled out of it."

"I beg thy pardon," I said. "Why in the world—"

"The subpraeceptor is no denser than the rest of us," Anora said sharply. "He could see as well as I could the reasons thou mightst have committed suicide."

I tried to say that was ridiculous and failed.

"Go and show him thou art alive," said Anora. Then he added in a softer tone, "He is thy friend also, Thara, if thou wilt but let him."

"I will go," I said. "I promise."

"Good," said Anora, and we parted smiling.

I had in fact intended simply to go to my room and thus to bed, but what Anora had said about Azhanharad disturbed me. I did not like to think of him worrying that I might have become one of the corpses pulled out of the Mich'maika, knowing that he would have a precise and gruesome understanding of what that meant. I decided sleep could wait a little bit longer and set out across the Airmen's Quarter for the Brotherhood Chapterhouse.

It was immediately apparent that the novices on door duty had heard that I was probably dead, for they backed away and made no effort to hinder me nor even to ascertain where I was going. I knew the way to Azhanharad's office and decided to try there first. If he was *not* there, I could worry about getting someone to tell me where he was.

But he was there, deep in a sheaf of reports.

I knocked on the partially open door.

He said, "No, Melobanar, you do not have to—" and at that point had raised his head far enough to see me. It was the first time I had ever seen Azhanharad so much as discomfited, and it was several moments before he was able to find words. "Othala Celehar," he said finally, then paused, then blurted, "Where have you *been*?"

"May we sit down?"

"Yes, please. Sit." He made an expansive gesture with the hand holding the pen. "Just so long as you tell us."

I sat and told my story for the fifth time that day. Azhanharad listened with great care and increasing horror. "But what will you do?" he said when I had finished.

"Witness for Ithalpherix," I said. "We swore an oath and it is our calling."

He gave me a troubled look. "The Clenverada have considerable power in Thu-Athamar."

"We know. Even more since the fall from favor of the Duhalada. But it cannot be helped."

"The prince will not listen to you."

"We think he will listen," I said, "although we do not expect him to act."

"The Clenverada will accuse you of being insane. Or a liar. Or both."

"It will not be the first time we have been accused of such things, and this is something we must do."

"Your calling."

"And our oath, yes."

"We would not see you hurt," Azhanharad said, so stiffly that I understood he meant, *I was worried about you*.

"The Clenverada are unlikely to think us so great a threat," I said. "One madman raving about a revethvezvaishor'avar?"

Azhanharad gave me a very long, suspicious look. "You have a plan," he said finally.

"Yes," I said. "But we will seek an audience with Prince Orchenis first."

I WALKED HOME. Merrem Istovaran the concierge said, "Othala Celehar! Where have you been?"

"I was called out of town unexpectedly," I said, which was the truth.

My post was a teetering stack of letters; I suspected that most of them were from Anora, demanding to know where I was. I took the letters up to my room, where there were no cats waiting for me. I'd been gone more than a week; it was hardly surprising, but I still felt a miserable pang of something like guilt, that they might have come for their sardines and I not been there.

I managed to get in the door without dropping my letters. I put them down on the table, where they spilled into chaos. As I was closing my door, a voice from the upstairs landing said, "Othala? Is that you?" and Thenavo came clattering down the stairs. "We thought you were *dead*."

"I was called out of town unexpectedly," I said.

"I fed the cats while you were gone," she said. "Here on your landing. And they came! The big brown one, too!" Even in the almost-darkness, I could see the delight on her face.

"But what did you do for sardines?" I said.

"I used my pocket money," she said with a shrug that

wanted to be casual but was not. "And Mother gave me an extra ten-zashan piece when Father was not around."

"That was very kind of you, Thenavo," I said, "and the prelates of Noranamaro blessed you with every bite."

It took her a moment to puzzle out my meaning, but it made her giggle.

"Thenavo!" a woman's voice called from upstairs. "Where are you?"

"I'm here, Mother. Othala Celehar has come back!"

"That is good news," said her mother, "but not an excuse for not being in bed. Come on, now."

"I have to go," Thenavo said with dignity. "Good night, othala. I'm glad you're back."

"Thank you for feeding the cats," I said. "Good night."

I closed the door, sat down, and began sorting through the letters. Four letters from Anora, one from Iäna, two from Azhanharad, one from Tomasaran, one from Vernezar, one from Othalo Ostilin at Ulnemenee, one from the Amalomeire. I looked at them, spread out like a hand of cards on the table, and thought, *Do I have to read these?* But I knew the answer was yes.

There was nothing particularly surprising in them, just people wondering where I was. (*Dear Thara*, Iäna had written, *I hope this letter finds thee well. Indeed, I hope this letter finds thee at all.*) Some were concerned, some annoyed; the Amalomeire's was a very formal letter wanting to know if I was forfeiting my stipend, and I was glad I had gone to the Office of the Treasury of the Amalomeire on my way to Tomasaran's boardinghouse.

By the time I had finished reading the letters, my five-zashan piece in the meter had almost run out, and I hurried to be in bed before darkness made the room into a stranger's.

In the morning, awake before dawn, I meditated, feeling as if I were trying to knit together a great raveled mass of yarn with my fingers; gladly took clean clothes and went to the public baths and then to the Red Dog's Dream, where they were startled to see me, for breakfast and orchor; took the tram up to the Amal'theileian in the midst of the great bumping crowd of clerks and bureaucrats. There, I realized I was looking for Captain Olgarezh only as I saw him and saw the surprise on his face at seeing me.

He had noticed my absence. The thought was ridiculously warming.

Tomasaran was already in her office. "Celehar," she said, "good morning. Is there a way in which I can help you with your insane plan?"

"I need to petition for an audience with Prince Orchenis," I said. "My paper is in the top left-hand drawer."

She opened the drawer and brought out the stick of wax and the bottle of black ink along with my few sheets of good paper.

"Thank you," I said.

My pen, I still had. It and my notebook had been in my inside waistcoat pocket rather than my inside coat pocket when the miners threw me to the dragon. I refilled my pen and wrote a petition to Prince Orchenis for a private audience—or as private an audience with the Prince of Thu-Athamar as one could get. Ideally, I would have preferred to wait until I had a coat of office again, but I wanted to gain this audience with all possible speed.

"What will you do next?" Tomasaran said as I sealed the petition with my signet—the skull within an eight-pointed star that was the signet of all clerical Witnesses for the Dead.

"Wait," I said. "I can do nothing else."

Anora let that go, only to pick up a different thread. "How thinkst thou thy calling was returned? For that, too, is something the Amal'othala will want to know."

"A miracle of Ulis," I said.

"Not the work of Othalo Rasaltezhen?"

I shrugged. "What she tried did not work."

"Not immediately," said Anora. "But who knows how such a thing might happen? Perhaps it needed some time."

"Art thou arguing against a miracle while I argue for?" I said, for that was not how our conversations usually went.

"I don't know. I wasn't there. But it is possible that Othalo Rasaltezhen deserves part of the credit."

"A *blessing* of Ulis, then," I said.

"That I will certainly agree with. And I am glad of it, whatever it is."

"Yes," I said. "I am, too."

I WENT HOME late and did not sleep. After an hour I got up again, dressed in the dark, and went out walking, because it was better than staring at nothing.

I walked to one of the larger and wealthier cooperative cemeteries in the Airmen's Quarter, Uldranavee, where the paths wound and twisted, almost like a maze, and I could walk for hours without having to retrace my steps. Uldranavee was also beautifully maintained, and the moonlight made everything crisp and clear and perfect. It was not better than sleep, but it was almost as good.

WHEN MORNING FINALLY came, I went to the municipal baths to wash off a sleepless night, went to the Red Dog's Dream for orchor (and breakfast), and then took the tram up the hill to Tomasaran's office. (Captain Olgarezh and I nodded to each other as if I had never been gone. I was aware of a ridiculous desire to tell *him* my story.) Tomasaran was already there. So was a courier wearing Prince Orchenis's colors, who bowed and handed me a sealed letter.

It was a summons. "Now?" I said to the courier.

"There is time before court if you come *now*," said the courier.

I hesitated a moment, but I could not keep asking Tomasaran to lend me her coat of office and the dark blue coat was respectable enough. Also, the fact that my own coat of office had actually been destroyed might be a fact that would catch the prince's attention.

I followed the courier back the way I had just come, from the Prince Zhaicava Building back to the Amal'theileian, and then through the Amal'theileian to the Cinnabar Room, where Prince Orchenis and his private secretary were waiting.

Prince Orchenis gave me a long, frowning look and said, "We are relieved to see that you are not dead."

"We are relieved not to *be* dead. But surprised that our petition reached you so quickly."

His expression changed to something that was almost amusement. "*All* our secretaries know that a communication from you goes directly to Mer Alcharanar."

"Oh," I said.

"But come," said Prince Orchenis. "We gather from your petition that you have a story you wish to tell us."

"Yes," I said.

And I told the story again.

I was glad I had had the practice with Iäna and Tomasaran and Anora and Azhanharad, for it helped me keep my place even in the midst of Prince Orchenis's questions, of which there were many.

When I had finished, he asked, "And you intend to witness for the dragons?"

"It is a rightful petition," I said.

"Against the Clenverada," he said, not really as a question.

"We do not witness *against* anyone."

"Sophistry," Prince Orchenis said impatiently. "You know that we cannot help you. The Clenverada are too powerful in Thu-Athamar."

"Yes," I said. "We know that."

"We do not think anyone less than the emperor can . . ." His voice trailed off.

"Yes," I said. "We know that, too."

His expression became mingled horror and admiration. "You intend to go to the emperor."

"As you just said, it is the only way."

He hesitated, choosing what he would say with some care. "Then go quickly, Othala Celehar. It will not take long for this story to spread, and the Clenverada will not agree that you are not witnessing against them."

"No, we don't expect they will. Thank you, Your Highness."

"For what?" said Prince Orchenis. "There is no help we can offer you."

"For good advice," I said, and he waved me away with an expression that was not a smile.

PRINCE ORCHENIS WAS correct that I needed to move quickly, but it was impossible to think of going before the emperor in this dark blue coat. I left the Amal'theileian and headed north to the Vermilion Opera. Iäna would not be there yet, but the Wardrobe Department worked on a different schedule and it was possible that the new coat was finished. Or that they could finish it while I waited.

The problem was that I had no idea of how to reach the Wardrobe Department. It seemed to me that every time he took me there, Iäna used a different route, and I could remember none of them.

As I stood in the great vermilion maw of the lobby, I realized that I could hear voices coming from the ticket office. I started toward the window, but the sound of my shoe heels quickly brought an inquisitive clerk.

"Othala Celehar!" he said. "How can I help you?"

"I need to speak to Merrem Adalharad," I said. "Can you spare someone to show me the way?"

"Yes, certainly," said the clerk. One of the part-goblin page boys came out into the lobby.

"Thank you," I said.

"It is truly nothing," said the clerk. "Zhana has nothing to do except wait for us to send him on errands."

The page boy smiled shyly and did not disagree.

He led me swiftly through the passageways and tunnels and stairs of the Vermilion Opera's backstage and brought me to the Wardrobe Department by a route I was sure Iäna had never used. Merrem Adalharad was seated in the doorway, doing embroidery with silver thread on a gray dress with a sweeping skirt.

"Othala Celehar!" she said. "I did not expect you until afternoon."

"I know," I said. "I cannot come this afternoon, so I dared to come early in hopes it might be ready."

"Of course," she said. "Really, there was nothing difficult about it. We put it here on the rack beside the door." She nodded to her right. "I would get it myself, except that it will be a five-minute job to extricate myself."

"If you don't mind?"

"Not at all," she said. "We have people in and out of here all day long. Sometimes they remember to tell someone what they've taken. Sometimes they don't."

I advanced, a little nervously, to the doorway and saw

that, as she had said, there was a standing rack beside the door with ten or twelve costumes hanging on it. But the coat of office was first in line.

"Try it on before you do anything," said Merrem Adalharad, and I returned to the tiny cubicle with a mirror, where I shed the dark blue coat and put on the coat of office. It fit perfectly.

I came out again and asked Merrem Adalharad, "What should I do with the dark blue coat?"

"You don't wish to keep it?"

I would have wished to keep it, except that my plan was to go directly from the Opera to the Amal-Athamareise Airship Company's mooring mast and purchase a ticket to the Untheileneise Court.

"No, but I thank you."

"Then just hang it on the rack. We'll get use out of it one way or another."

I carefully transferred the contents of my pockets from the dark blue coat to the coat of office, then hung the dark blue coat on the rack. I was a little startled to see that the page boy had waited for me, but said, "I am ready to go back to the lobby, if you will show me."

"Yes, othala," he said softly and led me back by a route that seemed different yet again.

"Thank you," I said when we reached the lobby. I would have offered him a five-zashan piece, but he had already disappeared. And there was someone waiting in the lobby, someone in the colors of the Amalomeire.

"You are a hard person to find, Othala Celehar," said the courier.

"We did not expect to be sought for," I said, accepting the letter she held out to me.

It was a summons to the Amal'othala's presence.

"Now?" I said.

"As soon as we can get there," said the courier.

I DREADED THE audience all the way from the Opera to the Amalomeire, all the way up the switchbacking stairs, and all the way down to the audience chamber the Amal'othala preferred today. It was one of the larger rooms, and the walls were all carved with peonies. The Amal'othala was sitting in a gilded chair at a gilded table; he raised his eyebrows when he saw me. "Well, Othala Celehar?"

"Well, Your Holiness?" I said, knowing it would irritate him but unable to guess what he wanted me to say.

"We understand that you vanished from Amalo for more than a week and have returned quite as mysteriously as you disappeared. We think it is not unreasonable of us to ask where you have been."

"Yes, Your Holiness," I said.

There was nothing for it. I told the story again. The Amal'othala listened in silence, but with a steadily darkening expression.

"That is your story," he said when I had finished.

"Yes, Your Holiness."

"And you intend to stand by your ridiculous determination to witness for these dead dragons."

"It is not ridiculous," I said. "We were rightfully petitioned."

"They're *dragons,* Celehar, not *people,*" the Amal'othala snapped.

"That is a matter of opinion."

"The Clenverada will squash you, and you need not think the Amalomeire will speak in your defense."

"We had no such delusion."

He glared at me. "We could forbid you . . ."

"No, you couldn't. We were appointed by the Archprelate."

"As you are so fond of reminding us. But do you really think the Archprelate will take your side?"

In truth, I was not sure. But I said, "The Archprelate is hardly going to support mass murder."

"Of *dragons,*" said the Amal'othala.

"Of beings capable of speech and rational thought."

We stared at each other for several moments.

"You really intend to do this insane thing," said the Amal'othala.

"Yes," I said.

"You must be planning to go to Cetho, then."

"Yes."

"We think you will be unpleasantly surprised by the Archprelate's response," the Amal'othala said as if the prospect pleased him. "But you are right. We cannot stop you."

"Your Holiness," I said, bowing, and escaped without having to correct his assumption that I meant to seek an audience with the Archprelate.

SOMEONE OF THE Clenverada probably knew about me by now. If nothing else, Canon Clenverin was going to know in a matter of minutes. What I did not know was how seriously they would take the threat I posed to them. Even to me, it seemed ridiculous, one Witness for the Dead, witnessing for 192 dead dragons, trying to shut down the Clenverada Mining Company, if not entirely, then entirely too close. I thought it was possible, but I did not know if the Clenverada thought the same, nor what they might be prepared to do about it. I was on my guard on my way to the Amal-Athamareise Airship Company office, but no one seemed to be following me or paying any particular attention to me.

As it turned out, that was because they did not need to. At

the front desk of the office, the extremely beautiful young elven woman looked at me and said, "You're the Witness for the Dead."

I could not lie in the service of my calling. "Yes."

"I'm sorry, othala," she said, although her face showed nothing of the sort. "We cannot sell you a ticket."

"Cannot?"

"Orders from the main office," she said and shrugged her perfect shoulders in a manner my governess would have censured for being unladylike.

"I see," I said, and I did see. The Clenverada were taking me seriously as a threat.

I walked away from the office without knowing where I was going to go. If the Clenverada had gotten to the Amal-Athamareise Airship Company, they would certainly have gotten to the coach companies. Finding a caravan heading south this time of year would not be impossible, but caravans were slow, and more than ever, I knew I needed to move fast. It was too obvious that the easiest and surest way of solving the problem was to get rid of me, and it seemed terrifyingly unlikely that the Clenverada had ethical principles that would stand in the way.

I stopped at a food cart and bought a tobastha, which I ate while walking toward Tarav'ostro. My route took me by Chonhadrin's barracks, and the association of ideas reminded me of what she'd said about stowaways.

Now, unexpectedly, I *did* want to stow away on an airship. And Chonhadrin's room was right there.

She wasn't home, but as long as the Clenverada didn't actually have anyone following me, and I felt reasonably sure they did not, this was as safe a place as any in Amalo to sit and wait. I went over the points of my story again to be sure I wasn't starting to leave something important out; the problem with telling a story repeatedly was that one did start to elide things from it, and I wanted to be sure that my one chance at telling this story to the emperor was not wasted.

Chonhadrin came home as the shadows were starting to lengthen; she said, "Hello, Celehar," as if it were not surprising to see me sitting outside her door. "Would you like to come in or would you like to go to the Pearl Dragon for tea?"

I badly wanted this to be a friendly visit that was suitable for a teahouse. "I would like to come in," I said. "I need to ask you a favor."

"A favor?" She unlocked her door and waved me in. "Well, sit down and tell me about it. If I can help you, I will."

"Thank you," I said and sat down at her small table. I told her about my audience with Prince Orchenis and my audience with the Amal'othala and then about my attempt to buy a ticket on the evening airship to the Untheileneise Court.

"They turned you away?" she said, horrified.

"They knew who I was," I said. "Someone in the Clenverada must know someone with power in the Amal-Athamareise Ashenavo Trincsiva."

Her ears flattened. "Mer Zhalanar, our treasurer, married a woman of the Clenverada."

"There we are, then," I said. "But that is why I need a favor."

She frowned in puzzlement. "But what favor can I do you?"

"I want to stow away," I said.

"Celehar!"

"I must get to the Untheileneise Court as quickly as I can, and if the Clenverada have gotten to the airships, they will have gotten to the coaches, too."

"That is most likely true," she said. "How much money do you have?"

"Money?"

"The easiest method of stowing away on an airship," she said, "is to bribe the captain."

THAT EVENING'S AIRSHIP to the Untheileneise Court was the *Strength of Rosiro*, the ship that had *not* blown up with the emperor on board. Surely, if I could look to omens at all, she was a good omen.

I followed Chonhadrin up the stairs of the mooring mast and into the wood-paneled main cabin. "Wait here," she said and went to knock on the door of the cockpit.

I waited. Chonhadrin was admitted into the cockpit. The two part-goblin crewmen cleaning the cabin gave me sidelong, curious glances. I tried to look calm. It felt like years, but it was really only minutes before Chonhadrin came back with a stout elven man who introduced himself as Captain Volbonar.

"The captain," said Chonhadrin, "is prepared to overlook some irregularity in the ticketing so long as the proper amount is paid to a representative of the Amal-Athamareise Ashenavo Trincsiva."

"Of course," I said. I judged the "proper amount" was probably twice the cost of a ticket, which used up almost all of the money I had.

The captain counted the bills, bowed, and said, "That covers the difficulty very nicely, othala. Please make yourself comfortable, and I will let the crew know not to bother you."

"It's that simple?" I said to Chonhadrin as the captain returned to the cockpit.

"It depends on the captain. You got lucky. Captain Volbonar is much more inclined to be flexible about such things than Captain Ulachenar. And Captain Porthanar is nosy." She smiled at me. "But you're set."

"Thank you for your help," I said.

She shook her head, still smiling. "You don't need to thank me. I hope your mad plan succeeds."

"So do I," I said.

I sat down. Chonhadrin, after a quiet word with the crewmembers in the cabin, left the way we'd come, and a few minutes later the properly ticketed passengers started entering the cabin.

There were not many of them. It was only since the advent of Edrehasivar VII that the Amal-Athamareise Airship Company had started, as an experiment, allowing the purchase of tickets by ordinary travelers, and the tickets were expensive. There was a goblin courier in Prince Orchenis's colors, an elven woman in deep mourning leading a beautiful part-goblin child by the hand, a prosperous-looking elven merchant and his part-goblin servant. The crewmen welcomed them aboard, but otherwise no one spoke.

The last passenger was very shortly followed by an elven crewwoman, an ashenin like Chonhadrin, who secured the cabin door and then went forward to knock on the cockpit door in a sharp rhythm. It was obviously a signal that they were about to cast off, for it was only a matter of moments after that that I felt the bump of the airship undocking.

I had no hope of sleeping, but I stared out the porthole at the great brooding darkness of the sky and did not mind.

THE MOORING MAST rose among the brightly tiled roofs of the Untheileneise Court like a slender jeweled sister to the Alcethmeret, the great tower that was the emperor's home. The *Strength of Rosiro* settled down beside the mast with a bob and a bump, and after an exchange of knocks, the crewwoman opened the outside door.

The fact that the mooring mast was part of the

Untheileneise Court did not mean that all airship passengers were bound for the emperor's court. After descending from the moored airship, I faced a choice of doors. One set, at the end of a long, roofed walkway, led to the palace; the other set—tall, arched wooden doors with wrought-iron vines coiling across them—led to the city of Cetho. The palace doors were guarded—having come to the throne by assassination and having survived an assassination attempt himself, Edrehasivar was cautious.

I was the only passenger who chose the palace doors.

The guards looked at me dubiously.

My urgent need was to get a message to Mer Aisava, the emperor's secretary, since submitting a petition for an audience with the emperor might take weeks, if it was granted at all. But there was no point saying so to guards on duty at the Ashenaveise Doors. I said, "We are Thara Celehar, a Witness for the Dead, and a kinsman of Csoru Zhasane. We seek entrance to our cousin's household." This was technically the truth; I wished access to Csoru's household, both because I knew I desperately needed to rebraid my hair before I tried to see the emperor and because a messenger from Csoru Zhasane would get farther quicker than would a Witness for the Dead. If I was hoping to avoid meeting my cousin—which I was—I did not have to share that if the guards did not ask, which of course they did not.

I could only hope that Ulis would accept the larger truth of which this almost-lie was in service.

"Certainly, Mer Celehar," said the right-hand guard. "Kibrenis will take you." Kibrenis was a part-goblin page boy, and I knew at least half of his job was to be sure I did not go anywhere *other* than Csoru Zhasane's household.

"Thank you," I said and followed Kibrenis.

My cousin Csoru was not housed in the Alcethmeret, a silent emblem of the emperor's lack of trust in her. At the arched grille that separated her household from the rest of the palace, I knew the liveried goblin doorman and could say, "Hello, Mathormened."

"Mer Celehar!" Mathormened said. "We weren't . . . were we expecting you?"

I said, "No. I have business with the emperor."

It sounded conceited and presumptuous to my ears, but Mathormened said, "Of course. Please come in. You are always welcome in Csoru Zhasane's household."

That was a lie, but a kind one, and more than I had anticipated. I had known Csoru's doorman would let me in—I *was* her cousin and it looked bad to leave me in the hall—but, considering she had thrown me out last winter, I had not expected to be *welcomed*. I bowed thanks to Kibrenis and said, "Is there a washroom I could make use of?"

"Just down the hallway to the left," said Mathormened.

"Thank you. And I need to send a message to Mer Aisava. Is there someone who could take it for me?"

"The page boys are just finishing breakfast," said Mathormened. "The two of them will be along probably in five minutes."

It looked like I might be able to do this without my cousin even knowing I was here. "Thank you."

The washroom had a ridiculously large mirror over the sink. I looked at myself and wished I hadn't. I took all the pins out of my hair, carefully putting them on the shelf beside the mirror, finger-combed my hair, dampened it to calm the curls, and rebraided it, tying off the ribbon with a sharp tug. Then I repinned it, trying to anticipate which strands would work their way loose of the braid first.

I looked at myself in the mirror again, after. My coat, at

least, was correct, and my hair was acceptable, if still a little wild-looking. A courtier would use maquillage to disguise the shadows under my eyes, but I was not a courtier. A prelate of the court would be wearing a round silver mask, but I was not a prelate of the court, either, and had never had such a mask.

I was about to open the door when I heard a clatter of heels in the hallway and my cousin Csoru's voice, sharply finding fault with one of her edocharoi. I froze, straining to hear—entirely expecting Mathormened to say, *Your cousin Thara Celehar is here*. But he did not, and the noise of Csoru's passage faded away.

When I returned to the grille, there were two page boys there with Mathormened, one elven and one part goblin with bright orange eyes. "Medra can take your message," said Mathormened, indicating the part-goblin boy, who looked nearly old enough to stop being a page boy and either take on an adult's responsibilities in the household or become a courier.

"Thank you," I said. "Good morning, Medra."

"Good morning, Mer Celehar," Medra said, his orange eyes lively with curiosity. "How can I help you?"

"I need you to take a verbal message to Mer Aisava. Can you do that?"

"Yes, I know the Alcethmeret guards. They'll let me by."

"Good. The message is simple. Just tell him that Thara Celehar, the Witness for the Dead, needs to speak to him urgently."

"I can remember a longer message than that," Medra said.

"No, that's really all I need. Will you?"

He nodded, recognizing the difference between "can" and "will." "I will."

"Thank you."

He left with a brisk stride.

I said cautiously to Mathormened, "You have done me a great favor, and I appreciate it."

He could easily have stonewalled me, but he did not pretend not to know what I meant. He said, "The way *I* was raised was to honor prelates." He left the comparison unspoken, but I understood him: Csoru had not the slightest respect for me or for my calling and had never hesitated to make that plain.

"I don't want to cause a headache for you," I said, too aware of the younger page boy within earshot to say, *I don't want to get you in trouble*.

"You are not," he said. "Most of the workings of her household are beneath Csoru Zhasane's notice."

There were several things I could have said in answer to that; I settled on, "Will you tell me the news of the palace?"

All doormen were gossips, crucial nodes in the network of knowledge that sustained the workings of the court. Mathormened could tell me in exhaustive detail about the preparations for the emperor's birthday and knew all the details about the jockeyings among the courtiers for Dach'osmin Ceredin's favor. With her marriage, she would become the mirror image of Mer Aisava, a negotiator with the world for the emperor—she among the nobility, Mer Aisava among the commons—both a shortcut to the emperor's attention, as I was attempting, and a last defense against those who would waste the emperor's time. No one was worried about Dach'osmin Ceredin's judgment, and as Mathormened said, "She will keep the wastrels from him." Neither Mathormened nor I pointed out that, even when she had been empress, Csoru had not been the emperor's partner in this way.

When Medra returned, he said, "You are to come with me, Mer Celehar. Mer Aisava says he can talk to you now."

That, too, was more than I had expected. "All right," I

said and was glad I had taken the opportunity to tidy my hair when I had it.

I followed Medra without even trying to remember our route. If the Amal'theileian was vast and confusing, it was a child's toy next to the Untheileneise Court, a palace the size of a city—a palace that *was* a city—and Medra led me from hallways floored in marble, to ancient stone passageways only wide enough for us to go single-file, to beautifully woodworked galleries, to a long stoa with caryatids supporting the ceiling, to, finally, the high-vaulted ceilings and parquet floors of the immediate approach to the Alcethmeret.

To my further surprise, Mer Aisava was waiting at the gates, an elven man with his hair in two respectable buns, wearing sober brown embroidered with flowers in deep purples and reds. His earrings were gold hoops with garnet drops. "Mer Celehar!" he said, offering his hand. "It has been an age since we have heard of you!"

I clasped hands with him and said, "We have been very busy."

"But come," said Mer Aisava. "We will go to my study. Have you had breakfast?"

Breakfast had not occurred to me. "No," I said, "but—"

"Allow us to remedy that, and then you can tell us what you need."

"Of course," I said, as arguing seemed singularly foolish.

Mer Aisava's study was on a landing off the main stairs of the Alcethmeret. It was wood-paneled and there was a fire already started in the marble-manteled fireplace.

"Sit," said Mer Aisava, pointing to the two chairs by the fireplace rather than the chair before his desk, and I sat in a deep leather chair, old but well cared for, and more comfortable than anything I'd sat on for at least twenty-four hours. He briskly pulled a bell-pull, which summoned a liveried servant, an elven girl whose cropped hair was as curly as mine. Mer Aisava told her to bring breakfast for two and a pot of orchor, and she nodded silently and departed, closing the door firmly behind her.

Mer Aisava sat in the other chair flanking the fireplace and said, "Now tell me how I can help you."

I tried not to look surprised at the shift in formality and said, "I need to speak to the emperor as soon as I can."

"That seems very urgent," said Aisava. "Why?"

I told the story again, this time adding on my failed attempt to purchase a ticket for the *Strength of Rosiro*. Aisava listened carefully, only asking questions at points that confused him, and said at the end, as if he wanted to be sure he had his facts straight, "You are witnessing for one hundred ninety-two dead dragons."

"Yes," I said.

"And you wish to petition the emperor to close all the mines in the Osreialhallan that were dragonholds."

"Yes." It sounded insane.

"Do you know how many that is?"

"At least a hundred and ninety-two."

Aisava made a face, appalled but not unsympathetic.

There was a knock at the door, and the servant girl returned with a tray holding two bowls of oatmeal with dried apricots and a beautiful deep blue teapot with two matching cups. She set it on the table between our chairs, which was just exactly big enough to hold it.

"Thank you, Celno," Aisava said, and she bobbed a kind of half curtsy and left, again closing the door with reassuring firmness.

"Eat," said Aisava, pouring tea, and as we ate we talked about lighter things. He had a different stratum of gossip than Mathormened and an insider's view of the preparations for the wedding, which were wide-spreading and intense.

He and Dach'osmin Ceredin's personal secretary were in charge of correspondence; they had sent out the notices of the wedding and now had nobles from dukes to petty gentry writing to say that they could or could not attend. "Plus the messages of good wishes from the common people, which have already started to arrive."

"You must be very busy," I said.

"Oh yes," said Aisava. "I mean, one is always busy as the emperor's personal secretary, but this is . . ."

"Like spring flooding."

"Exactly," he said. "Min Olivin and I are just trying to keep our heads above the water. She has developed a great chart, which takes up most of one wall in her study, where we can mark when we hear from a head of house and what their answer is. She says it will be useful for many other things when Dach'osmin Ceredin is empress, she having several times said that she wishes to be useful to the emperor."

"Laudable."

"And not a given," Aisava said, although he did not mention Csoru Zhasane by name. "But it is plain both that Dach'osmin Ceredin has the emperor's favor and that she means to be worthy of it, which is a great relief to both their households."

I was surprised when I realized I had finished the oatmeal. I put the bowl back on the tray and picked up the teacup. Aisava mirrored me, then leaned back in his chair and said, "Tell me why you think the emperor should hear this petition."

"Did I not just do that?"

"You explained what the petition is, not why it should be heard. I cannot simply give you an audience with the emperor because I trust your judgment. Well, I *could,* but it would ultimately be a weakness in your case."

"When the Clenverada come howling down out of the north to complain."

our heads, and he turned and gave me a half smile. "The center of the Alcethmeret is a rose garden. The emperor walks here when he wishes to be alone."

"But—"

"He has chosen to give you some of his time. Be sure you do not waste the gift."

"Yes," I said, feeling hollow now with the magnitude of the honor being done me.

Aisava led me around to another door, which was just opening. I recognized the man who emerged as one of the emperor's nohecharei, a tall, scowling soldier. He stepped clear of the servant holding the door open and turned to scowl impartially at Aisava and me. He nodded, a short, sharp jerk of his head, and the emperor stepped out into the rose garden.

He was as I remembered him: tall, with dark gray skin and pale gray eyes; he was dressed in white-on-white brocade with a froth of lace at collar and cuffs and wore amethysts on his hands and neck and ears and wound through the elaborate braids and buns of his hair. He looked tired.

"Mer Celehar!" he said, and he sounded pleased. Behind him, his other nohecharis came out, a maza in a plain blue robe, wearing thick spectacles.

"Serenity," I said and bowed deeply.

"Come walk with us and tell us what has brought you to the Untheileneise Court," he said.

"Serenity, we did not intend to intrude upon your—"

"We made the decision," he said mildly. "And it is not an intrusion if it is a friend."

I kept my face composed, but I knew my ears twitched wildly. "You do us a great honor, Serenity."

"You did us a great service," he countered. "Now come. We wish to hear your story."

I could hardly argue with the emperor. I walked beside

him, around and around the looping paths among the mostly bare rosebushes, and told the story again. He listened with great attention, asking no questions, and I was glad I had rehearsed the story earlier, glad I had had so much practice in telling it, for I knew how to keep everything clear and in order.

When I was finished, we walked a loop in silence before he said, "Why have you brought this story to us, rather than the Archprelate? Is this not rightly a religious matter?"

Someone had ascertained that I had not been to speak to the Archprelate. "The Archprelate does not have the power that you have, Serenity. He cannot make the Clenverada close down the dragonhold mines."

"That may be beyond our power, as well."

I felt my ears lower. "Serenity—"

"It would be an economic disaster to close down the Clenverada Mining Company."

"That is not what we are asking. Surely they have mines that are *not* dragonholds."

"We do not know. Csevet can find out for us. But even if they do, it may be a greater blow than their company can weather. And if the Clenverada fall . . ." He made a flattening motion with one hand.

"But they have been profiting from an atrocity for more than a hundred years."

"They have, and we do not like it any better than you do. But we cannot destroy the empire. The Clenverada will raise their banner against us, and they will win."

"Oh," I said, though I struggled to find a better response.

"And we must have jobs for all the workers. You cannot right a wrong with another wrong."

"Serenity—" I tried again, but he shook his head.

"This is no burden for your shoulders, Mer Celehar. You are the Witness for the Dragons, not the Witness for the Clenverada, nor the Witness for the Miners. In fact, it would probably be best if we appointed a judicial Witness for the Dragons as well, for there will be a great deal of work required."

"That wasn't actually a no," I said cautiously.

He had been looking at the last of the late-blooming roses, but now he turned to me. "It does not suit us that the Clenverada should continue to profit off a massacre. We will at least open the question, even if we cannot make assurances about the outcome."

"Thank you, Serenity," I said.

Our looping had brought us back to the door, and I knew the emperor was about to apologize for not being able to spend more time with me, but just as he was beginning to open his mouth, the door flew open and Aisava burst into the garden. "Serenity," he said, "we beg your pardon, but we feel you will wish to know of this immediately."

The emperor's eyebrows went up, but he said, "Then please tell us."

"We had remembered seeing something in the catalogue of the Imperial Treasury, and we looked it up in the index and found it again."

"And?" said the emperor.

"Serenity, it says there is a dragon skull in your vaults."

"A dragon skull?" I said. The emperor and I stared at each other in horror. "But who would—"

"It was a gift," said Aisava. "To the Emperor Varenechibel III from Tavenis Clenverar."

"Of course it was," the emperor said. "We wish to see it."

"We thought you might," Aisava said. "There is room in your schedule, but only just."

"Thank you, Csevet," the emperor said, and his smile was as lovely as I remembered. "Mer Celehar, do you wish to come with us?"

"We do," I said.

"Then come. Csevet, we trust you have found a page boy who knows the way."

"Yes, Serenity. Rachis will lead you."

"Thank you." He said to me, "We expect it will be years before we can find our own way through the Untheileneise Court—if we ever can."

"Many emperors do not," I said.

"It is a very lowering thought," said the emperor.

The page boy was elven. He had been in service in the Alcethmeret long enough not to be tongue-tied in front of the emperor; he was in fact eager to tell him about the results of an ombeth game the previous day, played between the page boys of the Alcethmeret and the page boys of the Ceredada and Celehada. The page boys of the Alcethmeret had been victorious, and the emperor was appropriately pleased that his honor had been upheld. I knew most of his mind had to be elsewhere, but it was entirely impossible to discern.

At the doors to the vaults of the Imperial Treasury, we were met by an elven man who introduced himself as Olta Tristivar, one of the curators of the vaults. He wore dark green with gold buttons and gold braid at the cuffs, and his hair, in a perfect, unostentatious bun dressed with small green glass beads, was a wig. It was clear that being this close to the emperor made him nervous, but he was staunchly ignoring it. He said, "We apologize, Serenity, but it is not quite clear to us what you are looking for."

The emperor said, "It is very simple. Is there a dragon skull in the Treasury vaults?"

"A . . . a dragon skull? Yes, Serenity, there is. In vault three, subfloor two. But why—"

"Show us," the emperor said crisply, and Mer Tristivar bowed and said, "Yes, Serenity. This way."

We followed him, the emperor, the emperor's nohecharei,

Aisava, and I, through two cavernous, well-lit vaults, filled with row upon row of shelves, and each shelf full of carved wooden boxes. Even without stopping to examine them, I saw that each box bore a brass plate with a combination of letters and numbers and sometimes a word or two. Probably this was not what anyone imagined would be done with the gifts they gave the emperor—had been giving the emperors for centuries—but on the other side, what else could the emperor do that would not involve the disrespect of giving the gift to someone else, or worse, throwing it away?

In the third vault, which was identical to the first two, Mer Tristivar pulled open a trapdoor, revealing a narrow staircase. It was as clean and well lit as the vaults, and we descended into another vault, this one full of what looked like furniture, but since everything here was covered with a drop cloth, it was difficult to tell.

Mer Tristivar mutely hauled open another trapdoor, and we descended again.

This vault held carriages, each body likewise covered with a drop cloth, although the gilding and paint on the wheels still showed.

"But how could you possibly get them in here?" said the emperor.

"We have another set of doors, Serenity, and a lift that can move large objects like carriages."

"Or dragon skulls," said the emperor. "Is this subfloor two, or have we another level to descend?"

"No, this is the correct floor." Mer Tristivar led us down a narrow aisle between hulking shrouded shapes and said, "Here it is, Serenity." He pulled the drop cloth off one of the shapes, revealing the shining black lines of a dragon's skull.

"Merciful goddesses," said the emperor. "Do we know . . . that is, what do we know about it?"

"Serenity," said Mer Tristivar. There was a tag tied through the eye socket; he consulted it and said, "It was given to the Emperor Varenechibel III one hundred and five years ago by the Clenverada. It comes from the mountains north of Amalo, from what was then the Clenverada's richest mine. The dragon's name . . ." Here, he faltered.

"Go on," said the emperor grimly.

"The dragon's name was Arquenethil."

"And they cut off its head and brought it as a present to our great-grandfather," said the emperor.

"Yes, Serenity," said Mer Tristivar warily. "The emperor was very pleased by the gift."

"From what we know of him, we are sure he was." The emperor turned to me. "Mer Celehar, what must we do?"

"The rest of its body must be long destroyed, and its spirit . . ." I laid one hand carefully on the snout. "Its spirit is gone as well. We think the best thing would be to give it an honorable burial, unless—does the tag say *which* mine?"

"No," said Mer Tristivar. "Only that it was at the time one of the Clenverada's most profitable."

"Hardly a useful distinguishing characteristic," I said, "even if true. Serenity, we think it should be taken to Revethora Vezvaishoroi and sealed in with the other dragons."

"That would be quite an undertaking," said Aisava.

"We would do it for an elven head," said the emperor. "We would do it for a goblin head, were one to be discovered in our vaults. How can we do less for this person murdered by the Clenverada with, apparently, our great-grandfather's approval?"

"Serenity," said his scowling soldier, "dragons are not people."

"They speak and have names and feel grief as well as anger," I said. "What more do they have to do before we cease pretending that they are animals?" I stopped, realizing both that my voice had risen and that everyone was staring at me.

"Serenity," I said, my face heating. "We beg your pardon."

"That was very well said," said the emperor. There was nothing pointed in either his tone or his words, but the soldier did not continue the argument.

THE EMPEROR HAD to go straight to his next commitment from the Treasury vault, but Aisava and I walked back to the Alcethmeret together. The next airship returning to Amalo was not scheduled until the next morning, so when Aisava invited me to dine with him, I accepted with both relief and gratitude, for it would otherwise have been a good question whether I got any dinner at all.

But first I had to go to the Untheileneisemeire and try to talk to the Archprelate.

It was always a toss-up whether one would find the Archprelate in the Untheileneisemeire or the Cethomeire. Technically, his prelacy was Cetho, and the Untheileneise Court just happened to fall within its bounds. In reality, his prelacy was the Untheileneise Court, and he did the best for Cetho that he could. I could not reach the Cethomeire without hiring a carriage for which I did not have the funds, so instead I got Aisava to lend me a page boy who knew the way from the Alcethmeret to the Untheileneisemeire.

Showing up unannounced and uninvited in front of the Untheileneisemeire was *not* the best way to petition for an audience with the Archprelate, and it took me more than an hour to get to someone who could actually tell me that the Archprelate was not in the Untheileneisemeire today. As I had known he might be, he was in the Cethomeire, hearing supplicants from the city of Cetho and doing the administrative tasks that inevitably piled up, even for archprelates and emperors.

"May we make an appointment for tomorrow?"

The elven canon looked at me assessingly and decided I did not have any family clout. "The Archprelate is very busy."

"We are sure he is," I said, "but we have come from Amalo and need to speak to him before the emperor sends us back."

"The emperor?" His ears said he didn't know whether to believe me or not. Even after months in Amalo, I had not lost the knack of reading the cues not hidden by the polished and uninformative mask.

"You can confirm with Mer Aisava," I said.

"We will do that," he said and marched away down one of the long straight identical hallways that made the Untheileneisemeire a nightmare of its own to navigate. I sat on the uncomfortable chair and waited, admiring the illusion the wooden walls gave of being marble, a trick entirely achieved with paint and a massive amount of someone's time.

The canon returned, ears looking even more irritated, and said, "Mer Aisava confirms your story. If you will come with us, we will consult the appointments ledger and see if space can be scraped out for you."

"We appreciate it very much," I said and followed him.

The appointments ledger, which had an alcove to itself, was a massive book. Each page laid out the hours of the day, and the different handwritings I saw on the current page explained how it was used. Any of the canons authorized to make appointments for the Archprelate could write the appointment in the book, and then the other canons would know they could not use that time.

The canon flipped the page, and I saw that tomorrow was already almost full. I wondered how many days into the future were already planned out.

"Here," the canon said, jabbing at the page with the long, lacquered nail of his index finger. "There is time for you here, if you do not waste it."

"We will not," I said, noting that the time was a half-hour window between one incomprehensible squiggle and the next (all the canons of the Untheileneisemeire were taught a secretary hand and a simple cipher that meant only another canon had any hope of reading what they had written). Half past eight in the morning was no hardship; I had been quite prepared to be told that the only time the Archprelate had for me was at five o'clock in the morning or eleven thirty at night. "Thank you."

The canon flicked his ears and said, "Is there anything else?"

"Actually, yes. The page boy who brought me here said that a novice could be found who could take me back to the Alcethmeret?"

Surprisingly, this request seemed to mollify him. "Yes, certainly," he said. "We will send Dalenis to you directly."

Dalenis proved to be a very young novice, and desperately shy. But he led me quickly and accurately back to the Alcethmeret and smiled when I thanked him.

AISAVA AND I were joined at dinner by the emperor's second nohecharei, Lieutenant Telimezh, who was tall and elven and unremarkable, and Kiru Athmaza, who was also elven, but both a maza and a cleric. And a woman. It said a good deal about the emperor that he had accepted her service, and I thought of that lunch at the Glass Phoenix and the discussion of people, like Coralis Clunethar, who might have found that choice immoral, even threatening, rather than laudable. Kiru Athmaza was a lively dinner companion, with a seemingly inexhaustible fund of stories, but she was also a sensitive listener. She asked how I came to be back in the palace, and although I did not tell her and Lieutenant Telimezh the whole story, I did end up telling them about the 192 dragons and the skull in the vault.

"It is dishonorable," Lieutenant Telimezh said stonily.

"Is it true that dragons ate people?" said Kiru Athmaza. "I don't disagree with you! I just want to know."

"They were certainly capable of it," I said. "Or of reducing a man to a smoldering pile of bones and ashes. But they were not aggressive. It was not the dragons attacking the Clenverada Mining Company."

"Maybe they should have," said Kiru Athmaza. "At least the wars of the Ethuveraz are conducted with honor."

"That would have required organization," I said, "and although they were not entirely solitary, they did not have anything we might recognize as a government."

"So they fought one by one," said Lieutenant Telimezh.

"And were killed one by one," said Kiru Athmaza, "until the Clenverada Mining Company decided to hurry things along a little."

"Yes," I said. "Avarice makes a monster of any man, I suppose."

"Or woman," said Kiru Athmaza. "But what will the emperor do?"

"I don't know," I said. "He's agreed to hear a Witness for the Dragons, but also Witnesses for the Mountains, the Miners, and the Clenverada Mining Company. And since I know he will listen to the Witnesses fairly, I cannot predict what he will decide."

"Yes," said Kiru Athmaza and added wryly, "The drawback to a just government is that it listens to all sides fairly, and thus one's own side does not always win."

"No," I said. "And I do not want to cause the economic collapse of the empire in order to avenge a century-old atrocity."

"One hundred ninety-two is a great many dragons," said Aisava, "but not all that many mines. And it may be that some of them are no longer in use. I do not think it impossible that the Clenverada Mining Company will be able to absorb the blow. But we will have to wait and see."

"Ithalpherix will certainly believe I have failed her," I said, "but I do not wish to go back to Revethora Vezvaishoroi until I can give her a proper answer."

"Also," said Aisava, "I beg of you, wait until the dragon's skull has reached Amalo. From what you have said, it would be murder to ask the men to take it into the mountain until you have explained the situation to Ithalpherix."

"That is most likely true," I said. "Although I think the area in which she can actually *kill* people is relatively small, I would certainly not want to wager anyone's life on my being correct. I will wait for Arquenethil before I return to the mountain."

"And I have to find a freight company capable of moving a dragon skull," said Aisava.

"Not a specialty one sees advertised in the newspapers," Kiru Athmaza said.

"Are there newspapers this far south?" I said. "I had thought them a northern phenomenon. Certainly, I did not think there were newspapers in the Untheileneise Court."

"No, there are not," said Kiru Athmaza. "They are banned, like photographs and fireworks."

"Fortunately," said Aisava, "when the emperor wants something done, it is not hard to find people willing to do it."

"Be sure they pack it carefully," I said. "The edges of the eye sockets are sharp enough to cut, and I do not know if this dragon skull is haunted as the ones in Revethora Vezvaishoroi are."

"Haunted?" said Lieutenant Telimezh with uneasy interest.

"Little hauntings," I said, "but those can be enough to kill with an object the size and weight of a dragon skull. Also, if it kills someone, the haunting will grow stronger."

"I'm not going to ask how you know that," Aisava said.

The server, a part-goblin boy with dark skin and blue eyes, finished clearing the plates, and an older boy, also part-goblin but pale-skinned with amber eyes, brought in a junket with caramel sauce. We were silent for some time before Kiru Athmaza asked me, "When do you plan to go back to Amalo?"

It was a simple question, but it froze me solid. I had no idea when—or *how*—I was going back to Amalo. I had no money for an airship ticket.

"Actually," Aisava said, sounding a little embarrassed, "I was going to ask you if you would take charge of the dragon skull for its trip to Amalo."

"Me?"

"As best I can tell, if I send a courier with it, they're going to be trapped in Amalo all winter. You, on the other hand, will not be trapped. You will be home."

Was Amalo home? I was not at all sure that it was, but that was not Aisava's point and it was not worth arguing over semantics. He was correct that I would not be trapped. "I can do that, I think," I said. It was foolish to wonder if Captain Olgarezh would notice I was gone again. "I hope this doesn't mean you want me to figure out how to pack it."

"Not at all," said Aisava. "The freight company will be in charge of that problem. I just, I don't know, I want a representative of the emperor to be there, not just the driver and the caravan guards. And, as the Witness *vel ama* for the Dragons, you really are the most appropriate person."

"I suppose I am," I said. "And anyway I don't see how I can refuse. I don't want to walk back to Amalo."

"The emperor's household accounts would provide you an airship ticket," Aisava said. "But if you are willing to go with the dragon skull, I would be very grateful."

“Yes,” I said. “I am . . . not *glad* precisely, but certainly most willing.”

“Excellent,” said Aisava. “And the Alcethmeret will house you until they are ready. No need to bother Csoru Zhasane.”

“No,” I said. “No need at all.”

In the morning, a page boy brought me back to the Untheileneisemeire in good time for my appointment. I was handed from novice, to junior canon, to senior canon, to another senior canon, to a group of three senior canons who were very annoyed that I was daring to bother the Archprelate, and finally through a doorway set into a wall more than a foot thick to a pleasant room hung with rose-and-gold tapestries. It had an elaborate circle, not unlike an Orshaneise corn maze, inlaid in the floor.

The Archprelate was sitting at a table by the window, but he turned and rose when I came in, crossing the room to greet me. “Thara, how pleased I am to see thee again!”

The canon who had escorted me looked stunned and backed away with a hasty mumble.

The situation with the Archprelate was complicated. He was both my immediate (only) superior and my chaplain, for he had agreed to act as such when I had come back to my calling, since I had done so partly on my knees before him, pleading for a second chance. No one else had had the authority, and no one else would have listened when I tried to explain what I wanted to do.

But at the same time, he was the Archprelate of Cetho, and I had never yet brought myself to “thee” him.

I bowed deeply. “Holiness.”

The Archprelate said, “Come sit down and tell me why thou art at court. And why I did not know thou wert coming.”

“That is my story,” I agreed.

I sat opposite the Archprelate and told the story again, leaving nothing out this time, including the interview with the Amal'othala and including the existence of Canon Clenverin. The Archprelate listened intently, and I had told the story so often that I told it cleanly and clearly—which was good, since we did not have very much time.

"And so thou art here," the Archprelate said when I was done, "to plead the case of thy one hundred ninety-two dead dragons with me?"

"Not . . . well, certainly your backing would be very much appreciated, but I do not expect it."

"Art prepared to defy me, Thara?"

The question was asked very mildly, but made a chill go down my spine that I felt out to my fingertips. "I am hoping it does not come to that, Holiness."

The Archprelate raised his eyebrows and made a little twirling "go on" motion with his fingers.

I said, very carefully, "It is my hope that the Archprelate of Cetho understands the nature of the calling of a Witness for the Dead—and honors it as he honors the callings of all his prelates—and that therefore he does not put the question direct."

"Thou meanst thou wilt defy me, if I force thee."

Baldly put, it sounded terrible, the worst kind of heresy. I said helplessly, "I have a rightful petition."

"So thou dost," said the Archprelate, "and I do not see that I have the authority to compel thee to abandon it."

"You don't?"

"Thy calling is between thee and thy god. No one has the right to step between you." He used an archaic, dual form of "you" which demonstrated his meaning: Ulis and me bound together. Unsunderable.

"The Amal'othala is not the only one among your prelates who will dislike your reading," I said.

"No, he is not. But none of them alone has the power to naysay me, and the Council of Prelates will do nothing but fail to come to an agreement about what they ought to do."

"Unless someone is willing to schism the church."

"True," said the Archprelate, "but unlikely."

"The emperor said that if the Clenverada rose against him, they would be followed."

"That's a slightly different problem. Those who actually have the power within the church to create a schism will not do so. Canst imagine the Amal'othala doing it?"

"No," I said. "But—"

"Thara," the Archprelate said. "I'm agreeing with thee. Thou needst not find all the reasons I should not."

I said nothing.

"It does not, however, suit me that thou shouldst continue to be paid by the Amalomeire."

"It doesn't?"

"Not when the Amal'othala is so clearly hostile to thy purpose. Not when thou art acting as my agent, rather than fulfilling a role that the Amalomeire ought to be paying for. And not when we know the Clenverada are there as they are at Prince Orchenis's court."

"I would be very grateful not to have to deal with the Amalomeire's Treasury," I said, "but, Holiness, I must eat somehow."

"I'm not abandoning thee. I shall write thee a letter to the Astravada bank there in Amalo that thou may'st have a stipend. *And* draw additional funds if necessary."

"I did not know the Archprelacy had an account with a bank in Amalo."

He gave me a tired smile. "There are many things about the Archprelacy it is not thy burden to know. But, yes. We have an account with the Astravada in every city they have a bank. I will write the letter now, so that thou canst carry it back to Amalo with thee. Thou needst only present it to one of the clerks."

"That is a great relief," I said.

He got up and went to a secretary-desk against one wall. While he wrote the letter, I looked out the window across the rooftops of the Untheileneise Court, rooftops of all heights and materials and centuries, some of them glittering in the early morning sun. From here I had a good view of the dome of the Alcethmeret, and for a moment I imagined the emperor and the Archprelate flashing each other mirror messages like something out of an adventure novel.

Returning to the table, the Archprelate handed me a folded and sealed letter, which I put carefully in my inside coat pocket. He said, more briskly, "I do have another problem for thee to solve."

"I have not dealt with Ulnemenee."

"Thou wilt. And this matter, I hope, should not prove as difficult."

"I am listening, Holiness."

"I received a letter from a scholar of the first rank at the University of Amalo, an Osmer Lisava Ormevar."

"I know him," I said.

The Archprelate nodded. "He writes that he has undertaken an archaeological project for which he needs to consult with a prelate of Ulis. Because the site is not technically within any benefice in the city of Amalo, he wrote to the Ulistheileian for assistance."

"And has received nothing in return," I said, because that was an easy guess.

"He says he considered consulting the Amalomeire but decided it was a waste of time when he already knew the outcome, and so wrote straight to me."

"His letter must have reached you very quickly."

"A letter from a scholar of the first rank may get preferential treatment," the Archprelate said. "I tell them not to, but they insist."

"What is it that Osmer Ormevar needs?"

"A consultant. Someone to provide the Ulisithalba's point of view."

The Ulisithalba—the worship-of-Ulis as a kind of entity separate from the men and women of the prelacy of Ulis—was a philosopher's term, not something I expected the Archprelate to say.

"It's a useful concept," he said mildly. "Certainly I wish to be able to discuss the worship of Ulis without having to discuss the current Ulisothala of Amalo."

"Can you not do anything about him?" I said, although I had meant to hold my tongue on the subject.

"Not until Amalo gets a new Amal'othala," the Archprelate said. "The current one has always been more interested in his political alliances than his duty, and he obstructs anything I try to do. But thou wert asking what Osmer Ormevar wants."

"Yes," I said.

"He wants someone to come to this tomb with him and tell him about the mosaics and the other things they've found."

"I thought so," I said.

"I cannot ask an Amaleise prelate without offending the Amal'othala and the Ulisothala, and while I *could* ask Vernezar himself, I would greatly prefer not to."

"No, that would be disastrous," I said, thinking of Osmer Ormevar's sharp eyes and sharper tongue.

"But thou answerest only to me," said the Archprelate, "and so I can saddle thee with all the worst tasks."

I looked at him, saw that he was making a slight joke, and managed to smile.

"I will attempt any task you ask of me, Holiness," I said.

"A dangerous answer, Thara, but I thank thee."

Someone knocked on the open door and pointedly cleared their throat.

"The rest of my day is becoming impatient," said the Archprelate, rising from the table and picking up the mask that was waiting for him. "Travel safely, Thara, and be well."

"Thank you," I said. My voice rasped into nothingness, and before I could say anything more, the Archprelate had donned the mask and was gone.

I WROTE LETTERS to Anora, to Iäna, to Chonhadrin, to Tomasaran, and to Shalicar, explaining why I was going to be some time in returning to Amalo—and in Shalicar's case, encouraging him to continue clearing the study in my absence. They were difficult letters to write, although easier than the conversations would have been, especially with Anora. But putting it all down on paper five times made it sound more than slightly mad, and I knew Anora and Iäna would be upset that I could give no good estimate of when I would arrive. But that was in the hands of Gorbelad and Sons Freight and Shipping, who had gotten the job of transporting the dragon skull because they were the only firm that did not even hesitate when asked to carry something to Amalo at this time of year. The person in charge of their Cetho office was one of the sons in "Gorbelad and Sons," a big, booming-voiced goblin who solved problems nearly as fast as they were presented to him.

His plan for transporting Arquenethil's skull was ingeniously simple. After swaddling it in a layer of newspapers and cotton, a task which drew blood more than once, he had his men (goblins, all of them) build a crate around it, lifting one end at a time with utmost care to slide boards underneath. There was a gap in the middle, but not one big enough to matter. Then, when the crate was finished and filled with more newspapers, they lifted the crate, one end at a time and with great care, enough to slide more boards underneath, which they then lifted to turn into sawhorses. They had an ingenious method of securing the crate to the sawhorses so that the crate would not move. Then they built the necessary wagon around the crate, put axles under it, put wheels on the axles. They even built a brake and a footrest for the driver at the front. The skull would leave the vault as if it were one of the carriages that had surrounded it for so long.

This all proceeded with only minor mishaps—missing tools, bent nails, the occasional hammered thumb—minor enough that I was not sure whether it was the skull causing them or not, but as soon as the horses were brought into the vault to be hitched to the crate, it became clear that the skull was haunted. They were a pair of draft horses, Chilconat Gray geldings, as placid as you could ask any pair of horses to be. But the instant they were led into the vault, both heads went up, and although they did not become disobedient, they were restless, with ears swiveling in all directions and much foot stomping. They were hitched to the wagon without incident, although their unease was almost like a visible fog around them.

The driver was a young Amaleise goblin man named Henet. He climbed up on the crate but yelped in pain before he had even sat down.

"What's the matter?" called Mer Gorbelad.

"A splinter," Henet called back.

I had explained to Mer Gorbelad about the skull possibly being haunted, and he'd said something to his men, although I didn't know exactly what. Whatever it was, none of them had complained or refused to work or simply not shown up. But I had impressed on him the need to be careful, and I thought that was why he said, "Do you need to get it seen to?"

Henet hesitated. "It's only a splinter."

"A splinter can kill you if you get blood poisoning," said one of the other men.

"'It's only a splinter' makes a rotten epitaph," said Mer Gorbelad.

One of the guards who had been set around the skull—a matter of procedure for anyone working in the vaults—said, "Doctor Ushenar's office isn't far from here, and he'll be quick."

It had been a fad of the late emperor Varenechibel IV to prefer doctors from the Alchemists' Guild over clerics of Csaivo, although he had not banned clerics as he had banned so many other things.

"Is that all right, Mer Celehar?" said Mer Gorbelad.

"Of course," I said, startled. "I have nothing against doctors, and from what I understand, this is exactly the sort of thing they're good at."

There were no doctors in Amalo. Between the Sanctuary and the csaivatheileian of the Dachen Csaivanat, the clerics were strong enough to keep them out. No one had yet said the word "heresy" about doctors, or at least not loudly enough to be noticed, but the enmity between the clerics and the doctors was deep and bitter.

A Treasury page boy, summoned, knew the way to the doctor's office. Out of curiosity, I went with Henet, who said uncomfortably, "It really is just a splinter."

"Don't take chances," I said.

"Then it's true?" he asked. "The skull is haunted?"

"The horses know," I said. "I hope you won't have too much trouble with them."

"This is a good pair," said Henet. "I've driven them before. But *something* was making them nervous."

"Horses are very sensitive to hauntings," I said. "Dogs, too, although not as much. Cats, maybe, but who can tell with cats?"

He laughed. "Well, I won't argue, I guess, but it's costing us time."

"Let Mer Gorbelad worry about that part," I said.

Doctor Ushenar was middle-aged, elven, thin and twitchy, with stains on his fingers and a pair of thick-lensed spectacles. He wore his Alchemists' Guild signet on a ribbon around his neck. He took Henet's splinter seriously, and indeed, when Henet showed his palm, the splinter was both thick and deeply embedded in the meat of his hand below the thumb.

"Tsk," said Doctor Ushenar. "Let us see if one of my grips can catch it, for I'd hate to have to lay your hand open pursuing it."

"I'd hate that, too," Henet said.

The doctor produced a case that had a gradated series of grips in it, from a pair barely larger than a needle to a set that could have been used in childbirth, if any mother, even in the Untheileneise Court, would prefer a doctor to a Csaiveise midwife. He selected the set he wanted and then fetched down a glass bottle with a clear liquid in it. "This is going to sting," he said as he poured the liquid on a small square of cotton, then applied it to Henet's hand.

Henet jerked back, I thought involuntarily, but put his hand out again. "Thank you," said Doctor Ushenar, and bent over Henet's hand with his chosen pair of grips. He worked quickly; although it took him a moment to catch the end of the splinter, once he did, he pulled it out and pressed the cotton back over the wound almost in one motion.

Henet made a noise through his teeth but held still.

Doctor Ushenar held his grips up with the splinter clenched in them. "That's an awful thing to have stuck in your hand," he said. "I'm glad you came to see me."

"Yes," I said. "What is the liquid?"

"Orthevar," said the doctor. "It's better than water at cleaning dirt away from a wound, although it does sting prodigiously." He pulled away his piece of cotton and examined Henet's hand. "Good, there's hardly any blood. I don't think we need to bandage it."

"Thank you," said Henet. "What do I owe you?"

"For a splinter?" said the doctor. "Even one the size of a table knife—no, I'm not going to charge for that. Just tell people that a doctor helped you, that's all."

"I will," said Henet. We exchanged bows and the page boy led us back to the vault, where Henet climbed at once back onto the crate and picked up the reins. One of the horses had manured in our absence, and I wondered who would have the job of cleaning that up.

"Ready?" said Mer Gorbelad.

"Yes," said Henet.

Two of the men removed the chocks from the front wheels, and the two men at the horses' heads stood away. Henet flicked the reins, the horses obediently started walking, and Arquenethil's skull, almost shockingly, began to move. I realized I'd been expecting one of the axles to break or some similar catastrophe, but perhaps that was beyond the reach of this haunting.

The trip back to Amalo was slower than I would have liked, but Henet and the horses, Aikara and Una, set a steady pace, which they maintained even when we walked into the snow I'd been dreading. Aisava had given me a good fur-lined overcoat, along with a valise of essentials and a pair of winter boots, and when I had tried to protest, he said, "Celehar, don't be ridiculous." Therefore I had accepted the coat, and I was grateful for it as we walked north and it got colder and the sky became gray and bitter.

Henet and the other wagon drivers and the caravan

guards—for Mer Gorbelad had said it was nonsense to send men north and not get full value for their work and had put together one last caravan for the season—spent a lot of time eyeing the sky. When I asked, Henet said, "Snow is snow. What we want to beat to Amalo is the winter's first blizzard."

"Surely it's still too early in the year for a blizzard," I said.

Henet made a face, expressive even in profile. "You can say that—and people say that every year and most of the time it's true. But every so often it's *not*."

"And you mislike the sky."

He shrugged one shoulder. "I have the utmost respect for Lady Winter," he said, giving Salezheio her Barizheise name, "and I'd be a liar if I told you we weren't all saying extra prayers to her, this trip. You might want to as well, if you can?"

"I'm a prelate of Ulis," I said, "not a *monotheist*. I will take your advice."

I did that night, lying awake in the bedroll. We shared them for warmth; tonight my partner was a goblin built exactly like a brick. His name was Traga. He had rolled over with his back to me and gone immediately to sleep. I lay for a while watching the stars through the breaks in the clouds and praying to Salezheio to keep the hounds of the blizzard off us until we reached Amalo.

My prayers were almost answered.

We could see the city when the snow started, and then within fifteen minutes we could not see the city at all. "I'd better lead the horses," Henet shouted to me over the howl of the wind—Salezheio's hounds, let loose from their kennels. "Will you stay up here and keep the reins from fouling?"

"Of course," I said and took the reins as he clambered down.

And at that moment, with the reins in my hands, I felt the

malice of the dragon skull in a way I hadn't since it had been packed in a crate.

"Henet! Get clear!" I said.

Something broke with a crack like a pair of giant hands clapping.

Una and Aikara both spooked violently. I gave in the reins so as not to jerk at their mouths and then got contact back in time to keep us from crashing into the tailgate of the wagon in front of us. Fortunately, Mer Gorbelad believed in leaving room between wagons and shouted at his drivers when they didn't.

I let the horses walk on several paces (to keep them from learning that if they spooked, the wagon stopped), and then drew them to a halt. Then took a deep breath and let it out slowly.

"Blessed goddesses, are you all right?" Henet demanded, coming to stand at the horses' heads while I carefully put the brake on. "I didn't know you could drive so well."

"I learned to drive a hearse when I was thirteen. Are *you* all right? I was afraid we'd run over you."

"No, I'm fine. What happened? Do you know?"

"I think a spoke must have broken," I said. "Can you check?"

"Yes," said Henet. I waited while he walked around the wagon. Una and Aikara, calm again, stood stolidly, though I kept the reins, just in case something else broke while we were standing here.

Henet returned and said, "Yes. One in the left rear wheel. We need a wheelwright."

"We're near the Sanctuary of Orshan," I said. "If they don't have one, they'll know how to find one."

"*How* near?"

"I'm not sure."

Henet grimaced. "I don't want to chance the wheel. Can

you stay with them while I run ahead? I have to let Mer Gorbelad know what happened."

"Yes," I said. "We'll be fine."

Henet started up the line of wagons.

Aikara and Una and I waited. They shifted their hips, cocking first one and then the other, and occasionally stamped. They twitched their skin to try to get the accumulating snow off; I did much the same and was grateful for Aisava's foresight in packing me a pair of gloves.

It seemed like a very long time before Henet returned, though he was out of breath and had clearly hurried both ways.

"Mer Gorbelad says to leave the wagon here because who's going to steal it? Then when the blizzard dies down, we can come back for it."

"We'll need a lot of shovels to dig it out," I said.

"We've got ten pairs of hands, not counting ourselves," Henet said. "I think it'll be all right. Will you come help me unharness the horses? Mer Gorbelad says we can lead them from the back of Suthana's wagon and ride to the Sanctuary. He says he knows where it is."

"Oh good," I said, the words completely inadequate for the relief I felt, and scrambled gracelessly down.

The Sanctuary of Orshan absorbed twelve guests and fourteen horses without any discernible difficulty. They gave us rooms, showed us where we could wash up, and promised us dinner.

"No walking the corn maze today, othala," one of the Orshaneisei said to me.

"Indeed not," I agreed.

I was anticipating that we would be at the Sanctuary for several days, but in fact the next morning dawned bright clear blue. The Orshaneise wheelwright was happy to work on our wheel. I did not know if it was any use for me to go out and watch them take the wheel off the wagon, but I felt better for having done so. Mer Gorbelad and the other wagons pushed on toward Amalo, but Henet stayed with me. "Our contract says we take the skull to a place of your choice in Amalo to wait out the winter," said Mer Gorbelad. "It does *not* say we abandon you to make your own way two miles out of the city."

So two days later, on another crisply beautiful morning, Henet and I drove Arquenethil's skull along the River Road north into Amalo, through steadily increasing crowds of people making their morning journey to work. I had Henet avoid the tramline, because I did not want to give the skull more to work with, so we skirted wide around the Amal-Athamareise Airship Company's massive compound, Una and Aikara working their way unbothered through the wheeled traffic we encountered—mostly delivery drays and the postal service's donkey carts. As we approached the great brick arch of the gate of Ulvanensee, we were both surprised to see someone standing in front of it, even more surprised when he turned at our approach, and we both recognized him.

"Zhorn'Iäna!" Henet said. "What are you doing here?"

Iäna looked equally surprised, also rather horrified.

I said, "You know each other?"

"He's in my—" Henet stopped with the next word almost visible on his lips.

I thought I knew, the pieces finally aligning. "Kelkinora?" I said, and both Henet and Iäna nodded, if rather reluctantly.

I asked Henet to wait and asked Iäna to walk with me. He complied, although his ears were down and he looked like a man bracing himself for a storm.

"Iäna," I said, "I've known thou wert Tahareise since the day we met."

This diverted his attention. "How?"

"We were talking about people who do not want to help catch murderers, and thou saidst they dishonored their ancestors. Even in Ethuverazhin, that is something only a Tahareise would say."

"And here I've been trying to hide it from thee," Iäna said ruefully.

"All thy zhornuzai?" I said, a number of things suddenly making better sense.

"I *could* have a large family in Amalo," he said.

"Thou couldst," I said. "But thou dost not?"

"My mother's family is all in Barizhan and I am her only child."

"And thy father?"

"No idea," Iäna said. "Mama won't say, and I admit at this point I don't want to know. We have done very well without him."

"Yes," I said, with even greater respect for Merrem Pel-Thenhior.

"But! Not the point!" Iäna said. "I thought Tahareise worship was heresy in the Ethuveraz."

"Mild heresy by the Amalomeire's standards."

"But not by thine?"

"My first prelacy was in Lohaiso, which is full of heretics. There were even rumored to be worshipers of Chevarimai, although I never met one."

"What of the Lohaisomeire?"

"It is a poor prelacy and stretched far too thin. And the Lohais'othala, though dearly beloved of his people, is old and not as strong as he once was."

We walked in silence for a few moments. Iäna's ears were up again, and he said, "Thou really art not bothered?"

"I'm really not," I said.

"And thou'rt not going to denounce me—and all my zhornuzai—to anyone?"

"No. Who would I even denounce thee *to*? I could denounce thee to Anora, who won't care any more than I do. Or I could denounce thee to the Amal'othala, who might care, I suppose, but who won't listen to me. No, thy secret is quite safe."

He hesitated a moment, then blurted out, "Mama is a priestess of water."

"Does she speak for the river?"

"She used to, when I was little, but she hasn't for a long time. That's why she puts up with Zhuleto."

"Zhuleto?"

"The girl thou met'st."

It took me a moment to remember. "The one that wanted thee to side with her?"

"That's the one. I don't dislike her as much as I disliked Arveneän, but that isn't saying very much. She really can speak for the river, though, even if she is a terrible pain." He gave me a sidelong look. "Thou knowest a great deal about Tahareise worship."

"For a morkol?" I said mildly, "morkol" being one of the less flattering goblin words for elves.

"For any non-worshiper," Iäna said.

"You all come to Ulis in the end," I said.

We'd made a looping circle around Ulvanensee and now returned to where Henet and Arquenethil's skull were waiting. Henet looked unabashedly glad to see us.

"But why art thou here?" I said. "I sent a message to Anora from the Orshaneise sanctuary, but . . ."

"I have been plaguing him," Iäna said. "Until he promised he would send me a message as soon as he heard from thee."

"Didst need to see me so urgently?"

Iäna shrugged and his ears went sort of sideways. "Did *wish* to see thee. Thou hast been gone for a long time, one way and another."

"Yes," I said. "I'm sorry."

"I do not *blame* thee. I am merely glad to see thee again."

"I am glad to see thee, as well," I said. "Is Anora performing a funeral?"

"Yes, but he said to tell thee the skull could go in the old carriage house. Which, opposed to the *new* carriage house?"

"Yes, actually," I said, "although the new carriage house is roughly six hundred and fifty years old, which Anora says is also the last time the Amalomeire spent money rather than hoarding it."

"Gracious," said Iäna. "And the *old* carriage house?"

"No one's sure. But there's been a cemetery here for over a thousand years. Maybe over two thousand. It used to be well away from the city."

"Dost know where the old carriage house is?"

"I do," I said and directed Henet widdershins around the wall of Ulvanensee to a secondary gate, which was closed but not locked. Iäna and I swung the doors open, and Henet drove through, across a small courtyard, and into the echoing space of the old carriage house, which was partly filled with barrels and crates and old furniture, but still had plenty of room for Arquenethil's crate.

"Why did they not tear it down?" asked Iäna as he looked around. "Surely Ulvanensee needs the space."

"There's a shrine," I said.

"A shrine to Ulis?" Iäna said, frowning. "That seems . . ."

"No," I said. "The whole cemetery is a shrine to Ulis, if thou wish'st to get technical about the matter."

"I don't," said Iäna.

"It's a shrine to Enthenevry—who even six hundred and fifty years ago was nearly a forgotten god, but whose worship was once intertwined with the worship of Ulis—and it was decided that it would be unpropitious to get rid of it."

"What is Enthenevry the god of?"

"Darkness and lost things," I said.

"A suitable patron for a dragon skull," said Iäna.

WE ALL HAD lunch together at the Chrysanthemum—Anora, his junior prelates, Henet, Iäna, and I—and then Iäna had to go back up the hill to the Opera, and Henet had to go to the Amalo office of Gorbelad and Sons, and Anora looked at me and said, "So."

"I should go find Tomasaran," I said guiltily, although I was not sure whether my guilt was at Tomasaran or Anora.

"No need," said Anora. "She'll be here for dinner."

"For dinner? Dost thou plan to keep me captive all afternoon?"

"I'm tempted," said Anora. "I would certainly like it if thou wouldst sit down and tell me the whole story from beginning to end—granting that it has not ended yet."

"All right," I said because I could hardly refuse.

We went into Anora's office and sat down, and I did my best to tell him the whole story, although from the number of questions he had when I was done, I did not do a particularly good job. Finally, he said, "Thou dost realize that thou art making an enemy of the Clenverada for good and all."

"Yes," I said, "but if I go back on my promise to Ithalpherix, I can no longer call myself a Witness for the Dead. And in any event, that part of the story is already done. I made an enemy of the Clenverada when I stowed away on the *Strength of Rosiro* instead of letting them defeat me."

"I hate to say this," Anora said, "but thou may'st wish to consider leaving Amalo in the spring. The Clenverada are powerful, and the miners will not love thee, either, no matter what the emperor's ruling is."

"No, I know," I said. "But I could not do differently."

"I know," he said with what looked like a mixture of exasperation and fondness. "I would not expect thee to. What wilt thou do now?"

"Well, I cannot go back to my room, since I have missed a month's rent."

Anora cleared his throat.

"What?"

"Mer Pel-Thenhior paid thy rent whilst thou wert gone."

"He . . . *what*?"

"Wouldst prefer we had left thee to be thrown out on the street?"

"Well, no, but . . ."

"He seems well able to afford it."

"That's not the point!"

"What *is* the point? That thou wilt not allow thy friends to help thee?"

"Anora . . ."

"I love thee, Thara, but sometimes thou art a hard man to be friends with."

"Anora, I don't—"

"I know. But thou didst *not* ask, so thou needst not feel guilty. Just remember that thou hast friends."

"I . . . I don't have any idea of what to say."

"Thank Mer Pel-Thenhior."

"Yes, but I suspect I should thank thee as well. I'm not sure it would have occurred to Iäna on his own."

Anora shrugged. "In any event, thou still hast a room."

"Then I should go collect my post."

"Dost want me to go with thee?"

"No," I said, "it's not necessary. They can't know I'm back yet. With luck, they won't know until spring."

"If thou'rt sure."

"Yes," I said firmly.

The walk was one I had made more times than I could

count, among the tenements and pawn shops of one of the poorer sections of the Airmen's Quarter. I was just walking into the courtyard of my building when a voice said behind me, "Othala Celehar?"

Even as I was turning, I knew it was a mistake.

The big goblin man grabbed me by the coat collar, like scruffing a cat, and flung me into the alley. My first thought was to run, and I tried, but the alley was choked with garbage cans and broken furniture, and I did not get far before he caught up with me.

He said, quite calmly, from behind me, "They're paying me good money for this," and something looped over my head.

The memory of Delthonar's bag got my hands up quickly enough that I caught my fingers between my neck and the cord, and I was still wondering confusedly what he was doing when the cord pulled tight, and I understood he was trying to garrote me.

Instant success was denied him, since my fingers were protecting my throat, but he was enough bigger—and stronger—than me that he could probably pull my fingers in tight enough to strangle me anyway. It would just take longer.

I had no breath to call for help, but I thrashed as wildly as I could against the cord and kicked both at his shins and at the metal barrels around us, trying to make as much noise as possible. Unfortunately, the residents of this neighborhood were accustomed to ignore the sounds of altercations in alleys. Nobody stopped or protested, and there were huge black spots taking over my vision when a man's voice roared, "What's going on here?" and I was suddenly on the ground, the cord loose around my neck, and my assailant nothing but the diminishing sound of someone running as hard as he could, the man who had interrupted him, crimson and gold, the colors of the Vigilant Brotherhood, running just as hard after him.

It felt like an eternity before I was able to pick myself up again, even to the extent of getting to my hands and knees.

A noise like sparrows fighting resolved into the voice of my concierge: "Othala Celehar! Othala Celehar! Are you all right? Can you stand?"

The answer to both those questions was *I don't know.* I didn't waste my breath trying to say so, knowing full well that Merrem Istovaran would not have stopped for an answer. She was a tiny elven lady, surprisingly well dressed for someone on a concierge's budget, and she never stopped talking. I let her voice go back to the twittering of sparrows and struggled to my feet. I was just starting to wonder if I could crown my success with actual movement toward one end of the alley or the other, when I was surprised by the support of Merrem Istovaran's shoulder beneath my arm.

"You needn't—" I tried to say, but my voice was so hoarse it was barely audible.

"Don't be ridiculous. You'll fall down on your own."

Since she was probably correct, I did not argue, but let her support me down the alley, around the corner, and into the concierge's office, where I was beyond grateful to be able to sit down.

Merrem Istovaran was in fact still talking when I was able to listen to her again, something about how it wasn't safe for decent citizens to walk on the streets anymore, and I wanted to tell her that decent citizens were in no danger, but that would involve explaining *why* I was getting murdered in an alley, and I shuddered away from the thought.

"Do you need a cleric, othala? I can send Ilora."

Ilora was her ten-year-old son, whom she used as an errand-runner when he was not in school.

"No," I said, straining to have any voice at all. "But a message to Ulvanensee?"

"Of course," said Merrem Istovaran. She went to the

door of the concierge's office and yelled "*Ilora!*" into the courtyard.

I tore out a blank page of my notebook and wrote on it, *I have been*

And there I stopped, unable to think of a word.

Ilora came tearing in—like most ten-year-old boys, he moved always at highest speed—and I did not have time for deliberation. From my options (assaulted, attacked, strangled, garroted), I picked "attacked" almost at random and went on: *I am not badly hurt, but I need some help in returning to Ulvanensee.* I signed with my initials and folded the paper into a screw.

Merrem Istovaran had been explaining his mission to Ilora, so he was ready when I handed him the screw and a ten-zashan piece. "I'll run all the way," he promised me and darted out of the office.

"He's a good boy," said Merrem Istovaran.

"Yes," I said, since I could hardly say no.

"That nice Mer Pel-Thenhior paid your rent."

"Good friend," I said.

"He said you'd gone to Cetho. Oh! Let me get your post." She disappeared into the back, returning with a fat hemp envelope.

"Thank you," I said.

"He said you had to leave in a tearing hurry, which was why he was paying your rent."

It was a semi-covert invitation to tell her what had happened, but, even if my voice would have held out, I did not want to share the story with Merrem Istovaran, who gossiped like rain—falling on the interested and the uninterested alike—and who might feel strongly about the Clenverada Mining Company. It was impossible to know who might have relations who worked for them.

I said, simply, "Yes," and was saved from further

interrogation by another tenant coming into the office with a complaint about water dripping down one of the walls of her room; Merrem Istovaran recoiled in horror like an opera ingenue before demanding to be shown the problem, and they rushed out of the office together.

I was very grateful to be left alone. I closed my eyes and did a very mild breathing exercise I'd learned as a novice, noticing the increasing stiffness and soreness of the muscles in my neck but in the exercise not being bothered.

I was still breath-counting when Anora's voice said, "Blessed goddesses, Thara, art thou all right?" and I opened my eyes.

Anora had brought two of his three prelates with him, and I said, "I don't need *that* much help."

Anora's eyebrows went up at the sound of my voice. "I think thou mightst. What *happened*?"

"The Clenverada," I said. "Garrote."

Anora stared at me for a moment, then visibly regrouped and said, "What dost thou need?"

"I can't stay here," I said. "I'm going to get my things."

"All right," Anora said. "We can do that."

"But—"

"Thara," said Anora, "thou didst the right thing in asking for help. Don't be a fool now and pretend thou dost not need it."

"Yes," I said, admitting defeat.

"We would be glad to help," Anora said, using the plural. He picked up the hemp envelope containing my post. "Dost need anything else down here?"

"No," I said. I tore out another page of my notebook and wrote on it simply *Thank you*. I left it on Merrem Istovaran's desk, and they came up with me to my room, which was cold and dusty but undisturbed. There, packing my things was mostly a matter of Erlenar going back down to get a peach crate from the lumber room for my books. My linen fit back into the valise I'd unpacked it from when I'd first moved in, and I was staring helplessly at my spare coats when Daibrohar said, "I can carry them."

"If we leave them—" I started.

"Thara," said Anora, "we are not abandoning any of thy belongings. Thy michenmeire can go on top of the books. Erlenar will carry the peach crate, Daibrohar will carry the coats, and I will carry thy valise. Thou canst carry thy post. Is there anything else?"

"No," I said. "For the next tenant."

"Very good," said Anora.

As we came out onto the landing, Thenavo came partway down the stairs and said, "Othala Celehar, you're leaving? But you haven't even been *back* yet."

"I have to," I said. "Are you feeding the cats?"

"Oh yes," she said.

"Here." I had a pocketful of five-zashan pieces that I would no longer need to feed the gas meter. "For sardines."

"Thank you," said Thenavo. She descended the rest of the flight of stairs and carefully transferred my five-zashan pieces into her own pockets.

"Good," I said and managed to smile at her.

"I am sorry to see you leave," she said, a phrase she was almost certainly copying from her mother. "But I will feed the cats."

"Thank you," I said.

She hesitated a moment, then turned and ran back up the stairs.

"What was that?" said Anora.

"I fed the local cats," I said.

"It does no harm to seek the blessing of Noranamaro," said Anora, "but remember that her children walk by themselves."

It had been the sardines they sought, more than my company. "I will miss them."

"At least you will be alive to do so," said Anora, and we started on the long walk back to Ulvanensee.

ANORA PRODUCED AN arnica ointment for my bruises and said, "What art thou going to do?"

"I don't know," I said. I'd never had anyone try to murder me before.

"Thou shouldst go to the Brotherhood."

"And tell them what? I didn't see the man clearly. I *think* he was sent by the Clenverada, but I have no proof." I coughed.

"Thara. Who else would be trying to murder thee?"

"I don't know," I said. "But I can't prove anything, and there's nothing for the Brotherhood to do—unless they actually caught him, in which case . . ."

"In which case, thou needst go to the Brotherhood and identify yourself as the intended victim," said Anora. "Otherwise, unless he is very stupid and confesses, they don't have anything to take to a Witness. I will go to the watchhouse now and see if Subpraeceptor Estrenar will come here."

"Thou needst not—"

"Wouldst rather go to the watchhouse thyself? I will go with thee, if it is thy preference."

I didn't want to move, but I saw the force of Anora's reasoning. "All right," I said. "Let's go."

The watchhouse was nearby, and I was grateful not to have to walk all the way to the Chapterhouse. Subpraeceptor Estrenar, an elderly elven man who looked still iron-hard as a handful of nails, took careful notes and said, "It will be tomorrow before we can discover if the man was caught. Where can we find you, othala?"

I hesitated.

Anora said, “A message to Ulvanensee will reach him.”

“Very good,” said Subpraeceptor Estrenar.

TOMASARAN ARRIVED NEAR sundown, as immaculate as ever. She was horrified by the burgeoning crop of bruises around my neck and on my hands, and I had to let Anora tell her that story along with the other.

For dinner, Anora took us to a teahouse called the Four Black Horses, which was clearly a place people came for privacy, since each table was in its own box of a room, lit by a five-candle chandelier—a perfect place to hide from the Clenverada’s assassin.

The proprietor of the Four Black Horses, a thin, gloomy-faced elven man, knew Anora and did not seem unduly alarmed at having three prelates come in together.

“You must come here to complain about the Amal’othala,” I said to Anora as we sat down.

“True,” Anora said, and I blessed him silently as he followed my lead rather than insisting that we talk about the man with the garrote. “The Four Black Horses is known for the discretion of their servers . . . and, to be quite fair, the excellence of their Okhransai tea.”

“Okhransai?” said Tomasaran.

“From Tan Okhrana in Barizhan. You don’t often encounter it this far north, and it can be a bit of an acquired taste.”

I had learned to drink Okhransai in Lohaiso. “I will share with you if Tomasaran does not like it,” I said.

“Good, good,” said Anora. “I suggest we get a dish of shorpan for the table. It is very good here, and it will be plenty of food.”

Tomasaran said, “I haven’t had good shorpan for a long

time. One of my sisters makes it very well, but she married a man from Kinreho, and I haven't seen her in more than two years."

"You are closer to Kinreho now," I said. "Perhaps you could meet halfway."

"There is a teahouse there," said Anora. "Halfway between here and Kinreho, I mean. So you wouldn't have to stand awkwardly on the side of the road."

Tomasaran laughed. "It is a good idea."

A part-goblin server stuck her head in, and Anora ordered for the table. "Would you like buttermilk biscuits to begin?" the server asked. "The new batch just came out of the oven."

"Yes, please," Anora said. "And we would like honey with those."

"Of course," said the server and disappeared again. She was back almost immediately with a platter of round biscuits and a crock of honey. We were silent for several moments, but after she had eaten half a biscuit, Tomasaran said, "Celehar, I need your advice very badly."

"What about?"

"The murder of Ema Dravenezh," she said. "I'm no nearer solving it than I was the day you first disappeared."

"Tell me what you've done."

"Well I went out to Paravi and talked to Orazheän Dravenezhen. She was . . . she was just *crushed* with grief. I felt terrible being the one to tell her."

"Part of your calling," I said. "Although as a Witness for the Dead, you won't have to do it often."

"I hope not. She is wild to have his murderer found and punished, but she says she doesn't know who his friends are. She says he never talked much about himself."

"So the only thing you know about Ema Dravenezh is that he was the lover of Tura Olora," I said.

"Yes," said Tomasaran. "And I don't know how to find out

anything else. I asked at the Opera, but the ushers all said he kept to his box and never had visitors."

"Well, he *wouldn't,* if he was angling for a chance to see Mer Olora after the opera," I said.

"Oh. I suppose not. But I just don't know what to do."

"Solving a murder is like untying a siren's knot," I said. "You have to start with whatever loose end you have. And the loose end *you* have is Tura Olora."

"Who is dead."

"But who—unlike Ema Dravenezh—had an array of people you can talk to. The other singers, his landlady—I'm sure Mer Pel-Thenhior knows where he lived. Mer Pel-Thenhior himself."

"Oh," said Tomasaran as she thought this through. "That's simpler than I thought it would be."

"Don't make it complicated unless you have to," I said.

She picked up the second half of her biscuit. "I still don't understand, though, why *anyone* would want to murder Mer Dravenezh."

"You've found no personal enemies, and no one seeking to harm the marquess by murdering his secretary, and it can't have been someone intending to kill someone else—"

"The Parzhadel crest on the door is hard to miss," Tomasaran said.

"And everyone knew that it was Mer Dravenezh who attended the opera."

"Anyone who knew enough about the marquess to want to kill him would know he wasn't there—oh dear, I phrased that badly."

"No," I said, "I understand you. It is not a secret that the marquess is confined to his bed. And you've found no hint of anything else Mer Dravenezh did, aside from attend operas?"

"Well, he must have been visiting Mer Olora," said Tomasaran, "but honestly I haven't found any hint of that."

"They kept their secret very well," I said. "Which makes you wonder what other secrets they were keeping."

"You think . . ."

"I'm speculating," I said. "But, yes, I am speculating that Mer Olora and Mer Dravenezh had other secrets, and it's one of them that someone thinks is worth killing Mer Dravenezh over."

"A secret they shared with someone else, then," said Anora.

"Yes."

"Three persons can keep a secret if two of them are dead," Anora said and sighed.

"But then how can I find out who murdered him?" Tomasaran asked plaintively.

"You hope there was a fourth person in their secret," said Anora.

I SPENT THAT night in the spare bed in the room shared by Erlenar and Daibrohar. (Vidrezhen had her own tiny room further down the hall.) Anora was apologetic about Ulvanensee having no actual guest room, but I was glad of the company, even if they slept and I (mostly) did not.

I did not know how frightened I should be. On the one hand, it seemed almost beyond belief that I was bothersome enough to the Clenverada to warrant hiring an assassin. On the other hand, it had *happened*. Would they give up after one failure, or would they send that man—or someone else—after me again? On the assumption that they would not stop at one try, what could I do to preserve my own life?

The obvious answer was to flee, and I was sure that was what the Clenverada expected. But dropping the petition was a betrayal both of my petitioner and of my god, and I could not do it.

The next most obvious answer was to hide until the emperor arrived in the spring. But how thoroughly did I need to hide myself? Since I had left my room, if I did not go to the Witness for the Dead's office, would they be able to find me? Would they have known to look for me at Ulvanensee? Was someone outside right now, waiting for me to show myself?

Calm thyself, Celehar. It was exceedingly unlikely that they would have moved fast enough to already have someone outside Ulvanensee; most probably, they didn't yet know that their first attempt had failed. So if I left the Airmen's Quarter (where would I go?) and did not draw attention to myself . . . would I be safe?

I was still wondering that when the sun came up.

LATER THAT MORNING, Iäna reappeared with a bag of jam-filled buns. "What *happened*?" he said, and I explained again.

I made tea at Ulvanensee's immense stove (on which Anora and his junior prelates used approximately two of eight burners). Iäna was talking about *The Dream of the Empress Corivero* when Anora came in, carrying my peach crate.

"Good morning, Mer Pel-Thenhior. Celehar, we left this in the corner of my office last night, but that's not really a good place for it."

"Good morning, Othala Chanavar," said Iäna. "What's in the crate?"

"Celehar's things from the room he no longer rents," Anora said.

"But if you don't have a room any longer," said Iäna, "where will you stay?"

"He can stay here," said Anora.

"If the Clenverada are paying people to kill me, this will be the first place they look," I said.

"Come stay in the Opera," said Iäna.

"What?" Anora and I said in accidental chorus.

"At least until you find something better," said Iäna. "It's not like there isn't room. And it's not a place anyone would expect to find a prelate."

"The Amal'othala's courier found me there," I said.

"Couriers and canons don't talk to each other," said Anora, "so Canon Clenverin will not know that. It is a good idea. Hopefully, when they do not find you in the Airmen's Quarter, they will think you left town. Which I would suggest you do, except that I know you won't. And you *cannot* go back to your office. Othalo Tomasaran told me, it must have been a week ago, that there were people who came looking for you and wouldn't say why."

"That is ominous," I agreed. "But I have no reason to go back to the Witness for the Dead's office, since I am no longer Amalo's municipal Witness for the Dead."

"You aren't?" said Iäna.

I explained about my conversation with the Archprelate.

Iäna thought for a moment. "What do you need to do?"

The question was a daunting one. "I'm not sure."

"I would recommend going to the watchhouse to learn if they found the man with the garrote," Anora said.

"A sensible suggestion," Iäna said. "Do you want me to go with you?"

"Yes," I said, before I could second-guess myself into silence.

"Nothing could be easier. Now?"

"No point in waiting," I said reluctantly.

"True enough."

The air was cold and crisp, and the walk would have been a more pleasant one if I had not been eyeing other pedestrians warily. I found I had no idea what my assailant had looked like, beyond that he had been a big man, goblin or part goblin, and there were a great many men on the streets of the Airmen's Quarter who matched that description. I thought Iäna was aware of my nervousness, but he did not say anything.

Subpraeceptor Estrenar was courteously pleased to see me, but had no good news to report. Brother Ivenarad had not caught the man with the garrote, and had really no better idea of what he looked like than I did. "If it's any comfort, othala," the subpraeceptor said, "a man who knew what he was doing with a garrote would have killed you before Brother Ivenarad realized he was witnessing a murder."

It was not any noticeable comfort.

"What now?" said Iäna when we had bid good-bye to Subpraeceptor Estrenar. "I will go with thee anywhere thou likest, and I still think thou shouldst come stay in the Opera, at least for a day or two."

"Thank you," I said. "I must also find the Astravadeise bank."

"It's most likely in the Glassmarket. We can take thy things to the Opera and go bank-hunting from there."

"That seems sensible," I said.

Since my belongings now consisted of two valises, three coats, and a peach crate, we took a cab—Iäna ungrudgingly paying the fare—to the Vermilion Opera, where, he carrying one valise and the coats and I carrying the other valise and the peach crate, Iäna led me to a side entrance rather than the lobby.

"The crucial thing," he said, "is that we find thee a room near the furnace so that thou dost not freeze to death overnight. But there's a rehearsal room that's too small for more than one or two people to rehearse in, and as far as I know, no one currently in the company uses it."

"Min Shelsin?" I said, guessing at what he wasn't saying.

"It was Tura's favorite," he said with a reluctant grimace.

"But I suppose thou dost not fear ghosts."

"If Mer Olora were to become a ghost, he would be on the roof," I said. "Which I suppose he might be, though I do not propose to go look."

"No, I thank thee," Iäna said with a shudder. We had come down a series of spidery flights of stairs, and now he led me up a broader set (which looked like they had been built by an apprentice carpenter), down a short hallway, and pushed open a door. "Here, if this will do?"

"I'm sure it will," I said. It was, as he had said, a small room, but it was warm and it had an old velvet daybed in one corner.

"I couldn't sleep on that," Iäna said, "but I suspect thou wilt be comfortable enough."

"I'm sure I will," I said, setting down the valise and the peach crate.

"Thara." Iäna eyed me doubtfully. "If thou wouldst prefer something different—"

"How would I even know?" I said. "Really, Iäna, I'm not difficult to please."

"No, and it worries me sometimes," he said. "I fear that thou wouldst not complain if thou *wert* uncomfortable."

"I admit I'm going to want a blanket," I said.

He laughed. "Yes, and I will show thee how to find the nearest washroom. And then I suppose we find this bank."

THE GLASSMARKET SOLD other wares than glass, but Glassblowers' Row was still its core. Iäna and I did not stop, but made our way to the market's long north side, where, Iäna said, we would find Moneybox Row.

We worked our way down one side of Moneybox Row and halfway up the other before Iäna said, "I think that's it! The building with the green awning."

A couple of steps closer and I could read the sign: THE BANK ASTRAVADA.

"I'll wait out here," said Iäna. "I'm unlikely to help thy cause."

"Iäna—"

"Truth is truth," said Iäna and flipped his long, beaded braids back over his shoulder. "Besides, it's nothing to do with me."

"Hopefully, it won't take very long," I said.

And it did not. Inside the brightly lit main room of the bank, where twelve elven clerks sat at desks in a tidy and ruler-straight formation, I presented the Archprelate's letter to the one nearest the door. He read it without excitement, as if he read letters from the Archprelate of Cetho every day (except for the tips of his ears twitching, just slightly, when he reached the signature and signet), and agreed to set up a stipend. "And the, ah, Archprelate says to start it from the beginning of *last* month, so we owe you money."

He counted out five hundred muranai, which was more money than I'd ever had physically in my hands in my whole life, then made it into a neat paper-wrapped bundle and tied it with a brown ribbon. Then he handed it to me, along with the letter.

"Please let us know if we can be of any further assistance, othala. The Archprelate's letter is quite explicit, so you need only present it to one of us," and he waved a hand at the room, "and we will be happy to help you."

"Thank you," I said, bowing, and then exited the building to rejoin Iäna, to whom I said, feeling a little giddy, "Let me treat thee to lunch."

AFTER LUNCH AT a teahouse called the Soldier and Serpent, we returned to the Opera, where Iäna led me on a strange expedition, half a tour and half a pirate raid, through practice rooms and storage rooms and a room behind and underneath the stage, where the singers stayed during a performance if they were not onstage themselves. They called it the Boiler Room as a joke, the actual boiler room being reached through a door set halfway up the room's back wall and a ladder-like set of stairs. Iäna showed me, but we did not go down.

Finally we returned to Mer Olora's practice room with an armful of blankets, a small table, and a wirework chair that probably would not have supported Iäna's weight. Iäna fussed over the placement of the table while I folded the blankets on the foot of the daybed.

"Wilt thou be comfortable, Thara? Truly?"

"Oh, yes," I said. "It is much better than the novices' dormitory at Tavolaree, and in any event I do not mean to stay here long."

"No," Iäna said, "but I would prefer thee not to suffer, all the same."

"I am certainly not suffering," I said and remembered to smile at him.

After some discussion, the note I sent with Zhana to the office clerk simply told Tomasaran to ask for Iäna at the ticket window, without any mention of me at all. Tomasaran did not come back with the messenger, but she followed close behind him. Iäna and I were backstage, trying to find a place from which I might watch the operas without either being visible from the audience or hideously in the way.

We heard Tomasaran call from the auditorium, "Is anyone there?"

We went out on stage. Tomasaran was standing uncertainly about halfway down the aisle.

"Mer Pel-Thenhior," she said, "I got your note and—oh! Celehar! What are you doing here?"

I explained.

"So you're going to stay in the Vermilion Opera all winter?" asked Tomasaran.

"No, no more than a day or two. Just long enough to find something . . . more conventional. It's safer than staying in Ulvanensee, which is my other option."

"Yes. Hopefully, the office was the only place outside the Airmen's Quarter where they will think to look for you."

"At this point," I said, "they can't stop the emperor from hearing Witnesses, no matter what they do to me. But I would still rather not encounter anyone the Clenverada have hired to find me."

"No," Tomasaran said with a jerky little twitch of her ears. "But I am glad to know where you are and that you are reasonably safe. And you have preempted the first task I had set for myself this afternoon, which was to find Mer Pel-Thenhior."

"Me?" Iäna said in considerable startlement. "Why?"

"I need to know about Tura Olora's friends," said Tomasaran. "Anything you can tell me."

"Friends? You mean aside from the other singers?"

"I don't know. Anyone he might have shared a dangerous secret with."

"A *dangerous* secret," Iäna said thoughtfully. "Let us perhaps not have this conversation in the auditorium."

"You are right," said Tomasaran. "But where . . . ?"

"I usually go for privacy to one of the boxes on the third tier," said Iäna. "If you're all right with that."

"I had better be," said Tomasaran.

Iäna and I came down off the stage, and the three of us went up the aisle and up a great many stairs to the third tier of boxes, where Iäna led us around to the box two stories above his own box.

"We have a better view of both the stage and the auditorium from here," said Iäna. "Now, explain to me about this dangerous secret."

I said, "Mer Olora," then remembered that I was not the Witness for Ema Dravenezh and looked at Tomasaran.

She nodded. "Mer Olora is the only loose thread in Mer Dravenezh's life, so Othala Celehar and I think it best to start there."

"Having nowhere else, yes," said Iäna. "And you think Mer Dravenezh was killed for a secret?"

"Mer Olora said his death was the only way to keep Mer Dravenezh *safe,*" I said, "and although there would certainly have been a *scandal* if it had come out that the Marquess Parzhadel's secretary was the lover of an opera singer, I don't think his life would have been in danger."

"So you think Tura was afraid of what else he might say once a Witness started asking him questions."

"There clearly *was* a reason to murder Mer Dravenezh," Tomasaran said.

"Yes," said Iäna. "Well, I know Tura was friends with Shulethis Dorenar—our senior principal baritone—and he was quite friendly with the young men of Dach'osmer Nedeva Cambeshar's circle. Not Dach'osmer Cambeshar himself, you understand, but the young men who are striving to emulate him. Which means in practical terms being critical of Prince Orchenis—which they all think is very daring of them—and solidly against things like women attending the University. They're all gamblers, too, and I remember asking Tura if he thought he could keep up with them, and he snorted and said he wasn't even going to try."

"Do you remember any of their names?" asked Tomasaran.

"Let me think," said Iäna. "None of them is as fond of the opera as Dach'osmer Cambeshar is, so I don't see them as often. But I know Osmer Dema Pashavar is one of them.

Tura spoke of him occasionally as having some sense, which he did not think true of all of them."

"Do you think Osmer Pashavar will speak to me?" Tomasaran said doubtfully.

"He might find the novelty of meeting a Witness for the Dead intriguing," Iäna said, rather dryly.

"All you can do is try," I said.

"But how do I *find* him?" she said despairingly.

"Look in the teahouses along General Shulihar Street. That's where most men of their class spend their afternoons."

"I can't go into those teahouses by myself!" Tomasaran said, horrified.

"Why not?" I said.

"I'm a *woman*. They might not even *let* me in alone."

"You're a Witness for the Dead. Witnesses go where their calling takes them."

"That's easy for you to say."

"It's true. Ask Witness Parmorin at the Judiciary. She could hardly do her job if she did not think of herself as a Witness before a woman."

"That is a good idea," said Tomasaran. "I will talk to Witness Parmorin. She might have . . . advice."

"I would go with you if I could," I said.

"No, no," said Tomasaran. "If the Clenverada are looking for you, that's the *last* thing you should do. I will manage. And I can ask Mer Olora's neighbors, if you can tell me where he lived?"

"I can, as it happens," said Iäna. "He lived in Tobazran. We used to tease him about his swank address, although of course it wasn't. It's the third stop before the University on the Cevoro line, and then you take the street directly in front of you when you come out of the station. Walk three blocks and go into the court on your left. I forget what it's called, but Tura lived in the three-story building, and his landlady was a terrible gossip, so that's actually a good place to try."

"And we don't even know that Tura Olora had anything to do with Mer Dravenezh's death," said Tomasaran.

"No, but you have nothing else," I said. "And it is good practice for you, even if it does not get *this* witnessing any farther."

"You *can't* enjoy it—the going out and asking strangers questions," she said.

"I find it easier if I think of myself as acting on behalf of the dead person. And the petitioner. And even justice, although I don't like to present myself in such grand terms."

"You found justice for Arveneän," Iäna said.

"Well, I found out that Tura Olora killed her. I'm not sure that I think what Mer Olora did was justice."

"You think he cheated the reveth-atha?" said Iäna. "It's always seemed to me that dead is dead."

"No, not that," I said. "I think that if he had gone before a judiciar, with proper witnessing, Mer Olora might have received a lesser sentence than the one he imposed on himself."

"He admitted he killed Arveneän."

"Yes, but he did it in a momentary rage, having been sorely provoked. I don't say he shouldn't have been punished, just that he preempted any chance of mercy."

"I didn't think you approved of mercy," said Tomasaran.

"I beg your pardon?"

"When we were discussing Osmin Tativin. You essentially said she deserved what she got."

"She did," I said. "She committed a pointless murder for selfish reasons. A pointless *premeditated* murder. Terrible though those photographs were, they were no reason to murder the Marquise Ulzhavel. Mer Olora killed Min Shelsin in a sudden overwhelming rage which Min Shelsin provoked, and he killed her at least partly to protect Mer Dravenezh. The situations are not the same."

"Are you saying *Arveneän* deserved what she got?" said Iäna.

"No, he shouldn't have killed her," I said. "But the factors involved in her murder make him, to me, less irredeemable than Osmin Tativin. But he thought Mer Dravenezh's safety more important than his own life."

"It's a pity how little time he bought," said Iäna.

"Yes," I said. "A great pity."

THAT AFTERNOON, WITH nothing to do—nothing I *could* do, not without leaving the Opera, which I did not know whether it was safe to do or not—I decided to treat as a day of rest, which I could admit it was possible I needed. I meditated and then read one of my fat Barizheise novels, and I was still reading when Iäna knocked and said, "Come to my office and have dinner. I brought food from the zhoän down the street."

He took me through the Opera on a route I did not know until finally we climbed a ladder through a trapdoor and came out on a platform halfway up the stage-right wall, just behind the proscenium. Iäna tugged me gently away from the view, and we turned down a hallway I hadn't even known existed. A little way along it, we came to a room that was self-evidently Iäna's office by the scores heaped everywhere. On the desk sat a Barizheise zharokan, a ceramic box in a wicker carrying case. The box had interior partitions, so several different things could be carried at once, including utensils.

"This zhoän must like thee very much," I said.

"They know where to find me," Iäna said, with enough of a smile that I knew he was joking.

He dumped a stack of scores onto the floor to clear a chair, and we sat down, one on either side of the desk, to eat.

The food was simple, soup and tobasthai and csabranai, but very good, and I was hungrier than I had realized. We ate, and Iäna talked about rehearsals, and for a little while I did not feel as if my life had been turned on end and shaken vigorously.

That night I lay in the strange darkness of the Opera and did not sleep.

In the morning, I had just finished dressing when Iäna appeared suddenly in the rehearsal room and said, "I know what thou shouldst do."

"Thou dost? Then I pray thee, tell me as well."

"Thou shouldst go speak to Prince Orchenis."

"Prince Orchenis? Why in the world . . . ?"

"Thara. Thou must surely know how grieved he would be by thy death."

"I suppose," I said, a little uncertainly. "But—"

"And also how *ag*grieved he would be to discover that it was the Clenverada who had killed thee."

"But that doesn't mean—"

"I think it might. And I think thou owest it to him to warn him of what the Clenverada are doing. For indeed, if thou wert the ruler of a principate, wouldst thou not wish to know that some of thy subjects were trying to murder a Witness for the Dead?"

"Yes," I said slowly. "I suppose I would."

"There," said Iäna. "I admit I do not know how one goes about seeking an audience with the Prince of Thu-Athamar."

"In general, one writes a petition for an audience and waits to be summoned. But I think in this case, if I am going to do it at all, I had best go to the Amal'theileian directly."

"Dost thou wish company?"

"Not for this," I said.

THE BUSY CORRIDORS of the Amal'theileian were nerve-wracking, even though I thought I was still ahead of the Clenverada's knowledge of my whereabouts. But I knew the way to the office of the secretaries of the Prince of Thu-Athamar, where a bored young elven man said, "Can we help you, othala?"

"We are Thara Celehar, a Witness for the Dead," I began and was startled when he suddenly became less bored.

"Othala Celehar! How may we help you?"

"We need to speak to Prince Orchenis," I said. "We are quite prepared to wait if there is any possibility of doing so today."

"Of course," said the young man. "We do not know if it is possible, but we will find out. Please be seated, and we will return as quickly as possible."

"Thank you," I said and sat down, wondering just what Prince Orchenis's secretaries had been told about me.

It took some time for the young man to return, but when he did, he said, "If you will come with us, othala, Prince Orchenis can spare you five minutes."

"Thank you," I said and followed him through a series of narrow private hallways that led eventually to the Cinnabar Room, where Prince Orchenis was dictating a letter to his personal secretary.

He broke off at the young man's tap on the door and said, "Come in, othala. We cannot give you much time, but we know you would not have asked if it was not urgent."

There was no time to lead up to it gradually. I said, "Someone tried to kill us the day before yesterday. We have no proof, but we believe he was sent by the Clenverada."

After a moment's stunned silence, Prince Orchenis said, "We are greatly relieved to see that he was unsuccessful."

"Thank you," I said. "We do not expect you can do anything, but a friend pointed out that we owed it to you to tell you."

"Yes, indeed," said Prince Orchenis. "And it is not that we cannot do *anything*. We can and will have a word with Dach'osmer Porana Clenverar about how very displeased we should be if anything were to happen to you. The Clenverada are greedy, but not stupid." He paused, frowning at me thoughtfully. "And yet that is not complete assurance that they will not try again. You need a guard."

"A guard?" I said.

"Like a nohecharis."

"Your Highness, we are surely not important enough to need a *nohecharis*."

"And yet you are the one who got the emperor to listen to your story about one hundred ninety-two dead dragons," Prince Orchenis said unanswerably. "Solavar!"

"Yes, Your Highness," said the young man, who had been lurking politely in the doorway.

"Go tell Commander Astrivar that we need a word with him. Quickly."

"Yes, Your Highness."

"We should have known you would take more than five minutes," said Prince Orchenis.

"We apologize," I said. "We did not intend—"

"Blessed goddesses, othala, don't apologize. *You* aren't going around murdering people. Or trying to."

"Well, no, but we didn't want to cause so much trouble."

"That's long past remedy," Prince Orchenis said dryly. "In any event, we would rather you were alive and causing trouble than being an untroublesome corpse."

"We admit, we prefer it ourself."

"As you should," said Prince Orchenis.

Perhaps not surprisingly, Commander Astrivar was not far

from the Cinnabar Room. He came in with Mer Solavar—a young elven man, younger than I had expected, but briskly competent. He listened to Prince Orchenis's summation of the problem, nodded, and said, "We will ask for a volunteer." He bowed and left, but was back almost immediately. I was shocked to see that he had Captain Olgarezh with him, along with a younger elven man.

"This is Captain Hanu Olgarezh," said Commander Astrivar. "He has some experience in this kind of work and has volunteered his services. And this is Armsman Ingavar, who will stand watch at night."

Captain Olgarezh bowed and said, "We are very pleased." Armsman Ingavar imitated his bow.

"Are you quite sure?" said Prince Orchenis. "This is not a task for which we want someone who is a volunteer only in name."

Captain Olgarezh almost laughed. He said, "No, truly, we are very pleased." I wondered how much of it was about escaping from the Amal'ostro, but that was an unfair question.

"Armsman Ingavar?" said Prince Orchenis.

Armsman Ingavar looked alarmed to be noticed, but managed to say, "Most pleased."

"Very well," said Prince Orchenis. "Unless you have an objection, othala?"

"None at all," I said.

"Excellent," said Prince Orchenis. "You will, of course, need rooms in the Amal'theileian."

"We will?"

"Of a certainty. Unless your current living arrangements include space for a guard?"

I thought of the practice room in the Opera. "No, you are correct. But—"

"We will invoice the emperor," Prince Orchenis said, "it

being on account of your witnessing for your dragons to him that you need a guard."

"Will that work?" I said dubiously.

"The amount involved is a drop of water in the imperial accounts," Prince Orchenis said. "Mer Solavar, will you find a set of rooms for Othala Celehar?"

"Yes, Your Highness," said Mer Solavar.

The rooms Mer Solavar found were in the south wing of the Amal'theileian, where the trams were audible as a deep rumble but nothing more. There was an antechamber with a desk and a sofa, a bedroom with a canopied bed, and a washroom. And then Mer Solavar and Armsman Ingavar left us alone, Captain Olgarezh and me, and I told myself not to be stupid. That I had longed to talk to him was no reason for him to have longed to talk to me.

Captain Olgarezh and I bowed to each other. He said, "It is an honor, Othala Celehar, to be properly introduced."

"We regret taking you away from your duties."

"But you are not," he said with what looked like genuine surprise. "Our duties are whatever Prince Orchenis commands them to be."

"Thank you. We will try not to be an unconscionable burden."

Captain Olgarezh bowed again and answered neither "yes" nor "no." He said, "Have we any chance of persuading you to stay in this room until spring?"

"By your phrasing, we suspect that you already know the answer is no."

"We have to ask. Guarding you here will be significantly easier than guarding you elsewhere."

"We cannot stay in this room until spring. We have tasks appointed us by the Archprelate that require us to go to other places. Do you really think the Clenverada will try to kill us with you present?"

"We don't *think* the Clenverada will try anything," said Captain Olgarezh. "But we cannot know it for a certainty, and it is possible to think things and be wrong. What are your tasks?"

I explained about Ulnemenee and the revethavar's tomb.

"And these are things you must do?"

"They are things we have promised the Archprelate we will do," I said.

"The tomb sounds easy to guard," said Captain Olgarezh.

"The University has guards on duty," I said, "and, yes, there is one and only one entry point."

"And the Hill of Werewolves is not far. What about Ulnemenee?"

"We have never considered it from this perspective before. Honestly, we do not know if there is more than one gate."

"That is something we must find out, then. For if we can establish a choke point, as we can with the antechamber here, you become much easier to guard. We must tell you, othala, that if the Clenverada truly wish to kill you, they will be able to do it. We can stop one swordsman. Maybe we can stop three, if we can establish a choke point. But we cannot stop five even then. And there is nothing to prevent them sending someone after you on the street. If you choose to go out."

"We understand. We do not expect you to be an invincible swordsman out of an adventure novel. Truly, we did not expect Prince Orchenis to appoint a guard at all."

"It is no honor on the prince's record if you are killed before the emperor's judgment."

"That is true."

I did wish, passionately but uselessly, that I had not somehow reached the point where I needed such guarding. And then I thought of the emperor, who was never without guards, even in his bedchamber, and felt ashamed of my griping.

Captain Olgarezh, having given his warning, accompanied me back to the Opera to collect my things without further objection, and, fortune favoring me, Iäna found us.

"Thara!" he said from the hall. "Didst thou—" He broke off abruptly as he found Captain Olgarezh in the doorway. "I didn't know you had any friends in the Principate Guard."

I caught myself before I said, *I don't.* "Mer Pel-Thenhior, this is Captain Olgarezh. He has agreed to act as our . . . guard until the emperor's judgment."

"Ah," said Iäna. "Then we are very pleased to meet him." They bowed to each other, and Captain Olgarezh stepped aside to let Iäna come in. "And you are . . . leaving?"

"Prince Orchenis has assigned us rooms in the Amal'theileian."

"That is excellent," said Iäna. "We are glad that Prince Orchenis is taking the matter seriously. May we help you transport your things?"

"Your help would be very welcome," I said, relieved that Iäna was not construing my removal from the Opera as a slight.

Iäna and Captain Olgarezh and I carried my belongings from the Opera to my new residence in the Amal'theileian. (Captain Olgarezh needed his sword hand free, but he carried one of my valises uncomplainingly.) By the time we got there, Iäna had discovered that, like many elves, if Captain Olgarezh had a weakness, it was for opera, and was cheerfully regaling us with stories of past opera disasters, including the time the Amal'opera's senior soprano's wig fell off in the middle of *Banetho*.

There was a note waiting from Prince Orchenis, which said merely, *Porana Clenverar admits no wrongdoing, of course, but we think it exceedingly unlikely that you will be troubled again. Please keep Captain Olgarezh with you, just in case.* I showed it to Captain Olgarezh, who said,

"We will continue to be watchful, but we do trust Prince Orchenis's judgment. Also his ability to make his displeasure plainly known." He sighed. "And now that the Clenverada know you are under Prince Orchenis's protection, it will not take them long to find out where you are, if they choose to inquire. And these rooms become merely *somewhat* safer rather than *markedly* safer. There are always windows."

"And are we not trapped here, if you are overcome?" I said. "Unless we go out a window ourself, which will also quickly result in our death."

"The goal, othala, is for us *not* to be overcome. But you are correct."

Iäna said, "This seems a very frightening way to live."

"It becomes less so with practice," said Captain Olgarezh.

I WROTE LETTERS to Anora and Tomasaran and Chonhadrin, telling them that letters to me should go under cover to Iäna, that being preferable (said Captain Olgarezh) to telling the world where I was by telling the post office. Iäna took the letters when he left, promising that they would go out by the evening post.

That night, not sleeping, I thought about Ulnemenee. I had asked the Archprelate for a task that would keep me in Amalo when I could no longer function as the municipal Witness for the Dead. Technically, I no longer needed such a task; my ability to hear the dead had returned, and I could resume my duties . . . except that in Tomasaran I had a fully capable replacement, and moreover I knew Captain Olgarezh would tell me the last thing I should do was start spending my mornings in the Witness for the Dead's office, where the whole point was that I was readily found and easily available. So I still needed a task to keep me in Amalo.

Besides which, the problem of Ulnemenee desperately

needed to be solved. Even leaving aside the people who currently had to scrape and scrabble to meet funerary costs because they had no municipal cemetery, it was a terrible embarrassment to Amalo to have the municipal cemetery of the city center be nonfunctional. Neither Vernezar nor the Amal'othala seemed to be bothered by this—nor by the bereft parishioners—but I was.

Captain Olgarezh and I went to Ulnemenee early next morning. I rang the bell in the courtyard, and Ostilin came from one direction and Hadrinar from the other.

"Othala Celehar!" said Hadrinar.

"Good morning," I said.

"We did not know you were back from Amalo," said Ostilin.

"I have only been back two days, and they have been . . . busy. This is Captain Olgarezh, who is guarding me."

"Guarding you?" said Hadrinar. "From what?"

"Attempted murder," I said and watched their eyes widen.

"But why would anyone want to murder you?" said Hadrinar.

"I petitioned the emperor on behalf of one hundred ninety-two dead dragons," I said.

Ostilin said, "But why . . ." and then I saw the moment she understood. "You mean it was the Clenverada."

"No one else has a reason to wish my death," I said. "But tell me—how have matters progressed in Othala Drinimar's study?"

"We have cleared off the desk," said Hadrinar. "But then Dach'othala Vernezar came on a visit—he was visiting all the municipal cemeteries—and Othala Shalicar locked the study and told Dach'othala Vernezar the key was lost. And he has not unlocked the study since."

"And the bones in the storeroom?"

"Are still there," Ostilin said with visible reluctance.

"Othala Shalicar will neither move them without the registers nor permit us to start a new one. And *we* can't . . ."

"No, it's no fault of yours," I said. "I must talk to Othala Shalicar."

"He's still in the refectory," said Ostilin. "Do you want me to go get him?"

"I would rather go to him," I said.

"This way," said Ostilin.

Captain Olgarezh and I followed her to the refectory, a room sized to contain at least ten more junior prelates, with a fireplace large enough to walk into, where Shalicar was sitting by the hearth with a cup of tea.

"Celehar!" he said, startling up when he saw me. "What are . . . who . . . ?"

"This is Captain Olgarezh," I said, "who is guarding me." I explained again, and Shalicar became quite agitated.

"Should you even be here?" he said. "Should you not be somewhere safer?"

And conveniently not bothering you? I thought, but chose to say, "Captain Olgarezh and I have discussed that question."

"This ulimeire seems safe enough," said Captain Olgarezh. "Is there another gate?"

Hadrinar said, "There is, but we keep it locked."

"Good," said Captain Olgarezh. "We noticed there are windows looking onto the courtyard. Might there be somewhere out of the wind where we would have a view of the main gate?"

"Yes," said Ostilin. "We can show you."

Captain Olgarezh bowed to me and said, "Then we need not disturb you, othala. Just let us know when you are ready to leave."

He and Ostilin left the room, and Shalicar said, "Celehar! What are you thinking? Ulnemenee is not worth your dying for!"

"If I thought it would come to that, I would not be here," I said. "But I really do not think the Clenverada will try again, now that they know Prince Orchenis knows they tried once."

"Ulnemenee does not need the disfavor of the Clenverada, either," said Shalicar.

"They aren't going to make any move against a municipal cemetery," I said. "Even one that isn't working."

"Celehar!" he said, as if I had said something shocking, rather than merely true.

"Why have you made no progress, Shalicar?" I said. "Why have you locked the door of Othala Drinimar's study?"

"I . . ."

"You're a reasonable man. You must have a reason."

For a moment, I thought he wasn't going to answer me, as his ears went flatter and flatter, but then he leaned in and whispered, "What if we find the body?"

I whispered in return, "What body?"

"Othala Csenivar! He disappeared without a trace! What if he's been in there all along?"

"Who was Othala Csenivar?"

"He was Othala Drinimar's junior prelate, fifty years ago. They did not like each other."

"It's a far step from there to murder."

"In his old age, Othala Drinimar would talk about having secrets. His junior prelates told me he told them that he could have gone to the reveth-atha, if anyone had known where to look."

"And you think they should have looked in the study."

"We think there could be *anything* hidden in there," said Shalicar.

"Even so, if we find Othala Csenivar . . . why is that a problem? Othala Drinimar is dead. And it isn't as if you've never seen a dead body before."

Ostilin came back in and joined Hadrinar in huddling by the fireplace and pretending not to listen.

"The Csenivada were not a powerful family fifty years ago, but they are now."

"Surely they could only be pleased to have their kinsman's body back."

"It looks terrible! They will rightly want to know how we could have had the body for fifty years and not *noticed* it!"

"You are spinning trouble out of straw," I said. "Clear the study first. If we find Othala Csenivar, deal with the matter then."

"Easy for you to say," Shalicar grumbled. "It isn't *your* benefice."

"Nor are they my parishioners who have been unable to bury their loved ones' bodies in their municipal cemetery for fifty years. Come, Shalicar. I said I would do it alone and I meant it. Where is the key?"

Ears sullen, Shalicar stood up, reached to the top of the mantelpiece, and took down a much-tarnished key.

"Thank you," I said.

"Ostilin and Hadrinar can help you," he said. "I don't want you here for the next five years. But *in the morning*! I need them in the afternoon."

"Why?"

"I beg your pardon."

"Why do you need them? Your ulimeire does not function. What is there for them—or you, for that matter—to do?"

Shalicar went red out to the tips of his ears. He muttered something of which the only word I could catch was "Vernezar."

I should have known. "You're doing something for Dach'othala Vernezar? What in the world . . . ?"

"When he showed me around the ulimeire," said Shalicar. "When he showed me Othala Drinimar's study and said, 'Of course, this is impossible, and I would not ask it of you,' he had another task which he said my junior prelates and I could help with."

"Which is?"

"The monthly reports from the municipal cemeteries. They're supposed to be put together in a quarterly report that goes to the Amalomeire, and Dach'othala Vernezar said he'd gotten shockingly behind."

"He didn't do them," I said.

"He said he—"

"He didn't do them."

"No, he didn't."

"So he has you and Hadrinar and Ostilin doing them?"

"They are terrible," said Shalicar. "Just when you get one batch written up, the next batch comes in. And we're *still* trying to get the old ones taken care of. I'm willing to give you Hadrinar and Ostilin in the mornings, because it is a task assigned you by the Archprelate, but I must have them in the afternoons if this quarter's report is to go to the Amalomeire on time."

"Very well," I said. "I appreciate the bind you are in." It was useless to suggest that he tell Vernezar no.

"Thank you," said Shalicar.

I turned and left the refectory, junior prelates in my wake.

I RETURNED TO the Amal'theileian late that afternoon, dusty and exhausted from a day of clearing Othala Drinimar's study, one piece of potentially important paper at a time, and I was not even properly begun on the task, which I was trying not to think about. Captain Olgarezh was alert at my side.

When we reached my rooms, Iäna was waiting in the hall; he had very sensibly brought a book, and it took him a moment to realize we were there.

"Ah, good afternoon," he said, putting the book in his coat pocket.

"Good afternoon, Mer Pel-Thenhior," I said. "What brings you here?"

"The noon post brought you a letter," he said, producing it from his other coat pocket.

The letter was from Tomasaran. It was oddly bulky, and she had folded and sealed it with obvious care, a combination which was both concerning and intriguing. When I opened it, it proved to enclose another letter, which I opened and skimmed to the bottom for the signature: Aäthis Rohethar. That was far from the worst possible answer to the mystery, so I went back and read the letter properly. It was a request for me to come talk to him about the Hill of Werewolves again; he said he had a number of new questions. I was dubious about my ability to *answer* new questions, since he had wrung my memory dry the last time we talked, but he had done so courteously and kindly, and I felt for him, prevented by ill health from doing his own investigating—although I would not have advised him to spend the night on the Hill of Werewolves, even if he had been able to do so. And I needed to find Osmer Ormevar, in pursuance of the second task the Archprelate had given me, and if he was not in his workroom at the University, I could at least be certain that he would return there and find a note if I left one.

Therefore, the next day, after a morning spent at Ulnemenee sorting through letters and timetables and newspapers, Captain Olgarezh and I took the tram out to the University and found our way to Osmer Rohethar's workroom.

He was a little surprised to see me—he had not expected an answer to his letter so quickly—but pleased. He was, naturally, more surprised to see Captain Olgarezh and horrified when I explained. Captain Olgarezh bowed and said, "You need not notice us. We will speak to no one of what we hear."

"It wouldn't really matter if you did," said Osmer Rohethar. "My research is hardly a secret."

"Still," said Captain Olgarezh. "It is a good principle." He retreated to the doorway.

I cleared a stack of books off the chair nearest Osmer Rohethar's desk in order to be able to sit down, and he said, "Periodically, I swear I'm going to organize my books and give away enough of them that the remainder will fit on the shelves, but I've never done it yet."

"Your collection is amazing," I said.

"Some of the books were my father's, and I had two uncles who were first-class scholars in history, *and* I have friends who know my interests. Osmer Ormevar is particularly kind about looking for books on my list when he goes trawling the used bookstores of Amalo. And indeed I don't know that I could bear to give *any* of my books away. But I beg your pardon; I didn't ask you to come so we could talk about my books."

"You said you had more questions."

"I do." He dug through the papers on his desk, finding the one he wanted at the bottom of a stack of essay books. "Yes. For I realized I had not asked you anything about the tomb."

"There were no ghosts there," I said.

"No, but we know from the surviving accounts that the Council of the Wolves of Anmura chose to raise a revethavar rather than tamely surrender their treasures, and I was wondering if anything of it remained."

I froze, like a water pipe in midwinter.

Osmer Rohethar frowned at me. "Othala Celehar? Are you all right?"

"Yes," I said hastily, although I knew my ears were still flat. "Yes, you just startled me. I wasn't expecting . . ."

"I *startled* you?" said Osmer Rohethar.

That had been a foolish answer. *Mind thy tongue, Celehar.* "I just meant I wasn't expecting questions about the tomb."

That wasn't much better.

"Well, I do beg your pardon for startling you," said Osmer Rohethar, still eyeing me uneasily, "but that must mean that you *did* encounter something, or else why would you be startled?"

I'd trapped myself. I said, "Yes, there was a revethavar. I . . . I destroyed it."

It sounded like the vilest kind of boasting—and in front of Captain Olgarezh, which was worse—and I knew I was turning red, but Osmer Rohethar did not seem inclined to doubt me. "How?" he said.

"The same way one quiets ghouls," I said and then, realizing that that might not be very helpful, I added, "You quiet a ghoul by finding the name of the person it was when it was alive and bidding them rest. It was the only thing I could think of to try against the revethavar, and it did work, although not in time to save my companion's life."

"Oh dear," said Osmer Rohethar, wide-eyed. "I *am* sorry."

"It's all right," I said. "I didn't . . . she was not a friend."

Osmer Ormevar's deep voice said from the doorway, "Rohethar, who *is* this?"

"This is Captain Olgarezh of the Principate Guard," said Osmer Rohethar.

I said hastily, "Let Osmer Ormevar in, please, Captain."

Captain Olgarezh stepped aside, and Osmer Ormevar came in.

"Why is there a captain of the Principate Guard in your doorway?" he said, which was a fair question.

I explained about the Clenverada again.

"That is very disturbing," said Osmer Ormevar. "Would you like me to have a word with Osmer Clenverar in the Department of Mathematics?"

"No, although I thank you for the thought. I would rather the Clenverada did not know I have ties to the University."

"Fair," said Osmer Ormevar.

"What brings you to my workroom, Ormevar?" said Osmer Rohethar.

Osmer Ormevar's face lit up. "You won't believe it."

"Won't believe what?" said Osmer Rohethar.

"We found an intact altar to Ulis!"

"You mean the revethgramal was still there?"

"Yes! And it's *round*!"

"Oh dear," said Osmer Rohethar.

"That's one in the eye for old Posilvar," Osmer Ormevar said with considerable satisfaction.

Osmer Rohethar said apologetically to me, "Ormevar and Posilvar have been at odds for years."

"And the revethgramal? A sort of mirror?"

"Seven hundred years ago, in the reign of Venet Clunethar, the Ulistheileian underwent a purge and the new Ulisothala was a man from a particularly harsh sect that said the revethgramalai were superstitious nonsense, and he had them all destroyed, just as he insisted that all priests of the city of Amalo go unmasked."

I thought of that empty plinth in the catacombs where Vernezar liked to hold clandestine meetings. "And what was a revethgramal, exactly?"

Osmer Rohethar made an expressive face. "That is what Ormevar and Posilvar have been quarrelling over. In Amaleise worship, mirrors used to be the principal signifier of Ulis, before Stohana's Purge. Posilvar has held the revethgramal to be a square mirror intended to reflect anyone who approached the altar, as the first step in any prayer to Ulis must be reflection on the self, while Ormevar says that it was a round mirror intended to symbolize the Moon. The texts we have are . . . not helpful."

"So this is a very important discovery."

"Very. Ormevar's excitement is not unwarranted."

"I am glad that something of worth has been found," I said.

"If a single looter had made it that far, it wouldn't have been," said Ormevar. "Or, at least, not found and made known to the University."

"The revethavar guarded his prison jealously," I said. "I don't think anyone made it far enough to loot."

Ormevar looked at me sharply. "Then the revethavar . . . it worked?"

"As I have just been telling Osmer Rohethar, yes."

"You need not go into the matter again, as I am sure you would prefer not to," said Osmer Rohethar. "I can relay your story to Ormevar later."

"That is very kind of you," I said. I was horrified to feel the hot prickle of tears and blinked them back fiercely.

Osmer Rohethar waved my thanks away with a flick of his ears. "You're the one who has done *me* the great favor. I can show you a little courtesy in return."

"In any event," said Osmer Ormevar, "it's a magnificent find and Posilvar will hate it. I have to go write up my notes, but it was a pleasure to see you again, Othala Celehar. Rohethar, I'll see you at dinner."

He was almost at the door before I could make myself say, "Osmer Ormevar!"

He turned. "Yes?"

"The Archprelate has asked me to assist you with your questions."

"He got my letter, then. Splendid! When would it be convenient for you to visit the tomb?"

"Whenever suits you," I said.

"Tomorrow morning? I will be in the tomb, well, most of the day really, but there are fewer interruptions in the morning."

"Yes," I said. "Tomorrow morning will be fine." I would have to send Shalicar a letter to let him know.

"Splendid!" said Osmer Ormevar. He bowed slightly to Captain Olgarezh, who bowed slightly in return, and was gone.

We were silent a moment; then Osmer Rohethar said, "Are you all right, othala?"

"I'm fine, thank you," I said, willing it to be true. "Did you have other questions?"

Osmer Rohethar frowned at his paper. "None of any significance. Or, at least, none that can be answered."

"What do you mean?"

"Ormevar's specialty—well, one of Ormevar's specialties—is the relationship of the Wolves of Anmura to the orthodoxy of their day, so he's been overflowing with delight about the friezes and the mosaics and now he's obviously found the chapel to Ulis—which they had not been able to find, and I'll have to ask him about that later—but my specialty is the history of the massacre, so I want to know things like when did they decide to make a revethavar and how did they persuade their Ulineise prelates to do it?"

"You might also ask why the Ulineise prelates knew *how* to do it," I said. "I cannot believe that it was an ordinary part of their instruction then, any more than it is now."

"That is very interesting," said Rohethar. "I admit, it had not occurred to me to wonder much about the prelates."

"They shouldn't have known how to make a revethavar. I don't know how, although I know the ritual exists. But that knowledge should have been contained only in the library of the Ulistheileian and known only to a couple of canons whose calling is the study of the deeper rituals. At least, that's how it is today. I know things must have been different in Hasthemis Brulnemar's day, but *that* different?" It was childish, perhaps, but I was proud of myself for saying the revethavar's name without faltering.

"You have raised questions I must ask other people," said

Rohethar with a smile. "Which—well done!—lets you off my hook."

"I don't feel hooked," I said. It was mostly true.

"No, I have asked enough of you for one day. Will you come talk to me again?"

"Of course."

"Thank you, othala."

"Good luck," I said.

We rode the tram in silence, Captain Olgarezh and I. It was not until we reached my suite that he said, "Are you all right?"

"We are, thank you," I said. "We are going to lie down."

He looked dubious, but, having already hung my overcoat on the coat rack, I went into the bedroom, closing the door behind me. I took off my boots, carefully hung up my coat of office, and lay down on the bed. After a moment I rolled to face the wall.

Sometime later, there was a murmur of voices in the antechamber, and then a tap on the door. Iäna's voice: "Othala Celehar? Are you awake?"

I said, "Yes," without moving.

There was a pause. "May we come in?"

"Yes," I said again, and I should have rolled over and sat up, but I did not.

The door opened, then closed.

"Art thou well?" Iäna said.

"I . . . I don't know," I said.

"What has happened?" I felt the bed dip under his weight and the warmth of his body against my back.

"Nothing important." But I still couldn't make myself move.

"I beg to differ," said Iäna. "Whatever this is, it is important. Wilt thou tell me?"

"Osmer Rohethar had questions about the revethavar," I said.

"And thou didst answer them?"

"They were not *harmful* questions."

"And yet thou seemst harmed."

"Folly," I said, and this time at least managed to roll onto my back. No one had lit the gas in the bedroom, so I saw Iäna only as a backlit silhouette.

"Thara," he said and stopped.

"It's destroyed," I said and inwardly cursed my voice for scraping into soundlessness on the last syllable of "destroyed."

"It nearly destroyed thee," Iäna countered. "I don't think there's anything wrong with not wanting to talk about it just to satisfy Osmer Rohethar's curiosity."

"It wasn't like that," I said. "He didn't know."

"No, but that still doesn't mean that thou hast to answer his questions."

"I could hardly run shrieking from the room."

"Is that what thou didst *want* to do?"

He had caught me. I said nothing.

"I do not wish to harangue thee," he said. "I came only to ask if thou wouldst dine with me—it's an off-night for the Opera."

"I am not terribly hungry," I said, sitting up.

"That does not mean that thou shouldst fast. Come to the Torivontaram, and my mother will make thee brev."

"What is brev?"

"Beef broth with an egg cooked in it. It's what she used to make for me when I was sick. I still find it comforting."

All at once it was too much, and I said, "What dost thou want from me?"

"I beg thy pardon?"

"This!" I said with a wide, probably mostly invisible gesture. "Thou com'st and worriest about whether I eat, thou givest me a place to hide, thou brokest into Osmin Temin's school with me! And I do not know what thou wantst."

"I thought it was obvious," Iäna said warily.

"Art thou marnis?" I had not meant to ask so directly—indeed, I had not meant to ask at all.

"No," he said. "Can I not simply be thy friend?"

"Thou art very . . . intense about it?"

"I promise I have no desire to have sexual relations of any kind with thee. I enjoy sex with women and they enjoy sex with me. It gives me friends among the opera singers and the demimonde. They all know I will not love them, so no hearts are broken."

"That young woman, Hetheno?"

"A faro dealer. A friend. We had an affair two years ago."

I hesitated.

"Ask," said Iäna.

"Dost thou love me?"

"I love thee, and it grieves me greatly to see thee hurt. And, to tell thee the truth, it worries me more than a little that thou findst this so unfathomable. Do thy other friends not love thee?"

"I have very few close friends," I said. "I suppose I don't know how the thing is done."

He laughed. "Dost wish a guidebook?"

"Thou hast no idea how much," I said. To my own surprise, I was smiling.

"And thou?" said Iäna. "What dost thou want from me?"

I said nothing; my throat had closed merely because he had cared enough to ask.

"Dost desire sex? I know thou dost desire men." He did not sound particularly bothered.

He said, "Thara. Do not *worry* so. Come and have dinner instead."

"Yes," I said, and we walked to the Torivontaram together, Captain Olgarezh watchful at my side. Although it had not snowed since the early blizzard, it was getting steadily colder and colder—it was already colder than the worst winter I had ever experienced. I was very grateful to get inside again.

The server—the goblin boy with eyes of Pelanran gold—led us to a table for three along the outside wall, but we had barely finished ordering a four-cup pot of isevren when the door swung open, admitting a cluster of opera singers and Iäna's assistant Thoramis. They were not rowdy, but they were definitely loud, and when they saw Iäna, they all waved vigorously.

Iäna muttered under his breath in Barizhin and said, "If we don't go to them, they will come to us. We'll be back as quickly as we can. If Garet wants to know, we always just order the house special and let our mother feed us what she likes."

"All right," I said, and he got up and crossed the room to the table of opera singers, saying, "Good evening, good persons," in a voice at least as carrying as any of theirs.

He was still there, having been dragged into some sort of extremely cheerful dispute, when Merrem Pel-Thenhior emerged from the kitchen and approached the table where Captain Olgarezh and I were sitting.

"Good evening, Merrem Pel-Thenhior," I said.

"Good evening, othala," she said. She raised her eyebrows at Captain Olgarezh.

I said, "This is Captain Olgarezh of the Principate Guard."

"Be welcome, Captain," she said. "I will take Iäna's chair for a moment." She sat down with the slight sigh of a person who spent their working day on their feet.

I realized I had become very still, like a rabbit seeing a

hawk's shadow—which was ridiculous. Merrem Pel-Thenhior was not a hawk, and I was certainly not a rabbit. I was about to prove it by saying something when she leaned across the table, fixing me with her golden eyes, and said, "Iäna says you know."

I had my wits sufficiently about me not to say, "Know what?" Instead, I said, "Yes."

"And you must not intend to say anything, or you would have done it already."

"Why should I say anything?" I said. "You're not doing anything wrong."

She gave me a long look, half skeptical and half curious. "You are an unusual prelate."

"Many have found me so," I agreed tiredly.

Iäna came back and said, "Nosy, gossipy . . . old women have nothing on opera singers. Mama, are you hounding Othala Celehar?"

"I merely wish to know him better," said Merrem Pel-Thenhior. "Othala Celehar, I thank you for your generosity of spirit."

"You need not thank me, Merrem Pel-Thenhior," I said.

"Maybe not, but I thank you all the same," she said, smiling, and got up to give her son back his chair.

Iäna sat down and said, "*Was* she hounding you? You look hounded."

"She was not," I said.

Iäna looked at Captain Olgarezh as if checking my veracity (in which case he gained nothing, for Captain Olgarezh's face was, as usual, unreadable), then smiled at the server, who had come quietly up to the table, and said, "The house special, whatever it is this evening."

"I will follow Mer Pel-Thenhior's guidance," I said.

"The house special tonight is gorshmast," said Garet. "Shall I tell Merrem Pel-Thenhior to prepare it for the table?"

"Do you object to a common dish?" Iäna asked us.

"No," I said.

Captain Olgarezh said, "Given how one eats in the barracks of the Anmur'theileian—no, not at all."

"Then, yes," said Iäna. "Oh, and tell her Othala Celehar needs brev."

Garet bowed and went to the kitchen.

I said, "Will you tell us of your opera?"

He smiled at me. "We observe that you know exactly how to distract us. But, yes, we will gladly talk about *The Grief of Stones*."

Garet brought the isevren, pot and three cups (none matching), and Iäna talked about *The Grief of Stones*.

After a night of patchy sleep, I rose early, bade Armsman Ingavar good morning as he went off to bed, let Captain Olgarezh lead me to a teahouse called the Harpy's Kiss for breakfast; then, reluctant but determined, I walked to the Hill of Werewolves. Things were different from the last time I had been there. The gardeners had made a real path around the side of the hill, so that one no longer had to skid down the drop-off, and it was possible to approach the tomb without crouching beneath a ceiling of thelavis vines. At the grille there were two half-goblin men on guard, wearing the University's livery, but they smiled and waved us past. One said, "Osmer Ormevar said to expect a prelate and a guardsman."

"Is he here?"

"Oh, yes. He always gets here when our shift starts at dawn."

"Thank you." No excuse to turn tail.

It was still an awkward squeeze between the grille and the stone, but I managed it without damaging my clothing.

Captain Olgarezh followed me. There were lights now, lanterns on tall poles, and it was some comfort to discover that the place was unrecognizable. It looked nothing like my nightmare memories.

I decided that the most likely place to find Osmer Ormevar was the crypt where the ancient books were. If he was not there, I would have to wander around calling for him.

I said to Captain Olgarezh, "There are no other egresses from the tomb. You do not have to come with us."

He was eyeing the friezes with disfavor. "By the same token, those two guards will stop anyone who comes. We will stay with you."

I could not deny that his company was welcome.

They had taken all the skeletons away, but I found I remembered their positions exactly, and then that right turn, and I was standing in the place where I had almost been torn apart by the revethavar.

I had not been sure how I would feel, and I still wasn't sure. It took a little effort to walk past the spot where Osmin Temin had died. Much as I had by then hated her, her death had been terrible. And it would be dreadfully easy to imagine that the revethavar was still there, waiting.

Which he was not, and I knew it. I marched firmly forward, only to be brought to a complete halt by the snarling stone wolves. I remembered my dream, the rasping way their eyes had rolled in their sockets, and for a moment I could not convince myself that they were not watching me. And with the revethavar destroyed, there was no one to command them not to fall on me and rend me bone from bone.

"Othala Celehar?" said Captain Olgarezh. He sounded worried.

"Nothing," I said. "Just too much imagination."

I forced myself to walk between the wolves. They were statues, nothing more, and their eyes did not follow me.

Osmer Ormevar was in the crypt, studying the lowest rank of revethmerai plaques on the wall to the left of the door. "Othala Celehar, Captain Olgarezh," he said, straightening from his crouch, "good morning!"

"Good morning, Osmer Ormevar," I said. "Do you make good progress?"

"We have no idea," he said cheerfully. "None of us has the least guess how much information there is to be gleaned from this tomb, so how can we judge? But everyone's been very good-tempered and cooperative, and the revethgramal is not the only discovery that has been made. Do you want to see it?"

"The revethgramal?"

"Yes. We wanted to ask you about the ulimeire anyway. Come on."

Captain Olgarezh and I followed him out of the crypt, past the snarling wolves, down the hall (past the place where I had almost died) and then to the right, where the way back out was to the left. We had advanced perhaps fifty feet down the corridor when Osmer Ormevar stopped and said, "Here."

"Here?"

"Exactly!" He stepped to the left-hand wall, pressed something among the wolves of the frieze, and a section of the wall rotated away from us, revealing a room, smallish and square. There were no decorations on the walls, and the mosaic floor, instead of being jaguars and bats and owls and wolves, was a simple sigil of Ulis. At the far end of the room was a plinth, and on the plinth, facing the door, was a round mirror. That, presumably, was the revethgramal.

"They hid the ulimeire?" I said.

"Doesn't make any sense, does it?" Osmer Ormevar said. "This was centuries before Stohana's Purge, so there was no need to hide the revethgramal, and it's not like this isn't a funerary complex to even the briefest of glances. That's why we wanted to talk to a prelate of Ulis."

"You know more about the Ulisithalba here than we do," I said. "All we can tell you is how it differs from what we do today—and you must know that already, too."

Osmer Ormevar made a face. "We know what other scholars have written in their books," he said, "but our own Ulineise prelate is a dimwitted lunk, and our efforts to talk to other Ulineise prelates keep jarring against the Ulisothala. We inevitably ask a question that they think the Ulisothala would not want them to answer, and then they stop answering questions at all."

"And of course Vernezar will not talk to you himself."

"We tried that, too," Osmer Ormevar said, "once, many years ago. It didn't go well."

"We are sure it did not. We will be glad to answer your questions, but we don't know how much help we'll be."

"More than you expect, because you have knowledge we do not," Osmer Ormevar said. "Everything that can be found by observation of this funerary complex, we will find. We've even found the names of the wolves, engraved on their bellies."

"Ata," I said, "and Eira."

Osmer Ormevar stopped and stared at me. "How did you know that?"

"We remembered it from a dream," I confessed, and his eyebrows shot up, as did Captain Olgarezh's.

"You dreamed about their names?"

"That wasn't what the dream was about," I said, "but he told them to let us past."

"'He'?"

"Hasthemis Brulnemar," I said, and then realized that, having said that much, I had to tell Osmer Ormevar the whole.

He listened attentively, and this was a story I had much practice in telling. When I was done, he circled back. "And in your dream, Brulnemar called the wolves Ata and Eira."

"Yes."

"'Ata' is an ancient word for spite," he said, "and 'Eira' for malice."

"What fitting guardians," I said, and my voice shook a little.

"One of our students is researching further," said Osmer Ormevar, "to see if we can piece together *why* the wolves are named Spite and Malice, but in the meantime that suggests some very interesting things about your dream. Do you often have true dreams?"

"Only when Ulis chooses to send one," I said.

He gave me a disapproving look. "That was not an answer."

"Once or twice?"

"More often than most people."

"We suppose so."

"Do you remember any other details of the tomb?"

"Nothing that was any different from how it is in truth."

"Pity," said Osmer Ormevar. "We find it interesting that Brulnemar was bound to his bones. Do you think *that* is also true?"

"It would make sense," I said, "although we hesitate to offer that as a measurement of truth."

"Hah. Do you think your dragon friend is bound to her bones, and that's why she can't just kill all the miners at once?"

"She did not tell us where her bones are," I said, deciding not to argue with him about whether Ithalpherix was a friend. "But, again, it would make sense. She must be bound to *something*, and her bones are the only thing left."

"Yes," said Osmer Ormevar. "In the wonder-tales, dragon bones are the only thing harder than diamonds."

I thought of the bone that had almost caved my skull in. "The wonder-tales may be right."

IÄNA WAS WAITING again when we reached my rooms in the Amal'theileian.

"You are very popular," he said and gave me three letters, all ostensibly from Tomasaran, although two of them were bulky enough that I knew they had enclosures.

"We did not mean to make you bring our post *every* day," I said.

"We do not mind," said Iäna, and I thought of what he had said about other men finding his friendship too intense.

"Would you like to come in while we read our letters? And then perhaps go to lunch?"

"Lunch seems like an excellent plan. We will be glad to wait."

I set the three letters down on the desk in the antechamber. I opened the bulky ones first. One enclosure bore the sigil of the Sanctuary of Csaivo on its seal, the other that of the Judiciary.

I opened the Judiciary letter and skimmed down to the signature. It was from Csathamar, which was surprising. I went back up to the top and read the letter properly. Then read it again.

"Mer Csathamar has been appointed the judicial Witness for the Dragons," I said to Iäna.

"That's good, isn't it? We remember that you have mentioned him."

"We are glad that it's someone we know," I said. "We just weren't expecting them to move so quickly."

"On a matter for the emperor's judgment?" said Iäna. "And the newspapers say he's going to come here."

I hadn't looked at a newspaper in weeks. *"Here?"*

"It was an appeal from the Clenverada. We think they thought it would be refused, and then they would have that to complain about."

"But the emperor went the other way." As the emperor often did. "Prince Orchenis must be . . ."

"Beside himself. The newspapers are full of speculation about what he's going to do about the Curneisei, given what *they* did the last time an emperor came to Amalo."

"Oh no," I said involuntarily.

"The *Standard* is predicting that the Brotherhood will be ordered to raid the A3 Co. housing."

"Oh *no,*" I said.

"It's where the Curneisei are. Or were. The *Arbiter* says they're disappearing in droves."

"As is only sensible," I said. "We hope they have the further sense to *stay* hidden and not do anything rash."

"The Brotherhood will be everywhere," said Iäna. "And the Principate Guard will be everywhere they're not."

"And the Imperial Guard," I said, trying to be comforted. "But what does Mer Csathamar say?"

"He wants to meet with us and requests that we come to the Judiciary as soon as we can."

"A risky idea," Captain Olgarezh said.

"We must meet with Mer Csathamar at *some* point before the emperor arrives," I said.

"Yes, but not in the chaos of the Judiciary. Write back and make an appointment for him to come here."

"All right," I said. "But how . . ."

"You'll have to have hours 'at home to visitors,'" Iäna said. He sounded amused. "Like the fancy society people."

"You are not making this situation more comfortable," I said.

"Could anything make this situation more comfortable?"

"Probably not. We will write a letter to Mer Csathamar

inviting him to visit us tomorrow between the hours of one and two."

"Very good," said Iäna. "What about your other letters?"

The second letter was from Othalo Rasaltezhen. She was writing in mingled concern and curiosity: she had not heard anything from me in some time and naturally wanted to know if I had noticed any change with regard to her and Doret Athmaza's working.

I did not know what to say to her.

"What's wrong?" said Iäna, and I realized my ears had gone flat.

"Nothing," I said hastily and probably unconvincingly. "It's from Othalo Rasaltezhen."

"That doesn't seem so terrible."

"She wants to know if her working had any success, and we do not know what to tell her."

"But her working *did* have success," Iäna said, frowning. "You can speak to the dead again."

"That was a miracle of Ulis. It had nothing to do with Othalo Rasaltezhen."

"Then shouldn't you tell her *that*?"

"Yes," I said reluctantly. "It is hardly fair compensation for the trouble she and Doret Athmaza went to if we do not tell them what happened. Must we tell her to come visit us as well?"

"It is your neck, othala," said Captain Olgarezh. "But you risk it every time you leave these rooms."

"That was a yes," Iäna said.

"Very well," I said, although my ears refused to lift. "We will write two letters."

"And the third letter?"

The third letter was from Tomasaran herself and detailed her progress in solving the murder of Ema Dravenezh. She had talked to the singers, gone back and talked to the marquess—

and I was both surprised and pleased that she'd found the courage to do so—and tried to talk to Tura Olora's friends.

All of whom had disappeared.

It is only two people, she wrote, *but it seems more than coincidental to me that Tura Olora is dead, the person who knew him best is dead, and two other persons who knew him have disappeared. It makes me think you were right about Mer Olora having a secret. I have been asking myself what that secret might be, and it occurred to me that there is another coincidence around these disappearances, which is that they happened at roughly the same time Coralis Clunethar escaped.*

That is a very big secret.

I am not sure that I am right—because I can't find anybody still alive to ask—and the Marquess Parzhadel's loyalty is unquestionable. On the other hand, it would not be the first time master and servant had disagreed. And it is certainly a secret that people would commit murder over.

My problem is that, while this excludes a good fraction of the population of Amalo from suspicion, it does not helpfully point me at anyone. I do not know the politics of Amalo, so I am writing to you to ask, is there someone I could talk to who openly supports Coralis Clunethar?

It was a question for Anora. I knew much more about Amalo's funerary practices than its politics.

I would have to write her back and tell her so.

"You will be writing three letters," Iäna said. "But first, lunch."

"And we must find a secondhand shop," I said.

"What do you need?" said Iäna.

"A warmer frock coat, among other things. And, no, we will not be 'borrowing' from the Wardrobe Department."

"As you wish," said Iäna, raising his hands palms forward in token of surrender. "We know of a couple of good secondhand shops that are very close, if we eat at the Wishbone Ring."

"All right," I said and looked at Captain Olgarezh.

"We must all eat," he agreed.

THAT WE TALKED about opera over lunch was not surprising. What *was* surprising was that Iäna somehow managed to get Captain Olgarezh to do the talking, telling us about the amateur operas put on by the soldiers of the Anmur'theileian. "There is a good deal of comic cross-dressing," he said, almost apologetically. "They have no other way of having female characters at all, since none of them can sustain a falsetto. But that doesn't matter if you're not trying to be convincing in the first place."

"But what are Anmur'theileneise operas *about*?" Iäna said in obvious fascination.

"They're silly things," said Captain Olgarezh. "The men aren't interested in performing in anything serious. It frustrates Lieutenant Estebezh a little bit, because he has grand ideas about actually writing an opera about the war—which would of course need all, or almost all, male voices—but he's very good at, oh, the kind of opera with a pair of young lovers who have to find a way to meet in secret. There's always a balcony scene, and the girl's father is a buffoon, and she has a dozen jealous suitors who are more interested in getting the better of each other than they are in her, and there's a chorus of villagers. Things like that, and with as many little two- or three-line roles as Estebezh can think of, so that everybody gets a chance to sing, since that's really the point."

"That sounds chaotic," I said.

"Oh yes," said Captain Olgarezh. He smiled at some memory, and my heart leapt a little, because there was my flame-eyed captain. He had been so relentlessly formal since taking up this guarding duty that I had thought he would never unbend.

After lunch, Iäna led us two blocks east to a row of respectable but not fancy shops. Two of them were secondhand clothes shops. Iäna nodded at one as we passed it, and said, "Prothanar does a brisk business in courtiers' clothes, especially with us and the other opera houses. I think, though, that Drezhkara's establishment is more what you meant."

Inside, Drezhkara's shop was brightly gaslit and smelled strongly of the corlincaira sachets used to keep off the moths. I was able quickly to find the things I needed—a better hat, a woolly scarf, a pair of fur-lined gloves—until it came to choosing a quilted frock coat, such as the Amaleisei wore in the winter, where the combination of a coat that would fit and a color I could bear proved elusive.

Finally I found a plum-colored quilted coat, warmer cousin of the coat Coralezh had given me, but one that fit me better.

"Not going to look for a second?" said Iäna as I folded the coat and put it on top of the store basket to take to the merchant's tall perch by the door.

I shook my head.

"Do you dislike bright colors, or is it just that you feel they're inappropriate?"

"A little of both?" I said. "We've grown so accustomed to wearing black that we don't feel comfortable in anything too bright. And we prefer our clothing not to attract people's attention."

The young woman at the perch totaled up my purchases and then made them into two neat parcels that I could easily carry.

Iäna and Captain Olgarezh and I walked back to the Amal'theileian together; there Iäna bowed to Captain Olgarezh (who bowed in return), hugged me hard around my packages, and set off north to the Vermilion Opera.

Captain Olgarezh and I returned to my (our?) rooms in silence. As we walked, it started to snow.

In the morning, through great white drifts of snow, it was back to Ulnemenee and the endless piles of paper in Othala Drinimar's study. Captain Olgarezh insisted on taking a different route to and from Ulnemenee, "Just in case. Indeed, othala, we wish you would not come here at all, but we understand that you feel you must."

"Do you really think the Clenverada might try again?"

"Once you are dead," Captain Olgarezh said bleakly, "you cannot be brought back, no matter what Prince Orchenis does. We worry that the Clenverada will reach the tipping point where they want you dead more than they care about the consequences. We agree they are probably not there yet."

In the afternoon, back in the Amal'theileian, I sat in the antechamber and waited hopefully for someone to visit. Promptly at one o'clock, Csathamar knocked on the door.

I said, feeling faintly ridiculous, "Please come in. I'm sorry I couldn't come to you but . . ."

Csathamar waved that away. He said, "I appreciate your agreeing to see me so quickly. I feel that I am starting this witnessing at a great deficit, and I am hoping that you will be able to help."

"Of course," I said.

And so I told the story again, this time to a trained Witness, who pursued every last detail with unflagging focus, unfeigned interest, and unfailing patience. By the time I was done, I felt as if I had been turned inside out and vigorously shaken. Captain Olgarezh listened to the whole, I noticed, although I could not tell what he thought.

Csathamar said, "The only problem I foresee is that you are the only witness—as well as the only Witness—to the truth of Ithalpherix's story. Can you take me to Revethora Vezvaishoroi?"

"Not until spring. Not at all if the miners are still there. They've already tried to murder me—I don't think they'll balk at murdering you as well."

"How extremely vexatious," said Csathamar. "We will have to ask Prince Orchenis to send the Principate Guard to clear them out."

"The Principate Guard?"

"It is a matter for the emperor's judgment. No one can afford to be behindhand in cooperation. Besides, they tried to murder a Witness."

"Technically, I wasn't a Witness at the time."

"That doesn't make throwing you to the revethvezvaishor'avar a good idea."

"No," I said. "It does not."

"Perhaps an expedition in the spring, if the emperor leaves us enough time."

"Yes," I said. "But for right now, do you need anything else from me?"

"I think you've got that backwards."

"But I'm not . . ."

"Witness for the Dead takes precedence," Csathamar pointed out.

"I'm not trying to *pull rank,*" I said, horrified.

Csathamar laughed. "You're quite doing the reverse, and you need not be so considerate of my feelings. Is there anything I can do to help you?"

"Do you not have other work you should be doing?"

"The four of us assigned to this matter have been told it

is our only concern until the emperor's judgment is made. Anything I can do to help you *is* my work."

"Then tell me the gossip of the court."

"Well, if there's one thing the Judiciary is full of, it is gossip," said Csathamar.

Coralis Clunethar still had not been found, making it all but certain that he was being hidden by someone. "And the Cambeshada and the Vernezada try to look innocent, not that Nedeva Cambeshar has been innocent since the moment he was born. But as to who's actually helping him right now, I don't know. They must have some sort of organization—not just a bunch of young hotheads storming Grivensee and striking off Coralis's chains. Not that he was chained to begin with, but you know the sort of nonsense I mean. That's not how it happened. There was planning involved, and someone clever enough to see that the weak point in Coralis's prison was the guards."

"And money."

"Oh yes. Someone *funded* this escapade. Which is what worries me about it. Not Coralis himself, but the people who may have decided to use Coralis Clunethar as a puppet."

"You mean the Tethimadeise conspirators," I said.

"It is what I worry about," said Csathamar. "Not the Tethimada themselves—their teeth have been pulled—but the people who supported them and did not get caught. In Amalo, such people had the cover of the Curneisei conspirators, and I don't think anyone went door-to-door asking what the household had planned to do when the Tethimada raised their banner."

"It is an alarming thought."

"Yes. The Tethimada—and the Chavada—were the houses left holding the bag, so to speak, but they were far from the only people who thought it might be very handy to have Eshevis Tethimar as emperor. And those people have not become less discontent as Edrehasivar's reign progresses."

"I suppose they would not," I said.

"Edrehasivar is not what anyone expected, and no one has any leverage with him. He didn't grow up with their sons and nephews; he has no fond memories of staying at their country estates in the summer. If it had taken longer to find an empress, they might have gained at least a little traction through their *daughters*, but as it is, only Ceredel has that advantage. But in any event, my point is that there are people in Amalo with power and money who would be pleased to have Coralis on the principate throne instead of Orchenis, and I am afraid they may have taken the first step toward achieving that."

"Of whom should I be suspicious?" I said. I knew the cemeteries of Amalo better than the court, and the mention of the conspirators had reminded me that there were more enemies in Amalo than I even knew to look for.

"The Rohethada, for starters. They badly want the princess freed from Bakhoree, and Coralis—speaking of traction and advantages—was one of the young men surrounding Sheveän Rohethin when it was fashionable to do so. But the Cambeshada have no love for Prince Orchenis, as I said, nor have the Imada. Oh, politics in Amalo is a wasp's nest—kick it and you won't be able to count the wasps that emerge."

"That's politics anywhere," I said. "It is why I prefer the company of the dead."

"Then let us speak of the University instead," said Csathamar.

The University's exploration of the tomb under the Hill of Werewolves was going about as one would expect: slowly and with much discussion.

"I spoke with Osmer Ormevar yesterday morning," I said.

"Then you probably know more than I do."

"No. Osmer Ormevar asks more questions than he answers."

"Well they're being very careful," he said, "since everyone agrees that the tomb is a valuable find. But I think at least three pet theories have been exploded in the last month, and there is a lot of shouting."

"Are you still acting as the Witness for the tomb under the Hill of Werewolves?"

"I was, until I got handed Witness for the Dragons. I handed off Witness for the Tomb in turn to Witness Mabrelar, who also comes from a University background, although he was a mathematician, not a historian, and usually witnesses for bank accounts and ledgers and the like. I told him it would be a nice change."

"I trust he knew better than to believe you."

Csathamar laughed. "Yes. But he isn't complaining."

I COULD NOT sleep that night. Under ordinary circumstances, I would have gone out and wandered the halls of the Amal'theileian, but I could imagine Captain Olgarezh's displeasure, and in any event, I could hardly ask Armsman Ingavar to wander with me.

I lit the sconce and read until dawn.

When I heard Armsman Ingavar leave, I went out into the antechamber and startled Captain Olgarezh. He raised his eyebrows. "Are you all right, othala?"

"Yes. We were just . . ." *Lonely* was ridiculous but true. *Thinking too much* was also true. "We suffer from insomnia," I said, again truthfully, "and we sometimes grow tired of our own thoughts."

"We can understand that," he said. "Lookout duty on the Anmur'theileian was like that, because you were entirely by yourself at the top of the topmost tower, and you had to stay alert but also not distract yourself from your duty to watch. So you had your esor of the strongest tea you could brew, and you had the vastness of the steppes. And your thoughts. There were men who would do *anything* to get out of lookout duty, and we have always thought that those were the men who had nothing in their heads to keep them company."

"Or too much," I said.

"Yes," said Captain Olgarezh. "Or too much."

"It sounds very lonely," I said hesitantly.

"Lonely?" He considered for a moment. "Yes, life in the Anmur'theileian was very lonely."

I was overwhelmed for a moment with a sense of recognition, almost of kinship.

Captain Olgarezh smiled at me. "We find this duty much more congenial."

I fumbled for something to say in reply and finally managed, "We are glad."

THE JUNIOR PRELATES and I worked in Othala Drinimar's study all morning. They were gradually becoming less shy of me; toward noon, Ostilin, who was the braver of the two, asked me what had happened to my voice.

"Sessiva," I said. "I caught it in Lohaiso when I was a junior prelate, and I am lucky that my voice is all that it wrecked."

"People go blind," Ostilin said.

"Yes. Blind or deaf—or both—or some people, it takes their wits. Or it could have killed me. I can remember lying there, before the fever got so bad I was delirious, wondering what it was going to take from me."

"How horrible," said Ostilin.

"Yes," I said. "The only good part about sessiva is that you can only have it once. So I need not fear its return."

"I suppose that makes it better than charcorsai," said Hadrinar. "You can have them again and again, and they might kill you any one of those times."

"Yes," I said. "It is not very much, weighed in the balance, but it is something."

"Does it ever feel like it isn't enough?" said Ostilin.

"The sessiva," I said wryly, "is the least of my troubles."

I HAD ASKED Othalo Rasaltezhen to come this afternoon; she appeared promptly at one and, unfazed by Captain Olgarezh, assured me apologies were not necessary.

We sat down, and she said at once, "And did we have any success?"

"Ah," I said and then decided there was no point in being anything but straightforward. "There was a miracle."

"A miracle?" said Othalo Rasaltezhen. "How so?"

I told the story again. Othalo Rasaltezhen listened carefully and said, "May I look?"

"Of course," I said, although there was nothing I wanted less.

The size of the antechamber meant our chairs were close together, so it was easy enough to meet her eyes and to feel her walk into my head as if it belonged to her.

"This is very interesting," she said after a moment. "You remember my metaphor of the document?"

"Yes?"

"It is here, where it ought to be in the room of your mind, and I can see where we mended it. But it is also . . . perhaps I must change metaphors again. I described it as a wall at first, and I think that was close. Imagine it as a dam, built by Ulis in your mind to hold something we'll call water, although that's not at all correct. When the revethavar broke the dam, all the water ran out, and when we mended the dam, we could not bring back the water. We didn't even know there was water that ought to be there."

"But the water is there now?"

"Yes! The reservoir has filled again with whatever kind of spirit force it is that lets you talk to the dead."

"A miracle," I said.

"Yes," she said. "I wonder if that might not have happened gradually over time, the same way that I wonder if the dam might not have rebuilt itself."

"You think it was not a miracle?"

"Oh, I didn't say that. The fact that it was full when you most desperately needed it to be . . ." She sat back, releasing me from her gaze. "You should make a pilgrimage to Ulis."

"I should," I said. "But I have done the only one I know of in Amalo, the Hill of Werewolves. Are there others?"

"The Dachen Csaivanat is a pilgrimage to Ulis."

"Not to Csaivo?"

"It's that, too. But there is a shrine to Ulis, only accessible when the well is low—as it is now, for it is high in the spring."

"That seems propitious. Thank you."

She smiled and said, "I appreciate your telling me what happened."

"I was taught that Ulis is parsimonious with miracles. It might be that if you had not mended the dam, the water would simply have run out again. If that is not too simple-minded a gloss?"

"No, it is certainly possible, and I admit I would be pleased to think that our working was of *some* use. I can't imagine that you will need my help again, Othala Celehar, but if you do, please don't hesitate to ask."

"And if there is anything I can do for you, although it seems equally unlikely, I would be honored."

"That is good to know."

We bowed to each other, and she departed.

There was, as the old song said, no time like the present. I said to Captain Olgarezh, "We are going on pilgrimage. Risky or not."

"We will not argue," he said mildly. "But we will accompany you at least part of the way."

"There's only one way into the well," I said. "You need not accompany us on the stairs."

"We will not deny that we are relieved," he said, and made me smile.

We went to the Amal'ostro and took the next tram, switching at the Dachenostro to the Vestrano line and out to the Dachen Csaivanat, with its vast and ancient wellhouse and the well that had nearly the circumference of the Alcethmeret, the emperor's tower in the Untheileneise Court. There was a waist-high wall around the well with a bench built into it. The wellhouse was surprisingly warm—surprisingly until I realized there was a hypocaust. There was a novice on duty at the single opening in the wall around the well, which was the head of the stairs. She bowed at our approach.

"Good day, othala. Do you wish to descend the well?"

"We do," I said. "We come on pilgrimage."

"Of course," she said and bowed again. "You will find it impossible to go wrong."

She looked questioningly at Captain Olgarezh. I said, "My friend kindly came with me, but does not seek to make the pilgrimage."

"The bench around the wellhead is suitable."

"Yes," said Captain Olgarezh and sat down next to the opening.

"Will you hold my overcoat?" I asked Captain Olgarezh.

"Certainly." I shrugged out of it, and he put it next to him on the bench.

The novice stood aside. I said, "Thank you," and started down the stairs.

It was warm in the well. The stairs were slick with moisture and greatly bowed with millennia-worth of feet going up and down them; the hand rail was a deep groove in the wall and as slick as the stairs. I did not make the mistake of looking down, but I proceeded very slowly, aware of the hard thump of my heart against my ribs. It was not a worthy pilgrimage to Ulis if there was not some danger involved. I had been worried about the water; it had not occurred to me to worry about the fall.

I followed the wide curve of the wall down and down and down, down so far that the oculus of the wellhouse became nothing more than a pinprick of light and my way was lit by great, elaborately carved sconces, each polished to a mirror-like shine, and I knew what the punishment duty was for the novices at the csaivatheileian.

I did not reach the end of the stairs. I reached the beginning of the water. The stairs continued on beneath it, and I could not see where they ended. I stopped and looked around. It was entirely possible that a pilgrimage to Ulis would include an underwater journey, but I did not think the clerics of Csaivo would want all those pilgrims getting in their water. And sure enough, I saw that five stairs above the waterline, I had gone past a waist-high hole in the wall.

Crawling was better than swimming. I went up five stairs and carefully fit myself into the hole—difficult to do without falling into the water. The passageway was short, mercifully for my trousers, and I was soon able to stand up again in something rather like a foyer, with two doors. One had one of Csaivo's sigils on it, and I guessed first that that was the way the novices on punishment duty got into the well, rather than having to go up and down all those treacherous stairs every time, and second that it was locked. The other had the sigil of Ulis in his aspect as the god of moonless nights, of darkness, the place where his worship overlapped with that of Enthenevry and had starved the lesser god out. That was the door I wanted.

It took both hands to work the heavy latch on the door, and I had to brace myself and shove to get it open far enough that I could squeeze through.

The shrine was lit by a single owl-light, so it was difficult to make out much more than a circle of mosaic floor and the walls stretching up on all sides. The pilgrimage tokens were easily found, in a bowl beneath the owl-light.

I took a token out of the bowl: a round cloth badge small enough to fit in my palm, embroidered with the sigil of Ulis on a blue background, the blue (I supposed) to represent the Dachen Csaivanat itself. I tucked it in my inner waistcoat pocket, then walked slowly around the circumference of the room. As I expected, I found nothing that seemed like an altar, nor, indeed, anything else. I chose a spot opposite the door and went through the series of moon prayers I'd learned as a child. Then I meditated on the miracle that had happened to me under Revethora Vezvaishoroi.

Was it truly a miracle? I had been taught that miracles were vanishingly rare and it seemed presumptuous to insist that I had experienced one. On the other hand, it had *happened* and Ithalpherix had not torn me to shreds. Could it be anything *other* than a miracle that my gift had returned to me exactly when I most needed it?

So, assuming it was a miracle, what did it mean? Why had Ulis cared enough about my survival to intercede? It hardly seemed likely that I was somehow his favorite among all his prelates and worshipers. He did send me dreams, on rare occasions—without my dream, I did not think the murderers of Varenechibel IV would ever have been caught. Perhaps Ulis found me useful? It might be that not everyone could receive a dream like that, in which case I could serve some purpose—even multiple purposes—that made me worth Ulis's attention.

That seemed conceited beyond anything reasonable, but then I thought, *It was a miracle*. Miracles were not reasonable occurrences. Therefore, perhaps I *should* be unreasonable in interpreting it. Perhaps I should accept as a hypothesis that I was useful to Ulis in a greater capacity than that of Witness for the Dead.

The idea, the idea of Ulis's attention resting particularly on me, made me want to hide—under a rock or in a closet . . . or at the bottom of the deepest well in the north of the world, where I was not hidden at all.

Hiding from your calling was impossible. I'd already proved that. This was a gift to be grateful for, or a burden to be borne, depending on how I wanted to look at it, but the only thing I could do, either way, was to continue to do my duty—to follow my calling—as it revealed itself to me.

I said the moon prayers over again. They were prayers that asked for courage and resilience, the strength to keep going as one's fortunes waxed and waned. I suspected I would need all of that and more to get through the winter and then the emperor's judgment.

And then whatever might come after, but it was impossible to think that far ahead.

CLIMBING BACK UP the stairs of the Dachen Csaivanat was worse than going down. I had to stop twice to rest my burning leg muscles and aching joints, and by the time I reached the top I was nearly crawling from step to step. It was a different novice on duty; she politely ignored me while I panted for breath. She was surely used to people coming up out of the well in all kinds of physical distress; probably there had been people who did not make it out at all. I wondered how they retrieved the bodies, but not enough to start a conversation. When I felt I could manage, I bowed to the novice (who bowed in answer) and turned to Captain Olgarezh, who had waited all this time without complaint. I said, "May we buy you a cup of tea?"

He hesitated a moment, then said, "Yes, we would appreciate a cup of tea."

We left the wellhouse, though we went no farther than the teahouse next door, the Lady of Rivers, where I ordered steamed buns and a two-cup pot of orchor and felt astonishingly grateful to be sitting down.

We sat in silence until the tea came. I poured for both of us. It turned out Captain Olgarezh, too, liked honey in his tea.

He said, "Do you think it was successful, your pilgrimage?"

I said, "Define 'successful.'"

"We suppose that is part of the question, though certainly you need not tell us what you hoped for."

"That is fortunate, for we don't entirely know. Often one goes on pilgrimage hoping for clarity of mind, and we suppose we did find that, at least."

"That is good." He hesitated, visibly weighing his options, then said, "You do not sound entirely satisfied."

"If so, the fault lies with us," I said. "We know better than to hope for the thunderclap of revelation."

"But you *do* hope."

"Always."

The server arrived with our steamed buns, and we both retreated from that moment of more honesty than I had meant to give.

In the morning it was Othala Drinimar's study again. With the desk and a chair cleared, it was almost like a functional room again. Except that there was still only room for one person, and that person had only two places they could go: the desk or the fireplace. The rest of the room was still filled with looming stacks of paper.

Hadrinar had brought me a stepstool, so that I could reach the top of the stacks without standing on the untrustworthy-looking desk chair. I was standing on top of the stepstool, surrounded by paper on three sides, to start the stack that stood between me and the wall behind the desk. I had gone through only three pieces of paper (a two-page letter from Vernezar that had to be saved and one of the ubiquitous tram timetables) when I realized I could see the lintel of a door behind the stack.

"I think there's a closet," I said to Ostilin.

"A closet?" said Ostilin. She considered a moment. "Do you think it's as full of paper as this room is?"

"I think it horridly plausible," I said. "He would have started by putting his pieces of paper where they *weren't* in the way."

"That would make sense," Ostilin agreed.

She and Hadrinar and I worked hard the rest of that afternoon, but it was still going to be days—possibly weeks—before we had cleared enough of the room to open the closet door.

It would be a goal to strive toward, which was helpful when facing a task as seemingly endless as Othala Drinimar's study.

In the afternoon, Tomasaran appeared at the door of my suite. She looked from Captain Olgarezh to me and swept a formal curtsy.

"Let her in, please, Captain," I said, my face heating. "We trust her."

Captain Olgarezh stood aside. Tomasaran came in and I pointed her to the other chair.

"I wasn't expecting a visit," I said.

"I didn't intend to come," she said. "I need to stop clutching the skirts of your coat and be a Witness for the Dead on my own."

"But?"

"Will you come with me to Ulvanensee? Or ask Othala Chanavar to come here?"

"Why? You can't possibly be nervous of Anora."

"It's not *that,*" Tomasaran said. "But I think he is lonely. He misses you."

"Me? But—"

"Celehar."

"All right," I said. "I will write him a letter asking him to come visit me tomorrow. His junior prelates are more than capable of running Ulvanensee for an afternoon."

"Yes," said Tomasaran, and some tension seemed to drain out of her.

We talked of other things, mostly gossip from Tomasaran's boardinghouse, where Min Nadin had started quilting the top I'd seen her piecing, and Min Ozharin, whom I had not met, was being courted by one of the men from the municipal water works across the street.

She said as she got up to leave, "I will be back tomorrow afternoon with Othala Chanavar. Thank you."

"No," I said. "You are the one to be thanked. It would not have occurred to me . . ."

"No," said Tomasaran. "I think you think of yourself so little that you don't see how you affect other people. But you do, you know."

She collected her overcoat, said, "I'll see you tomorrow, Celehar," smiled at Captain Olgarezh, and left.

"I . . . I have to write a letter," I said and fled into my bedroom.

"That isn't much of a crime," said Anora.

"He has the box on the other side of the prince's box from the Parzhadeise box," I said. "It would take him literally a minute. And I don't think he'd have any scruples about it, either."

"I thought you said you didn't know anything about Amaleise politics," said Tomasaran.

"I've met him," I said. "I talked to him when I was trying to find out who murdered Arveneän Shelsin. I remember thinking that if he murdered someone, the body would never be found."

"This was almost as good," said Tomasaran. "It's not like the body itself gave me any clues at all."

"No," I agreed, "that part was nearly perfect. *If* it was Dach'osmer Cambeshar, of which we have no proof."

"But we can talk to him," said Tomasaran.

I hesitated.

"Celehar?"

"*You* can," I said, "but showing myself to Dach'osmer Cambeshar is probably only one step away from showing myself to the Clenverada."

"Unfortunately, that is true," said Anora. "The two houses are intermarried, and while the Clenverada have never *openly* supported Coralis Clunethar, it is not a secret that they find Prince Orchenis sometimes frustrating, as they found his father."

"And Dach'osmer Clunethar would be less so?" I said.

"Almost certainly," Anora said. "Coralis would never dream of asking awkward questions about the welfare of the Clenverada miners."

"Yes," I said.

"Quite," said Tomasaran. "I admit I was hoping I would not have to go alone."

"I am sorry," I said.

"It's not your fault," she said. "But what do I do if he refuses to see me? Which he very probably will."

"His curiosity may get the better of him," I said. "If not, see if you can get a note taken in."

"A note?"

"'It is about Ema Dravenezh' should be sufficient," I said.

"Will you at least wait for me? Here, I mean?"

"Yes, of course," I said. "I have no other plans."

She lifted her chin bravely, although her ears showed her reluctance, and Captain Olgarezh let her out.

I TOLD ANORA about my pilgrimage to the Dachen Csaivanat, and we were still talking about pilgrimages—ones we'd completed ourselves, ones our friends had done, ones we'd heard of—when Tomasaran returned. Captain Olgarezh bowed and stepped aside to let her in.

"Well, that was horrible," she said, sitting down.

"Did he not see you?" said Anora.

"Oh, he saw me. You were right about his curiosity, Celehar. But what a dreadful man."

"He was rude?" I said, surprised.

"Not at all," said Tomasaran, "but I felt the whole time like there was a snake in the room."

"Venomous and possibly angry," I said, remembering my own interview with Dach'osmer Cambeshar.

"Yes, exactly!" said Tomasaran. "And in any event, he said he didn't kill Ema Dravenezh, and he didn't know who did, so it doesn't get us any farther."

"Did he say anything else?"

She thought for a moment. "He said the murderer was a fool. No, wait a moment. He said that even if he'd wanted Mer Dravenezh dead, he wouldn't have been such a fool as to murder him in the middle of an opera."

"It seems that I was right to begin with," I said. "If Dach'osmer Cambeshar had murdered Mer Dravenezh, we would not have found his body."

"And without the body . . ." Tomasaran said.

"No one can witness for a missing person."

She shivered. "Do you think he's done that?"

"I don't know," I said. "But I wouldn't be surprised."

SHORTLY AFTER ANORA and Tomasaran left, Iäna arrived.

"Are you not rehearsing?" I said as he exchanged bows with Captain Olgarezh.

Iäna laughed and said, "I let them go early. It doesn't hurt every once in a great while, and I wanted to talk to you."

"What about?"

He shrugged, a little uncomfortably. "Can you tell me if there has been any progress on finding the murderer of Mer Dravenezh?"

"Not very much," I said and told him about Tomasaran's visit to Dach'osmer Cambeshar. "The theory came to nothing. But we still think it is something to do with the escape of Coralis Clunethar."

"I agree that the timing is too good. I assume you thought of Cambeshar because he has a box on the same tier."

"And very close by."

"The same can be said of the Vernezada. They, too, favor Coralis, and much more loudly."

"The Vernezada? Was someone in their box at the premiere?"

"Someone was," said Iäna. "I noticed because it was someone I didn't recognize."

"Someone you didn't *recognize*?"

"Well, not *only* someone I didn't recognize. The dowager marquise was there, as she always is. But there was a young man with her, whom I guessed by their interactions to be one of her grandsons or great-nephews. There are at least a dozen of them."

"So a young man of the Vernezada, not an opera devotee, attended the opera that night. Has he been back since?"

"No," said Iäna. "It's been the dowager marquise and Dach'osmin Vernezin, her unmarried daughter, every night since, as it had been every night previously. I hadn't thought of it as anything suspicious, but I hadn't thought of Mer Dravenezh's murder being connected to Coralis's escape, either."

"It is certainly a suggestive coincidence," I said. "Tomasaran will have to go talk to the Vernezada."

"You won't do it yourself?"

"I am not the Witness for Ema Dravenezh, and I'm not going to show myself to the Vernezada any more than I am to the Cambeshada. I wouldn't be involved at all if Tomasaran had not asked for my help. If I write her a letter, can I ask you to post it?"

"Far more than that," said Iäna, "especially if it will get this murder solved."

"Is it affecting the Opera's business?"

"Oh no. If anything, ticket sales are up. But I liked Mer Dravenezh, and all of my singers are twitchy."

I DRAGGED ONE of the chairs around to face the desk Captain Olgarezh and I had put against the wall and wrote to Tomasaran. The letter ended up being a bit lengthier than I had expected, since I had to explain both how I had gotten from the Cambeshada to the Vernezada and that what we wanted, more than any of the dowager marquise's observations, was the name of the young man who had been with her. If Iäna and I were right, she had failed to notice her

slow process. I knew Hadrinar, at least, would have preferred to simply shove or throw all the paper blocking the door out of the way, but the only good thing I could see, in the nightmare of paper that was Othala Drinimar's study, was that the paper *was* in orderly stacks. "Whatever's in there has waited fifty years," I said. "It can wait a little longer."

"Does your curiosity not drive you mad, othala?" said Hadrinar.

"Most of a prelate's life is waiting for one thing or another," I said. "You grow accustomed. And I would rather do this properly now and save ourselves the headache later. Especially if it turns out Othala Csenivar is *not* in the closet."

"But then where could he be?" said Hadrinar.

"I don't know, but any ulimeire is full of hiding places, and this one is very old."

They thought about that for a moment and both shuddered.

I WAS NOT expecting anyone that afternoon, but the clock had barely struck one when Tomasaran came in, with a curtsy to Captain Olgarezh, and said without other preamble, "Nathalis Vernezar has also disappeared. Or, at least, no one in the Vernezada compound will admit to knowing where he is."

"That is very interesting," I said. "Did the dowager marquise have anything useful to say?"

"Aside from giving us his name? She certainly didn't admit she knew he did it, so no, not really. Just platitudes."

"Which itself tells you something."

"I don't have enough to go to a judiciar, do I?" Her slightly plaintive tone said she knew the answer.

"No, you have a set of suspicious circumstances. A judiciar will probably agree that they are suspicious, but no more than that."

"So what do I do?"

"That depends."

"Depends? On what?"

"On whether we can get some help. Come on."

"You're leaving the Amal'theileian?" she said, surprised.

"I think that we don't have time for letters and visits and all of that. If Nathalis Vernezar hasn't left the city already, he must be planning to do so. And once he's left the city, the person I'm thinking of won't be able to help us."

Captain Olgarezh said, "It is your neck, othala," but made no further argument.

We went south on the Zulnicho line to the Ulzhav'ostro, then a short walk to the Sanctuary of Csaivo. Ulzhavar was engaged in a journeyman's examination, but nobody objected to our waiting for him. There were padded benches along the outer wall, under the windows looking out over the snowy gardens, so Tomasaran and I sat and talked about witnessing, Captain Olgarezh beside me watching the passing healers, until a clatter of boots announced Ulzhavar's arrival.

I introduced Captain Olgarezh. Ulzhavar bowed to him before turning to me and saying, "I hear that you are healed!"

"I seem to be," I said.

"That is fantastic news. Rasaltezhen says you think it is a miracle."

"That I was healed exactly when I needed to be? I don't think 'miracle' is too strong a word."

"I'm inclined to agree with you," said Ulzhavar. "You are blessed of Ulis in the formal sense of the word."

"I suppose I am," I said reluctantly. It sounded so conceited and self-aggrandizing when said out loud.

Ulzhavar raised his eyebrows at me. "There comes a point where modesty ceases to be of benefit, Celehar, and I think you have reached it."

My face heated. "I don't want . . ."

"I know," said Ulzhavar. "And you needn't proclaim it in the squares. If it makes you feel better, you can think of it as Ulis having a particular purpose for you."

That was an almost eerie echo of the conclusion I had come to myself. "That *is* better," I said. "I would rather have a purpose than not, even if I don't know what it is."

"I think it will become apparent to you. But this is not why you and Othalo Tomasaran wanted to see me. How can I help you?"

I explained about Nathalis Vernezar. "Do you think Lenet Athmaza can help us?"

"I don't know," said Ulzhavar, "but we can certainly go find out."

LENET ATHMAZA WAS a small, elderly elven man who specialized in name magic. He was a friend of Ulzhavar's and also, as it turned out, a loyal subject of Prince Orchenis. When Tomasaran explained *why* Nathalis Vernezar might be hiding, Lenet Athmaza said, "If he is in Amalo, I can find him."

"Could you do the same for Coralis Clunethar?" asked Tomasaran.

"I have tried," said Lenet Athmaza, "but either he is not in Amalo or he has a blocking charm, which is a sensible precaution for anybody who does not want to be found."

My ears twitched.

Lenet Athmaza raised his eyebrows at me and said mildly, "I can make you a blocking charm, if you would like."

"I think it might be a good idea," I said, "but let's find Nathalis Vernezar first."

Lenet Athmaza got out the equipment he had used to find Broset Sheveldar: a filigree silver ball on a chain and a big map of Amalo. He wrote the name NATHALIS VERNEZAR on a slip of paper, which he tucked into the silver ball. Then he leaned over the map of Amalo muttering to himself. He began swinging the silver ball in a wide circle over the map; slowly, the circle got smaller and smaller, until the ball stopped over Paravi.

"Paravi," said Lenet Athmaza.

"Paravi," said Ulzhavar thoughtfully.

"Certainly not where I would have thought to look for him," I said.

"The city's too big," said Ulzhavar. "There are too many places a person can go. Which is why one seeks out alternative methods of looking."

"Yes," I said. "I suppose the question is whether we have enough to persuade Subpraeceptor Azhanharad to accompany us."

"Subpraeceptor Azhanharad?" said Tomasaran. "But why . . . ?"

"Finding Nathalis Vernezar is one thing," I said. "But we have no authority to apprehend him and nowhere to put him if we did. We need the Vigilant Brotherhood to keep him from just disappearing again."

"But *do* we have enough for the Vigilant Brotherhood?" said Tomasaran. "We still don't have anything that couldn't just be a coincidence."

"I think with such a *string* of coincidences, we might be able to persuade Azhanharad at least that there are some questions Osmer Vernezar needs to answer. That might be enough to get him to come with us."

"All we can do is try," said Ulzhavar.

WE MADE AN odd group—two prelates of Ulis, a cleric of Csaivo, a maza, and a guard captain—and at first the elven novices at the doors of the Chapterhouse wanted neither to let us in nor to go tell Azhanharad we wished to speak to him. Finally, irritably, Ulzhavar said, "We are the Master of the Mortuary, and we need to speak to Subpraeceptor Azhanharad *urgently*."

The novices blanched, and one said, "We will go fetch him."

"That should not have been necessary," Ulzhavar grumbled.

"Thank you for doing it," I said. "There was clearly no other way to budge them."

"It's bad manners," Ulzhavar said. "Any novice I caught behaving like that at the Sanctuary would wish I hadn't."

"Possibly," Lenet Athmaza said with a glance at Captain Olgarezh, "that is the difference between a house of Csaivo and a house of Anmura."

Captain Olgarezh shook his head, but said nothing.

Subpraeceptor Azhanharad, when he appeared, was scowling, but he said at once, "Our office is not large enough for six people, but please come with us and we will find a discussion room."

We followed him into the ancient bulk of the Chapterhouse, through the towering atrium, and into a long hallway with doors at intervals on either side. The first few doors were closed, but Azhanharad stopped at the first open one and beckoned us inside.

The room contained a table and a number of chairs, with a mural on the wall of Edrevenivar the Conqueror crossing the Istandaärtha. I realized that it was to a room like this that Balaro and Zinián and I had been brought on the night the revethavar was destroyed. I had noticed almost nothing of my surroundings at the time. It was only in retrospect and with the prompting of this similar room that I could piece that room together.

We sat down, and Azhanharad said, "Now, Dach'othala Ulzhavar, how can we help you?"

Ulzhavar looked at me. I looked at Tomasaran, who nodded. It took her a moment to assemble her thoughts, but she then explained the situation quite lucidly.

When she was finished, Azhanharad said, "You have no evidence against this boy."

"No," Tomasaran said. "Nothing but suggestive coincidences and the ability to find him, which is more than we have for any of the other people who have so conveniently disappeared since Coralis Clunethar escaped."

Azhanharad was visibly conflicted, his ears lowering. Finally he said, "We can make arrests on the evidence of a Witness for the Dead, but we cannot make arrests on no evidence at all, which is currently what you have."

"We were afraid you would say that," said Tomasaran.

"I don't know what kind of evidence we think we're going to get," said Ulzhavar.

"A confession is not impossible," I said. "People often panic when faced with a Witness for the Dead."

"And I suppose with *two* of you . . ." said Ulzhavar.

Lenet Athmaza, who had watched the whole scene with bright attention, said, "Being *found* is often very distressing to people who are trying to hide."

"That's true, too," said Ulzhavar. "But if he confesses, what then?"

"Then Tomasaran goes to the Paravi watchhouse to introduce herself to the subpraeceptor, while the rest of us stay to make sure Osmer Vernezar doesn't go anywhere."

"By force?" Ulzhavar said, alarmed.

"No," I said. "Force is not in my remit as a Witness for the Dead. If it would take force, I have to let him go."

"I don't," said Captain Olgarezh.

Considerably startled, both that he had spoken and that

he had abrogated formality, I turned to look at him where he was standing against the wall.

"I *am* a captain of the Principate Guard," he said. "If there is proof of his guilt, if I choose to use force to stop this boy from leaving, I am doing my duty. And, in fact, I would have some very pointed questions to answer if I let him go."

"That's true," said Ulzhavar. He laughed suddenly. "Do we even need to be here at all, Captain Olgarezh? Could you not arrest him?"

"I also need evidence," Captain Olgarezh said apologetically. "And I'd just end up asking the Brotherhood to hold him anyway."

"Can you give us a letter of introduction to the Paravi subpraeceptor?" I asked Azhanharad. "So he doesn't think we're just a band of lunatics."

Azhanharad snorted, but refrained from saying what he was thinking.

"Or at least," said Ulzhavar, "that we aren't willfully wasting his time."

"No, we believe that you are acting in good faith," said Azhanharad. "But do *us* the favor of not approaching Subpraeceptor Tholanezh until you have something he can act on."

"Of course," said Tomasaran.

"Then we can in good conscience write a letter for you," said Azhanharad. "Please wait here." He strode briskly out of the room.

Azhanharad came back within ten minutes, holding a letter sealed with the sigil of the Vigilant Brotherhood. He gave the letter to Tomasaran, who put it in her inner coat pocket. She said, "We appreciate your help."

"We must abide by the strictures of our calling," said Azhanharad. "But we trust Othala Celehar."

THE LONG TRAM ride out to Paravi was mostly silent, each of us sunk in our own thoughts. When we disembarked from the tram, Lenet Athmaza took the lead; the rest of us stuck close.

It did not take as long as the other such expedition I had been on with Lenet Athmaza, for Paravi was a newer district and was laid out on a more open plan than Penchelivor. Most houses we passed had gardens, and the signs on the shops were bright with gilt.

It was no more than half an hour of bitterly cold walking before Lenet Athmaza stopped before an elegant hotel called the Golden Fox and said, "He's in there."

"Now what?" said Ulzhavar.

I said, "Our calling forbids ruses and lies. Tomasaran asks for him at the front desk."

"Your calling is a harsh one," said Ulzhavar.

Inside, the Golden Fox had a floor of little marble squares, each a subtly different color, and wall hangings depicting the *Hunt of the Golden Fox*, which was a long poem an Amaleise courtier had written fifteen hundred years ago. The hangings were very modern in style and very new.

The elven man at the front desk, who was also very modern in style, watched our approach with raised eyebrows. Tomasaran said stoutly, "We are Velhiro Tomasaran, a Witness for the Dead, and we need to speak to Nathalis Vernezar about the murder of Ema Dravenezh."

The desk clerk considered his answer, looking from Tomasaran to Ulzhavar to Lenet Athmaza to Captain Olgarezh to me. Then he gestured to the nearest bellhop, an elven boy of about fifteen, and said, "Go find out if Osmer Vernezar is receiving guests."

The boy disappeared into the servants' corridor behind the desk.

We waited.

The wait felt endless, but it was probably no more than fifteen minutes before we heard someone on the main staircase and a young elven man came into the atrium. The family resemblance to Dach'othala Vernezar was quite strong, the same long nose and close-set eyes, but the boy wore his hair far more elaborately than Dach'othala Vernezar did, and he was wearing a gaudy purple coat that looked nothing like a prelate's coat of office.

He said, "We are Nathalis Vernezar. We understand you wish to speak to us?"

It was bravado, with fear showing through the cracks. If he had not been a murderer, I might have liked him for it.

"We are Velhiro Tomasaran," Tomasaran said. "We are the Witness for Ema Dravenezh and need to ask you about the night of his death." She and Ulzhavar and Captain Olgarezh herded Osmer Vernezar gently into a side parlor; Lenet Athmaza and I followed. There was no need to have this conversation in the lobby.

"We . . . we do not know who that is."

"The man who was murdered during the premiere of *The Dream of the Empress Corivero*. We know that you were there that night."

He hesitated, clearly recognizing the folly of pretending he didn't know a man had been murdered, but not sure what it would be safe to admit. He tried a different tack: "How did you find us?"

"Name magic," said Lenet Athmaza.

Osmer Vernezar's eyes widened, and he said, "You must wish to speak to us very much."

"We do," said Tomasaran, and then she had the sense to simply shut her mouth and make Osmer Vernezar figure out what to say next.

He looked from face to face, getting more nervous with

each passing second, his ears sinking lower and lower, and finally he blurted out, "We did not do it!"

Tomasaran and I looked at each other. "Didn't do what?" said Tomasaran.

"Kill Ema Dravenezh! Isn't that why you've gone to all this trouble to find us? You think we did it!"

"We could also ask questions," said Ulzhavar, "about why you're in a hotel all the way out here in Paravi."

Osmer Vernezar quivered like a plucked string. "What do you mean by that?"

Ulzhavar's eyebrows went up slowly. "What do you think we mean?"

"We do not know!" But it took no special powers of discernment to see that he was lying.

There was a fraught pause before Ulzhavar said, "Then why are you staying at the Golden Fox?"

The question needed only a simple lie, but Osmer Vernezar was too rattled to think of one. The silence stretched and stretched, and finally Ulzhavar murmured, "That is what we thought."

"You can prove nothing!" Osmer Vernezar said desperately.

"We haven't really begun to try," said Tomasaran. "Or do you imagine that we will not find *anyone* who will talk to us?"

His ear twitch said there was someone who would. "We swear we did not kill him!"

"If you did not," said Tomasaran, "then who did?"

Osmer Vernezar hesitated, then thought of someone. "Mithala . . . Mithala Plevar!"

"Plevar?" Tomasaran said.

"It has to be Plevar!" said Osmer Vernezar. "Killing Ema was *his* idea!"

There was a pause while we all noted that Osmer Vernezar had called Mer Dravenezh by his given name—also that there had been a plan to kill him, not merely a sudden whim.

"So you knew Mer Dravenezh," Tomasaran said. "Quite well."

"No, not at all!" Osmer Vernezar said frantically. "It was a slip of the tongue!"

"Yes, it was," said Ulzhavar. "But not one you would make with the name of a person you did not know. How did you know Mer Dravenezh?"

"We didn't! We have . . . we have read much about him in the newspapers while we have been in Paravi."

"Osmer Vernezar," said Tomasaran, "you must know that explanation is nonsense."

"All right," Osmer Vernezar said. "We knew him because of the Opera."

"The Vermilion Opera?" I said.

"Parzhadel's box is next to our grandmother's. We naturally spoke to Mer Dravenezh a good deal." Relief was as audible in his voice as it was visible on his face that he had found a good lie.

I said, "But Mer Pel-Thenhior did not recognize you."

"What?" said Osmer Vernezar.

"He knows everyone who attends the Opera regularly, and he had never seen you before the night Mer Dravenezh was killed."

"So it can't be that," Ulzhavar said. "Would you like to try again?"

"But," said Osmer Vernezar, though he could find nothing to follow it.

"Osmer Vernezar," Tomasaran said. "This is pointless."

"But we cannot . . . we did not kill him! We swear we did not kill him!"

"What will you swear by?" I said. I was mostly curious to see how far he would go, but the question took him aback almost far enough to literally stagger him. Therefore, I pushed: "Will you swear by Ulis in his aspect as the moon, which sees the truth behind all lies?"

He opened his mouth, but no sound came out.

"You need not swear by Ulis, though. You can always swear by Anmura in his aspect as the sun, which burns away falsehood to reveal truth. Or you can swear by Cstheio. Yes, perhaps that would be best. Swear by Cstheio that you did not kill Ema Dravenezh, and perhaps we will believe you." We wouldn't, but we would know we couldn't get the truth out of him.

Osmer Vernezar tried to speak, but either his voice failed him or he could simply find no words.

"Well, Osmer Vernezar?" said Tomasaran.

He tried again, but the words would not come. I saw the brightness of tears in his eyes before he turned away from us and knew he was crying for himself.

There was a long silence while Osmer Vernezar fought for self-control. Finally, he said, still facing away from us, "What happens if we admit . . . ?"

"You know that as well as we do," said Tomasaran. "The Vigilant Brotherhood arrest you. You are assigned a judicial Witness, who will find the truth of your actions. They and we will make depositions, and a judiciar will decide the case. If he finds that you did kill Mer Dravenezh, you will go to the reveth-atha. If he finds that you did not, you will be released."

"And if we do not admit that we . . . that we did it?"

"We are the Witness for Ema Dravenezh," Tomasaran said. "We will find the truth and the Vigilant Brotherhood will arrest you anyway, for we are afraid it is quite clear that you are the murderer."

"You have no proof," Osmer Vernezar said, but he said it feebly.

"We have your own actions," said Tomasaran. "And we

think if we find this Mithala Plevar, we will very shortly have more."

"It really was Plevar's idea," said Osmer Vernezar.

"Why?" said Tomasaran. "Why murder Mer Dravenezh?"

And Osmer Vernezar sighed and said, "Coralis wanted him dead."

AFTER THAT, THERE was no challenge in getting the story out of him, except the difficulty of getting the events sorted into some sort of logical order. To begin with, Osmer Vernezar had been part of the conspiracy to free Coralis Clunethar, along with Tura Olora, Ema Dravenezh, Mithala Plevar, and several other people whom Osmer Vernezar refused to name. "High-ranking people," he said proudly.

"Rich people," Ulzhavar said dourly.

"It was . . ." He caught himself at the last second. "It was a high-ranking person whose plan got Coralis out." He seemed to think that proved something, although I wasn't sure what.

Once they had been successful in freeing him, Coralis Clunethar naturally started planning to raise his banner in the spring. And while the rest of them threw themselves with enthusiasm into the preparations, Ema Dravenezh wanted no part of it. "He said that Orchenis had no right to imprison Coralis, but that Coralis had no right to rebel against Orchenis. He didn't make any sense."

They all tried to talk him down, but he would not be swayed. Tura Olora swore that he could persuade Mer Dravenezh to come back, and Coralis said he could try. But then Mer Olora committed suicide, and Coralis and the high-ranking person started arguing about Mer Dravenezh, whether it was better to leave him alone and trust that he would not betray them, since in betraying them he betrayed himself, or to kill him and thus make sure of his silence. They argued and argued and finally one evening when the high-ranking person was not there, Coralis said, just as he was bidding them good night, that he would sleep much easier if he knew that Mer Dravenezh would be silent.

And Osmer Vernezar and Mer Plevar and two or three others went to the Canalman's Dog in the Zheimela, where they could get both metheglin and a cheap private room, and they talked about how to make Mer Dravenezh be silent. The plan they eventually settled on was almost stunning in its simplicity: Osmer Vernezar would attend the opera with his grandmother, wait for a suitable moment when everyone's attention was on the stage, go shove a dagger into Mer Dravenezh's back, and return to his grandmother's box as if nothing had happened.

"Some god must have been smiling on you that that plan worked at all," said Ulzhavar. "By rights your dagger should have hit a rib and drenched you in blood and given Mer Dravenezh time to scream."

Osmer Vernezar shrugged. It *had* worked, he said, but it had made Dach'osmer—the high-ranking person furious. He said it would do nothing but draw attention to them and told Osmer Vernezar and the others involved that they had best go hide until he told them it was safe to come back.

"It would never have been safe," Tomasaran said, and I was glad that she had understood what I had tried to tell her about the duty of the Witness to the dead person they witnessed for.

"In the spring, when Coralis raises his banner, everything will change," said Osmer Vernezar.

Tomasaran and I exchanged a look. Osmer Vernezar was fooling himself if he thought he would still be alive by then, having confessed to both murder and treason.

"We had best go find Subpraeceptor Tholanezh," said

Tomasaran. She gave me an urgent come-along jerk of her head, and I followed her out into the lobby.

"How do I find the watchhouse?" she said.

"Ask the desk clerk," I said. "He'll know."

"Oh, of course." She went up to the desk; I went back into the side parlor, where Ulzhavar and Captain Olgarezh were blocking Osmer Vernezar from the door.

Lenet Athmaza, from the seat he had taken by the fireplace, said, "Come sit down, osmer. Be comfortable while you can."

Osmer Vernezar hesitated, looking from Olgarezh to Ulzhavar, clearly weighing his chances.

Lenet Athmaza said patiently, "If you run, do not doubt that we will find you."

Osmer Vernezar sat down and put his head in his hands, and he was still sitting there, not having moved, when the Vigilant Brotherhood came in to arrest him.

We all spent the rest of the day making depositions in the Paravi Chapterhouse. As we were leaving, Lenet Athmaza said to me, "I did mean it. If you wish a blocking charm, I would be happy to make one for you."

"I . . . that is, yes, I do. Can you do it now?"

"Easily."

Captain Olgarezh and I went with him back to his tidy flat, where he said, "The charm requires a sacrifice."

"A sacrifice?"

"A small one. In both senses of the word. Something small that you value, but not excessively. Many people have me use a piece of jewelry."

I thought for a moment. My earrings were brass, and I could not truthfully say I valued them. But . . . "Will a pilgrimage token do?"

"Mmm," said Lenet Athmaza. "Is there one you especially value?"

I thought through my little collection. I valued Tedoro's token, but that was because I carried it in memory of her murder. It was completely inappropriate for this purpose. Of the others . . .

I said, "I will never willingly make the pilgrimage to the Hill of Werewolves again, and I value this token as a proof that I survived doing it once. Is that acceptable?"

Lenet Athmaza held out his hand, and I gave him the token, a white glazed square with Ulis's sigil painted on it. He nodded and looked at me with bright, unmalicious attention. "And Thara Celehar is your true name?"

"It is," I said.

"This will not take long," he said. He left the room. I sat and looked at the maps of Amalo, to all scales and with widely varying degrees of detail, that hung on the walls. Some of them were obviously very old, some glossily new, and if there was a method behind their placement on the walls, I could not discern it. Captain Olgarezh stood with his back against the outer door; as usual, his face revealed nothing of his thoughts.

As he had promised, Lenet Athmaza was back quickly. "This will keep you hidden from name magic. To a lesser extent, it will hide you from anyone looking for you, with magic or without. But it will only hide you while you are wearing it."

"I understand," I said.

It was a locket, the cheap kind they sold ten for five zashan in the Silkmarket, strung on a narrow piece of black ribbon. There was nothing in any way remarkable about it. Lenet Athmaza said, "If you want to find something to put in it, so that people you know do not wonder why you are wearing an empty locket, that will not disturb the charm."

to play cards with me. We started with pakh'palar, but I proved hopelessly bad at it, so we switched to vedmennet, a game popular among the soldiers in the Anmur'theileian. It was simpler than pakh'palar and did not require players to guess whether the other players were telling the truth, and we played endless rounds. Captain Olgarezh and I celebrated Winternight—which was also now the Emperor's Birthday—with Iäna and his kelkinora at the Torivontaram, where they cleared all the tables out of the middle of the room and danced all night. Captain Olgarezh observed, but could not be persuaded to dance by any of the women.

Sometime well after midnight, he leaned over to me and said, "Will you come outside with us for a moment?"

"Outside?" I said.

"Just for a moment."

It seemed little enough to ask.

We got our coats and stepped outside. No one noticed us go.

There was a single street lamp outside the Torivontaram. By its light I could see snow falling in slow, fat flakes.

Captain Olgarezh stood for a moment looking down at me, his expression unreadable. Then he said, "We wished to thank you."

"To thank us? Surely the shoe is on the other foot."

"No," he said decidedly. "We have guarded other people and been treated like a lamppost. You have been courteous and thoughtful, and we appreciate it."

"But then why did you take the risk of agreeing to guard us?"

"We had a feeling about you," said Captain Olgarezh. "And we were right." He smiled at me.

I felt an upsurge of something like panic. "We'd better get back inside."

He reached out and gently brushed the snow off my hair.

"Yes, we'd better."

No one noticed us come back in. And the winter went on.

Captain Olgarezh politely but firmly kept the newspapermen out, which was a tremendous relief. They all wanted to ask questions about the emperor that I couldn't—or shouldn't—answer.

Iäna continued to bring me my post, which regularly contained letters from Anora, Chonhadrin, and Csathamar; I just as regularly wrote letters in reply. Anora wrote to me about Ulvanensee and politics in the Ulistheileian; Chonhadrin wrote to me about flying; Csathamar wrote to me about court gossip, and sometimes more important things.

One afternoon, the knock on the door proved to be for Captain Olgarezh: a nervous elven guardsman, who tugged Captain Olgarezh as far as the doorway and proceeded to whisper intently for a long time, while Captain Olgarezh's eyebrows rose higher and higher. Finally, Captain Olgarezh said, "Yes, I can do that." Then he and the guardsman came back into the antechamber, and Captain Olgarezh said to me, "We have been asked to take on a particular task this afternoon. We will hopefully not be gone long, but we will not leave you unguarded. This is Armsman Valomezh, who will stay with you."

"Good afternoon, othala," Armsman Valomezh said.

"Good afternoon," I said. "We are afraid you will find us a very boring duty."

"That's really all right," Armsman Valomezh said earnestly. "We will be happy to guard you against nothing."

"Good," said Captain Olgarezh. He nodded to me—I thought in token that he would come back—and left.

Armsman Valomezh said, "May we move this chair, othala?"

"Of course," I said.

Armsman Valomezh moved the chair so that it was blocking the doorway, and then sat down, his sword across his knees. He did not look like he wanted conversation; I said, "We will be in the bedroom, writing letters."

"That is very good, othala," said Armsman Valomezh, sounding relieved.

I went into the bedroom, where I did not write letters. I read a Barizheise adventure novel instead.

It was dark outside, almost time for Armsman Ingavar's shift to start, before Captain Olgarezh returned. I heard his voice in the antechamber and came out just as he was dismissing Armsman Valomezh with "Good night, and thanks."

"Good night, Captain," Armsman Valomezh said, gave me a nervous bob of the head, and strode away.

"Can you tell us where you were?" I said.

Captain Olgarezh gave me a thoughtful look. "We were not sworn to secrecy, and the news will be everywhere tomorrow. So. We were capturing Coralis Clunethar."

The capture of Coralis Clunethar was in all three newspapers, with varying degrees of shock and horror at the revelation that he had been in Amalo all this time. Captain Olgarezh was interviewed and very politely said nothing of use. Coralis Clunethar was *not* interviewed. He was in the Ancorlin, and the rumors said Prince Orchenis was allowing him no visitors.

The newspapers were also full of speculations about what Prince Orchenis was going to *do* with Dach'osmer Clunethar, who was currently both his heir and a traitor to his reign. He had tried relegation *last* time, and there was considerable doubt about whether he would try it again. No one liked to put the word "execution" in print, but it was almost the only option Prince Orchenis had left, Dach'osmer Clunethar having taken unfair advantage of every inch of clemency given him.

A couple of days after the capture of Dach'osmer Clunethar, Iäna brought me a fat letter from Csathamar that turned out to be mostly a copy of a letter he had received from Witness Parmorin, who wrote:

It took many hours of striving with Osmer Vernezar before he would admit even to things he had already confessed. He seemed to think that if he said nothing to me, his case could not go to the judiciar, which was a theory quite lovely in its wrongness but maddeningly difficult to dissuade him of.

Finally, I gambled a little and said, "Nathalis."

My use of his given name at least attracted his attention.

WITNESS: *You have already confessed to murder. We have depositions from a maza, a guard captain, two Witnesses for the Dead, and the Master of the Mortuary. Nothing you do or don't say to me now will change that.*
NATHALIS VERNEZAR: *Then why should I talk to you?*
W: *I can promise nothing, but if you cooperate with me, it may incline the judiciar to be merciful.*
NV: *You mean I wouldn't be executed?*
W: *Maybe. But it is better odds than if you persist in saying nothing.*

It was the right key to use on that particular lock. He went from sullen silence to anxious volubility, racking his brain for more details to give me, naming his friends without the least hesitation.

I let him talk and talk, and finally when the well seemed to be running dry, I asked him, "Where is Coralis?"

He froze.

I waited.

The silence stretched and stretched. Tears of panic and self-pity started to his eyes, but he had walked so far into the trap that he could not get out again.

NV: *I want a promise.*
W: *I can't make you any promises. I am a Witness, not a judiciar.*
NV: *But you're the one that tells the story. I want a promise that you'll tell them I helped.*
W: *I can promise that. I will tell them that you have given me all the information you have . . . if it's true.*
NV: *Dach'osmer Cambeshar is hiding him.*
W: *Dach'osmer Nedeva Cambeshar?*
NV: *Yes, in his flat. Cambeshar's servants are much too frightened of him to talk.*
W: *How long . . . ?*
NV: *Oh, from the beginning. It was the plan.*

And it was, I suppose, a particularly daring plan, depending on sheer audacity to succeed. Cambeshar has always had a reputation for enjoying deep play, and one cannot get significantly deeper than this.

I left Nathalis Vernezar with the injunction to think carefully through everything he had told me in order to make sure he had left nothing out, and returned from the Ancorlin, where he is being held, to the Judiciary. There I was fortunate, in that Judiciar Treshabar was free and could simultaneously take my deposition and make the correct arrangements for the information to reach Prince Orchenis. I only returned to my own office about ten minutes ahead of the summons to the Barlevar Courtyard, where a small detachment of the Principate Guard were getting ready to go knock on Dach'osmer Cambeshar's door.

Their captain was a part-goblin Ezheise man I did not know, tall and handsome except for the scar slashing across his face. He looked at me from under his eyebrows and said, "You're the Witness?"

WITNESS: *Yes.*
CAPTAIN: *I should tell you that I dislike having you along. I understand the legal necessity, but I don't like having an unarmed person in the middle of something this tricky, and I will be grateful if you stay by me and do not wander off somewhere on your own.*
W: *I promise. No wandering.*
C: *Good. I am Captain Hanu Olgarezh.*
W: *Zhodeän Parmorin. Have you been in the Principate Guard long?*
C: *No, not even a season.*

And he might have gone on, but his lieutenant came up to him with a question, and Captain Olgarezh visibly forgot about me.

It was not much longer before we were ready to go. Captain Olgarezh divided his small detachment even further, sending his lieutenant and two men off with instructions to find the back of Dach'osmer Cambeshar's building. That left the captain, two guardsmen, and me to start walking toward the front of Dach'osmer Cambeshar's building. Fortunately I had my good winter boots on.

It was not a long walk. I stayed close to the captain, as instructed, and we talked about opera, of all things.

At Dach'osmer Cambeshar's building, the elven gatekeeper made no protest about letting us in. Captain Olgarezh got the page boy to take us to Dach'osmer Cambeshar's flat.

I had been in this block of flats before, witnessing in an unrelated matter, so I was expecting the soft luxury of the carpets and the elegance of the wallpaper. When we reached Dach'osmer Cambeshar's door, Captain Olgarezh told the boy to go, which he did with alacrity.

Captain Olgarezh knocked on the door, a reasonable, polite knock that had nothing to do with the Principate Guard.

The door was opened by a servant in the Cambeshada livery, whose face transfigured from annoyed to aghast in barely a second.

CAPTAIN: *Good afternoon. We are Captain Hanu Olgarezh of the Athamareise Principate Guard. We are looking for Dach'osmer Coralis Clunethar.*
SERVANT: *For . . .*
CAPTAIN: *Dach'osmer Coralis Clunethar. We have reason to believe he's here.*
SERVANT: *We . . .*

The servant seemed to be simply unable to find any useful or relevant words, and he gave way when Captain Olgarezh started forward. The guardsmen and I followed close behind.

I hadn't asked Captain Olgarezh if he had a plan, and I wasn't sure if he did. If he did, it consisted of opening every door he came to and looking in. We found the house-

keeper that way, and two more servants. We didn't find Dach'osmer Cambeshar, because he found us.

NEDEVA CAMBESHAR: *What is the meaning of this?*
CAPTAIN: *Dach'osmer Nedeva Cambeshar?*
NC: *Yes.*
C: *We are Captain Hanu Olgarezh of the Athamareise Principate Guard. We seek Dach'osmer Coralis Clunethar.*
NC: *You won't find him here.*
C: *We're under orders to look.*
NC: *We will speak to Prince Orchenis.*
C: *You have every reason to do so, but we must search all the same.*
NC: *Very well. But you will not find him.*
C: *Perhaps not.*

Captain Olgarezh continued his search. He had only opened two more doors before there was a great commotion from the back of the flat, and the two guardsmen he had sent to find the back entrance of the building emerged, one on either side and each gripping an arm of a man with the unmistakable Clunethadeise nose. Captain Olgarezh's lieutenant brought up the rear.

"Dach'osmer Coralis Clunethar?" said Captain Olgarezh with the same relentless politeness he had shown throughout.

Coralis Clunethar swore at him.

IT WAS INTERESTING, to see Captain Olgarezh from another person's perspective. It did nothing to quiet the strange, foolish feeling I had for him, nor to lessen the hope that behind his formality, he might harbor a similar feeling for me.

Thou art ridiculous, Celehar, I told myself. Pining after my own guard, like the ingenue in the stupider sort of opera. But I could not deny—at least, not to myself—that Captain Olgarezh lit something inside me that had been cold ashes since Evru's death, something that I had not expected would ever kindle into life again.

So it might be ridiculous, but I hoped all the same.

A FEW DAYS LATER, Tomasaran appeared an hour after noon and said, "They're executing Nathalis Vernezar tomorrow."

"The judiciar was not swayed by his help in finding Coralis Clunethar?"

"No," she said. "He said treason is treason."

"You sound dissatisfied."

"No," she said, although not with confidence. "That is, I agree, treason is treason. But on the other hand, he *did* help."

"It was a second betrayal," I said.

"How do you mean?"

"First he betrayed his prince—and the emperor behind him—by plotting with Dach'osmer Clunethar. Then, after committing a murder, he turned around on his own shadow and betrayed Dach'osmer Clunethar and everyone else involved in the hopes of saving his own head. Whether it helped or not is immaterial."

"You are harsh," Tomasaran said, as she had said to me before.

"Treason is treason," I said, and we were both silent for a moment.

"Do you feel you must go to the execution?" I said.

She made a frustrated gesture. "No, I don't, but yet I do."

"If it was my witnessing, I would go. Witness that the murderer is . . ."

"Yes," said Tomasaran. "It feels like I'm not *done* yet."

I knew the feeling she meant, and I was glad of this sign that she had a true calling to be a Witness. "Do you want me to go with you?" I did her the courtesy of making it a question even though we both knew the answer.

"Yes," said Tomasaran.

"You went with me to see Osmin Tativin executed," I said. "It's only fair." I looked at Captain Olgarezh. "We hope you do not mind witnessing an execution."

"We have witnessed far worse," he said. "And, yes, if you are determined to go, we will not impede you."

THE NEXT DAY, just before I needed to leave, Hadrinar and Ostilin and I finally succeeded in clearing enough of the floor that the closet could be opened.

"Do you think there's really a body in there, like Othala Shalicar says?" asked Ostilin.

"Honestly, I have no idea," I said. "Let's find out."

The door was locked.

We looked at each other in no little dismay.

"Maybe the key is in one of the desk drawers," Ostilin suggested.

"Maybe," I said, but when Hadrinar, who was closest, tried to open the drawers, we discovered that the desk was also locked.

"If the keys are in this room, we will never find them," said Hadrinar.

"Oh, we'll find them," I said. "It will just take a very long time. And before we make that assumption, are there other places in Ulnemenee that keys might be hidden?"

"Any number of places," said Ostilin.

"We can ask Othala Shalicar," said Hadrinar, and since I really did need to go, we left it there, with their promise to ask Shalicar about keys and also to look themselves everywhere they could think of.

I made it back to my rooms with time to wash my hands and face before Tomasaran showed up, which she did an hour before noon.

"Shall we go? We'll get there before noon if we start walking now."

"Yes," I said.

We walked quickly and reached the plaza in front of the Ulistheileian with several minutes to spare. The wind was bitterly cold, but the sky above us was a brilliant blue. The plaza was crowded, but not as jammed as it had been for Osmin Tativin, and we found a good vantage point without too much trouble.

"I don't know why we're bothering," said Tomasaran. "It's not like I *want* to watch."

"It seems illogical," I said, "but it's much worse if you can't see what's happening."

"Really?"

"*Much* worse," I said.

"Yes," said Captain Olgarezh.

None of us purchased an execution pamphlet.

When they brought him out, Nathalis Vernezar was obviously determined to maintain his dignity, even though he was almost too scared to be able to walk. The crowd's volume increased, but they were not howling for his blood; apparently, Prince Orchenis had managed to hold back the fact that Osmer Vernezar was a traitor as well as a murderer—and a turncoat as well as a traitor. I had seen executions in Lohaiso that had almost become frenzies: a band of elven men who had gang-raped and murdered three prostitutes before they were caught. The crowd had nearly succeeded in taking matters into their own hands, and I had no doubt they would have torn those men apart. No one was feeling that kind of rage toward Nathalis Vernezar, and that could only be because no one knew the full extent of what he had done.

Except the three of us.

Tomasaran said, "Why did the judiciars not sentence him as a traitor as well as a murderer?"

"Does it really matter?" I said. "The end result is the same."

"Yes, but it seems dishonest."

"I think," I started, but then the Brothers dragged Osmer Vernezar up the steps to the dais, and I lost the thread of what I was saying.

Tomasaran, Captain Olgarezh, and I watched in silence as Osmer Vernezar knelt in front of the reveth-atha and after a second's worth of hesitation, laid his neck across the stock. The executioner did not wait, but immediately dropped the top half of the stock into place, and the second after that the blade sliced down, and the execution was done.

We walked to the zhoän where Tomasaran and I had eaten the last time we watched an execution. We ate in silence until she said, "But he *was* a traitor. He was sure he'd be pardoned when Coralis had the throne."

"He was. I think Prince Orchenis is trying to keep from having to pass judgment on Dach'osmer Clunethar. After all, if Osmer Vernezar is a traitor, he's far from the only one."

"You don't think he'll let Coralis get *away* with it!"

"Not without some penalty. But the sentence for treason is death, and Prince Orchenis seems somewhat reluctant to kill his cousin."

"Dach'osmer Clunethar's whole faction will say it is murder," Captain Olgarezh said.

"Oh certainly," I said. "It will look bad to people who want it to. And others as well."

"But Coralis is a traitor."

"Yes, and not executing him will look bad to a different faction. Prince Orchenis is stuck."

Tomasaran sighed. "I wish it were easier simply to do the right thing."

"First you have to have consensus on what the right thing is," I said, thinking of Ithalpherix.

"That's what I mean," said Tomasaran.

BOTH JUNIOR PRELATES were waiting for me in the morning. "We found the key! Well—we found several keys," said Ostilin. "But we are sure one of them must be the right one."

"But we waited for you," said Hadrinar. "It is your task for the Archprelate. You should be the one to open the closet."

"Thank you," I said, absurdly touched, and followed them to the study.

The third key matched the lock. It was stiff, but I was finally able to twist it over and open the door.

Like the room, the closet was full of paper, which came out in a small avalanche. I was about to say we should have expected as much when Ostilin grabbed my arm and said, "Othala Celehar, *look*!" I looked the direction she was pointing, toward the floor, and saw what she had seen: the toes of two boots like boulders in the drifted paper.

Shalicar was right after all.

"What do we do?" said Hadrinar.

"We exhume him from all this paper and then—assuming this *is* Othala Csenivar—we write to the Csenivada and ask them what they would like done with the body."

"Surely we must also tell the Ulistheileian," said Ostilin.

"Yes. *Someone* will want to know that Othala Csenivar has been found. Although I'm afraid this also means telling the Ulistheileian that Othala Drinimar was a murderer, which will not be a welcome piece of information."

"At least Osmer Drinimar is dead," said Hadrinar.

"And we need not entertain the city with the prosecution of a Ulineise prelate for murder? True enough."

"We have to tell Othala Shalicar," said Ostilin.

"Also true," I said. "If you two will start unburying Othala Csenivar, I will go tell Othala Shalicar that his worst fears have been confirmed."

SHALICAR DID NOT gloat that he had been right and I wrong. He was horrified and insisted on coming to see. By the time we got back to Othala Drinimar's study, Ostilin and Hadrinar had cleared away enough paper, by dint of picking it up in great armfuls and dumping it on the floor we had worked so hard to clear, to show that Othala Csenivar was seated in a chair and on his lap held the long-missing registers.

"But this is terrible," said Shalicar. "How can we possibly use them now?"

It was a good question. Othala Csenivar and the paper around him were long-dry, but the damage to the registers from his reveth'osrel, if one could call it a reveth'osrel when the body had never been buried, was evident without touching them, and I wagered grimly with myself that the pages would be stuck irretrievably together.

"I am afraid," I said, "that you really are going to have to start new registers." It was a terrible thing to have to say, a terrible loss to admit to—there was going to be a chasm in the record of the practice of Ulnemenee—but, having *found* them, we were out of choices, out of hope.

"Oh, but Dach'othala Vernezar—"

I turned and looked at him, and he did not finish the sentence. "You can start," I said, "with those poor people in your storeroom."

"Celehar, it's—"

"Not your fault," I said firmly. "It is Othala Drinimar's fault, and there's nothing for it but to mend the situation as best we can. And that means new registers."

"We haven't any blank ones."

"Then send Hadrinar or Ostilin to the Ulistheileian to get more. Really, Shalicar, you have to stop dragging your feet about this *sometime*."

He reddened, but swallowed his protest. "Very well. Hadrinar, go to the Ulistheileian and tell them we need blank registers."

"How many?" said Hadrinar.

"Two for certain," said Shalicar.

"You can always go get more," I said. "Hopefully, you'll have to, when Ulnemenee starts functioning properly again."

"What do we do about the map of the graveyard?" Shalicar said despairingly.

"Well, find it, first of all. And if you need a new one, can't you ask the Cartographers' Guild? They could send a journeyman."

"You have answers for everything."

"I have common sense. The other thing that must be done is that you must notify the Csenivada that Othala Csenivar has been found."

"Must I?" Shalicar said, even more despairingly.

"Really, Shalicar," I said. "Yes. You must. Ostilin can take a letter if you truly cannot face going yourself. I would suggest that you do that while I see if I can find anything salvageable of Ulnemenee's apparatus."

"I do not envy you your task," said Shalicar, looking sidelong at the papers around Othala Csenivar.

"And I do not envy you yours," I said, "but they are both things that must be done."

THE REMAINDER OF Ulnemenee's apparatus—the map of the cemetery and the timetables and all the rest of it—proved to have been stowed carefully behind Othala Csenivar's chair, where they had been spared the worst of the damage. Somewhat to my horror, the closet kept going; it was another of these Amaleise closets that stretched the length of the wall. It was full of paper all the way back.

I was still examining the papers around Othala Csenivar the next day, in case there was something else important that Othala Drinimar had chosen to stash here, when there was a tap on the door of the study. It was Shalicar, accompanied by a young elven man in good but not overly fancy clothes. After a puzzled moment, I recognized him. He was the Mer Csenivar who had been an admirer of Arveneän Shelsin. We bowed to each other.

"Blessed goddesses, this is dreadful," he said, looking at the stacks of paper around him as he picked his way through the study to the closet door. "Surely Othala Drinimar must have been sick in his mind."

"We think so, yes," I said and moved aside so that he could see his kinsman.

To his credit, he recoiled only a step. He said nothing at all for several moments, then asked, "Can you tell how he died?"

"The Master of the Mortuary might be able to," I said, "or he might not. Some methods of murder leave no trace on the skeleton at all."

"And as a Witness for the Dead, you can't . . . ?"

"It's been decades too long," I said. "There's nothing of his spirit left here."

Mer Csenivar nodded. "We suppose there's no point in hoping it wasn't violent."

"No," I said. "Not really."

"No," he said. "Well, we will have to have him transported

to Ulprasalee, which is the cemetery the Csenivada have shares in. Although we don't quite know . . ."

"The prelate of Ulprasalee will be able to arrange it," I said. "That is part of their duties."

"On behalf of ourself and our junior prelates, we are so very sorry," Shalicar said.

"It's no fault of yours," said Mer Csenivar. "As we understand the situation, you inherited him without knowing he was here."

"Essentially," said Shalicar.

"It would be different if you'd known all this time."

"We assure you we did not," Shalicar said; I did wonder if the Csenivada would ever have known what had happened to Othala Csenivar if I had not been here to insist.

"Exactly," said Mer Csenivar. "We thank you for finding him," using the plural "you." "It does not look as if it has been pleasant labor."

"It is tedious," I admitted. "But it must be done."

"A laudable philosophy," said Mer Csenivar.

"We follow our calling."

"Then your calling brings you to some very strange places," he said, and with that I had to agree.

Ulnemenee finally had new registers, but my work was not done. First and most obvious, the registers had to be filled with the names of the dead—*only* the names, since we knew nothing more about them. Then plaques had to be made for the revethmerai, which also meant ascertaining whether Ulnemenee could afford the plaques, and what I did if it could not, I did not know. Then to the Violet Street entrance to the catacombs and hope that the catacombists there remembered after all this time that they had been told to look for bones from Ulnemenee.

And once the bones were sealed in their revethmerai, there *still* remained the problem of Ulnemenee itself and how it was to become a functioning ulimeire again. And that required Shalicar to say no to Vernezar, which I was not entirely sure was possible. But he could not possibly be a proper prelate of a ulimeire if he was eternally writing reports about other prelates' ulimeirei. I had known the Ulistheileian was inefficient and unhelpful; I hadn't known the problem was so bad that Vernezar was co-opting the time and energy of his beneficed prelates.

The problems of the Ulistheileian were thankfully not within the bounds of the task the Archprelate had set me.

I said to myself, *Start with the first thing,* and showed Hadrinar and Ostilin how they should put entries in the register, this situation being rather different from the ideal circumstances they would have been taught.

"But what do we do with the bones?" said Hadrinar.

"Keep them in order," I said, "and find somewhere to put them until the plaques can be made."

Ostilin started to object. "But you can't get the plaques made until . . . oh."

The plaque-maker couldn't make the plaques until they had a list of the names to be engraved, and it was customary among Amaleise prelates to use the register sheets as the list—which wasn't a problem, ordinarily, because the name would have been entered in the register at the time of the funeral, five years before the plaque would be needed.

"We'll have to do them in batches," I said, "one register sheet-worth at a time."

"Othala Celehar," said Ostilin, "*when* are we going to do this? If we are clearing the study in the morning, and working on reports with Othala Shalicar in the afternoon . . . are we to stay up all night making entries in the register?"

"No," I said. "I will talk to Othala Shalicar. It is time for him to stop doing Vernezar's work for him."

PREDICTABLY, SHALICAR WAS horrified. "Celehar! We cannot just . . . *stop*."

"Certainly you can," I said. "Pack up these reports and send them back to the Ulistheileian. Hire a courier if you don't want to send your junior prelates. You shouldn't be doing them in the first place, and Vernezar knows that as well as you do."

"But . . ."

"Either that," I said, "or you should admit that you are Vernezar's clerk and let this ulimeire go to someone who will tend it properly."

"Celehar!"

"The Archprelate wants Ulnemenee to function as a ulimeire again," I said. "That is more important than what Vernezar wants."

"Well, yes, but—"

"No," I said. "This isn't something you can equivocate about. You cannot do both things, Shalicar. Pick one."

Shalicar sat silently for several moments, ears flat and expression hunted. Finally, he visibly came to a decision, and his ears lifted a little. "I must choose Ulnemenee," he said and added under his breath, "for I hate being Vernezar's clerk."

THE NEXT DAY, all of Vernezar's papers were gone.

A WEEK AFTER the execution of Nathalis Vernezar, Tomasaran brought me a letter that had not come through the post.

"A novice brought this from the Ulistheileian," she said in the tone of one disavowing all responsibility.

"Thank you," I said. I toyed for a moment with the idea of setting it on fire at the gas fixture without reading it, but in the end I opened it and read it quickly. It was from Dach'othala Aiva Vernezar, the Ulisothala. He wanted me to meet him in the plinth room of the catacombs that evening. He did not specify a reason, but did add ominously that it would be better for Amalo's Witness for the Dead if I complied. He did not mention the Clenverada, whether because he had already told them everything he knew or because he was not going to, I could not judge.

I gave the letter to Tomasaran, who read it and said, "Is he *threatening* you?"

"No," I said. "He's threatening *you*. You're Amalo's Witness for the Dead."

"Me?" She stared at me, her disbelief obvious in her ears. "Why would he threaten me?"

"Because he thinks it will make me do what he wants."

"Will it? I mean, will you go?"

I handed the letter to Captain Olgarezh, who read it quickly. "Do you know where this room he specifies is?"

"Yes," I said.

"We actually have fewer qualms about your going places in the catacombs. Someone following you down there will be as obvious as an ink blot on a white sheet."

"Then, yes," I said to Tomasaran, "I will go, if Captain Olgarezh is willing to act as a witness."

"As a witness?" he said.

"Anora persuaded us some time ago not to go to one of these 'informal' meetings of Vernezar's without a witness, if you'll forgive the pun."

"Ah. Yes, we will not let you out of our sight regardless, so we might as well be your witness."

"Thank you," I said.

We went together that evening to the room of the catacombs that must once have contained a revethgramal and now contained an empty plinth. Vernezar was already there, and he was horrified to see Captain Olgarezh.

"Who is this? What is he doing here?"

"This is Captain Olgarezh, who is acting as our witness," I said, deciding to leave out the more complicated part about why I needed guarding. "He is not here to arrest you. Now what is it you want?"

"Not with him here," said Vernezar.

"Then not at all," I said.

"Wait, wait, wait!" Vernezar almost clutched at me but thought better of it. "Celehar, you have to help us."

I had expected this to be about Shalicar, but clearly it was not. "Actually," I said, for I was still irritated by that threatening letter, "we do not 'have' to do anything."

Vernezar stared at me in mingled disbelief and horror.

"We are a Witness for the Dead. We have to tell the truth about our witnessing. Nothing more."

Vernezar had lost all momentum. "But . . ."

"No," I said. "You are not our superior, and we are not in your debt. But with that understood, why did you want to see us?"

Vernezar gave me an ears-lowered, resentful look. "Someone has to tell Prince Orchenis we are not a traitor."

"Why can't you?"

"Do you think he will even *see* us, after what that little idiot Nathalis did?"

"Have you tried?"

"We do not wish to be dragged away by the Principate Guard," he said, eyeing Captain Olgarezh. "That's why we want *you* to talk to him."

"We are not going to plead for you with Prince Orchenis."

"Celehar!"

"No. We are a *Witness*. We will tell him the truth, but nothing more."

"But it *is* the truth. If we had had any idea what Cambeshar had planned, we would have told Orchenis immediately!"

I stared at him until his ears twitched and he looked away. "Be careful what you ask. Unless you want to be witnessed for, with all that entails."

Vernezar shuddered. "But can't you just—"

"No. You want us to talk to Prince Orchenis because he will believe us. But he will believe us because we are a Witness."

"He'll believe you because he likes you," Vernezar muttered.

I stared at him.

"Oh, don't be tiresomely disingenuous, Celehar. It's hardly a secret that Prince Orchenis likes you better than any of Amalo's native prelates."

"Liking has nothing to do with trusting my probity."

Vernezar snorted. "Only you would say that," he said, not as a compliment.

"That's why Prince Orchenis can trust him," Captain Olgarezh pointed out.

Vernezar glared at him, but Captain Olgarezh returned his gaze unapologetically, and Vernezar swung back to me. "So you will not help us?"

"We do not think you need help," I said, "and, no, we will not do what you want."

Vernezar said, "Are you sure that's wise?"

"We do not care if it is or not. We are not going to be threatened into lying to Prince Orchenis."

"We don't want you to *lie* to him!"

"You want us to tell him something we don't ourself know the truth of," I said. "The difference isn't all that great."

"Do you really think we are a traitor?"

"No, but if you want us to witness for you, we must be more certain than that."

"We don't want you to *witness*," Vernezar said.

"Yes, actually, you do. That's what you mean."

He started to say something, stopped. Started to say something else, stopped. Said resentfully, "Well, if you don't want to help us, we suppose there is nothing more to be said."

"No," I said. "There isn't. Good-bye, Vernezar."

Captain Olgarezh kept up with me easily, and we left Vernezar standing by the empty plinth, alone.

WITH SHALICAR FINALLY playing his proper role, I was able to focus on clearing out the study, which Shalicar was now going to need, since the morgue was going to have to revert to its proper function and not act as an extension of the Ulistheileian. Hadrinar and Ostilin kept me apprised of the progress they were making with the bones in the storeroom and proudly brought the first full sheet of the register to show me.

I had had time by then to ask Anora and so was able to tell them where to find an engravist to make the plaques. "And be sure you tell them you need the register sheet back. You'll need to record it when each person's bones are placed in their revethmer—especially with these bones, where so much of the ritual has been lost."

"And then the bones in the graves?" said Ostilin.

"There are still bones in the graves?" I said, although I couldn't say why I was so surprised. It was of a piece of the fifty years' mismanagement of Ulnemenee.

"Oh yes," said Ostilin. "After Othala Drinimar fired the sexton, there was no one to disinter them. Hadrinar, we're going to need to hire a sexton."

Hadrinar took a notebook and pen out of his inner coat pocket and made an addition to what looked like quite a lengthy list. I was pleased that the two of them had been wise enough to know—without being told explicitly—not to leave everything to Shalicar.

"Hire someone in the neighborhood," I said. "That will be the best way to start spreading the word that the ulimeire is working again."

"Ooh," said Ostilin, "what a good idea," and Hadrinar made another note.

Some days later Iäna said over lunch, apropos of nothing, "You are an actual prelate of Ulis, are you not? Not just a Witness for the Dead?"

"All clerical Witnesses of the Dead are prelates of Ulis," I said.

"No, what we mean is, you can conduct a funeral?"

"We can."

"Because—and you'll do one for one of our mother's kelkinora?"

"Yes, of course," I said. "Why do you ask?"

"One of Mama's deacons has been sick all winter—all fall, too, for that matter—and has finally died. We shouldn't put it like that, but the poor man was in a great deal of pain. In any event, he has died, and his prelate refuses to perform his funeral."

"Why?"

"She doesn't approve of the Tahareisei."

"But she hasn't denounced you."

"She doesn't approve of that, either," said Iäna with a shrug. "The point being, we need *someone* to perform Aktara's funeral, and we thought perhaps you might be willing."

"When?"

"Tonight?"

"We have no other engagements," I said. "Tonight is fine."

Thus I ended up at sundown in a small collective cemetery in Habronan, performing a funeral for a man I'd never met. Captain Olgarezh did not approve, but came with me all the same. He stayed by the cemetery gate and had kept Iäna at his side until the ceremony started, to tell him if anyone tried to come in who was not known to him.

I knew several Barizheise funerary rituals, and Merrem Pel-Thenhior had told me which one was most appropriate. Fortunately, it was a simple one by Barizheise standards and did not take long—important in the winter, when night came early and fast and cold.

Afterwards, we all returned to the Torivontaram, and the mourners combined goblin and elven customs by holding a wake. It was kind of Merrem Pel-Thenhior to invite me—even kinder of her to include Captain Olgarezh in her invitation—and so we stayed, though we sat at one of the three-person tables along the outer wall, and I, at least, hoped we would go unnoticed. Which we did, save for Iäna swinging by periodically, until the second hour after midnight, when Zhuleto found me.

I knew how much Iäna disliked her, so I was wary from the moment she approached. At the same time, she was a practicing priestess, even if her sect was not one I was supposed to approve of, so that I did not want to be needlessly rude.

She sat down in the third chair without waiting for an invitation and said, "Iäna thinks very highly of you."

"We think very highly of Iäna," I said cautiously.

She gave me a narrow-eyed stare. I was fairly sure she was looking for weaknesses. I gave her back a blank face.

"We don't know what you think you're going to get from him," she said.

"Get?" I said, genuinely startled. "Why do you think we want to get anything?"

"You must want *something*," she said, which told me more about her than it did her about me.

There were several different responses I could make. I chose the one most frustrating for her, which was silence.

After a moment, she seemed to realize she wasn't going to get anywhere and rethought her strategy. "But we were forgetting! We haven't been introduced yet," she said; her false smile might have been convincing if I hadn't seen the scowl that preceded it. "We are Zhuleto Korborad."

"Thara Celehar, a Witness for the Dead. And this is Captain Olgarezh." With someone else, I might have picked up some of the burden of the conversation, but every passing moment made me more certain that I did not want to become entangled in a conversation with Zhuleto Korborad, and I did not want to let my guard down.

"Oh, everyone knows the famous Othala Celehar," she said poisonously, and I could only hope it wasn't true. It made me, for an instant, almost understand how Broset Sheveldar could have changed his name so many times. "Is it true"—and she'd clearly thought of another grievance—"is it true that only a Witness for the Dead can destroy a ghoul?"

"Not exactly," I said, and I was saved from having to explain what "not exactly" meant (or the difference between "quiet" and "destroy") by Iäna appearing out of nowhere and saying, "Zhuleto, my mother would like to have a word with thee."

Zhuleto gave him a resentful look, but got up without argument and crossed the room to where Merrem Pel-Thenhior was sitting.

Iäna took her chair. "What did she want?"

Captain Olgarezh was watching the dancing with a distant expression. I leaned closer to Iäna, so that we could have something resembling a private conversation under the noise of the dancers and musicians. “I don’t know,” I said. “To cause trouble?”

“Probably. She has no great love for elves. I have been lectured about associating myself with the morkolai, and I admit I laughed in her face. ‘Associating myself with the morkolai’ is, from some angles, the entirety of my job.”

“Thou writest operas,” I said.

“Morkol operas for a morkol audience.”

“Not *Zhelsu*.”

“Point.” He brightened perceptibly. “And I have a brilliant idea for the opera after *The Grief of Stones* that will give Othoro another leading role. Also, I want to perform *Harimar,* let her play Mulibaro, and leave act two, scene five, exactly as it is.”

It took me a moment, but clearly he meant the great love scene. He could mean nothing else. “Dost *want* another riot in thy opera house?”

“I will take it,” Iäna said. “Anything that means people are paying attention.”

He had said something of the sort before. I said, “Is that what you think the purpose of art is?”

“Not a bit. The purpose of art is the expression of the soul. Opera performances, on the other hand, must do more than express the soul if the opera company is going to stay solvent. I will do anything that will get people to buy tickets. And, of course, I want to give Othoro every opportunity I can to sing roles that are worth her talent.”

“That’s a lot of different things to be doing with one opera.”

“It is,” said Iäna. “That’s why I like doing it.”

“Thou likest difficult things,” I said.

“I do. Present company included.”

My face heated, but Anora had said much the same.

"Truly, Thara," Iäna said. "I am teasing, not complaining."

"That's good," I said, "for I don't know how to change."

"I know," he said and gave me a smile that said he truly didn't mind.

We sat and watched the dancing together for some time.

WITH THE FIRST signs of spring came imperial Witnesses: Witnesses for the mountains, the miners, the Clenverada, the dragons. The imperial Witness for the Dragons, who met with Csathamar and me in my rooms almost before his luggage was brought out of the *Strength of Rosiro,* was elven, tall and diffident, his blue eyes half-hidden behind the thick lenses of his spectacles. His name was Rada Sorohar, and although I did not think the diffidence was a pose, it was definitely a shield behind which Mer Sorohar hid his intelligence, which was as sharp and slicing as a reveth-atha. He listened to my story, asking questions like a man prising crumbs out of corners, and taking page after page of notes.

When I was done, he said, "And you think the claim of the dead dragons can be placed in the balance with the Clenverada Mining Company?"

"I swore to witness for her," I said. "It just turned out to be . . ."

"Do you not consider the massacre of a hundred and ninety-two dragons worth mentioning?" Csathamar said.

"Not what I said," Sorohar said, quite mildly. "But the Clenverada's position is clearly going to be that, no matter how unfortunate and regrettable the events of a hundred and twenty years ago, they have no bearing on the present."

Csathamar said, "The Clenverada Mining Company's notable success *not* being based on a massacre?"

Sorohar said, "All the men who participated are long dead."

"And yet their profits live on," I said dryly.

"Ah," said Sorohar. "Yes. That is the weakness in the Clenverada position, that they continue to profit from murder."

"They can claim they didn't know."

"They can," Sorohar agreed. "But now they *do* know. And that is the situation we are all faced with."

"I don't want to bring the empire down in ruins," I said, "but I also must put forward the fact that my petitioner would not care if I did."

"Perfect justice is unobtainable," said Sorohar, "since the people who ought to have been punished *are* all long dead." He paused, flipping back through his notes. "I will say that I have noticed, in witnessing before the emperor, that you do better with him if you can suggest a compromise outcome. And that way, the compromise is of our choosing, not of the Clenverada's."

"I see what you mean," said Csathamar. "But I also see Celehar's point about Ithalpherix. Is our job to find a way out, or is it to witness for the dragons?"

Sorohar said, "If we witness for the dragons exactly as the dragons would wish to be witnessed for, we will simply lose, because the emperor cannot afford to bankrupt the Clenverada Mining Company, no matter how much they may deserve it. If we come up with a compromise, we may be able to get as much justice as is possible—that is, we may be able to make the Clenverada *do* something."

"Rather than nothing," Csathamar said, "which is all we will get if we hold to a justifiable but unreasonable position. Celehar? You are the principal Witness, after all."

I said, "I am not sure dragons have much to do with compromise. But I understand you, and I personally would rather get something out of the Clenverada than nothing. Perhaps even enough to satisfy Ithalpherix, although I doubt it."

"I have been doing some research," said Sorohar, "and of the one hundred ninety-two dragonhold mines, one hundred thirteen are actually not in use at all. So that's one hundred thirteen mines that the Clenverada will attempt to appease us with, whereas we want to keep our eyes on the seventy-nine mines that are still active."

"Are they profitable?" said Csathamar.

"Another good question," said Sorohar with a quirk of a smile. "Fifty of them are making negligible contributions to the Clenverada Mining Company's annual profits. So there are twenty-nine mines that the fight is actually about. Those, I regret to say, include three of the Clenverada's top five producing mines, and one of them, the Aglatheno, is the Clenverada's best mine."

"Aglathenning," I said. "I walked through their bones."

We were all silent for a chilled moment.

"This," said Sorohar, "is where we need to have an alternative suggestion. The Clenverada will have a thousand reasons why they should not be forced to shut down three of their five best mines, and some of them will even be good reasons."

"The Witness for the Miners will probably also speak against closing mines," Csathamar said. "And argue very persuasively that it isn't fair to the miners, who had nothing to do with the massacre."

"Yes," said Sorohar. "The Witness for the Mountains will argue, as the Witness for the Mountains always *does* argue in mining cases, that the miners are tearing apart the bones of the world, and will not be listened to."

"Because it's inconvenient," I said. "Like one hundred ninety-two dead dragons."

"In fairness, it's more than just inconvenient," said Sorohar. "You said you didn't want to cause the ruin of the empire."

"But I would like it if the Clenverada had not managed to get themselves so intertwined with the empire that ruining one means ruining the other."

"Yes," said Sorohar. "Wouldn't we all."

I WANTED, VERY badly, to finish clearing the study, including the closet, before the emperor arrived. It was still necessary to examine each piece of paper, even though *most* of them were not relevant to Ulnemenee. Every time I considered simply taking paper by the armfuls to the refectory fireplace, I would find something—a letter from the Ulistheileian, an itemized bill from an engravist—that needed to be kept. All correspondence from the Ulistheileian, or the Amalomeire, was supposed to be preserved, and the engravist's bills might, if we were lucky, help to patch the chasm of the ruined registers.

So I kept going—when not meeting with Sorohar and Csathamar—now with Shalicar's help as well as Ostilin's and Hadrinar's, and we did make far more rapid progress, until finally, two days before the emperor was due to come to Amalo, I picked up the last piece of paper off the floor of the very back of the closet and found it was a laundry list.

"Burn it," I said to Ostilin, and then we all stood and stared around the empty study in disbelief.

Finally, Shalicar said, "Othala Celehar, do you feel that your task for the Archprelate is complete?"

"Provisionally," I said. "All the obstacles to Ulnemenee's functioning have been removed or resolved. The question is now whether it functions or not. And that's up to you and Othala Hadrinar and Othalo Ostilin. But mostly you."

His ears dipped, but he said, "You can trust us."

"Yes," I said. *I hope so,* I thought.

THE EMPEROR ARRIVED on the airship *Loyalty of Lohaiso,* along with his secretary and his nohecharei. If any of them was thinking of the last time an emperor came to Amalo by airship, they did not show it. A second airship, the *Honor of Csedo,* brought the remainder of the emperor's retinue.

It was what the Amaleisei called the true thaw; the ice on the Zhomaikora had melted and the cobbles of the streets were visible again. Caravans were starting to move in and out of the city, heading north as well as south, although the tremendous mud made this still a treacherous employment.

The emperor and his retinue were housed in the ancient imperial suite in the main octagon of the Amal'theileian, which had been aired out and ferociously cleaned and installed with modern furniture. And the first thing that happened was not the judgment of the dragons and the Clenverada. It was the judgment of Coralis Clunethar. Prince Orchenis had found a way out.

I attended the judgment with Anora and Tomasaran (and Captain Olgarezh) and listened carefully to it all: the testimony of guards and servants and, at great length, the Witness for Nathalis Vernezar. The testimony of the Witness for Coralis Clunethar clearly showed how difficult it had been to find the truth through his obscurations, misleading statements, and outright lies, and that itself told its own kind of truth.

The emperor listened carefully and courteously. At the end, when he was quite sure all the Witnesses had finished, he said: "We see no ambiguity in this case, nor any difficulty in judgment. Coralis Clunethar has committed treason, not once but many times, and the sentence of treason is death."

He looked around the room at what must have been a sea of horrified faces and said, without a scrap of apology, "There is nothing else to say."

Dach'osmer Clunethar tried to argue, but the emperor held

up his hand, and Dach'osmer Clunethar was taken away by the Principate Guard.

"It is understandable that the emperor has strong feelings about treason," I said.

"Any emperor would," said Tomasaran.

THE EXECUTION WAS the next day at noon, in the Barlevar Courtyard of the Amal'theileian. Coralis Clunethar's rank entitled him to privacy in his death, as would Nedeva Cambeshar's, when he in turn was judged.

A steward of the Amal'theileian had brought me an invitation to the execution with a note at the bottom in a precise hand, *We would appreciate your presence.* It was unsigned, but I did not need a signature to tell me that that was the emperor's handwriting.

I went, Captain Olgarezh beside me.

There were not many people there aside from the Principate Guard: the emperor and his nohecharei; Prince Orchenis; a selection of the Clunethada, women weeping ostentatiously on their husbands' shoulders. Captain Olgarezh. Me.

I drifted around to stand beside Kiru Athmaza, who gave me a glance to be sure I wasn't a threat to the emperor, and then a flicker of a smile before she returned her attention to the courtyard as a whole, watching for danger. Early emperors had been assassinated; later emperors had had attempts made on their lives stopped by their nohecharei. Edrehasivar himself had survived such an attempt. The nohecharei seemed an antique custom, but they served a real and often dreadful purpose.

Instead of the reveth-atha, persons of high rank were executed with a sword; Coralis Clunethar had the right to be executed with the sunblade of the Clunethada, which normally stayed in the innermost vault of the Athamareise treasury, and it was very like him that he had insisted on it. In centuries past, Prince Orchenis would have performed the execution himself; nowadays the honor, if honor it was, went to the municipal executioner, a part-goblin veteran of the imperial army. Even he handled the sunblade with caution bordering on terror.

At noon precisely, Dach'osmer Clunethar was led out, his hair cropped and his shirt collar turned back to expose his neck. He was yelling from the moment he was within earshot, trying to make his case to the emperor for why he should not be executed. The two Principate Guard captains escorting him, whose function was supposed to be ceremonial, instead were almost wrestling him to keep him from flinging himself at the emperor's feet. The emperor watched stonily as they dragged Dach'osmer Clunethar to the block and pinned him across it.

Abruptly, he stopped fighting. The two captains froze, not trusting him.

"All right," said Dach'osmer Clunethar. "It's all right. You can let go."

They straightened up warily, but Dach'osmer Clunethar stayed as he was. And stayed as the executioner, wasting no time, stepped forward and brought down the blade.

The sunblade sliced through Coralis Clunethar's neck as if through paper.

Afterwards, while two liveried servants anxiously cleaned the sunblade in preparation for taking it back to the treasury, the emperor turned and said, "Mer Celehar, we would speak with you."

"Yes, Serenity," I said—the only possible answer. I was allowed past Kiru Athmaza into the carefully empty space the emperor lived in. Captain Olgarezh took a step back, to make it clear that he was not trying to crowd in. I bowed.

"Are you well, Mer Celehar?"

"Yes, Serenity."

"You come with a guard, and we are told you have been guarded all winter. Do you truly feel the Clenverada intend you harm?"

I explained about the garrote, and the emperor's brows drew together. "And why are we only hearing about this now? You cannot think we would approve of your being murdered in an alley."

"We did not think Your Serenity would approve, but we were also afraid that by the time you found out, it would be far too late."

He gave me a sharp look, his pale eyes, as always, slightly unnerving. "There are such things as letters, Mer Celehar. We know you know how to write them."

I felt my face heat. "Serenity—"

"Is it that you did not wish to be beholden?" He sounded slightly hurt.

I said, "No, Serenity. But we did not wish to trouble you when Prince Orchenis was already doing everything that could be done."

He looked unconvinced, but said, "Are you in danger now, do you think?"

"We do not know," I said. "The Clenverada would have to be awfully bold to do anything in the imperial presence. But we do not know how bold they are."

"Hence your guard."

"Yes."

The emperor said, "It is not perfect, but perfection is unobtainable."

"Yes, Serenity," I said. "Between Captain Olgarezh and Prince Orchenis's warning to Dach'osmer Clenverar, we think the Clenverada will not do anything before the judgment."

"And after the judgment?"

"That depends entirely on what Your Serenity decides."

"You think they will seek vengeance if our decision is not to their liking?"

"We think it very possible. They are not accustomed to being crossed. And it *is* our fault."

"That is, we suppose, one way of looking at it. But we do not think you are at fault for following your calling, any more than we think you are at fault for finding the massacre of one hundred ninety-two dragons objectionable. Is the skull safe?"

"Yes, Serenity," I said.

"Good. Are you still willing to take the skull to Revethora Vezvaishoroi?"

"Yes, Serenity, when the roads north are made of something other than mud."

"Yes," said the emperor, and might have smiled.

THAT AFTERNOON, IÄNA herded me gently into the bedroom, sat down in one of the wingback chairs, leaned back, and said in an unwontedly serious voice, "Thara, hast thou thought? What wilt thou do after the judgment? Wilt thou have Captain Olgarezh to guard thee for the rest of thy life?"

I *had* thought, sleeplessly on some nights, as my position became worse and worse. I said, "I truly don't want to leave, but I don't think there is any way I can stay in Amalo. Or even in Thu-Athamar, really."

"The Clenverada own half the principality," Iäna agreed. "But what wilt thou do?"

"Go back to the Untheileneise Court and ask the Archprelate to give me another job."

"And start all over again?"

"Yes, I suppose."

He considered that for a long moment. "Wilt thou write to me?"

"Yes, of course, although I doubt I'll have anything interesting to tell thee."

Iäna stared at me, then burst out laughing. "And I'm sure thou wouldst say the same about thy tenure in Amalo. I do not fear that thou wilt be a boring correspondent." He turned serious again. "But I am sorry that thou canst not stay. I will miss thee."

"I will miss thee, too," I said, swallowing against a lump in my throat. "Thou art . . ."

"Intense," he suggested, smiling crookedly.

"Indispensable."

"Thara . . ."

"If thou art allowed to be intense, then so am I," I said. "I would not leave and have thee think I did so lightly."

"Thou dost nothing lightly. And I know thou wouldst not leave if thou hadst a choice."

"I would not," I said. "And I will write."

IN THE MORNING was the emperor's judgment on the matter of the dragonhold mines.

Captain Olgarezh and I got quite early to the great formal octagonal hall that was the center of the Amal'theileian. It was just as well, since this time I was not audience, but Witness, and the stewards of the hall had a great many people to organize before the judgment could begin.

The first to come in were the judiciars, who sat in chairs on the broad steps of the dais. One of them, Lord Orshevar, was there to organize the proceedings; the others were there for the dignity of their office.

Csathamar and Sorohar arrived not long after and were escorted to join me at the table of the Witnesses for the

Dragons. "I haven't been nervous about a hearing in *years,*" said Csathamar, "but I confess I'm a little nervous about this one."

"This is a judgment quite unlike any I have ever taken part in," said Sorohar. "But the emperor is what I was taught to call a 'strong' listener. He retains the things one tells him—which is more than one can say for a great many judiciars. And he has proved the wisdom of his judgment many times."

The Witnesses for the Miners came in, followed by the Witnesses for the Clenverada (and one non-witnessing representative who had petitioned for and been granted permission to speak) and then the Witness for the Mountains. They were all elves. I thought of Tomasaran and Parmorin and was more specific in my thoughts. They were all elven *men*. Which was no manner of surprise.

Behind the tables of Witnesses, the audience filled in rows and rows of chairs: the emperor's retinue, the courtiers of Prince Orchenis, the Clenverada, the newspapermen, clerks and page boys and opera singers, prelates of all kinds—even the Amal'othala appeared, borne in a jeweled palanquin worth enough to feed the Airmen's Quarter for a week. I saw Iäna standing with Anora and his junior prelates; more to my surprise, I saw Shalicar and *his* junior prelates. Tomasaran eluded the stewards long enough to reach our table and say good luck.

When the emperor and his nohecharei mounted the steep steps behind the dais, the entire hall fell silent except for the great susurration of everyone bowing at once. The emperor, in his white-on-white brocade coat, was again wearing smoky amethysts on his hands and in his ears and had a chain of them woven through his elaborate piled braids. He sat down on the throne of the Prince of Thu-Athamar, made a gesture easily interpreted as *Please be seated,* and directed an inquiring look at Lord Orshevar.

Lord Orshevar stood up and said, "Serenity, the question before you today is the disposition of one hundred ninety-two mines, said to be dragonhold mines, in the possession of the Clenverada Mining Company." He went on from there at considerable length and to little purpose about the honor done to Thu-Athamar by the emperor's presence, making it sound as if the principality had requested the emperor's judgment rather than being informed unilaterally that they were going to receive it. The emperor sat through it all with perfect posture and an unreadable face.

Finally, Lord Orshevar ran out of things to say and proceeded to the Witnesses. He introduced us all and started, "We will begin with the Witnesses for the Dragons," when the emperor interrupted him, firmly and unapologetically, and said, "We would prefer to begin with the Witness for the Mountains."

Orshevar looked for a moment as if he'd swallowed a toad, then said, "Yes, Serenity. We will begin with the Witness for the Mountains."

The Witness for the Mountains looked nearly as surprised as Lord Orshevar—customarily, the Witnesses *vel ama* went last, not first. But he gathered himself and stood and said, "Serenity, your lordships, we speak to you today on behalf of the Osreialhallan, the mountains of Osreian's Spine. The mountains, Serenity, desire only to be left alone, their ores left undisturbed, their caverns left untrammeled. We know that this is an impossibility, but we must speak the truth of our witnessing."

"Thank you," said the emperor. "You have witnessed with honor."

The Witness for the Mountains bowed and sat down again.

"*Now* the Witnesses for the Dragons," the emperor said (and in fact throughout the judgment, he did his own organizing, leaving Lord Orshevar nothing to do but go along with it).

I stood and said, "Serenity, we apologize for our voice."

"Do not apologize," the emperor said. "Proceed."

And thus I told my story again, this time formally and this time to receive the emperor's judgment, not merely his agreement to hear what I and the other Witnesses had to say. It seemed like a very long story in the silence of the octagon hall.

"Witness Celehar," said the emperor, "how came you under the mountain?"

"Serenity," I said. "We were brought there by a group of miners."

"Did you go willingly?"

"No, we were kidnapped."

A little murmur ran through the audience.

"Thank you, Witness Celehar," said the emperor.

I sat down, almost limp with relief that he was not going to make me explain about the revethavar and the miracle.

"Witnesses Csathamar and Sorohar, have you anything to add?"

"Not at this time, Serenity," said Sorohar.

The emperor gave Sorohar a stately little nod and said, "Next, we think, the Witnesses for the Miners."

There were three Witnesses for the Miners, one, Halanezh, to speak for the thousands of Clenverada employees; one, Tholabar, to speak for the miners who had died in the eisonsar explosion beneath Revethora Vezvaishoroi and in other mines; one, Remavar, to speak for the men who were actually mining Revethora Vezvaishoroi. Remavar had interviewed me several times. He had also done a hero's work in getting to Tanvero before the thaw and finding Halhathvered and his friends. He had somehow persuaded Halhathvered to put on skis and trek with him to Revethora Vezvaishoroi, where the miners refused to speak with him.

"Refused to *speak* with you?" the emperor said. "Do they not understand what an imperial Witness is?"

"Serenity, we do not know. We camped inside the mouth of Revethora Vezvaishoroi for a week and sent many messages—for Mer Halhathvered most earnestly counseled us not to attempt to go to the mining camp ourself—and the only message they sent back was that they would not speak with us. And we had no ability to compel them."

"No, of course not," said the emperor. "We suspect you are lucky they did not think it worthwhile to murder you."

"Yes, Serenity, that thought did occur to us."

"Very well," said the emperor. "You have done as much as anyone could do. What is your testimony?"

"Serenity," said Witness Remavar, "these miners are poor men who had to pool their resources to buy a mountain the Clenverada no longer wanted and who were and are desperate to find a vein of ore valuable enough to repay their money and time. Thus far, they have not succeeded, and it is our testimony that this endless searching in the depths of the mountain has driven Mer Delthonar and his followers insane."

"Insane?" said the emperor.

"Serenity, they do not behave like sane men. They attempted to murder Mer Celehar, they refused to speak to us, and they continue their search for ore despite repeated failures and despite knowing that there is a creature in the mountain that will kill them horribly if it can. None of these is the action of men in their right minds, and it would be unfair of us to claim otherwise. On the other hand, they did purchase the mountain legally from the Clenverada, so their claim to it is futile—in our judgment—but legitimate. That is the extent of our witnessing." He bowed and sat down.

The emperor considered for a moment, then said, "It is unlikely but possible . . . is Mer Halhathvered here?"

Silence—the deep sort of silence that came about because everyone was afraid to twitch—until a voice from the depths of the audience said, "We are here, Serenity."

"Splendid," said the emperor. "Will you come forward?"

Halhathvered did. He stopped at the gap between the table of the Witnesses for the Miners and the Witnesses for the Clenverada and said, "How . . . how may we serve you, Serenity?"

"By telling the truth," said the emperor. "Do you agree with the Witness for the Miners that Mer Delthonar is mad?"

Halhathvered was clearly terrified, but also trying to think. He said, "On the subject of Revethora Vezvaishoroi . . . yes, Serenity."

"Thank you," said the emperor. "Do you still own a share in the mountain?"

"None that we care to claim," said Halhathvered.

THE SECOND WITNESS for the Miners was the Witness for the Dead, for those who had died because of the Clenverada's actions—for eisonsar, aside from being lethally dangerous, had no legitimate use in mining. It had been introduced into the mines solely to kill dragons, and some unknown and unknowable number of miners had died as well. Tholabar spoke passionately about the waste of life, and although he did not go so far as to accuse the Clenverada of murdering their own employees, he did call them negligent and suggested that they simply had not cared.

The third Witness for the Miners, Halanezh, was the Witness for the living employees of the Clenverada Mining Company. He had a great deal to say, and he said it at great length, with figures and quotes from testimony he had gathered, but what it came down to in the end was that, although most of the miners did not want to be part of an ongoing atrocity, they also needed their jobs.

Which left the Witnesses for the Clenverada. Norathar

emperor said in a voice that carried no further than the tables of Witnesses, "We noted in the testimony of Witness Halanezh that many of the dragonhold mines are not even in current use."

"One hundred thirteen," Sorohar muttered.

"Thank you, Witness Sorohar. One hundred thirteen abandoned mines. So that much we can grant without difficulty. Those mines will be sealed."

The representative of the Clenverada scowled.

"But what of the remainder?" said the emperor. "We cannot close seventy-nine working mines. It is unjust."

"Serenity," said Sorohar, "according to what we have discovered, fifty of those seventy-nine mines make only negligible contributions to the Clenverada's profits. Might it be possible to close those as well?"

"What of the men who mine them?" said Halanezh.

"Surely jobs can be found for them at other mines," said Sorohar.

"Even an unprofitable mine can employ more than two hundred miners," said Halanezh, "and it is not so easy to find jobs for that many men at once."

"It need not be all at once," said Sorohar. "The mines could be shut down gradually, on a schedule, which would provide time for jobs to be found for the men."

"Jobs we create out of what?" said the Clenveradeise representative. "Our hat?"

"You need not think our judgment will not include a burden for your shoulders," the emperor said, and he almost sounded irritated. "The Clenverada are guilty of an atrocity, an atrocity which you continue to profit from, and even if retribution is not something we are willing to inflict, restitution is."

"We cannot make restitution to dead dragons!"

"People make restitution to the dead all the time," I said.

"It's part of our calling."

"As we understand it, the dead are usually not quite so specific about what they want," Csathamar said.

"They can be," I said. "But they aren't as complicated. Ithalpherix has her living intelligence, not the fading memory of being alive. And she has had more than a hundred years to contemplate the question."

"We do not suppose we could negotiate with her?" the emperor said.

"We do not think there is anything to be negotiated," I said. "She has said what she wants. It's not as if one could substitute in different mines for the ones that were dragonholds."

"We see your point," said the emperor.

"You could let us expand to the east," the Clenveradeise representative said with sudden hope.

The emperor looked at him. "Into imperial lands? No."

"Besides," said the Witness for the Mountains, "what if there are dragons there?"

"No," the emperor said. "In justice—to the workers if not to the employers—we cannot ask the Clenverada Mining Company to take a blow greater than they can absorb. Witness Norathar and Witness Grenelar, you have done great work, and we would ask you to make your notes available to the imperial auditors."

"Auditors?" said the representative of the Clenverada.

"It is the only way," said the emperor. "We wish as many dragonhold mines closed as is possible, but we do not wish to destroy the Clenverada Mining Company. Our auditors will find the answer."

"What of the miners who then have no jobs?" said Halanezh.

"The imperial government will create jobs for them," said the emperor, "for the imperial government has its share of guilt."

The representative for the Clenverada looked like he'd taken a mortal wound. "Serenity, you cannot mean—"

The emperor raised his voice and pronounced judgment, declaring the Clenverada of 120 years ago guilty of the cruel and abhorrent murders of 192 dragons, murders from which their descendants were still profiting. He specified their sentence: an imperial audit to determine how many of the dragonhold mines could be closed without bankrupting the Clenverada Mining Company. And he made a promise that any miner for whom the Clenverada could not find a new job would be employed by the imperial government.

He rose—and there was another great susurration as everyone bowed—and retreated down the steps behind the dais, his nohecharei in careful attendance. The judgment was done.

Immediately, a babble of voices filled the octagonal hall. Under the clamor, Csathamar said to me, "I know it is not the bold stroke of justice it would be in a novel, but is it acceptable?"

"To me? Yes, it is the best answer he could give. To Ithalpherix? I suppose it depends on what the auditors find. She won't care whether the Clenverada Mining Company survives or not."

"And in any event," said Csathamar, "you cannot tell her what the auditors find until they have found it. Meaning you are stuck in Amalo."

I glanced over my shoulder at Captain Olgarezh. "We regret that you are stuck guarding us."

"We do not," said Captain Olgarezh.

THAT EVENING, FOR the first time in fifty years or more, there was a funeral in Ulnemenee: an old woman whose family could not afford shares in a cooperative cemetery. They were deeply grateful not to have to go all the way to Ulvanensee to bury her.

All of the preparations had been properly made (Ostilin assured me when Captain Olgarezh and I came through the gate). It only remained to hold the ceremony to commit the woman's body to her reveth'osrel. I chose a spot well to the back and reminded myself that if things did not go well, that was not actually my fault. The Archprelate had asked me to restore Ulnemenee to functionality. He had not included the competence of Ulnemenee's prelate in my remit.

The old woman had been a member of a relatively obscure elven sect; when I had been at Ulnemenee that morning, Shalicar had been panicking about memorizing the funerary ritual. This sect *did* believe in ghouls, unlike the Vikhelneisei, and a good portion of the funeral service was devoted to measures meant to prevent the old woman from turning into one. I didn't have the heart to tell anybody they were so much nonsense; what would keep her from becoming a ghoul was her name engraved on her headstone.

Even with the useless parts, the ceremony was not unreasonably long. Shalicar was visibly nervous, even with Ostilin and Hadrinar loyally beside him, and his voice shook and wavered; I wished I could have done it for him, but I was not the beneficed prelate of Ulnemenee. Despite his nerves, he did not forget any words, and he did not lose his place. He made it through to the end without any misstep bad enough to offend anyone, and Hadrinar and the newly hired sexton lowered the coffin into the grave.

As Captain Olgarezh and I walked back to the Amal'theileian, I thought the thing had gone as well as it could. And Shalicar would improve with practice.

Not my fault, I reminded myself. And, with a sense of relief, not my problem. I had done what the Archprelate asked of me.

THE IMPERIAL AUDITORS arrived in Amalo the day after the emperor and his airship of retinue departed. They descended on the offices of the Clenverada Mining Company like a swarm of polite and highly efficient locusts, and then, to switch metaphors, they began to dig. Witnesses Norathar and Grenelar had done a good deal of digging themselves, but (they said to Sorohar, who passed it on to Csathamar, who passed it on to me) they were not trained in the way that imperial accountants were trained, and the auditors rapidly discovered corners of the Clenverada Mining Company that Norathar and Grenelar had completely missed.

One of those corners was a fund labeled "CC," which was not recorded in the general ledger, but was nourished in small amounts from a dozen different sources—or had been, until the day Coralis Clunethar was apprehended. The auditors found this coincidence suspicious, dug deeper, and discovered a file of correspondence that someone should have burned and hadn't: letters from Coralis Clunethar to Porana Clenverar asking for money, going back years. We had wondered who had funded Dach'osmer Clunethar's escape. The evidence of the ledger and the letters showed very clearly that it had been the Clenverada.

The auditors reported to the emperor and the Corazhas, and the emperor did the only thing, at that point, he could do, which was to seize the entire Clenverada Mining Company for the imperial crown. He reiterated his promise to find or create jobs for all the miners, and he instructed his agents, as part of the process of dismantling the company, to begin shutting down all the dragonhold mines.

All the branches of the house of Clenverada were furious, and Iäna and I spent a long afternoon trying to decide if they were going to raise their banners against Edrehasivar or not.

"He could just execute them for treason, starting with Porana," Iäna said.

"I think, and I expect he thinks, that if he does that, they *will* rebel, because what will they have to keep them loyal?"

"Clemency is all very well, but people take advantage of it. Certainly, you can count on the Clenverada taking advantage of it."

"He'd have to get them all at once, and they are a very wide-flung family."

"Some of whom have already gone into hiding, yes," said Iäna. "But they're not going to forgive him."

I said, "I expect he knows that."

But the emperor's decision came at an auspicious time, for spring was far enough advanced that we could, with patience and some luck, get Arquenethil's skull to Revethora Vezvaishoroi. The guardsmen drew lots to see who would accompany Captain Olgarezh and me to guard the skull: two young elven men named Ivoranar and Nevetezh. They seemed pleased at the chance to get out of the palace after the long winter, and I hoped that made up for this apparently pointless guard duty. I tried to convince Prince Orchenis that since we were leaving Amalo, neither I nor the skull needed guarding, but he was unimpressed with my reasoning.

"The men will not complain," he said.

That wasn't quite what I was worried about, but I didn't know how to explain myself, and Prince Orchenis said, "Othala Celehar, it would be a great kindness to us."

To which there was nothing I could say but, "Yes, of course."

Later, Captain Olgarezh said, "Think of it this way. It's better to have us and not need us than need us and not have us."

"Our grandmother used to say that about umbrellas," I said.

He smiled and said, "We think the analogy holds."

We were part of a larger caravan headed to Revethora Vezvaishoroi: the emperor's demolitions experts from the Clockmakers' Guild going to blast the mine entrance closed had two wagons of supplies (one of which also carried Halhathvered, who had volunteered to serve as a guide) and a carriage for the experts.

Gorbelad and Sons were continuing their contracted job of getting Arquenethil's skull to Revethora Vezvaishoroi. I had hoped we might have Henet and Una and Aikara again, but it was a different young goblin man, Ernu, and an odd pair, a Vedencreise black and a bright bay Elgorat who matched him in size. "They work well together," Ernu said, and I agreed that that was the most important thing. The Vedencreis was named Orla, and the Elgorat rejoiced in the name Starstannover, after a folk hero of the northern badlands. The morning of the demolitions caravan's departure, Captain Olgarezh and Armsman Ivoranar and Armsman Nevetezh and I took the tram south to the Ulvanensee stop, walked to the Gorbelad stable, collected Ernu and Orla and Starstannover, and walked to Ulvanensee, where Anora was waiting for us, despite the fact that it was before dawn. He walked with us around the outer wall to the old carriage house, where Arquenethil's skull was waiting.

"I will not be sorry to see it go," Anora said. "The little hauntings have been a misery all winter."

"You could have said something," I said.

"And then what? Where else were you going to be able to store it?"

"Still."

"No serious harm was done," Anora said, and if we'd been alone, I would have pressed him to explain what he considered "serious" harm. "But I am glad you are taking it away."

Ernu succeeded in hitching the horses to the wagon, although neither of them liked the skull. They stayed obedient, and I knew from my experience with Aikara and Una that they would become more accustomed to whatever it was they sensed as the miles passed.

Ernu and I climbed up to the driver's seat; Captain Olgarezh and the armsmen used the footholds behind to take their own seat on top of the crate. I warned everyone to be careful, and Ernu asked the horses to walk forward.

We joined the demolitions caravan in the Glassmarket, where—to my relief—we were not the last people to arrive. The caravan master, an elderly part-goblin man named Hama Kepgorod, put us where he wanted us in the line (at the end), and we waited for the last clockmaker to show up. He was an hour late, which Mer Kepgorod said was not as bad as it could be, and we were underway before the sun fully cleared the horizon.

Orla and Starstannover proved to be willing workers; Ernu's chief problem was in keeping them from catching up with the wagon in front of us. Captain Olgarezh, sitting just behind us, could not be enticed into conversation for more than a minute or two, but he was unbothered when the skull's malice periodically found a small stone to throw at us.

"It would do more if it could," I warned him, and told him about the wheel spoke.

"The Anmur'theileian is haunted," he said. "Mostly it's little things like these stones, but every once in a while, one of those little things happens at, say, the top of a staircase, and then the results can be very serious."

"Yes, exactly," I said.

That night, Captain Olgarezh and I shared one room in the nameless hotel that marked the halfway point between Amalo and Tanvero, and the armsmen shared another. We went to bed early.

I was very tired and he was very warm against my back, where the dip in the mattress had slid us together, and instead of sleeping, I was thinking about the way his scar had come so dangerously close to being across his eyes. *Go to sleep, Celehar,* I said impatiently to myself, but it was a long time before I could follow my own advice.

Another day's travel brought us to Tanvero, where I thought about visiting Osmer Thilmerezh and then thought again. Captain Olgarezh would have to come with me, and I would have to explain why he was there, and although Osmer Thilmerezh already knew much of the story, I did not want to tell him the rest. We had another early night.

The road from Amalo to Tanvero had been surprisingly good; the road from Tanvero to Revethora Vezvaishoroi was not. There was mud and more mud. The horses strained and sweated. We all got down and walked and were soon muddy from toe to eartip. We slept that night in an extremely makeshift camp; Captain Olgarezh and I huddled together beside the fire, one overcoat underneath us as a ground cloth and one overcoat on top of us as a blanket. Nothing could make it not miserable, and I was grateful when Mer Kepgorod insisted that we start moving again as soon as there was enough light to see to hitch the horses to the wagons.

We reached Revethora Vezvaishoroi just past dusk of the fourth day since we had left Amalo, and our first sign that something was amiss was that there was no light in the watchman's shack. Halhathvered swung off the wagon and went up to bang on the door of the shack. There was no answer. He tried again, and when that still failed to rouse anyone—and it was hard to imagine even the soundest sleeper sleeping through the noise Halhathvered was making—he opened the door and looked inside. He then came back to the wagons and said, loudly enough for everyone to hear, "Empty. Not even supplies."

"What about the stable?" said Mer Kepgorod.

Halhathvered went and checked and came back shaking his head. "All the mules and all their tack are gone."

"Then at least we can use the stalls," Mer Kepgorod said pragmatically. "Come on, boys, let's get the horses put away." That done, lanterns lit, and the wagoners and caravan guards also settled—"Go near a place called the Tomb of Dragons?" said Mer Kepgorod. "I think I'm plenty near enough already, thank you"—we walked the rest of the way to the mine entrance, which was as silent as the tomb it was named.

I did not want to try to talk to Ithalpherix tonight, for all kinds of reasons, so I was careful to stay outside while the others looked around, the clockmakers muttering to each other about places to put their powder, Halhathvered and Captain Olgarezh looking for signs of life. They came out again to where I was standing with Armsman Ivoranar and Armsman Nevetezh, and Halhathvered said, "Nothing. Not even a burned-out torch."

He and I exchanged a glance, something we had both been being careful not to do. But we both knew the most likely reason for this desolate silence.

"It is a mystery that I vote waits until tomorrow," said Sol Nivinar, and the rest of us agreed. We all ended up spending the night in the stables, since no one wanted to sleep in the shack by himself, and there were enough clean stalls for everyone, as long as we shared. Captain Olgarezh and I slept close together, our overcoats layered to serve as a kind of haphazard blanket.

In the morning, we returned to the mountain. Having

persuaded Ernu that he did not have to do something he so clearly did not want to, I was driving the skull's carriage, and although Orla did not like the mine entrance, he and Starstannover gamely pulled Arquenethil's skull into the mine. I said, "Are you there, dragon?"

We are here, Thara Celehar, the dragon said immediately. *Who are these strangers you have brought to Revethora Vezvaishoroi?*

"They are the men who are going to seal the mine."

There was a pause. I'd startled her.

Then you succeeded?

"We did. The emperor decided to close all of the dragonhold mines."

We would disbelieve you, except why would you come back to Revethora Vezvaishoroi only to tell us lies?

I couldn't think of a reason I would be so stupidly foolhardy, either.

And what is this strange vehicle you are driving?

I wished mightily that I did not have to tell her, but I said, "It is the skull of the dragon Arquenethil."

Arquenethil? He never made it here. A pause while she thought about what I'd said. *They cut his head off? As a trophy?*

"Yes."

And you brought it here?

"We do not know where the rest of his body is, if it is anywhere. Bringing the skull here seemed the most honorable thing to do."

A long, considering pause before she said grudgingly, *We suppose it is the best thing you could have done.*

"We are sorry," I said, feeling helpless. "The men who did this terrible thing are long dead."

It is past repining over, she said. *So you are going to seal the mine?*

"Yes," I said, and here was another difficult topic. "But we have to be sure that everyone is out, first."

She made no sound, of course; it was the memory of a sound, but even as a memory, dragon laughter was horrific. *You needn't worry about that.*

"*All* of them?"

All those who remained beneath the mountain. Some were wise enough to flee, and we do not know what became of them.

"But . . ."

They misjudged the reach of our strength.

I made an involuntary warding gesture and turned to the others. "Ithalpherix says there is no one left alive in the mine."

The clockmakers looked at each other. "Do we trust what she says?"

"Since what she says is that she tore them all to pieces, I tend to think yes."

Everyone made warding gestures. Halhathvered said, "Would it hurt to check? I hate to think of sealing someone in here alive."

"It might," I said. "She says they misjudged the reach of her strength, so I don't have any idea how far it's safe to go. And I cannot promise that she will not tear you to pieces, given the chance."

"If you came with me?"

"She might tear you to pieces with me standing right next to you. Or she might tear both of us to pieces—my bargain with her is complete, so there is nothing to keep her from killing me."

"Ah," said Halhathvered.

"But, truly, I think in this she is trustworthy. If you will forgive my being blunt, she had no reason to leave any of them alive."

"That is very true," said Halhathvered.

"Are we ready?" said Sol Nivinar.

"Yes," I said. "Let us seal this tomb."

First we had to unhitch Orla and Starstannover from Arquenethil's carriage. Captain Olgarezh helped me with that, and he and I walked them out and back to the stable.

("There's no need to wait, is there?" said Sol Nivinar.

"No," I said. "None at all.")

Ernu came out, and we unharnessed the horses and curried them and put them back in their stalls. Then Ernu cleaned tack. I sat in the dooryard and enjoyed the sunlight after the endless dark of Revethora Vezvaishoroi. Captain Olgarezh guarded me, and although I wanted to tell him he did not have to, I could not think of a way of doing it that would not sound like I wanted to be rid of him.

We'd been there maybe half an hour when the clockmakers appeared, unrolling a kind of cord off a spool as they went.

"Are you *quite* sure you're ready?" said Sol Marchipar. "Once we light the fuse, there's really no going back."

"Quite sure," I said.

"And everyone's here?" said Sol Nivinar.

The third and youngest clockmaker, Sol Tesibar, went into the stable and came back leading a bewildered lot of wagoners and caravan guards, plus the armsmen and Halhathvered. "This is everyone," said Sol Tesibar. "I counted twice."

"All right," said Sol Marchipar, and Sol Nivinar took out his lighter and held it to the end of the cord.

"In three," he said. "Three, two, one." His lighter sparked and the cord immediately started burning, back down the slope and around the corner out of sight.

"How long . . ." I said.

"Maybe a minute," said Sol Nivinar. "It's a fast-burning fuse."

We all waited, frozen. Sol Marchipar was counting slowly under his breath. He'd gotten to seventy-five when there was a noise so tremendous I felt it in the ground. The stable wall shook; the horses screamed and banged into their stalls trying to bolt.

The dust settled slowly; the ringing in my ears subsided. "Blessed goddesses," said Mer Kepgorod. "Was that the mountain coming down?"

"Not the whole mountain," said Sol Nivinar. "But hopefully enough."

Presently, after the drivers had checked on the horses to make sure they hadn't hurt themselves, the clockmakers and Captain Olgarezh and I walked down the path to what had been the mine entrance, and of the mine entrance there was no sign.

"It worked! It worked!" the clockmakers congratulated each other. Captain Olgarezh and I just stared. I had imagined the mine entrance being filled in by rubble, but this was a solid slab of rock. If it hadn't been for the path, there would have been no reason to think there had been an entrance to *anything*.

That afternoon, Captain Olgarezh came with me to find Jormentauren's Door. There was nothing left of it but a kind of cubbyhole in the mountain, but it was large enough that I could step inside.

"Ithalpherix?"

We are here, Thara Celehar.

"The mine is sealed."

Yes, she said. *The mine is sealed and the tunnels have collapsed.*

"We will be leaving in the morning, but before we go, we wanted to ask you."

Ask us what?

"If you remember, we are able to quiet ghouls, and our

ability worked on the one revethavar we have encountered. Do you wish to be quieted? It seems to us that you are going to be very lonely."

We are already lonely. But Revethora Vezvaishoroi is truly sealed, and we need not watch any longer. A pause and she admitted, *We do wish greatly to rest.*

"Is that yes?"

A long silence. Then she said, *Yes. If you can do it, quiet us. Let us be done.*

"Ithalpherix," I said, "we know your name. We know your death. Ithalpherix, you have been wrongly kept from your slumber. You must rest, Ithalpherix, let the darkness take you."

I felt the memory of her body thrash, like the death throes of a snake.

"Ithalpherix, let the darkness take you," I said. "Sleep now. You need stand guard no longer."

They were the right words. I felt the last of her resistance erode away.

"Sleep, Ithalpherix," I said, and she dissolved into darkness and was gone. I exhaled with a strange mixture of feelings. This was the last, long-delayed piece of a terrible tragedy, but I could not help being relieved that she had never decided to tear me to shreds, as she could so easily have done. So I did not mourn her as a friend, but rather as an enemy with whom I had had a mostly amicable truce.

But at least she would not be lonely from here until the end of time.

ANOTHER NIGHT SPENT sleeping against Captain Olgarezh's warm and unyielding backbone.

In the morning, Ernu tied Starstannover and Orla to the back of the clockmakers' second wagon, the one that did not contain blasting powder. Ernu sat with the driver, and Captain Olgarezh and Armsman Ivoranar and Armsman Nevetezh and I sat among the bundles and crates or walked alongside as the caravan traveled back to Tanvero—two miserable, cold, muddy days—and then, having grafted itself onto a larger caravan, back to the nameless hotel, and then on the morning of the day that should have seen us back to Amalo, on a particularly overhung and gloomy section of the road, we were attacked by bandits.

They came surging out of the forest, grabbing at the horses' heads to keep us from trying to run.

Captain Olgarezh said to me, "Stay put," and he and the armsmen slid off the back of the wagon and vanished into the chaos of bandits and caravan guards and wagoners. I stayed where I was. As I had said to Chonhadrin the *last* time this had happened, I would be worse than useless in the melee and trying to run would merely draw attention.

I got down as far as I could among the bundles, in case any of the bandits had a bow. And then I waited—until I heard someone saying, "Where is Thara Celehar? Do you know where Thara Celehar is?" to Menharad, the driver of the wagon.

"Who?" said Menharad, and I took the second's advantage I had to scramble out of the wagon and fling myself into the woods. If they were asking for me by name, they had been hired to find me, and since the only people I could think of who would hire bandits to find me were the Clenverada, it followed that they'd been hired to find *and kill* me.

Poor planning on the bandits' part: there was nobody at the end of the wagon train to see if they flushed me out.

I did not run far, since death by starvation in the woods would not actually be very much preferable to death by bandit, but farther than I thought the bandits would go in searching for me. I lay down behind a tree, so that someone looking into the woods would not get flashes of my white skin, got as comfortable as I could, and waited.

Eventually, the sounds of fighting died down, and sometime after that, I heard Armsman Ivoranar calling for me: "Othala Celehar? Are you there?"

"Armsman Ivoranar?" I said, getting up. "Is that you?"

"Yes. Where are you, othala?"

"Just here," I said, stepping around the tree. "Thank—"

I discovered I was looking at the point of a sword. "Ivoranar?"

"We are sorry about this, othala," Ivoranar said, although he did not sound very sorry. "The Clenverada are paying well for your death."

I backed up a step and jarred hard against the tree.

"If you hold still," said Ivoranar, "we can do this quickly."

"That's a terrible bargain," I said.

"It's the only bargain you're going to get," Ivoranar said, coming a step closer. He was not sorry, but he did not seem comfortable with the idea of killing me, either; someone who was accustomed to killing people would have done it by now.

I was just wondering if this meant I might be able to distract him when Captain Olgarezh roared, "Celehar, *down*!"

I dropped as Ivoranar wheeled to face the threat. "Captain," he said, "Captain, this isn't what it looks—"

Captain Olgarezh slashed hard, not across his face, but across his throat.

Ivoranar crumpled to the ground in a gout of blood as Captain Olgarezh stepped back.

"He killed Nevetezh," Captain Olgarezh said. "Blessed goddesses, Othala Celehar, are you all right?"

"I think so," I said, sitting up. "He hadn't actually worked himself up to kill *me* yet."

Olgarezh cleaned his sword and resheathed it, then crouched down next to me. "We are in a world of trouble," he said, using the plural.

"The Clenverada are paying people to kill us," I said, pulling myself back up to the correct level of formality. "Yes."

"And if Ivoranar was willing to take their money, how can we trust anyone else at all?"

"We appreciate," I said delicately, "your use of plural 'we.'"

He gave me a bright-eyed, sardonic look. "If we had any desire to kill you, you'd already be dead."

"That is what we thought."

"But we can't go back to the caravan."

"You don't have to stay with us," I said.

His eyebrows went up. "Just leave you out here to die on your own?"

"Things aren't *that* dire . . . or well, yes," and I decided it was ridiculous to maintain formality in this situation, "I suppose they are. I don't have any idea what I should do."

Captain Olgarezh regarded me for a moment, as if deciding what to do with my shift in formality. "You can't go back to Amalo."

"I . . ." Ridiculously, the first objection that came to mind was that I had promised to consult with Osmer Ormevar again on my return from Revethora Vezvaishoroi. "No, you're right."

"Unless you want to become a hermit . . . that *is* a thing prelates of Ulis do, isn't it?"

"It is," I said, "but it is not my calling."

"Good. If you *don't* want to become a hermit, the best thing to do is to go to Ezho, where it will be easy to find transportation of some kind to the Untheileneise Court. Do you have any money?"

"I do." The habit of carrying all my most important things in my inside waistcoat pocket was ingrained—which appeared, under the circumstances, to be a good thing. And I had my letter of credit from the Archprelate, getting slightly dog-eared as it was, so that when we reached Ezho, hopefully there would be an Astravadeise bank where I could draw funds.

"Then that part's all right. We just have to get to Ezho. Come on."

"Just like that?"

"No, but we need to get farther away from the caravan. If they find us, first, we will have a lot of explaining and arguing to do and, second, someone will know what we're doing." He stood up and offered me a hand. I was glad of the help. "In any event, I know that Ezho is west of here, and west is that way." He pointed, and we started walking. I felt ridiculously warmed by his use of "I."

THE MORNING WAS rough going. Tree roots were everywhere under the carpet of dead leaves, and the leaves themselves were sometimes slick. I did not fall, but I came close several times.

In clearings, where we could see the sun, Olgarezh checked his navigation, and we were always heading west.

"Can all soldiers do this?" I asked.

"Are we taught to navigate in the woods, you mean? No, although we are taught to navigate by the sun. I happen to have a good sense of direction." He shrugged a little. "Luck, I suppose."

"It is certainly lucky for me," I said. "My sense of direction is completely baffled by these trees."

"When I was a child, there used to be stories about the Osrentantal—the woods between Amalo and Ezho."

"Do I want to know?"

"Most of them were really just warnings about ghouls. Don't bury people in unmarked graves. Don't forget where your loved ones are buried. Things like that."

"Are there ghouls in the Osrentantal?"

"I don't know. Probably? There are fur trappers, and they tend to be Vikhelneise."

"Idiots," I said, with more force than I had intended, and that was how I ended up telling Olgarezh about my ghoul hunt in Tanvero.

"That cannot have been your first ghoul hunt," he said.

"No, I quieted several when I was the prelate of Aveio."

"Aveio?"

"It is a small town in the prairies south of the Evressa. I can tell you nothing to recommend it," I said, thinking of Evru—and of the coil of Evru's hair in my room in the Amal'theileian. I had put that strand of his hair in Lenet Athmaza's charm mostly as camouflage in case anyone asked, but now it was, ironically, quite genuine. "But it was good practice for ghoul hunting."

"Yes, should one wish to take that up as a hobby," he said dryly.

"It has proved useful," I said. "Without that, the dragon would probably have shredded me."

"True enough. I . . ." He cocked his head. "I hear running water. Come on."

I followed him off to the left, up a slight rise (when I began to be able to hear water as well), and then down a long, steep hill to a sizeable and very rapid stream.

"We'd want to boil it before we drank it," said Olgarezh, "and we have nothing to boil it in. But where there's water, there are more likely to be people."

"People?"

"People do live in the Osrentantal, and I think we will do better to find them than to try to reach Ezho on our own."

"I am in full agreement," I said. "But how can you be sure anyone at all lives near this river?"

"I can't be. But it's flowing roughly west to east, so if we walk upstream, we won't be doing ourselves any harm anyway."

"I have no better ideas," I said.

We started upstream.

It was hard going at first, rocky and steep in places and in others impassable due to trees clustered close together or tremendous briar bushes. But we persevered and eventually the hill became less steep and the briar bushes less frequent, and then we came to a shallow place with stepping stones and a clear path down the hill on our side and up the hill on the other.

"Your gamble paid off," I said.

"I got lucky, you mean. And you're correct."

"*We* got lucky. Which way do you think we should go?"

"Let's cross the stream and go up the hill and see if we can see anything helpful from there."

The stepping stones were good ones, wide and flat and well anchored. We crossed the stream from what I thought was the north side to the south and climbed the hill, which was considerably taller than the hill we had come down. I was out of breath by the time we reached the top.

"Sit," said Olgarezh. "Let me investigate."

"I think I'd rather we stayed together," I said, panting. "Just give me a moment."

He considered and said, "I cannot in all fairness argue with that."

He waited until I said I was ready. Then we started down the hill on the far side from the stream, still heading south. I confirmed our direction with Olgarezh.

He said, "South is better for our purposes, I think. North just gets us farther and farther into the mountains, where we have no desire to go."

At the bottom of the hill, our path encountered another, much wider path, this one running east–west. "West again," said Olgarezh, and we followed that path, winding among the trees, until finally we came to a cabin, four-square and well made, with smoke rising from the chimney.

I caught at Olgarezh's sleeve. "What in the world are we going to tell them? We went out for a walk and got lost?"

"I was planning to tell them we're trying to get to Ezho. I don't think we need to say anything else."

I was dubious, but I had forgotten to reckon in the effect that Olgarezh had on people encountering him for the first time. The elven woman who came to the door of the cabin didn't ask any questions at all, but was happy to tell us to follow the path to the next town, which was Benisho—happier still when, having asked permission and drunk from her well, we thanked her and went on our way.

"'Town' is likely to be an overstatement," said Olgarezh. "Six houses and perhaps an othasmeire is more likely."

"If there's an othasmeire, the othas'ala will probably give us shelter for the night."

"That would be most welcome," Olgarezh said.

We passed other cabins, one with a goat grazing on the new spring grass of its sod roof, but did not stop except once, at a particularly large and prosperous-looking cabin, to trade a two-muranai coin (that being the smallest coin I had in my pockets except for a scatter of half-zashan pieces) for a loaf of bread and a half-wheel of cheese.

"My cheese is good, but it's not worth that much," said the elven housewife.

"Do you have use for the money?" I'd counted at least five children, and she was clearly pregnant with a sixth.

"Yes," she admitted.

"Then consider us even," I said. "I have no use for a two-muranai coin and very good use for your bread and cheese."

"All right," she said, "but let me make you tea to go with it. It's still not a fair trade, but it's better."

"We would welcome tea," I said.

We sat at her kitchen table and ate bread and cheese and drank strong kolveris while the woman did laundry and her children peered at us shyly around the door. She did not ask questions, either, but that seemed to be more out of good manners than intimidation. She warned us that Benisho was better described as a hamlet than a town.

We reached Benisho, which was, indeed, six houses and an othasmeire, just before dark. The five-spired clapboard othasmeire showed considerable craftsmanship and was well-maintained. The great arched doors were open. Olgarezh knocked on one and called, "Hello? Is anyone there?"

"Strangers?" The voice came from above us, which made us both jump. "What in the world are *strangers* doing in Benisho? Don't go anywhere! I'll be right down!"

We waited obediently, listening to the thud of feet along the gallery and down a set of stairs, and then the othas'ala plunged into view and said, "Greetings! I am Othala Gorvera."

He was a young elven man, aquiline of nose and weak of chin. His hair made a deep widow's peak, but his prelate's braid was as thick as a bell-rope to his waist. His eyes were a bright inquisitive blue. The form of his name, as well as his accent, said that he hailed from Thu-Tetar, hundreds and hundreds of miles to the south. He had probably been assigned here, as I had been assigned to Aveio, because *someone* had to fill the position and he had no benefice to step into in his own principality.

"I am Othala Celehar," I said. "This is Captain Olgarezh. We are traveling to Ezho."

I saw the question form and saw him decide, with a glance at Olgarezh, not to ask. "How can I help you?"

"We're seeking a place to sleep for the night," I said, "and hoped the othasmeire might welcome us."

"Of course! Of course! But you need not sleep in the othasmeire. My house is small, but I can at least provide blankets and a fire."

"Both of which would be greatly welcome," said Olgarezh.

"And you must be in want of dinner. I know I am."

"We don't want to—" I started.

"Nonsense!" he said. "I am only too happy to have company. The good people of Benisho are faithful parishioners, but they do not seek me out."

"We are glad to trade company for a meal," I said.

"Splendid!" said Othala Gorvera. "Come with me, I'll give you the tour."

We followed him across the sanctuary of the othasmeire to a narrow door behind the altar which led, by a narrow passageway that curved and angled around the wall, to a door that opened onto Othala Gorvera's kitchen.

"I'm afraid you will find the food uninspiring," he said. "I have to eat my own cooking most of the time, although the good wives of Benisho provide me with jam and pickles in canning season, and the hunters keep me supplied with venison. But I have learned how to bake bread, and so I can offer cold roast venison and bread fresh this morning and the last of the winter jam and tea. I have isevren *and* orchor."

"Isevren or we'll be awake all night," said Olgarezh.

"Since I can make orchor either terribly weak or terribly strong but nothing in between, you're probably right. But let me show you the rest of the house."

There wasn't much. Another room downstairs on the other side of the chimney stack and then two rooms upstairs, again one to each side of the chimney. The other downstairs room was the formal parlor, which any prelate with parishioners had to have. The rooms upstairs were Othala Gorvera's

waiting for an opportunity to escape. Was it still eating only the dead?"

"No one in Benisho is missing," said Othala Gorvera, "but beyond that I have no idea."

The sunken tombs had been dug into the side of a hill just to the north of Benisho, like the beginnings of a catacomb. One of them, well lit by fire, had a terrified adolescent elven boy standing outside it.

"Has it come back?" said the parishioner.

"No," said the boy. "Father, I'm sorry!"

"You'll be sorrier if it kills anyone. Othala, what must we do?"

Othala Gorvera looked at me.

"It will be hungry," I said. "Is this Benisho's only cemetery?"

"Yes," said Othala Gorvera.

"Then it won't go far," I said, "and it *will* come back."

"What if it *has* started eating the living?"

"Then there's us," I said. "Easy targets. Just let the fire die down."

"Should we not let Mer Ophanar and his son go home?"

"Safer to stay here," I said. "If they leave and it follows them instead of coming after us—"

"I'm not such a fool as to leave," said Mer Ophanar.

We stood against the hill, Mer Ophanar's lantern at our feet, all of us straining to see or hear something out in the darkness that would warn us of the ghoul's approach. After some time, Othala Gorvera whispered, "You've done this before?"

"Yes," I said.

"Good."

He said no more, and we waited.

We did not actually have to wait very long. The ghoul was hungry and not smart enough to wait until we got careless.

It was, however, smart enough to attack from the one direction we weren't expecting.

I felt it, the moment before it crashed into Olgarezh, felt the anger and hunger and raw chaos that made up a ghoul's mind, but didn't have enough time to realize that it had gone up the hill and gotten above and behind us, certainly not enough time to give a warning.

Olgarezh staggered, but he was drawing his sword even as he dropped and rolled. The ghoul's clumsy rib-fingers had not dug in, and he was able to get free of it, although he was bleeding heavily from a bite wound on his shoulder. I did not know whether to thank Anmura or Ulis, his god or mine, that the ghoul had missed his neck.

I was reaching for its name, reaching and finding nothing but chaos. This ghoul was on the verge of simply falling apart; it was the name that held the assemblage of meat together. But it was not falling apart *now*. Its shapeless head swung from Olgarezh to Elmet, and it lunged for him.

His father yanked him out of the way, and by then Olgarezh was on his feet and his sword blade arcing around to a solid blow just below the ghoul's right shoulder.

Its arm fell off and began to writhe toward Olgarezh on the ground.

Olgarezh looked wildly at me.

"I just need another moment!" I said, reaching again into the chaos, reaching farther, deeper, reaching with a sudden access of desperation and *there!* finding a name.

"Ulgrana Morenthar!" I said. "Ulgrana Morenthar, I know your name! I know your death!" Iärditha, caught on a trading journey to Amalo, but waiting until the deep loneliness of the forest to worsen and worsen. Ulgrana Morenthar had died alone and had been buried by the next trapper who stopped by his one-room cabin. Vikhelneise, of course, the both of them. "Ulgrana Morenthar, you are wrongly woken from your sleep! You must rest again! Ulgrana Morenthar, let the darkness take you!"

The ghoul fell on top of its arm.

"Let the darkness take you, Ulgrana Morenthar," I said. "You must rest."

And the ghoul collapsed. The fingers of its severed arm spasmed one last time and then simply fell apart.

"There," I said. "It's done. Captain Olgarezh, are you all right?"

"I will be," Olgarezh said. "I'd be bleeding *much* worse than this if it had hit anything important."

"Lucky," I said.

"Very," he agreed. "Benisho doesn't have such a thing as a cleric, does it?"

"No," said Othala Gorvera. "Just Merrem Isbralaran, who knows something about herbs."

"She might have a tincture of varath," Olgarezh said. "That's what I want to wash this bite out with."

"We can certainly find out," said Othala Gorvera. "Elmet, can you remember that long enough to go and ask her?"

"Yes, othala," the boy said and darted away.

Merrem Isbralaran, who insisted on coming with Elmet back to the cemetery, was a stern-faced middle-aged elven woman. She washed the bite out with a marigold-smelling tincture, salved it with something else, and bandaged it neatly. "You were right about the varath," she said to Olgarezh. "Hopefully it'll keep the corruption out."

"I've seen it work before," Olgarezh said. "So it can't hurt to try."

"Anything gives you a better chance than nothing," said Merrem Isbralaran.

Olgarezh woke mildly feverish the next morning, so we

spent two days in Benisho with Merrem Isbralaran keeping a close eye on the bite. The first day, he quite literally caught me as I was leaving the room, coming up on his elbow to get a hard grip on my arm, and said, "You won't leave, will you?"

"Leave?" I said, considerably startled. "Why . . . ?"

"You could, you know. Othala Gorvera could give you directions."

"I don't want to go to Ezho by myself," I said and winced.

But it seemed to reassure him. "All right," he said and released my arm.

It seemed conceited to imagine that he was worried I would abandon him, but I said, "I promise I won't go anywhere without you," and saw him relax.

He lay down again and said in a more normal tone, "I don't know what you're going to find to do in Benisho."

"Gorvera will tell me," I said and got about half a smile from Olgarezh before he fell asleep.

I let Gorvera show me his othasmeire (we climbed up all five spires) and his collection of books (which was impressive for a prelate in a benefice this small), and we talked and talked. I told him about being a Witness for the Dead in Lohaiso and Aveio and Amalo (without mentioning my stay at the Untheileneise Court); he told me about growing up in a town near the Barizheise border and how he'd ended up in Benisho—it had been as I had imagined: he didn't have the connections to get a benefice anywhere better. "And it is not truly so bad," he said. "Or, at least, it could be much worse."

"Yes," I said, thinking of Aveio.

I also spent a great deal of time with Olgarezh, who seemed to rest more easily if I was in the room. At one point on the second day when I thought he was asleep, he said, "I am sorry you have to leave Amalo."

"Thank you," I said. "I am . . ." I tried to decide how I

felt. "I am sad, but also I can write to the people I care about once we have reached Ezho, so I am not cut off from the most important part of my life there. And in truth, I don't know how much longer I could have stayed in Amalo anyway. The Archprelate *cannot* have an infinite list of problems that would keep me there."

"I suppose not," said Olgarezh. "Could you . . . could you have asked for a ulimeire there?"

"I don't want one," I said. "I am happier leaving Amalo than being saddled with a benefice."

Anora or Tomasaran might have questioned my use of the word "happy"; Olgarezh merely said, "That's good," and fell asleep. And it was true. Much as I regretted leaving Amalo, much as I resented the Clenverada for making it necessary, leaving—to become whatever the Archprelate asked of me—was far, far better than being trapped as a beneficed prelate in the politics of the Amalomeire and the Ulistheileian.

Was I happy? I flinched away from the word: it had been so long since it had seemed applicable in anything but the ugliest contrast. But it felt *possible*.

On the third morning, Olgarezh woke up unfeverish and eager to be off. Instead of simply striking blindly west, we now had directions to the next hamlet, nearly a day's walk away, and a letter of introduction to its prelate, who was Gorvera's literally closest friend. In this way, prelate to prelate, we were able to follow a chain of hamlets through the Osrentantal to the hilly farmland that lay beyond. There we hit a town large enough to have a coach stop, and the next day we found ourselves, a little bewildered, in Ezho, in a teahouse called the Crimson Hare, sitting at a two-person table along the outer wall and staring at a pot of golden orchor and a plate of round cakes called sarenthers that were the local specialty.

"I'm starving even if you aren't," said Olgarezh and picked up one of the cakes.

"No, I mean, yes," I said and took one myself. They were sweet and creamy and very good. "Let me pour the tea."

I poured the tea carefully, set the pot back down, and blurted out, "What wilt thou do?"

His eyebrows went up.

I hadn't meant to "thee" him, and my face was heating, but I did not take the question back.

"I thought I would stay with thee," he said, "at least until thou reachst the Untheileneise Court safely."

"But thou'rt a Principate Guard."

He shrugged. "I was for a season. But I never intended to stay longer than it took me to find something better."

"And I qualify as better?"

"In thy company, I have attended the emperor's judgment, been haunted by a dragon skull, blown up a mountain, survived the Osrentantal, and fought a ghoul."

"But that's . . ."

He grinned and picked up another sarenther. "Interesting."

"Not on purpose, I was going to say."

"It need not be on purpose to happen. Besides, other than thou going back thyself, the quickest and surest way for the Clenverada to find out thou art still alive is for *me* to go back, because where have I been all this time?"

"Thou couldst lie," I said hesitantly.

"Well, I could make the attempt," he said. "But I am a very bad liar and invariably get caught out. And thou *must* know that Prince Orchenis will not be satisfied with, 'He died in the woods, so I buried him and came home.'"

"Thou couldst say thou leftst me in Benisho?"

"Prince Orchenis would have my head. And in any event, without knowing how *committed* the Clenverada are to thy death, I hesitate to give them clues. It does not take a clever man to reason that if thou wert in Benisho, thou must have been heading to Ezho, because where else couldst thou possibly go?"

"I see thy point," I said and took another sarenther.

"Once we have reached the Untheileneise Court, I might write to Prince Orchenis to apologize for leaving in such a fashion. But a Principate Guard is not like a nohecharis. There is no oath-swearing. They can't. They're desperately short-handed as it is. Otherwise they would never have taken me."

"A soldier from the imperial army? Surely thy credentials are impeccable."

"And my eyes are the wrong color. I am lucky that they need officers so badly."

"Why didst thou leave the army?" I asked and winced.

"It's a fair question," he said, unbothered. "Oddly enough, it wasn't the blow to the face. Or the living year-round in a haunted palace. It was just . . ." He made a gesture of helplessness. "It's a perfect stalemate. The Nazhmorhathveras can't get us out of the Anmur'theileian, and we can't catch the Nazhmorhathveras. We skirmish, but they're far too smart to send *all* their warriors against us at once. Even if they did, they couldn't win. And we can send all our soldiers *out*, but the Nazhmorhathveras just melt away like fog. It just goes around and around and around, and men suffer and die, and it's for nothing. So I served my twenty years and I left."

"Thou still wearest thy hair like a soldier."

"And maybe I should stop," he said, startling me considerably. "A prelate and a soldier traveling together draw attention, which just at the moment we don't want."

"I don't want thee to have to change on my behalf."

He shook his head. "Change isn't bad. Lack of change is stagnation, and stagnation is death, literal or just as a metaphor. But I think it is meaningful that the Anmur'theileian is haunted."

I poured the last of the tea into our cups. "Well, I have no right to tell thee what to do in any event. But I thank thee."

"For what?"

"For not burying me in the woods and going back to Amalo," I said. "It would have been much easier. *And* more profitable."

His brows drew together for a moment, but then he caught my meaning. "I am not interested in the Clenverada's money."

"I know," I said. I ate another sarenther, mostly to give myself time to think. "What wilt thou do for money, though? I cannot imagine the Archprelate providing me a stipend large enough for two."

He shrugged. "Perhaps the Archprelate will agree with me that thou needst a guard."

"I do not," I said.

"Thara," he said. "Really."

"I used not," I said, conceding.

"But if he does not agree, it isn't hard for a man who's good with a sword to find a job. Unless thou endest up somewhere like Benisho."

"Unlikely," I said. "The Archprelate's original intent was for me to be a sort of . . . problem-solver, and that takes a more complicated situation than poor Gorvera alone could possible generate."

"Then how didst thou end up as the municipal Witness for the Dead in Amalo?"

"That was the problem," I said. "That there wasn't something like a municipal Witness for the Dead, I mean. And now there is. But I have no idea of what the Archprelate may ask me to do next."

"There, thou seest?" said Hanu. "Interesting. And I think

almost certain to stay that way."

I caught his meaning only a moment or two later, and could not help the smile that spread across my face. "I will make every endeavor," I said and dared for a fleeting moment to touch his hand.

To Iäna Pel-Thenhior, greetings.

It is very likely that thou hast thought me dead for some days by the time thou readest this, and I apologize for that. We did not dare return to Amalo. The Clenverada had succeeded in suborning one of the Principate Guard, and there was no way to know whom we could trust among the drivers or the guards or even the clockmakers.

I am also writing to Othala Chanavar, Othalo Tomasaran, and Min Chonhadrin, those being the other people in Amalo I am certain I can trust. The enclosure is a letter to Prince Orchenis, who must be told that the Clenverada are bribing the Principate Guard. I would ask that thou not tell anyone else that thou hast heard from me. I regret it, but I think it may be much safer if the rest of Amalo believes that I am in fact dead.

I am writing to thee from Ezho, from beneath an exceptionally handsome black-and-silver tabby cat belonging to the proprietor of the hotel. Captain Olgarezh and I are about to join a trading caravan headed to Cetho, where I will seek an audience with the Archprelate. Yes, before thou askest, I will also seek an audience with the emperor and tell him the Clenverada are willing to pay people to murder me.

I am afraid it will be a terrible nuisance, but I am hoping thou wilt do me a favor and see if thou canst get my belongings from the Amal'theileian before they're sold or burned or otherwise disposed of. It may be that it is already too late, but I would be sorry to lose them and would be most grateful for thy help.

I know thou hast questions, but it would take more paper than I have to answer them. Captain Olgarezh says to tell thee that I am safe and not destitute and I will write thee again from the Untheileneise Court, and perhaps those are the most important things to say.

With all good wishes and the certainty of true friendship,

Thara Celehar

ACKNOWLEDGMENTS

The Tomb of Dragons was a particularly arduous book to write, so my gratitude for everyone who supported me is particularly keen.

My heartfelt thanks go out to:

Ambar, Heather Gardener, Oliver Barrett, Catherine Fraas, Sharis Ingram, Achariya Rezak, Anne Froyen Mowery, LionessElise, Paige Morgan, ScottKF, Seth Carlson, Katherine Magruder, Jesper Stage, Katy Kingston, Laura E. Price, Magdalena Stojek, Teresa Doyle Kovich, Marisa Gnadt, Liza Furr, Lydia Applegate, Katie Jones, Mandy Brasher, Liz Novaski, Kimi Wallace, Gordon Tisher, H. E. Wolf, Hilary Kraus, Sabine Moehler, Brennan C Mallonee, Gail Morse, Judith Pruski, Aeryn Morgan, green, Jeff Frane, Sarah Shope, Kris Ashley, Linda Martínez, Evelyn R Symons, Jay Parlar, Yerin Kim, Elaine Blank, Garret Reece, Lindsay Kleinman, Luzia Mathez, Clifton Royston, Bill Ruppert, Margaret Johnston, Fred Paffhausen, Laura Bailey, Becky Ward, Redhound, Simone Brick, CL Deichmann, Megan Prime, Julia Gruber, Elizabeth Woodley, Erin Lytle, Cecil Roth, Ruthanna and Sarah Emrys, Amy Miller, Amy Treber, LCL, H. Holmquist, Ruby J. Jeffery, Ariana Mercer, Jennifer G Tifft, Natalie Cole, Devyn Attwood, Morgan Ladd Harlan, Allison Ruvidich, Laia Pedreño, Anna Davidson, Christie Young, Burdock Broughton, Abigayle Ploetz, Lisa Junker,

Asia Wolf, Alexandra Kwan, Kathy V, Lesley Hall, E.S.H, Brittany Sims-West, Sasha Lydon, S.M.Bree, J.A. Nguyen, Kitty M, Laura Ownbey, and all my other Patreon patrons.

Allen Monette and Sarah Wishnevsky, who read the book in draft and provided invaluable feedback.

My agent, Cameron McClure.

The amazing people at Tor: my editor, Oliver Dougherty; cover designer, Esther S. Kim; interior designer, Greg Collins; managing editor, Rafal Gibek; production editor, Megan Kiddoo; production manager, Jim Kapp; copy editor, Christina MacDonald; proofreaders, Terry McGarry and Devi Lir; marketing team, Emily Honer, Becky Yeager, Rachel Taylor; and publicist, Desirae Friesen. Also the wonderful cover artist, Chris Gibbs.

My writers' group: Elizabeth Bear, C. L. Polk, Arkady Martine, Vivian Shaw, Jodi Meadows, Ryan Van Loan, Scott Lynch, Celia Marsh, Alex Haist, Devin Singer, John Chu, Benjamin C. Kinney, Fran Wilde, Fade Manley, Amanda Downum, Jamie Rosen, Tochi Onyebuchi, Stella Evans, Clarissa CS Ryan, John Wiswell, Liz Bourke, Max Gladstone, Amal El-Mohtar, Deanna Hoak, Arula Ratnakar, R. S. A. Garcia, and S. K. Terentiev.

And to all my readers: thank you!

About the Author

Katherine Addison's short fiction has been selected by The Year's Best Fantasy and Horror and The Year's Best Science Fiction. Her novel *The Goblin Emperor* won a Locus Award. As Sarah Monette, she is the author of the Doctrine of Labyrinths series and coauthor, with Elizabeth Bear, of the Iskryne series. She lives near Madison, Wisconsin.